ZARA BLACKWELL

Mine to Break

First edition

ISBN: 979-8-9989660-0-2

This book was professionally typeset on Reedsy.
Find out more at reedsy.com

Trigger Warning

Mine to Break is a dark romance for mature audiences (18+). This book contains themes, scenes, and dynamics that are emotionally intense, morally complex, and potentially triggering. Please proceed with care.

Main Content Warnings:

- Abduction / Kidnapping
- Non-consensual confinement
- Emotional and psychological manipulation
- Dubious consent and CNC (Consensual Non-Consent)
- Coercion and threats
- Obsessive, controlling behavior (Yandere traits)
- Toxic relationships
- Mental and emotional breakdowns
- Past domestic abuse
- Pregnancy and mentions of past miscarriage trauma
- Gun violence and murder
- Parental death
- References to childhood neglect and trauma
- Intense power imbalance and possessive dynamics
- Violence, including torture and murder
- Gun violence
- Choking and breath play
- Praise kink ("Good girl")

- Dom/brat dynamics
- Degradation kink (spitting, name-calling, humiliation)
- Rough sex and overstimulation
- Breeding kink and pregnancy-focused dialogue
- Anal sex
- Public teasing
- Obsession-fueled intimacy
- Possessive dirty talk and primal language
- Somber sex following trauma
- Manipulation through sex

These scenes are meant to reflect the flawed, obsessive, and extreme morally grey nature of the characters. They are not examples of healthy relationships and are not meant for all readers. This book is intended for **18+ mature audiences** only. Please take care of your heart and mental health while reading. You know your limits better than anyone—honor them.

Author's Disclaimer

This is not a love story wrapped in flowers and forgiveness. It's wrapped in barbed wire, power, and hunger. It's twisted, toxic, and intense. The characters make questionable choices. They are not role models—they are shadows of the things we hide, the things we crave, and the things we survive.

If you want a story that's safe and sweet, this isn't it.

But if you want to bleed with them—if you crave fire, ruin, and the ache that comes with loving something that might just destroy you...

Welcome to the chaos.

Playlist

Just pretend- Bad Omens

IFHY- Tyler, The Creator, Pharrell Williams

Introvert- Brakence

Deja Vu- RealestK

Every Time You Leave- I Prevail, Delaney Jane

HOPE- NF

Down With The Sickness- Disturbed

Car Radio- Twenty One Pilots

E-Girls Are Ruining My Life- Corpse, Savage Ga$p

The Kings of Ruin Series playlist can be found on Spotify

Chapter 1

<u>Sabrina</u>

I look in the mirror, questioning how I got here. My reflection resembled someone braver than I felt. My heart pounded against my ribs like a warning bell.

I once had a respectable job.

I was engaged.

Now I'm single and working at Velvet Inferno. I have only been working at Kalel Marchetti's club for one week, and it already felt like I was dancing on the edge of a knife—because the Marchetti name alone could make men twice my size tremble.

You may be asking, who is Kalel Marchetti? He is more myth than man. A whispered threat, a ghost in a suit. The type of danger you didn't see coming until his hand was already around your throat leather-gloved, precise, and unforgiving. Yet, here I am, working for him.

I take a breath. "Pull it together, Sabrina," I muttered. Confidence has always been my armor. Sass, my shield. And tonight? Tonight, I was bulletproof. Not because I wanted to be, but because I have to be.

I hadn't always needed armor.

Hadn't always needed to become someone else just to survive.

I had a normal life once—at least, the closest thing to it. As a teacher's assistant, I overworked and underpaid myself, yet felt proud. I loved the structure, the routine, the sense of purpose. I thought if I

1

kept my head down and worked hard enough, life would reward me with stability. Even if I would get slapped around once I got home. Even when he told me he loved me after making me wish I was dead. I've lived through worse.

Until I left Liam.

He hadn't taken it well. Not when I packed my bags. Or when I tried to avoid him. And not when I said, "Enough." The possessiveness that had once felt like passion twisted into something way uglier and more violent than I thought possible.

He started blowing up my phone. Waiting outside my apartment. Sending voicemails that swung from desperation to threats in the same breath. Then he came to my job drunk and high—storming into the hallways, accusing me of things in front of students, starting fights loud enough to draw attention.

And the attention? It didn't help.

I was the problem, not him. I was the distraction. I was the one they let go, gently, with a "we wish you the best," and that felt like a slap in the face. Why was I paying for his irrational and illogical behavior? It wasn't fair.

I left that office with my head held high and a hole in my chest. No job. No savings. No one to call.

I started bouncing between couches so I didn't run into Liam. Never home for more than a few days so Liam didn't see a pattern. I skipped meals and blocked Liam's number over and over again. But a blocked number doesn't stop fear from crawling under your skin at night.

And that's when I found Velvet Inferno. It appeared like a dare on my screen.

No experience needed. High pay. Late hours. No questions.

It sounded dangerous. But desperation doesn't listen to warnings.

I auditioned in my friend's lingerie and borrowed heels and danced like my rent depended on it—because it did. The lights were hot. The air, so thick that it became hard to breathe. I refused to make eye contact with anyone, just in case I ran into someone I knew. Did I want to be chosen? No, I wanted to disappear into the dark, but they chose me.

Was I happy? No? Yes? I don't know. All I knew was that I needed money, and fast. Questioning my dignity? I'm sorry to tell you, but that was the first thing I learned to sell. Velvet Inferno was supposed to be temporary. Just until I find something else. Just until I got back on my feet. That was the lie I told myself to soothe the subtle ache of worthlessness. The ad said they paid well. I didn't ask questions. I couldn't afford to.

The first time I stepped into the club as a newly hired stripper, it felt like walking into the mouth of something beautiful and deadly. Red velvet. Low lighting. Secrets soaked into every wall. I kept my head down, danced my sets, and didn't make waves. For an entire week, I had gone out of my way trying not to run into Kalel and succeeded. I hadn't run into him the whole week, and for some stupid reason, I thought that meant I was safe, but safety is an illusion in a place like this.

I didn't know Kalel Marchetti watched everything from the shadows like a king surveying his court.

* * *

The music hit like a heartbeat—deep, pulsing, alive—and as I stepped onto the stage, the spotlight swallowed me whole. It was like I became someone else — someone sultry and untouchable. Someone in control. I moved with purpose, every sway deliberate, every roll of my hips a calculated game. A way to make them ache for me.

Then I saw him.

Front and center. He was watching me.

A man in an immaculate suit, posture relaxed but eyes locked on mine like a predator who had just found prey worth chasing. His gaze burned into me. My skin prickled, and my stomach tightened, leaving a low, constricting feeling. I dropped to my knees and crawled forward. Our eyes locked and never broke, not when other dancers begged for attention, and not when I begged for him to look away. His lips parted slightly, almost in reverence. I could feel the electricity— dark, magnetic, dangerous, but addictive.

My heart pounded in my ears and other places I'd sadly rather not mention. I slid off stage and turned to target someone else. When I saw him whisper to another man. Bigger. Broader. Dangerous, but in more of a casual way. Like he'd kill you for miss spelling his name, but also planted flowers in his free time. I knew him to be Angelo, Mr. Marchetti's enforcer. Also known as Ghost because you never seen him coming until it was too late.

The air shifted.

Angelo walked toward me. His tailored suit clung to his body built for war, every movement coiled with purpose. Fuck! What could he want with me?

"Follow me," he said, his voice both low and lethal.

I should've run. Why didn't I run? How far could I get? I push my thoughts down, deep down.

Instead, I chose to follow.

He led me to a private room cloaked in shadows and decadence. With barely a breath, Mr. Marchetti sat with his legs spread wide and fixed on me with a devouring gaze. A king on his throne.

The Kalel Marchetti.

I knew, and he knew that I knew who he was. He didn't need to announce himself. He was the announcement, and he reveled in the fear it put in people.

4

Climbing onto his lap, I acted as though I wasn't terrified or shaking inside. I moved slowly. Seductively. Every brush of my body, deliberate, a challenge wrapped in temptation. His hands found my hips, strong and possessive, and I forgot how to breathe. Not from fear, but because my body yearned for more. His fingers gripped my chin, forcing my eyes to his.

Piercing. Starving. His voice, rough like gravel and sin, rasped out, "You don't belong here." I tilted my head, playing coy. "I work here." He smirked. A wicked smile that I know has brought many women before me to their knees. A knowing smirk that made me want to test my limits. What is wrong with me? He's a Mafia boss. Get it together, Sabrina.

Before I could pull myself down from doing something I couldn't return from —" no", his hand sliding up my thigh. "You belong with me." He said confidently.

Oh, he's good.

I lean in, lips grazing his ear, "Whatever you say, Mr. Marchetti". He tightened his grip, silencing me. "Kalel." He said, correcting me.

I look at him, and I let the name curl on my tongue. "Okay, Kalel," I echoed, then slid off his lap with a slow smile. "This was nice, but unfortunately, our time is up."

"Okay."

Just one word. Soft, almost amused—but it sent a shiver down my spine, like a hand at my nape. As I left, I felt his eyes scorch a trail down my back. As if he'd already claimed me as his own. Like he'd already planned something.

* * *

He didn't seem as bad as everyone said. I wonder why I was so scared.

I head back to the stage; moving with sharpened edges. Every sway, a sensual rebellion. Every flick of my hips was a challenge.

I wanted to see how much I could get away with. I've been with men like him. Men who think they own women, but Kalel didn't blink. He watched—like a man watching his favorite sin take shape. After a while, I danced just to get through the day, but every time I looked, there he was. I shot him a glare, and he smirked. You can't be serious. His smirk was slow and smug. What an infuriating jerk.

After my final set, I changed quickly—ripped jeans, crop top, sneakers. I looked in the mirror, admiring my curls, hazel eyes, and curvy figure. My body was one of the few things I've ever been proud of. My body was the only part of me that I could change, because changing my mental state has always proven to be the hardest and without his gaze, the backstage air felt easier to breathe.

As I stepped outside, my blood turned cold.

Liam, my abusive ex, was back and stood leaning against a lamppost as if he had a right to be back in my world. I froze, panic coiling tightly in my chest. Fuck. I slammed the door shut. Pressed my forehead against it. Breathe. Just breathe.

"Everything okay, Sabrina?" I spun and see that Kalel is standing behind me, hands in his pockets, gaze unreadable but undeniably sharp. He caught everything.

Before I could stop myself, I blurted out, "My crazy ex is outside."

"I really don't want to deal with him right now." I say faster than I can breathe

Kalel tilted his head slightly, with a ghost of a grin tugging at his mouth. "Ah. I see. I saw him lurking around like a coward. Want me to make him disappear?"

I blinked. "What?"

"To make sure he understands you're off-limits." His voice dropped an octave.

"Yes," I breathed, before logic could stop me.

"Need a ride home, too?" He said, looking at me with a smirk. Is he having fun right now? I should've said no. A giant, screaming NO. But Liam was out there—and Kalel was in here.

"... Sure."

He placed a hand at the small of my back, and my entire spine lit up.

* * *

I didn't miss the way Liam stiffened when he saw us together. I also didn't miss the way Kalel stared him down like death incarnate, and I can't lie it was hot.

The car was waiting at the curb. Sleek, black, and expensive. Angelo, held the door, he didn't say a word. Kalel helped me in, his fingers brushing my waist a moment too long.

He slid in beside me, casual and calm. "Where to, sweetheart?" I gave him an address that obviously wasn't mine, heart thundering. I was not going to give him my actual address.

"Thanks for dealing with Liam." I said with a smirk.

Kalel's smile was slow and dark as he said "It was my pleasure."

When the car rolled to a stop, I climbed out quickly. Kalel watched me, eyes burning a whole in me. "Stay safe, Sabrina," he murmured. I looked him in the eye, sincerely, yet still flirtatiously. "I always do." I said with a wink.

The moment the car vanished, I spun on my heel and bolted toward my actual address, pulse still racing.

Whatever danger Liam posed...

It was nothing compared to Kalel Marchetti.

* * *

Kalel

The bass thrums low and steady, vibrating through my chest like a war drum as I sit back in the chair, half-listening to the chatter of clients and girls. My fingers wrapped loosely around a crystal glass I haven't touched in twenty minutes.

They all dance for attention.

For power. For the illusion of control, but I'm not impressed. Not until she steps onto my stage. The moment her heels click against the floor, my pulse stills, then spikes so fast it feels like a goddamn car crash in my chest.

Sabrina.

I hadn't seen her in years. I still remember the first day I saw her. She reminded me of someone I once knew. Someone I loved more than anyone in my life. I knew it wasn't her, but I couldn't convince myself to move on. She was eating a sandwich on a bench at a park during what I could only assume was her lunch break. That day was the day the park became my favorite place to go. I went there every day, hoping to see her. When I saw her, I knew she was mine. I watched her for months before I became The Kalel Marchetti everyone now knows.

Sabrina had the kind of body that made men stop mid-sentence and women size her up twice. She wasn't delicate. She was *intoxicating* in her curves—hips that didn't lie, a waist that begged to be gripped, and thighs built to break a man's resolve. Her ass? Fucking sinful. Full. Firm. The kind of shape that turned slow walks into damnation.

Her breasts weren't oversize or modest—they were *perfect*. Enough to tease without offering, soft enough to cradle, full enough to press tight against silk or sin.

And her stomach? Flat, but not rigid. Soft where it needed to be. A canvas of temptation beneath every crop top she threw on, like armor.

Her skin was warm caramel, kissed by shadows and light—smooth as hell, a fire under fingertips. Her legs were long enough to tempt, strong enough to run, but she didn't. She *never ran.*

And that mouth...

Full. Coquettish. Made for sass and sin alike. The kind of mouth a man dreams of tasting and fears being ruined by.

She didn't walk—she *swayed.* Didn't move—*she danced.* Every part of her body spoke in fluent seduction, even when she wasn't trying, and she was now in my strip club, dancing for me.

I let her go before so I could focus on becoming the head of the Marchetti family. I let her go unassumingly , but now? I want to know everything. I want her blood type, her apartment number, the scent she leaves on pillows. I want to know how she likes her coffee and how she sounds when she cries.

* * *

Her hips roll, making my cock throb. Her thick curls catching the club lights as she moves—fluid, effortless, hypnotic. Her hazel eyes scan the room, and when they lock onto mine, something inside me snaps. She doesn't look away. She dances like she knows she's mine already.

Her mouth curves into a smirk—cocky and defiant as I shift in my seat, cock twitching, jaw clenching. She does not know who she's teasing. No idea who she's dancing for, but she'll learn. And when she does, it'll be too late. "When did she start working here?" I ask, my voice low, controlled—but tight with restraint. Angelo leans in without taking his eyes off the stage. "Sabrina? She's new. One of your good ones."

A slow, twisted smile curves my lips. "Bring her to the back room." I don't wait for confirmation. I'm already moving.

Inside the room, I sit back in the leather chair, legs spread, heart pounding like a countdown. My fingers curl into fists at the idea of her grinding on anyone else tonight.

Then the door opens—and there she is. She hesitates just slightly. I catch the flicker of recognition in her eyes. Good. She knows who I am, knows what the name Marchetti means. But that doesn't stop her. No—this girl's pride won't let her back down. That's my girl.

She straddles me with slow, seductive precision, like she's testing my control on purpose. Her body molds against me, making my pants feel a little too tight. My hands find her thighs, gripping tightly. Every inch of her ignited something primal inside me.

"You don't belong here," I rasp, dragging her gaze up to meet mine. She flinches, but recovers quickly. "I work here."

"You belong with me." The words leave my mouth like a brand. Final. I mean them more than I've meant anything in my life. I had let her go, and the universe sent her back to me. That was all the confirmation I needed. She leans in, her breath a tease against my ear. "Whatever you say, Mr. Marchetti." I growl low in my throat, my grip tightening on her skin. "Kalel." I say correcting her

"Kalel" She says it like a promise. Like she enjoys the way it sounds. Kalel.

My name on her tongue makes me want to melt. I wonder how it would sound when I make her beg for me. Her voice was addictive.

She slides off my lap like she didn't just change the course of her life and mine. "But our time is up." Sabrina says as she walks away, and I let her.

Only because I know she'll be back. I watch her on the floor again, dancing for another man like I don't exist. Like she didn't just make my blood boil with need. I needed her.

She shoots me a glare, and that fire in her eyes? I want to snuff it out—and then light it again. Over and over. Until she forgets who she was before me. From the shadows, I leave the room and track her. I'm not the man who begs or pleads. I take, and tonight, I'm taking notice.

* * *

After her final set, I waited. When she emerges from the dressing room in ripped jeans and a crop top that makes me want to rip them off just to remind her she's not walking around like that anymore. Not when she's mine. She steps outside, and then she freezes.

So, I follow her line of sight. I'd seen that guy lingering around here for the past few days. I just didn't know why.

Calmly, I approach, hands in my pockets, slow and deliberate in my movements, but inside? Inside, I'm already planning how I'll make Liam scream.

"Everything okay, Sabrina?" She turns to me, eyes wide. For the first time, I see something other than sass in her expression—relief. "My crazy ex is outside. I really don't want to deal with him."

I nod once, already deciding. "Want me to make sure he knows you're off-limits?"

"Yes," she breathes.

Dangerous girl.

She does not know what she has just agreed to. "Want a ride home, too?" She hesitates, then nods again. Good. I guide her to the car, my hand on her back, searing through the layers of her clothes. Liam watches, and when his eyes meet mine, I don't blink. I don't smile. I warn him. She is mine.

One look. That's all it takes, and he pales. Oh, so he's a bitch. This— is going to be fun. Angelo's already in the car. He doesn't ask questions—he knows better. Sabrina climbs in, giving me a fake address. She's smarter than I thought. I don't call her out. I already know where she lives. The second she walked off that stage, I made certain of it. When we pull up, she slips out fast, thanking me like I didn't just rewrite her future.

As she disappears inside someone else's building, I lean forward. My voice is low. Final.

"Bring me her ex."

* * *

Hours later, at the safe house, it is silent but heavy. Liam's breathing disrupts the stillness—shaky and panicked. Angelo throws him into a chair, duct-taping his wrists behind his back. "W-what the hell is this?" he blurts, squirming. I step from the shadows, gun loose at my side.

Liam's eyes widen. "Mr. Marchetti, I didn't—"

"Shut. The fuck. Up." He freezes. "You've been harassing someone who belongs to me," I say flatly. "Showing up where she works. Watching her. Making her afraid. Are you going to leave her alone?"

"I didn't know. She's crazy, man, she's—"

I tap the barrel of the gun against his temple. He stops talking. Immediately. "That's not what I asked," I chuckled. "I'm in a good mood today, so I'm going to ask you the question one more time." I say, voice soft—deadly. "This is your last chance to answer right." He nods furiously, tears brimming.

"Are you going to leave Sabrina the fuck alone?"

"Yes!" he screams. "Yes, I swear!"

I stare into his eyes. "Right answer." I say smiling "Was that so hard" I ask chuckling. Then—

Bang.

The sound rings out, final and merciless. Blood paints the wall. Liam slumps forward, a useless sack of regret. "I don't like to ask more than once." I say, disgusted.

"Get rid of him." I tell Angelo, already turning for the door. As soon as I get outside, I inhale the cool air and let it settle in my lungs. She'll never know what I've done. She'll never see the monster in the shadows, but from this moment forward, she is mine. I'll kill anyone who dares touch what belongs to me.

Chapter 2

In the morning, I was surprisingly calm as I headed to work. I heard the birds chirping on my way here. The sun shined perfectly, making the day seem way more optimistic than it should have been. I walk to the dressing room, ready to change and go on stage. I put my black strappy top on with my black strappy bottoms, which left way more to be seen than what needed be. Threw on my black thigh-high boots like it was armor and went to walk toward the stage, only to see Angelo walking toward me. "Kalel wants to see you."

I sigh "For?"

He smirks, "You won't know until he tells you."

"Touché" I said.

My heels clicked against the polished marble floor of the strip club's back hallway, my pulse racing with every step. Angelo's silent presence beside me did nothing to ease my nerves. What could he possibly want from me? The bass of the club music vibrated faintly through the walls, an ominous undertone to whatever awaited me behind Kalel's office door.

Angelo opened the heavy wooden door, gesturing for me to enter. I squint my eyes at him as I stepped inside. It felt like I was entering the lion's den, and he was the one who had brought me here. Kalel sat behind a sleek mahogany desk, his broad shoulders tense beneath his dark suit, attention fixed on the papers sprawled before him. Angelo closed the door, leaving me alone with the man who seemed to hold my fate in his ruthless hands.

Kalel's gaze lifted slowly, those piercing grayish-brown eyes locking onto mine. A predatory smirk curved his full lips. "Did you hear from your crazy ex again?" Kalel asked.

Relief washed over me momentarily. He just wants to know about Liam. "No, I haven't," I replied evenly, forcing my voice not to shake.

"Good," he drawled, leaning back into his chair, confidence radiating from him. "Because I took care of it. You won't be hearing from him again."

A chill slithered down my spine, curiosity fighting dread. "What did you do?" I asked cautiously. As if I didn't already know the answer.

His smile grew darker, eyes glinting with secrets I probably didn't want to know. "What I did is none of your business, Sabrina." His voice held an unmistakable warning. "The real question is—how are you going to pay me back? I don't do favors for free."

My stomach twisted into knots. Is he serious? Meeting his gaze defiantly, I lifted my chin. "I can work for you until it's paid off."

He chuckled softly, a low, menacing sound. "Is that really repayment if you're working for me? Sounds more like I'd be paying myself." He rose from his chair, his tall, muscular frame unfolding with predatory grace.

Anxiety clawed at my chest. What's with him? I struggled to hide it behind a mask of bravado. "Well, what else can I offer? I have nothing useful for someone like you."

Kalel closed the distance between us, each step deliberate, powerful, suffocating. My breath hitched, heart hammering violently in my chest. His eyes raked over me slowly, igniting an unwelcome warmth beneath my skin. One that I know I shouldn't feel for him, but I do. "I can think of something," he murmured darkly, his voice a velvet threat.

15

I recoiled instinctively, eyes wide. "I'm not sleeping with you," I hissed, anger creeping into my tone despite my best efforts to hide it. Does he think I'm some sort of prostitute? Like, I'd sleep with him because he helped me?

He stopped mere inches from me, his scent enveloping me—intoxicating yet dangerous. He leaned in close, his voice dropping to a possessive whisper. "It's not about just sleeping with you, Sabrina. It's you I want. You belong to me now."

Shock froze me in place, rage bubbling hot, in my veins. "Like fucking hell I do!" I spat furiously.

His hand shot out, fingers gripping my chin with firm dominance, forcing me to meet his penetrating stare. Fear surged within me, yet I refused to let it show, refusing to cower. Kalel's voice became quiet and, shall I say, seductive. "We can do this the easy way or the hard way. And believe me, you won't enjoy the hard way, and I'd rather not make things messy."

I hated the tremor in my breath, hated how his touch burned against my skin, hated how helpless he made me feel. A reckless defiance surged within me, but logic made it clear. I was trapped. This was Kalel fucking Marchetti; A fight was pointless.

With bitter resignation, my voice icy and dripping with disgust. "Fine. Can I at least pack my bag?"

His thumb brushed softly across my jaw, eyes holding triumph and dark promise. "Good choice. You can, but Angelo will accompany you."

He released my chin, stepping back just enough to let me breathe again. But even then, as I looked into those stormy eyes, I knew I'd just lost the battle, but I would not lose the war. He may have my body, but if he wanted my mind, he was going to have to fight through hell to get it.

* * *

After Angelo and I finish packing my things, we headed to Kalel's place.

To find out it's not just a house—it's a fucking fortress. A sprawling estate in Bellavora that looks more like a palace than a home. A place built to keep people out. Or, worse, to keep them in.

As we drive past the gates, I glimpse the security—guards stationed at every turn, cameras hidden in places they think I won't notice. An icy chill slides down my spine. This isn't just a mansion. It's a goddamn prison wrapped in luxury.

When we pull up, Angelo steps out first. I hesitate before following, my stomach twisting as I take in the sheer size of it all. The wood steps, the towering pillars, the overwhelming silence of the place. It was overbearing.

I step inside, and the scent of leather and expensive cologne washes over me. Everything about this place is him. "This is where you'll be staying," Angelo says, leading me through endless hallways. I mumble "puñeta madre" under my breath, laced with all the irritation I feel, but Angelo only chuckles.

"I heard that." Angelo says.

I roll my eyes but say nothing, too busy surveying the space, committing details to memory. My room is beautiful, of course. Everything is, but beauty means nothing when you can't leave, and I can't fucking leave. The moment I'm alone, I throw my bag onto the bed with a sharp thud.

"Fuck."

My breathing is uneven. My chest is tight. I rake my fingers through my hair and whisper, "Fuck, fuck, fuck, fuck."

What the hell am I supposed to do? Just sit here and wait for whatever twisted plan Kalel has for me? I need a way out. I don't have time to waste, so I slip out of my room, walking through the hallways with careful steps. I don't expect to escape now. That would be stupid, but I can at least study the place. I could figure out where the weak spots are. If there are any.

The halls are quiet, but I feel the security. I can practically hear the unseen eyes watching me. A wrong turn leads me to a dead end. Another turn, another locked door. Ugh!

I clench my fists. Of course. I exhale slowly, about to turn back— and slam into something solid. Someone. A firm hand grabs my wrist before I can stumble back. Before I can run.

Kalel.

His grip is cold. Unshakable and absolute. I swallow hard as I look up, meeting his eyes—those beautiful Greyish-brown irises that always seem to see too much. How could he be so dang dangerous with such beautiful eyes? Dang it, girl, bring it back. He's your kidnapper. I know you seem to always fall for the bad guy, but get it together. Snapping myself back to reality, his eyes were unreadable. Something about them unsettled me.

He doesn't speak right away. He just looks at me, like he's memorizing my face, drinking in every shift of my expression, every flicker of emotion.

Then, softly, he says, "Trying to escape already?"

His tone is so calm it makes my skin prickle. There's no anger, no amusement. Just certainty. Like he expected this. Like he's been waiting for me to make my move.

My pulse thrums. I refuse to let him see how rattled I am. I tip my chin up, crossing my arms over my chest. "Would I get far if I tried?" I throw out, forcing sass into my voice.

He watches me. His grip on my wrist tightens just enough for me to notice, but not enough to hurt.

"No," he murmurs, his voice as smooth as silk. "You wouldn't."

The way he says it—so matter-of-fact, so final—sends ice crawling down my spine.

I scoff, trying to shake off the way my body reacts to him. "Is that so?"

Kalel steps closer. The warmth of his body almost presses against mine, caging me in. My back almost touches the wall. He doesn't even need to force me there—I feel trapped already.

"You don't understand, Sabrina." His voice is low, like a whisper meant to brand itself into my skin. "You're already mine. You were mine the moment I decided to help you."

I swallow hard. "You don't own me."

Something flickers in his gaze—dark amusement.

"Of course I do." He lifts a hand, brushing his fingers against my cheek. It's soft, almost gentle, but it feels like a warning.

"Every exit you find?" he murmurs. "I already know about it." His fingers trace down my jaw, sending a sharp shiver through me. "Every escape plan you think up? I've already considered it." His thumb brushes my lower lip, and I feel myself freeze. "You don't stand a chance, sweetheart." His voice is calm. Unshakable. He means every word.

And the worst part?

He's right.

I rip my wrist from his grasp, stepping back even though the heat of his touch still lingers on my skin. My breath comes too fast, my heart pounding against my ribs, but I force myself to stand tall.

"God, you're delusional," I spat, my voice laced with disgust. "You really think you own me? That I'll just sit here and be your perfect little prisoner?"

Kalel doesn't react. Not at first.

Then, slowly, he tilts his head. His gaze drags over me, like he's studying me. He's studying me as if I were something he's carved his name into long before I ever knew.

"I don't think, Sabrina." His voice is calm. Certain. "I know."

That certainty—it does something to me. It fuels my rage. I clench

19

my fists at my sides, nails digging into my palms. I hate the way he talks, the way he moves, the way he looks at me like this is all some inevitable conclusion.

"Go to hell," I snap. "I'll get out of here. And when I do, I swear—"

"Swear what?" Kalel interrupts, voice laced with steel. He steps forward, slowly, deliberately, cutting off the space between us inch by inch. "That you'll run? That you'll fight me? That every second, you'll fight against me and hate me?"

He's so close now, his body almost touching mine. The air between us is tight, electric—I want to step back, but I won't. I refuse to give that to him.

"Yes." My voice shakes, but not from fear. From rage. "I will never stop hating you."

Kalel exhales a quiet laugh, low and dark, like I just told him a secret he already knew.

"I hope so." He says smirking at me.

That catches me off guard. My brows furrow, my pulse stumbling for half a second. As he leans in, his breath grazing my ear. "I don't just want your love, sweetheart. I want all of you. Your fire, your anger, your hate. I want you to fight me repeatedly." He tilts his head, brushing his lips against the shell of my ear in a whisper-soft touch. "Because at the end of the day, you're still mine. No matter how hard you try to run—you're mine."

And I snap.

I shove him—hard—my hands hitting his chest with all the force I can muster. He doesn't stumble; Doesn't even flinch. But the moment I push him, his eyes change. The playfulness is gone. Something darker, hungrier, more sinister settles over his face, and before I can react—he has me caged against the wall again.

A sharp gasp leaves my lips as my back hits the cool surface, Kalel's hands braced beside my head, trapping me. I brace myself for pain, but it never comes. He doesn't hurt me. He just stares. Long and unyielding. Like he's daring me to fight harder. Like he wants me to. What a sick bastard.

It's like he's waiting to see how much more of him I can take before I break.

"I don't care how much you fight me," he murmurs, voice almost too soft for how terrifying it is. "I like it when you do." He shifts, his body brushing against mine. "But don't forget who's in control here, Sabrina. It's not you."

I glare up at him, refusing to back down. "Then kill me." His gaze darkens. For a second, something flashes behind his eyes—something raw and feral.

Then, to my horror, he smiles.

"Kill you?" he echoes, amused. "Now, why would I do that?" His fingers brush against my cheek, his touch mocking. "You'd look so pretty screaming my name instead."

My breath catches. I hate the way my stomach twists, how my pulse betrays me for half a second.

And he notices.

His thumb traces my lower lip, barely there, like he's testing me. Pushing me.

Seeing how far he can go before I snap again.

"You can hate me all you want," he murmurs, so close now. "But you'll never escape me. And deep down—" His lips barely graze my skin, his breath warm. "You already know that."

I slap his hand away, fury and panic churning inside me.

Kalel just smirks, stepping back. Like he won.

Like he always knew he would.

"Go ahead, try again," he says, stepping away, but his presence still suffocates me. "Try to run. Try to fight. Make this more fun for me." He gestures toward the hallway. "I'll even give you a head start."

I grit my teeth, rage bubbling beneath my skin. I don't run. I won't give him the satisfaction. Instead, I lift my chin and walk past him, refusing to look back as I return to my room.

* * *

The moment I shut the door, my hands shake. Because what the fuck was that? What the hell am I supposed to do now?

This isn't over.

Not even close.

For the next few days, I make it my mission to stay the hell away from Kalel. If I hear his voice down the hall? I turn around. If I spot him at dinner? I don't eat. If I get a glimpse of him walking through the estate? I disappear into my room. I refuse to give him another chance to get under my skin. To touch me. To push me. If he wants to play his little game of ownership, he can do it without me feeding into it.

And at first? It works.

The mansion is vast. Easy to avoid someone if you plan it right, and I plan it right.

When I wake up, I listen for footsteps outside my door before stepping out. If I see a maid coming from the east wing, I know Kalel's probably on that side, so I go the opposite way. I even time my movements, waiting until I hear him in his office before sneaking past to go to the garden, to the library—anywhere he isn't.

For days, I haven't seen him. Not once. Not even a glimpse, but I feel him. His presence is everywhere. In the guards watching me a little too closely. In the way the staff avoids meeting my eyes, like they know something I don't. In the shifts in the air, like he's there even when I can't see him.

And it's driving him insane. It happens on the fifth night. I'm in my room, flipping through a book I don't give a damn about, pretending

I'm not starving because I skipped dinner again.

Then—the door swings open. Hard. Like it's been ripped from its hinges. Kalel stands in the doorway, his broad frame casting a long, menacing shadow across the room. He's slightly undone his shirt at the collar, rolling up his sleeves as if he's just been in a fight. The veritable storm is in his eyes.

Was dark and unrelenting. He's furious, but worse. He's calm about it. For a second, neither of us speaks. The air crackles, thick with something dangerous. Then, in a voice too quiet for how angry he looks, he says, "Are you done?" No.

My fingers tighten around the book. "Excuse me?" Kalel steps inside, closing the door behind him with a deliberate click. I immediately step back, heart pounding. "What the hell do you want?" I ask.

He doesn't answer. He just keeps moving, slowly like a wolf finally cornering its prey. I back up again until my legs hit the bed. Shit. So, I walk away from him, closer to the window. I refuse to be trapped.

His lips curl—not in amusement, not in arrogance. In something else. Something so much worse. "You're avoiding me," he says, voice deceptively soft. I tilt my chin up. "Took you this long to notice?" Kalel lets out a slow breath, running a hand down his face, like he's fighting the urge to do something reckless. Then, his eyes snap back to mine, and I swear the temperature in the room drops.

"You're testing me, Sabrina," he murmurs, stepping closer. I try to move, but there's nowhere to go. I'm trapped. My throat tightens. "Oh? Am I now?" I ask sarcastically.

Kalel exhales sharply, like he's reached his limit. Then—he moves his hands slamming them against the wall on either side of me. Caging me in. I inhale sharply, my entire body locking up as he looms over me, heat radiating off of him like a storm about to break. His scent, his presence—it's all-consuming. "You think you can avoid me?" His voice is low, dark, and possessive. "You think you can pretend I don't exist?" I glare up at him, refusing to shrink under his presence. "I don't have to pretend. You're nothing to me." A muscle ticks in his jaw. Oh, that pissed him off.

Then, without warning—his fingers wrap around my throat. Not tight. Not choking, just holding. A warning. A reminder. That he could. That if he wanted to, if I pushed him hard enough, he would. My breath stutters. My pulse hammers, and—he notices. Of course, he notices. His thumb strokes along my jaw, almost gently, but his eyes?

Feral.

"You belong to me, Sabrina." His voice is barely above a whisper, but it's the most suffocating thing I've ever heard. "You can run, you can hide, you can ignore me all you want." His thumb presses just a fraction harder, and I feel it everywhere. "But at the end of the day, you'll still end up right here. With me." I suck in a shaky breath, hating the way my body is making me feel.

Hating the way my skin burns where he touches me. Kalel leans in, his lips just inches from mine. It takes everything in me not to hit him. "If you want a war," he murmurs, "you've got one." Then, suddenly, he releases me. Stepping back like he wasn't just two seconds away from ruining me. I blink, disoriented, my breath still uneven. Kalel watches me with a look that seals my fate. He's done being patient.

The real game starts now.

Chapter 3

Sabrina

Days after Kalel's confrontation, I feel his presence like a noose around my neck. He won't let me ignore him anymore. If I try to eat alone? He's there. If I try to walk in the garden? He's suddenly beside me. If I spend too long in my room? The door opens, and his voice cuts through the silence. Come. Now.

It's suffocating.

He's suffocating, but I don't break. I won't.

Instead, I do the only thing I can—I study. Every hallway. Every exit. Every blind spot. I memorize the guards' movements, watching the subtle shifts in their patrols. Not all of the guards maintain discipline. Some of them get lazy. Some do not check certain corners. Some take smoke breaks at the same time every night.

I keep track of it all, and when the opportunity finally presents itself—I take it. It's just past midnight when I slip out of my room. Moving fast and silently, I stick to the shadows. I calculate every step I take. I head toward the back of the estate, where the servants' entrance is. It's rarely used at this hour, and if I time it right, I can slip past the blind spot between the cameras. The adrenaline pumps through my veins, my heart slamming against my ribs. I can taste freedom.

I'm so close.

The cool night air hits my skin as I reach the door. It's unlocked.

Yes!

My breath catches. I did it. For the first time since Kalel took me, I have a chance. I push the door open, stepping out into the crisp darkness. My feet hit the gravel, my pulse thrumming—and then I hear it. A slow clap. The sound is sharp and deliberate.

Mocking.

My stomach drops as a shadow moves from the corner of my vision, stepping into the dim glow of the security lights.

Angelo.

His arms are crossed, his posture relaxed—too relaxed.

That smug bastard.

He's been waiting for this. He knew I was going to escape. I freeze, my breath coming in sharp bursts as he cocks his head, amusement flickering across his face. "Really, Princess?" His voice is casual, but there's an unmistakable edge beneath it. "You thought you'd make it past me?"

My fingers curl into fists. "You could always just let me go. Pretend you saw nothing."

He raises an eyebrow, unimpressed. "Let you run? Kalel would have my head. And honestly?" He sighs, shaking his head. "I like my head."

Rage burns through me. "I don't care what Kalel wants." My voice is sharp and full of venom. "You can either move, or I'll—"

"You'll what?" He's suddenly in front of me. Geez, he's fast. I guess Ghost was the right nickname for someone like him. Before I can react, he grabs my wrist. Firm. I jerk back, but he doesn't let go. I swing at him with my free hand, but he dodges effortlessly, catching my arm like it's nothing. Great, Sabrina...Good job.

"Easy, sweetheart," he mutters, twisting me around. Then, I feel it. The cold press of metal. Did he just put fucking handcuffs on me? I thrash, but it's too late. The cuffs snap into place around my wrists, locking them behind my back.

No. No, no, no —

Panic claws at my throat as Angelo sighs, like he's dealing with a reckless kid instead of a desperate woman. "You really thought you would get away from us that easily?" he murmurs against my ear, voice almost sympathetic. "Kalel told me to monitor you. Especially after you started avoiding him."

Bastard.

I bite my lip hard enough to taste blood, breathing ragged. "Don't take it personally, Princess." Angelo adjusts his grip, holding me steady. "It's just business." I snarl, thrashing again. "Let me go, Angelo!" But he doesn't. Instead, he lifts me like I weigh nothing. My feet leave the ground as he throws me over his shoulder, carrying me back toward the mansion like a misbehaving child.

"You're gonna regret this," I growl, kicking. Angelo just sighs. "Yeah, yeah, you'll kill me, gut me, burn my corpse—I've heard it all before."

I scream in frustration, my fists clenching against my back." Put me down!" I was so close, so fucking close. But now, I know one thing for certain. Kalel is going to find out, and he is going to make me pay. The moment Angelo drops me onto my feet inside the estate, I know what's coming.

Kalel is waiting.

He stands in the center of the room, arms crossed, his eyes dark with something unreadable. He doesn't move. Doesn't speak.

But the air is thick—too thick.

Angelo, the traitor, smirks. "She gave me a little trouble, but nothing I couldn't handle." Kalel doesn't even acknowledge him. His focus is on me. I square my shoulders, refusing to look weak. "Go ahead. Say whatever bullshit lecture you've got planned, then get out of my way."

Kalel's expression doesn't change, but I see it. The slight tic in his jaw. The way his fingers flex at his sides, like he's holding himself back.

Then—his voice cuts through the silence. "Remove the handcuffs." Kalel demands.

Angelo hesitates. "Kal, are you sure? She—"

"Now."

Angelo sighs but does as he's told, unlocking the handcuffs. The second my wrists are free, I rub the sore skin, shooting Kalel a look of pure hatred. "Happy?" I sneer. Kalel doesn't answer. Instead—he moves. He grabs me by the throat, lifting me off the ground like I weigh nothing, and slams me into the wall, easy enough not to hurt me. Just enough to warn me. Then he lets go and a startled gasp rips from my lips as my back hits the nearest wall.

Kalel's body pressed against mine, one hand braced beside my head, the other gripping my chin—forcing me to look at him. His eyes are molten fire, burning into me. "Do you have any idea," he murmurs, voice too quiet, too dangerous, "how much trouble you've been causing me?" My breath is uneven, my pulse hammering.

I try to shove him, but he doesn't budge. I hate how he makes me feel small. Hate the way my body reacts to him. "I wouldn't have caused you any trouble if you'd just let me go," I hiss.

Kalel laughs. A low, dark sound.

"Let you go?" He leans in, his lips almost brushing against my ear. "Kitten, I don't think you understand the situation you're in." His grip on my chin tightens—just enough to make me gasp. "You don't get to leave me," he murmurs, his breath warm against my skin.

Something flickers in his eyes—something disgustedly satisfied. Because he sees it. The way my chest rises and falls too fast.

The way my lips part just slightly. The way my body, traitorous and weak, shivers under his touch.

"Fuck you," I breathe.

His smirk is slow and dangerous. "Not yet," he murmurs, and then— he pulls away. His sudden withdrawal of his heat makes me dizzy, as if

28

someone cut off my oxygen. Before I can process what's happening, he grabs my wrist and drags me through the hall.

"What the fuck is wrong with you? Let go of me!" I yell as I twist, struggling against his hold, but his grip is iron. "You wanted to run? There was an unnerving stillness in his voice. "You are going to learn your lesson." He shoves me into my room, and I spin, ready to throw every curse I know at him—but the moment I do—he slams the door shut and locks it.

The sound of the deadbolt sliding into place sends an icy chill through me. I know he didn't just lock the fucking door! I rush forward, yanking at the handle, but it doesn't budge. My stomach drops. "Kalel!" I snap, pounding on the door. "Open this fucking door!" I scream from the other side, his voice was too casual. "You're going to stay in there until you learn to behave." He says. Rage burns through me. Who does he think he is? I don't even listen to my father. What makes him think I'll listen to him? "You can't just—"

"I can." He says and I hear the shift in his weight as he's leaning against the door. Like he's enjoying this. Like he's taking his time.

"Sleep tight, sweetheart." His voice is mocking and amused. "You're going to need your energy." My entire body tensed. "For what?" I asked.

He pauses. Then—he chuckles. "You'll find out soon enough." And then—his footsteps retreat. Leaving me locked away.

Leaving me trapped.

And the worst part? I don't know what he's planning next.

* * *

I wake up the next morning to the feeling of someone standing over me. The air is too still, heavy with the scent of spiced cologne. His

29

scent. My eyes snap open, heart pounding—and Kalel is there.

He stands at the edge of my bed, his eyes unreadable. One hand tucked into his pocket, the other rolling up the cuff of his crisp white shirt, casual, like he hasn't just scared the life out of me.

"Get up," he says, smoothly. "Get dressed."

Confusion fogs my mind. My body is still stiff from yesterday, from being locked in this damn room like a misbehaving pet. I push up on my elbows, glaring at him. "For what?" I ask. Kalel watches me for a long moment, then—with a smirk. The slow, calculated one that makes my stomach twist. "I'm giving you another way to pay me back." I freeze.

The weight of his words sinks deep into my bones, an unease curling in my chest. Another way? Something in his tone makes my skin crawl. Still, I refuse to show weakness. I shove the blanket off and stand barefoot on the cold floor, staring him down. "If this is another one of your games, Kalel—"

He tilts his head, amusement flickering in his gaze. "Let's see if you'll win or lose, sweetheart because I always win." The warning sends a chill through me. I grab the first outfit I can find—a simple dress, nothing special, nothing inviting—and head toward the bathroom, but before I can shut the door, his voice follows me.

"Wear something pretty." I hear as I slam the door shut. Now he wants to control what I wear, great.

* * *

The drive is quiet, but the tension sits thick between us. Kalel is calm, fingers drumming against the steering wheel, his body relaxed. He is calm, too calm for my liking. I just know he's planning something and the worst part is that all I can do is wait. Wait for the inevitable. "Where are we going?" I ask glaring at him. His lips curl, but he doesn't look at me. "You'll see."

I hate how the answer makes my stomach drop. The car slows, and when I glance outside. That's when I see it. The flashing neon lights. Faint music thrummed in the background. The dark-tinted windows, the shadows of women moving inside. A strip club, but not just any strip club. I know this place. Everyone does. We are going to La Morsa and I panic because La Morsa is more than just a club. It's a known brothel. Shit. Shit. Shit. He wouldn't, right?

Panic grips my chest. I turn to Kalel, my breath shallow. "Why are we here?" I ask, as he finally looks at me, his expression unreadable. "Business." he says, like I have nothing to be worried about.

The scent of cheap perfume and alcohol hits me instantly as soon as we walk in. It's dimly lit, all plush red velvet and flashing lights, women in barely there outfits draped over men with dead eyes and too much money.

I hate it.

Kalel doesn't react. He moves through the club like he owns it, like he's above it all. And I hate that, too. We're led to a private booth in the back, away from the main floor. The club owner is already waiting for us. A large man, with greedy eyes that rake over me the moment we sit down. I shift in my seat, every muscle in my body screaming, this is wrong.

Kalel leans back in the booth, the picture of ease—legs spread, arm draped over the seat like he owns the entire fucking city. "Do you still need a new girl for the back?" he asks, voice smooth. The club owner let out a bitter laugh, rubbing a hand over his scruffy chin. "You don't know how hard it's been to find girls lately. None of them wanna work here—too many rumors. It makes my job a nightmare."

Kalel hums thoughtfully. Then—without looking at me—he says, "You can have her."

I freeze. The words make little sense at first. They hit too softly, too casually.

You can have her. What the fuck?

I blink at him. There was no smile. No laugh. No hint of a joke. Just calm certainty. Like I'm a glass of fucking wine he's offering to pass across the table. The club owner perks up instantly, interest gleaming in his eyes. "You serious?" Kalel sits up, meets his gaze, and nods once. "Completely." My breath catches. My skin prickles.

No. No. No.

What the fuck is wrong with this man?

The man turns to me slowly, gaze sweeping down my body like he's already undressing me. "I'd treat you better than he probably does," he says, voice slick and revolting and I want to scream. He reaches for me—fingers brushing the bare skin of my arm—and every cell in my body recoils. I yanking my arm away. "Don't touch me" I say demanding and enraged.

I look at Kalel begging him to do something, say something—but Kalel doesn't move. He watches. Not with anger. Not even with indifference.

This sick bastard is amused by this and If I make it out of here, I am going to kill him.

His eyes glitter with quiet, terrifying delight. Like, this is entertainment. Like he wants to see what I'll do. My chest rises. "What the fuck is wrong with you?" I snap. Kalel still doesn't move, but now, finally, he speaks.

"Hold on," he murmurs, voice soft. Almost bored. The club owner pauses.

"What?" the man asks.

Kalel leans further back, exuding complete control but clearly feigning. "You can have her... if she wants to go."

The room goes still and the man's eyes shift to me—eager, expectant. Ha, he's testing me! Me! The one he kidnapped.

Kalel's eyes stay locked on mine. His voice drops, smooth and silken, yet laced with the faintest mockery. "You have five seconds, Sabrina."

He can't be serious.

"Five." The blood drains from my face. "Four." He's serious. He's really doing this. "Three." My throat closes. I can't breathe.

"Two."And I realize — this isn't about giving me a choice. It's about showing me I don't have one. I'm not free, not really. Never was. "I want to stay with you," I choke out, the words tasting like poison.

Silence.

Kalel's gaze darkens. Then—he smiles. Not with joy. Not with affection, but with satisfaction. He felt like a man who had just confirmed what he wanted to know.

"I guess she doesn't want to go with you," he says, voice dismissive as he turns back to the club owner. The man sighs and clicks his tongue. "Shame. She would've made me a lot of money." Kalel's hand clamps around my wrist—tight and unforgiving—as he pulls me to my feet and leads me from the booth. I don't resist. I'm too angry to move. Too humiliated to speak.

Outside, the chilly air hits me like a slap. My breath escapes in a harsh, ragged exhale. When we reach the car; I rip my wrist from his grip and whirl at him, fury cutting through the fog of fear. I punch him in the face, hard. Before I can think about what I've done. Because what the fuck had I just done, but I can't back down now. I'm too angry.

"What the fuck was that?" I hiss, but Kalel doesn't blink. He just smirks as the car unlocks with a soft click. "That," he says calmly, licking his bottom lip, "was a lesson." I stare at him, heart hammering. "Will you need another one?" He asks with a smirk.

A lesson.

That's what that was to him. He wanted me to beg to stay. He wanted me to choose him—even when the other option was being handed over like a piece of meat. He wanted me to know that even if I hated him... I'd still pick him. Because the alternative was worse.

He doesn't need to chain me. He doesn't have to cage me. He just has to show me how little power I have. Then smile while I try to pretend I'm the one in control. Little did he know I won't go down without a fight. Even if I don't know if I've ever hated him or feared him more.

Because now I know—Kalel Marchetti isn't just dangerous. He's deliberate, and I'm already too deep to escape.

Normal people would get the message, but me? I wish I would let him think he could do any and everything to me without a fight. Fucking dickhead.

Chapter 4

Kalel

Sabrina sits beside me in the car with her arms crossed tight over her chest, jaw clenched, staring out the window like it might offer her an escape. She punched me, and I liked it. I love the fight. I love that she that thinks she won something tonight. She thinks she made a choice. We both know she didn't, but that punch? It makes me want to bring her to her knees and make her beg. I want to see how much fight she will have once I make her beg for someone to save her. Only to find out the only savior she will ever have is looking at her right now. I sigh. Right now, she thinks she holds some ounce of control in a situation I created just to take it from her.

But the truth?

I chose for her.

She was never leaving me. Not for that man and not for anyone. She'll realize that soon.

I watch her from the corner of my eye. I see the way her fingers tap against her thigh, like she's trying to release all the tension clawing at her inside.

Good. She should be tense because I'm calm now. Which is always the most dangerous side of me.

When we pull up to the estate, she doesn't wait. She gets out fast, like she's trying to outrun the night or me and I let her. I give her that space. That illusion of control she's so desperate to cling to.

She walks ahead of me, moving like every step takes effort. Like the weight of tonight is finally sinking in. I follow in silence, close enough to touch her, but far enough to make her wonder when I will. She avoids looking back. "Are you done?" she asks, annoyed.

"Shouldn't I be asking you that?" I say, holding in my amusement, or trying to. I sense her temper rising and it brings a smile to my face. One I can no longer hide.

I've never been affected by women. Never cared enough to let it affect me. As I think about all the women, I've fucked, and there's been many. There has been no one to keep my attention like she does. Sabrina sighs, bringing me out of my thoughts.

Her punishment is subtle but effective. She thinks her silence is a weapon, but I don't need words to win. I just need proximity. We reach her door and she opens it. Hands trembling, and that's when I do it. Just a touch—my hand brushing the back of her neck. Her gasp is perfect.

Soft and guttural.

Her entire body locks up, her fingers going tighten around the doorknob. She feels it and hates it. The shift in the air. The sharp, silent understanding that I let her walk ahead. I let her get to the door.

That I let her think she is safe, but she isn't. Not from me. I step closer, my breath brushing the shell of her ear as I lean in—close enough to feel the tremble in her spine. Her breathing hitches again. She's fighting it. Fighting me. She hates me.

And I love it.

I smirk as she stares up at me, her hazel eyes flashing with emotion—fear, confusion, fury, all tangled together. "I hope you learned something today, Kitten." She doesn't answer. Instead, she watches me like I'm something unholy. I smile, releasing the door, and she slams it shut in my face.

I chuckle, slipping my hands into my pockets, the sound low and amused as it echoes down the hallway. This is going to be fun. She thinks the door is enough to keep me out.

Cute.

I'll let her cling to whatever scraps of control she thinks she still has. Let her believe she's safe. For now.

* * *

When the house falls quiet and the night settles over the water like a heavy shroud, I go to her. The door is unlocked. She can't be that mad, or maybe she wanted me to come. Either way, she made it easy.

I step inside, slowly and silently, letting the door close behind me with a quiet click.

The room is dark—quiet. Only the soft sound of her steady breathing greets me. Moonlight cuts across the room in silvery streaks, casting soft shadows over her sleeping form. She's curled on her side, a sliver of bare skin exposed beneath the thin blanket. Her curls are wild and messy, her face soft with sleep.

She looks fragile like this. Defenseless.

Mine.

I move closer—my steps soundless on the floor. I don't need to rush. She isn't going anywhere.

Not now. Not ever.

I lower myself into the chair beside her bed, elbows resting on my knees, eyes locked on her. Watching her like this is ten times better than watching her from afar, I think as I admire her. She is incomparable. For hours, I could be content watching her like this. She stirs slightly, breath shifting. I lean forward, my voice a whisper soaked in control. "You looked peaceful." Her breath hitches.

There it is—that beautiful reaction. The instant awareness that slams into her before she even opens her eyes. Her body tensed, going rigid beneath the covers. She feels me. She knows. Not by touch. By instinct.

Then—slowly—she blinks awake. I can sense her anger and fear before she says anything.

I smile. "I almost didn't wake you," I murmur, my voice smooth, possessive. She shoots up, scrambling backward, the blankets tangling around her legs.

"What the fuck!"

I tilt my head, watching her. Has she not realized how fucked up I actually am? She's breathless. Disoriented and perfect. I let the moment stretch, let her feel the weight of my presence, let her realize how long I've been sitting here. Watching her.

Her chest rises and falls fast, her hands clenching the sheets. "Why are you in my room?" she breathes. I lean back, stretching out, owning the space. "You left the door unlocked," I say casually. "That's practically an invitation."

She blinks.

"Get out." She says deadpan.

I hum, amused. "Not yet." I say.

Should I see how annoyed I can get her? She swallows hard, trying to mask the way she reacting to me. Trying to pretend she's not terrified, but I see everything.

I let my gaze drag over her, slow and deliberate, before locking onto her eyes. "You were so still," I murmur, voice soft. "So peaceful."

She rolls her eyes.

"And yet," I continue, tilting my head, "I wonder... were you dreaming about running?" I smile slowly, mockingly.

She stares blankly.

"You can't run from me, Sabrina." I lean in, my voice dropping to a whisper. "Not even in your sleep."

Her lips part. Her breath shudders. She freezes, good. I reach out, trailing my fingers along the edge of the blanket, watching her reaction.

"Are you always this melodramatic?" She says with a mocking look in her eyes. "If you missed me, you could've just said that." She says annoyed. "And if I do?" I say as I lick my bottom lip. Eyes trailing from her lips back up to her eyes.

"well it depends on if you miss me or if you want to scare me," she says as her strap slides off her shoulder. Is she teasing me? She's now sitting up on the bed on her knees. My cock throbs and I want to show her how much I really miss her, but I can't. Not yet.

I get up from the chair and walk towards her. "You don't like this, do you?" I murmur, my fingers barely brushing against the fabric of her pajamas up to her chin, bringing her eyes up to mine. The look in her eyes threatening my unravel. "you don't like me being in here. Watching you sleep. Knowing you're completely at my mercy." She swallows while I am holding on to whatever shred of self control I have.

I smirk.

"You should lock your door next time," I whisper. "Unless you want me to come back." Then—I turn to leave. Her breath rushes out in a shaky exhale as she watches me, waiting, unsure of what I'll do next.

I pause at the door, glancing back. Sabrina's still waiting for me to pounce. I chuckle.

"Sleep well, sweetheart."

And then—I leave.

I let her wonder if I'll come back. Let her know that next time? She won't be so lucky. I don't knock and I won't announce myself.

The next morning I come into her room, the doors still unlocked. She's still sleeping, curled in the sheets, her hair sprawled like silk over the pillow. I let my eyes trace her, dragging over the soft rise and fall of her chest, the exposed skin of her shoulder, the way her lips part slightly in sleep.

Peaceful.

That's about to change. I step closer, grabbing the edge of the blankets and rip them off her. She gasps, body jerking awake, hands flying up in defense as she scrambles back disoriented and confused.

Perfect.

"Get up."

She breathes raggedly, her body tensed, but she glares at me, her hazel eyes flashing with anger as she realizes where she is.

"What the hell, Kalel?" Her voice is rough with sleep, but the venom is still there.

I smirk, arms crossed, as I tower over the bed. "I gave you a night to yourself. You should be grateful."

She clenches the sheets, jaw tight.

I lean down closer, invading her space, my hand bracing against the mattress beside her. "But the little game you played?" I let my fingers ghost over her wrist, just enough to feel her pulse—fast. "That ends today."

Her body tenses under my touch. I can feel it, the heat. The resistance. The panic. She hates this. She wants to fight me.

And I want her to.

Her chest rises sharply as she tries to twist away, but I grab her arm, holding her still.

She freezes.

And then, her voice drops—low, biting. "Let. Me. go." I tilt my head, studying her. She's so small beneath me, her body rigid, her muscles coiled with fight.

I love it.

I lean in, my lips hovering near her ear, my voice dropping into a smooth, mocking whisper.

"No." I say.

Then—I pull her up, dragging her out of bed.

She thrashes, yanking against me, but I barely feel it. She's trying to fight against a force she can't control.

"Kalel!" I throw her over my shoulder. She gasps, her fists pounding against my back as I carry her out of the room.

"Put me down!" She demands.

I chuckle, unbothered.

"Not a chance, Baby." I drop her into the dining chair, watching as she fumbles to catch herself. She breathes fast.

She looks furious. She should be, but it's her own fault. I grab a plate, sliding it in front of her. "Eat."

She glares at me. "I'm not hungry." I let out a slow sigh, stepping behind her chair.

She stiffens when my hands graze her shoulders, fingers brushing against her skin.

I grip the chair, leaning down beside her.

"You don't get to ignore me, Sabrina," I murmur, voice like silk. "Not in this house. Not anywhere." I feel the way she shudders, the way her breathing faltered for a split second.

She thinks she's strong enough to resist me, but her body?

Her body already knows who owns her. She snatches the fork, stabbing into the food aggressively. I smirk, Good girl.

The moment she finishes, she tries to escape. She stands fast, ready to bolt, but I catch her wrist. As I yank her into my lap, she gasps. She lands hard against my chest, her breath slamming out of her in a sharp exhale.

She freezes, but she doesn't move.

I let go of her wrist and put my hand on her thigh and slide it to her waist. I feel the tension in her spine, the rapid beat of her pulse. My grip tightens around her waist, fingers spreading over her hip. "Where do you think you're going?" My voice is low, edged with amusement.

Her body burns against mine, every part of her rigid, locked in place. She smells fucking intoxicating.

I let my fingers drift, trailing up her ribs, grazing the soft curve of her waist.

"You don't get to run from me, remember?" I murmur. "Not today. Not ever."

She snaps. Her nails dig into my arms, trying to push away, but I don't let her go. Instead, I lean in, my lips grazing her ear, my breath warm against her too-hot skin.

"You feel that?" I whisper, my hand pressing flat against her stomach. "The way your body reacts to me?" She trembles. Her breath hitches.

I grin.

"You hate me," I murmur. "But not as much as you wish you did." Her sharp inhale is my fucking victory. She throws herself off me, stumbling back, her chest rising and falling fast. "Are you going to tease me again?" I ask.

I watch her, my smirk slow and deliberate.

"Go ahead, sweetheart," I murmur, watching the way her hands shake at her sides. "Run."

She hesitates.

Just for a second. Then she storms away, fists clenched. "Pendejo!" she yells and I smirk, letting her go.

For now, but she knows the truth now. She can fight me all she wants. She'll always lose.

Because she's already mine.

* * *

Sabrina

42

I hate him! I hate him with everything in me. But hate doesn't feel strong enough anymore.

Hate means I have some kind of control. It means I can hold on to my anger like a shield, like a weapon.

But after today—after the constant pressure of him, of his presence, of his hands on me—I feel like I've lost something.

Or worse.

Like he's taken it. I slam the door to my room so hard that the walls shake. My ragged breath and trembling hands force me to press my back against the door to stay upright.

What is wrong with this man?

Breathe. Breathe.

How can I breathe when my body is betraying me? My skin still burns where he touched me. My lips are still parted from the way he whispered in my ear, from the way his breath grazed my throat. "You don't get to ignore me, sweetheart." The thought rumbles in my head. I press my fists against my temples, trying to shove his voice out of my head.

It's not working, he's everywhere. He's inside me now.

And I don't know how to get him out.

My body is still buzzing. Hot and restless, too aware. I should shake with rage. I should plot my next escape. Instead, I press my thighs together, swallowing down the memory of his fingers brushing my stomach, his hands playing against my ribs. Of how effortless it was for him to hold me down. How my breath hitched before I could stop it.

A warm wave of disgust rolls through me.

Not at him. At myself. I let him win, even if it was just for a second. Even if it was just my body betraying me. Which it was. Even if I know— I will never give in to him. I shove away from the door, pacing the room, restless to sit still.

I have problems.

Did I not learn from Liam?

He won't let this be the last time he corners me, the last time he forces me into his space, into his touch. Because now he knows. He saw it. The way I reacted. The way I froze.

The way my body—my traitorous, weak, fucking body—shuddered under his hands. And now? He'll never stop. I cross the room and grab the dresser, yanking at the drawers, searching for something—anything—that could give me an edge.

A weapon. A way out. A way to stop him.

If I don't, I won't survive this. Not the way I need to.

Not the way I want to. The worst thing about Kalel isn't his control. It isn't his strength.

It isn't even the way he plays with me, like a cat with a mouse he refuses to kill. The worst thing about Kalel is that he knows me. It's how weak he makes me feel without actually having to do anything to me. And if he keeps pushing—

If he keeps breaking me down — if he keeps forcing me to want him

One day, I might not fight him anymore. And that? That terrifies me more than anything else.

I don't leave my room for the rest of the day. Not because I'm scared. I just refuse to give him the satisfaction of seeing me like this. Of seeing how I still feel him on my skin. Of seeing how he's inside my head now, and I can't shake him loose. I've always had a soft spot for the bad boys, but this girl? Get it together! I pace the room, every muscle coiled tight, every breath feeling too shallow.

I can't let him get to me.

I won't.

I need time. Space. I hear a knock at the door. I freeze. Then—the handle turns. My stomach drops. The lock doesn't turn. Because I never locked it.

Fuck.

The door swings open, and there he is. Kalel steps inside, closing the door behind him, his gaze locking onto me like a hunter finding his prey.

I sigh. "Get out." His lips curve slowly and mocking. "No." He says.

I take a step back. "I don't want to see you." He exhales a slow breath, tilting his head like he's amused. "That's cute." I grit my teeth. "I'm not in the mood for your games, Kalel." His eyes darken. "Who said this was a game?"

I swallow hard. Fuck me, man. He moves forward. Slow. Deliberate. I move back instinctively.

His smirk deepens. He loves this. He loves the way I react to him. The way I can't stop reacting to him. I hit the dresser, my breath catching as I realize there's nowhere else to go.

Kalel stops in front of me, one hand bracing against the wood beside my hip. Caging me in.

My heart pounds. I refuse to look up at him. I refuse to let him see what this is doing to me; But I can feel it. The weight of his gaze. The warmth of his body, too close, too solid, too much. Then—his fingers brush my chin.

A slow touch. I jerk my head away.

His grip tightens. Not enough to hurt. Just enough to say I own you. Enough to make my breath stutter.

He forces my chin up, his eyes burning into mine. "Look at me."He says.

I shake my head. "Fuck you."

"Say it again."

I don't, because suddenly, my entire body is thrumming with something I don't want to name.

Something dangerous. Something he feels, too. Because his eyes— they change.

They go darker. Heavier. More possessive.

His thumb traces the edge of my jaw, slow and calculated. I don't know why I do it, but move, get on my tippy toes and lick him.

"Did you just lick me?" he murmurs with a smirk. "Why?"

I clench my fists. Because why did I do that? "Too much tension." I smirk, panicking inside. "If you want to play games, then let's play." I say.

He chuckles, soft and dark. "Is that so?" Then—he leans in. Too close. His breath brushes my lips, sending a full-body shiver through me. My heart slams into my ribs. I turn my head at the last second, my breath uneven.

Wrong move. His lips graze my throat instead. A slow, deliberate brush of warmth against sensitive skin. I go still. My pulse jumps in more than one place. God help me.

Kalel notices. Of course he does. His lips curve against my skin. "You hate me." Kalel says, as I suck in a sharp breath. "Yes."

His hand slides to my waist, his fingers spreading against my ribs, holding me still. I tremble. His voice drops. "Then tell me, baby..." His teeth graze my neck. A soft, teasing scrape that sends a full-body shudder through me. "Why does your body say otherwise?"

I make a sound—**a sharp, strangled gasp—**and that's when I know. I know I've lost. Because that sound? That's exactly what he wanted. Kalel pulls back just enough to look at me. Really look at me. His gaze scorches over my skin, his pupils dark and hungry.

"Say it."

My ragged breathing made it hard to speak. "Say what?"

His thumb brushes my lower lip. "Tell me you don't want this." I snap back to reality. My jaw locks. My hands clench into fists. I shove at his chest, forcing space between us. "I don't. I never will."

His smirk is slow and mesmerizing. "Liar." He says.

I glare at him. "Get out." His eyes glint. "Not yet." I breathe hard, hating myself for feeling like I need air. He watches me for a long

46

moment.

Then, slowly, he steps back. I let out a breath I didn't realize I was holding. But before I can regain my composure—

He leans in one last time, his lips hovering over my ear. "One day, you'll stop fighting, Sabrina." His breath burns against my skin. "And when you do?" His hand ghosts over my stomach, teasing, lingering— then gone.

I shudder.

"You'll beg me for more." Then—he turns and walks away. Leaving me breathless. Shaking and terrified, not of him. Of myself. Because, for the first time, I wonder—if he might be right. Will I be the first one to break?

Chapter 5

<u>Sabrina</u>

I woke up slowly, stretching out beneath the soft, warm sheets. Sunlight streamed through the curtains, bathing the room in the gentle glow. For a moment, I almost forgot where I was—until reality slammed into me with a harsh reminder.

With a sigh, I pushed myself out of bed, shuffling toward the bathroom to shower. As the warm water cascaded over my skin, my mind began racing, searching for a new plan. Every day felt more suffocating, each attempt at freedom more desperate.

I dressed quickly, pulling on a simple outfit and twisting my hair into a loose bun. With a deep breath, I headed downstairs to the dining room, where breakfast awaited me. You've got this. Kalel is already there, sipping his coffee calmly, his posture annoyingly relaxed.

I took a seat opposite him, grabbing a fork and aimlessly pushing scrambled eggs around my plate, my appetite nonexistent. Kalel's gaze settled on me, his eyes unreadable.

"You know," Kalel began casually, his voice breaking the heavy silence, "you can leave the house if you want, but Angelo has to go with you."

My head snapped up, heart racing with sudden hope, only for suspicion to swiftly follow. "I'm not a child. Why does Angelo have to come?"

Kalel's expression didn't waver, his eyes fixed on me with a mix of amusement and warning. "It's an offer, Kitten. Take it or leave it." Kalel says.

I huffed, folding my arms over my chest, frustration bubbling inside me. "That's just trading one cage for another."

"Think of him as your very intimidating shadow," Kalel drawled, leaning back in his chair, his eyes glittering dangerously. His voice remained deceptively casual. "Your only other choice is staying here, with me."

Frustration boiled beneath my skin, but suddenly, a thought sparked in my mind. If Angelo was the only guard, maybe I had a chance. My heart thudded, and I quickly masked my excitement with feigned resignation. "Fine."

Kalel studied me for a moment longer, a faint smirk curving his lips. "Good girl."

A few hours later, I call for Angelo because I'm ready to leave this hellhole. And then I walked out of the room, Angelo falls into step beside me, his presence comforting yet irritating. This better work because if it doesn't, this might be my last glimpse of freedom I will ever see. I glanced sideways at him, forcing a cheerful voice. "I want to go to that diner on Fifth. You know, the one that serves those milkshakes you hate."

Angelo chuckled softly. "If you insist."

We drove in silence, my mind racing. When we arrived, Angelo shadowed me inside, his presence drawing curious stares from the other patrons. We sat down and placed our order, but all I could think of was my escape being a success. Once the waitress brought our meals, we ate, the atmosphere deceptively casual. After a few minutes, I excused myself casually. "Bathroom break. Be right back." I said.

Angelo's eyes met mine briefly, unreadable. "Sure."

In the bathroom, my pulse pounded. I glanced at the small window above the sinks—small but manageable. After a quick struggle, I pushed myself through, dropping to the ground in the alleyway behind the diner. Adrenaline surged as I straightened, a triumphant grin spreading across my face.

"Really? The bathroom window?"

My heart plummeted. I spun around, finding Angelo leaning against the wall, arms crossed, eyebrow raised in mild amusement. Ugh!

"That's about as cliche as it gets, Sabrina," he sighed, pushing off the wall and stepping closer. "Did you really think I wouldn't be watching?"

My shoulders slumped, irritation flooding my features. "It was worth a shot."

Angelo guided me firmly yet gently back toward the car. Closing the door behind me and I take off running out the other side of the car. Angelo sighs, but I am gone, running as far as I can before Angelo catches me. Which is shortly after. God, why is he so fast? He picks me up and throwing me over his shoulder. "You couldn't make this easy for me, could you?" as he drops me into the car. "Stay" He demands.

As we drove home, I leaned forward earnestly, my voice pleading. "Hey, Angelo. You're not going to tell Kalel, right?. It was just a stupid impulse. He doesn't need to know."

He glanced at me in the rear-view mirror, his eyes softening slightly. "You know I can't do that."

I groaned, sinking into the seat. "He's going to be impossible to deal with."

Angelo shrugged apologetically. "Next time, maybe choose something less predictable." I glare at him. "Or maybe you could let me go."

The rest of the ride was quiet, my thoughts a storm as I mentally braced myself for Kalel's reaction. It couldn't be that bad, right?.

Angelo parked the car and opened my door, offering me a sympathetic look. "Time to face the music."

I squared my shoulders, determined despite the anxiety curling in my stomach. Kalel stood waiting, expression cool and unreadable. His eyes flicked briefly to Angelo, who nodded silently.

"I hear we had an adventure today, Kitten," Kalel murmured, voice calm. I raised my chin defiantly, eyes meeting his. "I wouldn't call it an adventure." His lips curved slowly into a wicked smirk. "Oh, wouldn't you?"

The moment Kalel's hand closes around my wrist, ice floods my veins.

This isn't like before.

He's dragged me through these halls countless times since I first tried to escape—pinned me against walls, cornered me into submission, locked me away to remind me exactly who owns me.

But this?

This is different.

Because he's silent. Unnervingly and dangerously silent. I can read him.

His grip is firm and controlled. Not painful—yet unbreakable.

Panic claws up my throat as we pass my bedroom without slowing. "No," I whisper, voice trembling, heels digging uselessly into the polished floors. "Kalel, please—"

He doesn't respond. Doesn't even spare me a glance. His stone-like face, every line etched with ruthless determination, greets me as we approach his room.

The one place I swore I'd never enter.

My heart crashes against my ribs as he reaches for the door. "No." I plead.

Kalel pauses. Finally, those storm-Grey eyes turn to mine, stripping me bare.

51

"You don't get a choice," he murmurs quietly, his voice velvet wrapped around steel.

The door swings open, a sinister invitation. With brutal inevitability, we step inside, and the lock clicks into place behind us—a sound that echoes like a death sentence.

The room smells faintly of leather and his cologne—dark, rich, and intoxicating. Every surface screams power, dominance, control—dark marble, polished wood, the stark minimalism reflecting Kalel's cold command. I jerk free from his grip, chest heaving. He doesn't stop me.

Because he doesn't have to.

Desperately, I scan the room. But it's useless—he's left nothing to chance. Great, just my luck. Every weapon, every advantage, stripped away before I could even think to reach for them.

I whirl to face him, adrenaline pumping wild fury into my veins. "Don't you want to let me go?"

Kalel calmly shrugs out of his suit jacket, casually tossing it onto the chair as if he hasn't just trapped me in hell.

I snap.

Storming toward him, I shove both palms against his solid chest, fury burning in my fingertips. "I WON'T STAY HERE!"

He doesn't flinch. Doesn't even sway under my force. Instead, a slow, deadly smirk spreads across his lips. "You will." He says

"You can't keep—"

His fingers threading firmly into my hair, tilting my head back with effortless control. I gasp, gripping his wrist, but his touch is strangely gentle—a twisted mockery of affection.

He leans in, breath warm against my ear. "You're sleeping here from now on, sweetheart."

A shiver races down my spine, my defiance cracking. "I hate you." I hiss.

His chuckle vibrates through me, dark and intimate. "You say that now," he whispers, fingers tracing down my throat, lingering over my racing pulse, "but it doesn't look like you do."

My breath catches painfully. Heat blooms under his fingertips, traitorous desire battling my anger. He sighs. "If you really hated me, would you really be doing things that lead me to punish you?"

He releases me suddenly, turning away as if I pose no threat. Rage and humiliation surge inside me, overwhelming rational thought. I sprint toward the door, twisting the handle desperately. It's locked, of course. I sigh. "I'm really getting tired of this!"

Behind me, Kalel chuckles, dark and knowing. "You always do that." he says.

"Do what?" I snap, chest heaving as I face him.

His gaze meets mine, intense and possessive.

"Try to run."

He slowly unbuttons his shirt, exposing the sculpted muscle beneath—marked by scars, a story written in every line. My traitorous heart stumbles.

I despise myself for noticing.

"You're not leaving, Sabrina," he murmurs, eyes darkening as he slips into the bathroom, leaving me trembling and trapped.

The sound of running water fills the heavy silence. I pace helplessly, searching in vain for an escape. But there's nothing. Every exit, every possibility, meticulously erased by him.

The water stops.

My pulse spikes as the door opens, revealing Kalel in nothing but low-hanging sweatpants, droplets of water glistening on his bare skin. My throat dries instantly. How can he be this attractive yet fucking psychotic? And why did I notice?

He towels his hands slowly, eyes tracking my every twitch with lazy amusement, fully aware of the effect he has on me.

"Get in bed," he commands softly.

My stomach knots violently because I want to listen. Girl, you need to get railed because this is insane. I pull myself together. "I'm not sleeping with you."

Kalel smirks, arrogance curving his lips. "I didn't say you were."

Relief wars with dread as he tosses a pillow onto the leather chair in the corner. "Relax. I'm not touching you." His voice dips dangerously. "Yet."

That single word ignites a firestorm inside me, and I hate myself for the traitorous heat pooling in my core. Slowly, bitterly, I slide under the sheets, rolling away from him, my back rigid. When this is over, I am so going to therapy.

Minutes pass in tense silence until darkness fills the room. The bed dips slightly with his weight. My entire body hums with awareness.

And then, his voice—dark silk in the shadows. "You can fight me all you want, Sabrina." My breath stalls. "You can keep running."

He shifts closer, his warmth seeping into me, intimate without touch. His voice caresses the back of my neck, possessively and unbearably intimate. "But you'll never escape me." My heart thuds painfully as his quiet promise settles deep into my bones. He's right. I already know it. I can't stop hearing his voice. Can't stop feeling him. Because for the first time since I got here, I realize Kalel doesn't need to trap me with chains. He already owns me. And there's nowhere left to run.

* * *

I should've known this was a mistake.

From the moment Kalel threw that dress onto the bed this morning— a silky black thing, scandalously tight, indecently short—I knew he was planning something. This wasn't a date. It wasn't even about showing me off.

This was about control.

Every muscle in my body tensed as we sat in the dimly lit, expensive restaurant. Kalel's powerful presence pressed into me, suffocating every attempt at independence. His arm rested possessively across the back of my chair, casual and yet utterly domineering. The men across the table spoke quietly about business—territories, shipments, violence. I blocked out their voices, focusing instead on the frantic rhythm of my pulse.

I shifted in my seat, desperate for space, for a breath that didn't taste like him. Even though I know that's not going to happen. Kalel's fingers brushed my bare shoulder lightly, sending a traitorous shiver down my spine.

Casual, but possessive.

Great. Like I needed another reminder. He didn't even glance my way, but I could feel his subtle warning.

I set down my napkin, my voice strained. "I need the bathroom." I say.

Kalel didn't pause in his conversation. His fingers tightened ever so slightly on my skin. A quiet threat. My stomach clenched. God forbid I take a leak without supervision. As I stood, I felt his stare branding me, even though he pretended to focus on business. Each step away from the table was like walking through thick syrup, my heart hammering against my ribs.

In the narrow hallway near the bathrooms, I inhaled shakily. And then—

"Sabrina?"

A familiar voice, bright and warm. My heart stumbled. Turning, my breath caught at the sight of Luca, a face I hadn't seen since college. He smiled, eyes brightening as he stepped forward, pulling me into a warm embrace.

"It's been forever!" he said, pulling back, gaze traveling over me with surprise and admiration. "You look incredible."

For a heartbeat, something inside me relaxed. It was a glimpse of normalcy, freedom, something untouched by Kalel's suffocating presence.

"I'm surviving. How have you been?" I say, smiling.

"Good!"

Then everything shifted.

My skin prickled with awareness, and dread curled deep in my stomach. Luca was still speaking, but his voice blurred, distorted by my heartbeat. I glanced past his shoulder, my blood running cold at the sight of Kalel sitting at our table, chair shoved back, his jaw clenched so tightly it looked carved from granite. His eyes locked onto mine, and I recognized the look immediately.

Oh fuck.

I guess I should kiss freedom goodbye. Again.

Slowly, purposefully, he strode toward us. Luca seemed oblivious, his voice cheerful as he talked about the past, but I couldn't hear him. Kalel's intense, feral gaze drowned out everything else.

"Luca," I interrupted shakily, "I have to—"

Kalel's hand wrapped around my wrist, suddenly and ruthlessly. Luca stepped forward, concern clouding his features. "Is everything okay?" Luca asked

Kalel didn't even glance at him. His eyes burned into mine, possessive fury simmering just beneath his carefully controlled facade. "We're leaving," he growled softly.

"Kalel—" I protested, but his grip tightened painfully, a warning that halted any further resistance.

He yanked me toward the nearest door. Which happened to be the bathroom. The door slamming shut behind us. My back hit the icy wall, breath knocked from my lungs as Kalel crowded into my space, his body heat overwhelming, intoxicating.

His hand curled around my throat, gentle but firm—just enough to remind me he could crush me if he chose.

"Who the fuck was he?" Kalel's voice was dangerously calm, the quiet threat clear beneath the surface.

"Just an old friend," I whispered, struggling to keep my voice steady.

"Did he fuck you?" His voice was a raw edge, eyes blazing with jealousy.

"Kalel—"

His grip tightened slightly, silencing my protests. His thumb slid across my jaw, forcing my gaze to his. "Did he touch you?"

My breath hitched. I pushed weakly against his chest, desperate for space, for clarity. "You need to calm down." I demand.

He laughed sharply, darkly amused. "Calm down? Another man touched what's mine."

"I'm not yours," I snapped defiantly, my voice trembling despite my effort to sound strong.

Kalel's expression turned lethal, his voice dropping to a dangerous whisper. "Say that again, Sabrina."

Swallowing hard, I met his eyes, stubbornness masking my fear. "I don't belong to you."

His hand slid to my waist, fingers biting into my skin possessively, branding me through the thin fabric. "Oh, Baby, you had the chance to run. You didn't take it. You stayed," he breathed into my ear, sending tremors racing through me. "Stop pretending you're anything but, mine."

Of course, my brilliant life choices come back to haunt me again.

I hated the way my body responded to him, hated that despite my mind screaming to fight, every nerve in my body sparked under his touch.

He released me abruptly, but before I could draw a relieved breath, his hand was around my wrist again, dragging me through the restaurant. The drive home was painfully silent, filled only with simmering, dangerous tension.

Once we got inside the house, I tried to pull away, to create distance, but he held firm once we got to the room. He spun me until my back collided with the dresser, lifting me easily onto it, pinning me between his powerful thighs. His grip bruised, his eyes dark with need and rage.

"Say you're mine," he demanded, voice low and dripping with dominance.

My body betrayed me, heat pooling deep inside even as I shook my head defiantly. "No."

His lips crashed down on mine, brutal and possessive. Taking my breath away. I should have fought, should have screamed, but instead, I melted beneath his ruthless claim, moaning softly as his hands gripped my thighs, rough and possessive. My pulse skipped traitorously, my body arching toward him instinctively, desperately.

Great, Sabrina. Way to stick to your guns.

"Say it," he growled against my mouth, pulling back just enough to force my eyes to his.

The words lodged in my throat, pride warring with desire, hate mingling with undeniable need. I shook my head weakly, struggling to resist him, to resist myself.

Kalel smiled wickedly, knowing he'd already won. His touch was slow, calculated, torturous.

Perfect. This is exactly how I envisioned my night going. With Kalel pushing me past the edge.

I was trapped. Body and soul, by a man who claimed me as his own, and I knew then—I was completely and devastatingly lost. I shake my head defiantly, even as my breath comes ragged and my pulse is a wild drumbeat beneath my skin.

"Never," I hiss, the word dripping with venom.

Kalel's gaze darkens dangerously, his eyes turning stormy, molten with barely contained hunger. "Wrong answer, Kitten."

A sharp gasp escapes my lips as he grabs my wrist, yanking me forward until my body collides with the hard wall of his chest. Heat floods me instantly, mingling with the hate I desperately cling to. His mouth crashes against mine, devouring the protest I'd planned to scream.

And God help me—I kiss him back.

My lips part instinctively, welcoming the brutal invasion of his tongue, even as my mind screams to fight him. His fingers dig into my hips, rough and possessive. Branding my skin through the thin fabric of my dress. His thumbs skim dangerously along my inner thighs, leaving trails of molten fire in their wake. He swallows my moan, claiming it like a trophy—like he's claimed everything else.

My nails dig into the rigid muscles of his arms, intending pain but betraying me by pulling him closer instead. I wrench my head back, breaking our kiss, only to gasp desperately for air.

"You're an asshole," I pant.

A slow, dark smile curls his lips. "And yet you're dripping for me."

Heat floods my cheeks as his hand moves higher, fingers slipping beneath the silk of my panties, brushing unapologetically against my slick, aching pussy. I shudder violently, fury blazing brighter as humiliation mixes perversely with desire.

"Fuck you," I grit out, voice shaking.

He chuckles, dark and low, eyes gleaming victoriously. "Maybe later."

Then he pushes a finger inside me without warning.

I arch against him, a strangled moan ripping free before I can silence it. Pleasure pulses traitorously through my body, deepening the flush in my cheeks, making me want to claw his smirk from his face.

"Still think you don't want me?" Kalel whispers, adding a second finger, twisting and stroking, until I tremble uncontrollably. His other hand fists in my hair, forcing me to look at him, to acknowledge his control. "Tell me again how much you hate me."

"I—I hate you," I spat breathlessly, voice weak.

He laughs softly, dipping his head to trail passionate kisses down the side of my neck. "Your" kiss "body" kiss "begs" kiss "to differ." kiss.

The slow, tortuous rhythm of his fingers intensifies, and I grip his shoulders, shaking as pleasure coils tight, hotter, and unbearable.

Just as I'm about to shatter, surrendering completely to this humiliating bliss, he withdraws abruptly, leaving me aching. Empty and furious.

"Kalel," I choke, fury tangled hopelessly with need.

He raises his hand. His gaze locked provocatively on mine as he slides his glistening fingers into his mouth, tasting my betrayal and savoring it slowly.

"You taste like surrender," he murmurs darkly, eyes burning into mine, stripping away every barrier between us.

I glare at him, pride forcing my spine straighter despite the trembling weakness in my knees. "Enjoy it now, asshole. It'll never happen again."

His smirk deepens, pure, wicked confidence radiating from every fiber of his being. He leans in close, lips brushing softly, tauntingly against my ear.

"It will happen every single time I touch you, Sabrina. You're mine. Your pretty little mouth can lie all it wants, but your body never will."

Then, he steps away, leaving me slumped against the wall, chest heaving, knees trembling, and mind utterly wrecked.

And worst of all, I realize with absolute horror and undeniable yearning—he's right.

Because despite all my resistance, all my stubborn defiance... I already crave him.

Chapter 6

Kalel

Sabrina is shaking. Not in fear. Not in anger. In something far more stimulating. Something primal. Something inevitable. This is only for me. The one thing I've been craving and obsessing over every damn night since she first defied me.

Her chest rises and falls rapidly, each breath a sharp little gasp. As her eyes lock onto mine, dark and glittering with raw vulnerability. Her thighs remain parted from where I couldn't help but have her, and the sight is almost too much to bear.

She looks ruined. Wrecked. And, fuckkkk, it's the most exquisite thing I've ever witnessed.

My chest tightens, hunger roaring inside me. Every fiber of my being aches to push her back against the dresser, and finish what I couldn't help but start. To devour her entirely, but I restrain myself—that sweet agony will make my victory even more satisfying.

I couldn't help but lift my fingers to my lips, savoring her taste, letting her watch my tongue glide over the evidence of her surrender. She shudders visibly, cheeks flushed, eyes blazing with anger and desire. God, she's fucking beautiful when she fights herself like this.

She hates this. For letting me in, she hates herself. The undeniable truth written clearly across her flushed skin and trembling limbs—but I won.

And she knows it.

I step closer, inhaling the intoxicating scent of her desire, feeling it settle deep in my bones, branding me just as thoroughly as I've branded her. I lean in, my lips brushing lightly against the sensitive shell of her ear, letting her feel my breath warm her skin.

"You're mine, Sabrina.." I say.

She freezes, doesn't even breathe. I couldn't help but linger, savoring her reaction, her stunned silence.

Pulling back just enough to meet her gaze, I smile slowly, my smirk full of promise and wicked intent. My fingers are still slick from her arousal, glistening with proof of her submission. I lift an eyebrow knowingly.

Her pupils dilate further, nails scraping desperately against the dresser behind her as she tries and fails to close her thighs, to erase the ache I've seared deep within her.

I made sure she wouldn't forget me so easily. I straighten and step back, allowing a cold distance to rush between us, reminding her exactly who controls this moment. Because Sabrina isn't going anywhere.

And now.

She fucking knows it.

So do I.

I walk away without looking back, keeping my control. I hold the upper hand. But, fuck—I don't want to. My body screams to stay, to take more, to own her in every way that matters.

My hands twitch with the need to touch her again. To push her over the edge and hear my name ripped from her throat. To ruin her so completely that there's no coming back. No denying what we are. What she is to me.

Without another word, I force myself to put distance between us, my muscles tight with restraint. Every step away from her is torture, but I know what's coming.

She'll try to fight this. Try to fight me And I'll enjoy every second of breaking her down. Because when she finally admits the truth, when she finally stops lying to herself and fucking surrenders, it won't just be her body that belongs to me.

It'll be everything.

Her mind. Her heart. Her fucking soul.

I don't need to stay to see her frustration, to watch her pull herself back together. I already know she'll grit her teeth, shake her head defiantly, and curse my name under her breath. But she'll also ache for me. Because I'm inside her head now, permanently.

She'll lie to herself tonight, pretending it meant nothing. Convince herself that she despises me. But when her eyes flutter closed? She'll remember my fingers buried deep inside her. When she breathes? She'll feel my lips brushing against her throat, possessively and relentlessly. When sleep finally comes? I'll haunt her dreams, vivid and demanding.

And when I come back for more—because I will—she'll break even easier, surrender even quicker.

That's the fundamental difference between us. She still thinks she needs to fight me, but I don't have to fight because Sabrina was mine the moment I decided to take her.

I storm into my office, jaw clenched, hands fisted at my sides, trying to like hell to get the sound of her moans out of my head. But it's useless. My dick throbs, aching, demanding relief. She's wrecking me, and she doesn't even know it.

I lasted all of ten minutes before giving up and going to take a shower. The cold shower does nothing to numb the need clawing at me, the hunger that won't fade. My palm wraps around my cock, and a guttural curse rips from my throat as I stroke myself to the thought of her— Sabrina, panting, writhing, pushing at my chest while her lips spit venom. "I hate you." We both know that's a fucking lie.

I squeeze my grip, tilting my head back as the fantasy coils tighter, hotter. Her mouth, her body, the fire in her eyes when she fights with me. She wants to hate me, needs to, but her body betrays her every time.

"Fuck—" My hips jerk, as pleasure rips through me like a live wire. Her name leaves my lips as I come, thick and hot, against my palm.

I breathe hard, water washing away the evidence of my weakness. By the time I make it back to the bedroom, she's asleep. She looks so small in my bed. So fucking perfect. I sit beside her, watching the slow rise and fall of her chest, the way her dark curls spill across the pillow. My fingers twitch, needing to touch her, to claim her. I reach out, brushing my thumb across her cheek, my voice a whisper in the dark.

"You are so fucking beautiful." I whisper

She stirs, but doesn't wake.

I couldn't help but smirk, shaking my head. She does not know what she's done to me and no idea what I'm going to do to her.

Sliding into bed beside her, I close my eyes to get some sleep, but it doesn't come easily. Not when the hunt is still fresh in my veins. I'll wait though because soon she'll be mine completely.

The next day, I wake up before she does as usual. I got a little sleep, I've been thinking. Planning. Because last night? That wasn't a punishment. That was a reminder. She still thinks she has choices. She still thinks she can resist me, escape me. I'll let her keep that delusion. For now.

But today? She's going to understand. I turn to look at her. She's still sleeping, her breathing soft, her body wrapped in the sheets. For a second, I let myself watch. Let myself take her in. She looks so peaceful in my bed. It was as if she had always belonged there. I exhale slowly. Then I get up and rip the sheets off of her.

She jerks awake with a sharp gasp, her hands scrambling to grab the blanket that's no longer there. She blinks, confused and then—she sees me. Her whole body locks up. I couldn't help but smirk. "Morning, kitten." She sits up fast, pushing her tangled hair out of her face. "What the fuck—" I grab her wrist, pulling her out of bed before she can finish. She stumbles, tripping over her own feet as I yank her against my chest. She sucks in a sharp breath.

I grip her waist, keeping her flushed against me. "You're spending the day with me." She glares at me. Then she shoves, but I don't budge. Her anger flares, her hands pressing against my chest, trying to create space. "Like hell I am!"

I chuckle, tilting my head. "I don't remember giving you a choice." She Bares her teeth, furious. "You can't just—" I cut her off with a whisper against her ear. "I can do whatever I want. I own you."

I feel her breath hitch. She tries to hide it, but she can't. Not from me. Not when I have her right where I want her. I slide my hands down to her hips, holding her there, fingers pressing into the soft skin.

"You ran into another man yesterday," I murmur. "I let you walk away after last night. Now, you think you're going to spend the day pretending I don't exist?"

I tighten my grip. "You're not running from me, Sabrina." I lower my lips to her ear, whispering slow, deliberate words I know will sink deep inside her. "I won't let you."

I take her to the dining room, where I've set the table with all her favorite foods. Fresh fruit, warm pastries, eggs cooked just how she likes them. She steps in cautiously, eyes scanning the spread before locking onto mine.

"What's all this?" she asks, suspicion laced in her tone. There's a glint in her hazel eyes—mistrust, but something else, too. Something curious.

"Breakfast." I say, as I pull out a chair for her. "Sit." She crosses her arms, tilting her head. "I'm not a dog. I'll sit if I and when I want to."

Defiance. My favorite fucking thing about her.

I slide my hands into my pockets, giving her a slow, measured look. "You can sit on this chair," I say, voice calm but edged with warning. "Or you can sit on my lap. Those are your only two options. You have three seconds, kitten."

Her lips part in disbelief, like she can't decide whether to argue or test me.

"Three..." Nothing.

"Two—"

She drops into the chair before I could say one, rolling her eyes as she grabs a fork.

"Good girl." I say with a smirk. She tries to hide her amusement behind irritation, but I see the way her lips twitch, the way her breath catches just a little too quickly. She likes this game just as much as I do.

I take a sip of coffee, watching her. "Eat." I demand.

She doesn't move right away, just narrows her eyes at me like she's trying to figure me out. I let her, because she never will.

"After this, get dressed," I continued. "We're going out."

She raises an eyebrow. "Out?" I nod. "I have an event tonight. You're coming with me. We need to make sure you have something to wear." She stares at me for a beat, then tilts her head with a slow, teasing smile. "Look at you," she muses. "It almost looks like you have a heart, but no."

Something tightens in my chest, but I ignore it. She's not winning this round. I push off the table and turn away. "It wasn't a choice, Sabrina." I glance over my shoulder, my voice dropping to something darker. "Be ready in an hour. I wouldn't want to lock you back in that room."

Her smile vanishes. Her back straightens. And there it is—fear. Anger. A storm was brewing in her expression. I let it linger before leaving the room. She'll fight me, but we both know how this ends. An hour passes. She slides into the car with an exhale, arms folded across her chest, legs crossed like she's already regretting agreeing to this. She doesn't want to be here, but she came anyway. I guess she didn't like being locked in the room. I win.

Angelo shuts the door, and as the car pulls away, she glances at me. "So... where are we going?"

"A gala," I say, not looking up from my phone as I finish a text. She lets out a sharp, disbelieving laugh. "A gala? Are you insane? I'm not the type of person who goes to a damn gala." She shakes her head, shifting in her seat. "You might actually have to lock me in the room this time." That gets my attention. My fingers are still over the screen, but I finally look up at her.

"Why?" My voice is calm, but there's an edge to it. "You're with me and I'd love for them to say something to me."

She chews on her lip, a tell I recognize now—she's not just pissed off. She's nervous. I don't like it.

It's not the gala. It's her. She doesn't think she belongs in rooms filled with high society, the elite, the people who throw around money like it's nothing. Like she isn't worthy of the attention that'll come with being on my arm. It makes me wonder who made her feel like that?

Her deadbeat father? That useless ex of hers, Liam? Maybe both.

A slow smile pulls at my lips as I think about them—the men who used to have a say in her life. They don't anymore and they never will again.

"We're here," Angelo announces, catching my eye in the rear-view mirror.

I step out first, scanning the area, then extend a hand to her. She doesn't take it right away, but after a second, she sighs and lets me help her out. Her fingers are warm and hesitant, but she doesn't pull away. Awe look at that were progressing.

She turns, and I watch the exact moment the boutique steals her breath.

This isn't some department store.

The interior screams power and excess—white marble floors polished to a perfect shine, floor-to-ceiling mirrors with gold trim, and racks of designer clothing displayed like museum pieces. Rows of tailored suits, high-end street wear, and luxury accessories sit under soft-lit displays, each item crafted for people who don't need to check price tags. Leather armchairs and velvet sofas sit in front of private dressing suites, and a well-dressed associate greets us with a glass of champagne on a tray, waiting to serve.

Sabrina takes it all in, her hazel eyes flicking over the racks, landing on a leather jacket, then a silk blouse, then a pair of heels with red soles. I can see her wanting things, but she won't admit it.

"Pick whatever you want," I tell her.

She hesitates, glancing at me. "For the gala?" Sabrina asks.

"For whatever the fuck you want."

Angelo steps up beside me, arms crossed, his lips twitching like he's holding back a laugh. "This has nothing to do with the gala, Kal." Angelo says amused.

"She needs clothes," I say, watching Sabrina as she brushes her fingers over the sleeve of a tailored blazer. She likes it. But she won't grab it.

"She refuses to buy anything willingly. And she only packed a handful of things to take with her."

Angelo exhales a quiet chuckle. "Shouldn't you be following her?"

I flick him a glance. "Make sure everything and everyone are on time. We'll get ready once we're back at the estate." He nods, dropping his eyes to the floor, but still smirking. "Got it." I turn back to her—my girl, my problem, my goddamn obsession. She still hasn't picked anything. Still pretending like she doesn't want to.

I couldn't help but smirk. She'll learn. By the end of tonight, everyone in that room will know exactly who she belongs to.

Chapter 7

Sabrina

I don't belong here.

Not in a place where the floors shine like mirrors and the air smells like wealth and exclusivity. In such a store, they hide the price tags like a dirty little secret because if you have to ask the price, you can't afford to shop there.

Kalel doesn't fit in either. He dominates. His presence takes up space, like he owns the place the second he steps through the door. And maybe he does, in a way. Men like him don't browse. They acquire.

Meanwhile, I hesitate at every single rack, my fingers brushing over the softest silk and the smoothest leather. I don't grab anything, though. I tell myself it's because I don't need it. I don't need another reason to owe Kalel.

But the truth is, I do. I've never been the type of girl who drops thousands on designer clothes. My closet back home—if you could even call it that—didn't contain luxury brands and tailored pieces. I had clearance-rack finds, secondhand treasures, things I had to make work, and I did.

So, when I spot the jacket—soft, black leather, buttery to the touch, cropped just right—I almost convince myself to walk past it. Almost.

Kalel's standing right behind me, watching my internal struggle. "Get it," he says. I turn, tilting my head. "No, it's okay." His eyes flick

70

to the jacket, then back to me, unreadable but firm. "If you want it, get it." He says.

I let out a soft scoff, shaking my head. "I didn't say I wanted it." He smirks like I just proved his point. I cross my arms. "What?"

"You think I didn't notice the way you touch things when you like them?" His voice is low and teasing, but there's something else there, too. Something knowing. He's studying me...Great. "You do that little swipe with your thumb."

I glance down at my hand. Annoyed that he caught me so easily. I roll my eyes. "Oh, so now you're an expert in all my little habits?" He leans in, his voice low, just for me. "I've been studying you since the day I took you, kitten."

My breath catches. He doesn't move away, but I do. Turning back to the jacket, I stare at it for a second too long. "It's probably stupidly expensive." Kalel sighs, like I'm exhausting him, but I hear it—the patience underneath. "I said, get it."

"I don't need—"

His hand brushes my lower back, a light touch, barely there, but it makes my stomach tighten. "Sabrina." His tone is lower now, softer, but there's no room for argument. "You don't have to earn everything. If you want it, it's yours." I swallow.

He makes it sound so simple. Like it's easy for him because it is. He probably never had to work for what he wanted, never had to question how expensive something was before buying it. But I did. I struggled and now he is talking to me like I deserve to have things.

Like I'm allowed.

The worse thing is, I don't know whether I should believe him or if this is another one of his games.

Slowly, I pick up Jacket and it's heavier than I expected; the quality screams luxury, and something in my chest tightens as I hold it.

"Good," Kalel murmurs.

I glare at him. He smirks and moves past me, leaving me standing there, trying to ignore the warmth his words sent through me.

* * *

An Hour Later

I couldn't help but stare at the receipt, my stomach twisting.

$68,932.

Holy. Shit.

The stylist bags the last of my things, carefully folding a silk dress into a box like she's handling something sacred. Meanwhile, I'm doing mental gymnastics, trying to process how the hell I just let that happen.

I look at Kalel. He's lounging on a leather chair, completely unbothered, scrolling through his phone like he didn't just drop seventy grand on me. Oh, I am never going to pay off my debt to him at this rate. I sigh.

I swallow hard, turning toward him. "Kalel"

He doesn't even look up. "Hmm?"

I shift on my feet, the weight of the shopping bags feeling heavier than before. "I—I didn't know it would cost that much."

Now he looks at me. Slowly. Lifting his gaze with the kind of deliberate ease that makes my stomach flip.

I try again, my voice quieter. "I'm... I'm sorry. I didn't mean to—"

His brows lift slightly, like he genuinely can't believe what he's hearing. Then, with a slow smirk, he leans forward, resting his elbows on his knees. "You should be sorry." He says.

I blink. My stomach knots harder. He tilts his head.

"Next time, don't go easy on me." His voice drops, his smirk deepening. "I'm not broke, kitten. And I don't want people to think I am." Heat spreads up my neck. I fight the tiny smile threatening my lips, but he catches it anyway. His smirk grows. "You were about to smile." He says.

"No, I wasn't." He leans back. "Liar." I purse my lips, crossing my arms. "I wasn't."

"You were." He says with a smirk.

I huff, shaking my head. "In your dreams." He stands, stepping into my space, looking down at me like he knows exactly how he affects me. "You are in my dreams." I exhale, gripping the bag straps tighter. One minute he's the most infuriating person I know, and the next he's making me forget why I hated him.

Then I remember. He is my captor. God, is this what Stockholm Syndrome feels like? Kalel smirks, like he's already won. Like I'm just some game he enjoys playing. Tighten my grip on the shopping bags, I lifting my chin. "I'm here because you decided freedom wasn't in my future." I say.

His gaze darkens, that slow, dangerous kind of darkness that makes my stomach clench. He steps closer, forcing me to tilt my head to keep eye contact.

His voice drops to something softer, smoother. "Then why does it feel like you're choosing me?" My breath hitches, but I refuse to break first. He wants me to back down. To flinch. To give in. That's not happening. I square my shoulders. "Maybe I just like the free clothes."

His smirk curves into something sharper, more knowing. "Lie to yourself all you want, kitten." Before I can fire back, Angelo clears his throat. "You two done eye-fucking each other, or should I leave?" Heat rushes to my face. I turn so fast I nearly smack Kalel with a shopping bag. "We're leaving." I say.

Kalel chuckles—actually chuckles, like he's enjoying this way too much. He takes the bags from my hand without asking, carrying them like they weigh nothing, and nods at Angelo. "Car."

Angelo sighs like he's dealing with children, but he leads the way. The car ride home is silent. Not the awkward kind, but the thick, loaded kind. I stare out the window, pretending not to feel Kalel watching me. I swear I can feel his gaze dragging over my skin, slow and deliberate. He's so fucking annoying, but my heart is still hammering in my chest.

I hate that he gets under my skin so easily. How he reads me better than I read myself. That for a second—just a second—I couldn't help but almost believe him. That I could just... Take. Want. Belong. I cross my arms tighter, shifting in my seat. No. That's not my world, that's his.

Kalel exhales beside me, the sound smug and amused, like he knows exactly what's going through my head.

"You're quiet." Kalel says.

I roll my eyes at the window. "And you're observant. Look at us." His low chuckle makes my pulse stutter. "You're thinking about it." I frown "Thinking about what?" I ask.

"That you liked today. You liked me spoiling you." I snap my head toward him. "I never said that."

"You didn't have to." He tilts his head, studying me like I'm a puzzle he already knows how to solve. "Next time, don't hesitate." I scoff. "There won't be a next time." Kalel smirks, like he's already decided otherwise. Angelo glances at us in the rear-view mirror, clearly holding back a comment.

"What." I snap. He shrugs. "Nothing. Just wondering how long you're gonna keep pretending you don't like it when he takes care of you."Angelo says.

I gape at him, then whip my head toward Kalel. He looks pleased. They are having too much fun with this. I groan, dropping my head against the seat. "I hate both of you."

Kalel chuckles again, and this time, it's downright smug. "You say that, kitten." He leans in, his voice brushing my skin like silk. "But you didn't tell me to stop." I swallow hard. This car is too small and my pulse is too loud.

And what's worse is.

He's right.

The car slows as we pull through the estate gates. I straighten in my seat, already dreading whatever Kalel has planned next. The man loves control—loves telling me where to go, what to do, and apparently, what to wear. But nothing prepares me for what's waiting inside.

As soon as Angelo opens the car door, I step out—and freeze.

Three women stand in the grand foyer like a damn glam squad. One of them is wheeling in a rack of dresses. Another woman carries a sleek leather case filled with makeup worth more than my entire life. The third is holding a set of hair tools that look like they belong in a celebrity dressing room.

My stomach drops.

I whirl around to Kalel, my arms folding tight across my chest. "What is this?"

He strides past me, casually rolling up his sleeves. "Your team." He says.

I blink. My what?

He nods toward them like he didn't just say something completely insane. "Your stylist, makeup artist, and hairstylist."

My jaw nearly unhinges. "Are you kidding me?" I ask.

One woman, a tall blonde in a perfectly tailored dress, steps forward with a dazzling smile. "Miss, we'll be getting you ready for the gala tonight."

I glance at her, then back at Kalel, confused but flattered. "Are you serious?"

He smirks. "Why wouldn't I be?" He asks.

"Because I don't need this, you already spent so much money Kalel!" I gesture at the team, at the literal rack of designer gowns, at the insanity of this entire situation. "I can do my hair and makeup. And I can pick out my dress."

75

Kalel steps closer, voice calm. "Did you though?" He asks.

I narrow my eyes. "What?"

He lifts a single brow. "Did you pick out a dress today?"

I open my mouth, then shut it. Because—fuck. He's right. I'd spent the entire trip walking past gowns, avoiding heels, pretending I didn't want any of it.

Kalel smirks, leaning in slightly. "You keep acting like you don't want this, kitten. But you do. You just don't know how to accept it yet."

My pulse hammers. I swallow, trying not to let him see that his words hit something deep.

I shift on my feet. "This is excessive, but thank you."

His gaze flicks over me, slow and deliberate. "You deserve excessive."

I hate the way my stomach flips. The way his words linger, how they feel like something I shouldn't believe, but want to.

The stylist claps her hands. "We should get started! We only have a few hours."

I look at her, then back at him.

Kalel nods at the team like he's handing me over. "Make sure she looks like she belongs on my arm."

I scoff. "Oh, so this is about you?" His lips curve, slow and dangerous. "Everything is about me." He says.

I roll my eyes, but before I can protest further, the glam squad is ushering me upstairs, herding me into a massive dressing suite filled with full-length mirrors and gold-trimmed vanities.

I catch one last glimpse of Kalel before the doors close, and he is still smirking. Maybe he isn't as bad as I thought.

Chapter 8

Sabrina

A few hours later, I stare at my reflection and Holy. Shit. The girl in the mirror doesn't look like me. She looks... expensive. The kind of woman who belongs at a gala, who turns heads, who doesn't hesitate to take up space in rooms meant for the elite.

She was not me.

My skin glows under the vanity lights, my makeup soft but striking— eyes sharp, lips full, cheekbones sculpted like I was born for this. My hair falls in perfect waves, glossy and effortless, like I walked out of a magazine spread.

And the dress—It makes me look like I could own any room I walk in.

A deep, satin black gown, hugging my body in all the right places. The fabric feels like amazing, draping over my curves, dipping scandalously low in the back, with a slit that runs dangerously high up my thigh.

I feel powerful. Stunning. Like someone I don't recognize. Then the door opens, and I remember why — Kalel. The moment his eyes land on me, the smirk vanishes.

His gaze darkens, his chest rising slow and deep, like he's trying to keep himself in check. He steps inside, shutting the door behind him, the click echoing in the room.

Silence.

I cross my arms and smirk, trying to act unaffected. Trying to ignore

77

how handsome he looks. "So? Do I look like I belong on your arm?" His jaw ticks, eyes dragging down my body. "You look like you belong to me."

And fuck me, because for the first time when he says it. I am wondering how far he will go to actually make me his.

My breath catches, my pulse out of control. He's presence is too much, filling the entire space like oxygen doesn't exist without him. I clear my throat, forcing myself to roll my eyes. "You're so full of yourself." I say.

He smirks, reaching out. His fingers skim my bare shoulder, barely touching me, but my skin ignites.

"I'm not full of myself, baby. I'm full of you. Every smirk, every fight, every time you try to run... It all proves it. You already belong to me. You just haven't admitted it." He leans closer. "But you will and when you do, don't bother fighting it. I always get what I want."

I shiver, my thighs pressing together. His smirk deepens. "Ready, kitten?" I swallow hard, pretending like I don't want him to ruin me. "For what?" His eyes flick to my lips. "To make them all jealous." And just like that, I know exactly what kind of night this is going to be and I'm here for it.

* * *

I can still feel Kalel words on my skin as I step out of the dressing room, my pulse slightly erratic.

"You look like you belong to me."

Arrogant bastard.

I try to shake it off as I walk down the grand staircase, my heels clicking against the marble. As I reach the bottom, Angelo lets out a low whistle.

"Damn, princess." He smirks, crossing his arms. "If I didn't know any better, I'd say Kalel's got some competition tonight."

Kalel, standing just behind me, exhales sharply. "Good thing you know better." Kalel says and Angelo chuckles, but I don't miss the warning edge in Kalel's voice.

I smirk, shifting my weight. "Thank you, Angelo. At least someone here knows how to give a proper compliment." Kalel's gaze flicks to mine, dark and heated. "You're really testing me tonight, kitten." I raise an eyebrow, ignoring the way my stomach tightens. "Am I?"

Instead of answering, he simply reaches for my coat and drapes it over my shoulders, his touch lingering just long enough to make my breath hitch. Then he leans in, his lips brushing just below my ear.

"You have no idea."

I swear he enjoys watching me struggle to keep my composure. Angelo clears his throat. "Hate to interrupt the foreplay, but we have a gala to get to." I roll my eyes and step ahead, feeling both men trail behind me as we make our way outside.

Once the car door clicks shut, sealing us in, and we pull away from the estate, I realize something. Kalel is too damn close. The SUV is spacious, but with the way he's sitting—his legs spread wide, his body turned slightly toward me, his arm draped lazily along the back of the seat—he might as well be devouring me whole.

I exhale slowly, forcing my eyes forward. His fingers brush my thigh. I jolt. "Kalel." He doesn't even look at me, just continues tracing slow, agonizing circles along my bare skin. "Hmm?" I glare at him, shifting my leg away. "Are you having fun?" I ask.

His smirk deepens. "Yeah, I am...watching you pretend you are unaffected when your thighs are already begging to stay open for me." His voice is a low, gravelly hum, all dark promises and control.

His fingers slide higher, just beneath the slit of my dress. "Keep asking questions like that, princess, and I'll show you the kind of fun that makes you forget your name." I suck in a breath.

"Are you sure you can?" I smirk. Teasing the devil.

He leans in, his lips hovering just over my jaw. "You wore this knowing every man in the room would want to fuck you," I stiffen, my pulse hammering. He chuckles, dark and low. Like he enjoys my reaction.

"But you also know they won't dare to touch you because they know exactly who you belong to," he murmurs. "Be honest, princess. You wore it for me. To see if I'd lose control and remind you just how good it feels when I do," I swallow, hating that my body is already reacting. "Or maybe I wore the dress to see who else would lose control."

He exhales and clenches his jaw. His hand spreading over my thigh. "And yet, you're still letting me touch you.... Still clenching your thighs like you're one second away from begging." I should shove his hand away, but don't. This is the tension and danger I secretly crave. I always have. It's the danger and adrenaline only a dangerous guy can provide.

That is how I ended up with Liam, after all.

Instead, I part my lips to object, but nothing comes out. Because his fingers slide higher. "So, either admit you want me, or keep pretending while I drag the truth out of you inch by inch," I scoff and shift away slightly. "I'm not going to beg," I warn, my voice barely a breath.

He leans in closer, fingers teasing up my thigh as he says in a low, smooth voice. "Want to test that theory?"

"Yeah, actually." I glare at him, shifting my legs to block his touch. It doesn't phase him— he smiles darkly as his grip tightens, forcing my legs apart again.

I shift, but his hand tightens to stop me from moving again. A low sound rumbles from his chest as if he knows. Because he does. My brain screams at me to stop this before I lose whatever sliver of control I have left and Kalel, that smug bastard, knows it.

He leans in, his breath warm against my ear. "Go ahead then, kitten." His fingers slide higher. "Tell me to stop."

My breath hitches. I hate that I can't. I suck in a sharp breath as his thumb skims higher, just barely brushing the inside of my thigh, dangerously close to where I need him most. A low, pleased sound rumbles from his chest when he feels the way my body reacts.

"Careful, baby," he murmured. "You can lie to yourself all you want, but your body? She's already mine."

Ugh! Bastard.

My nails dig into my palms, my breathing uneven. "You're such a—"

"Say it," he taunts. I snap my head toward him, furious that I can feel myself getting wet. "You're such an asshole." He chuckles, his fingers trailing higher.

"You love it." Kalel says.

I open my mouth—to deny it, to argue, to do something—but his hand suddenly moves, just a little further, just enough—

And then—

"Alright, lovebirds," Angelo's voice slices through the thick, unbearable tension. "We're here." I snap my legs shut so fast it's a miracle I don't crush Kalel's hand. Kalel exhales sharply, visibly restraining himself. His jaw clenches, his fingers curling into his palm like he's physically holding himself back.

I stare straight ahead, mortified, my cheeks burning. Angelo turns, his expression way too amused. "Perfect timing, don't you think?"

I turn toward Kalel. He's not smirking anymore. No, his expression is darker now, his control slipping just enough for me to see what I've done to him.

I love it, but I don't have time to dwell on it before he reaches for the door and steps out. Then he turns to me, offering his hand.

I hesitate.

His voice drops, low and husky. "Come on, kitten." I place my fingers in his and the moment I step out, he leans in close, his lips brushing my ear. "You owe me for that ride." I inhale sharply. "I don't owe you anything. You did that to yourself." He chuckles, dark and dangerous. "We'll see." As we step onto the carpet, all eyes turning toward us.

* * *

Kalel

I still feel the heat of her thighs and the way she trembled beneath my touch in the car, the sharp bite of her glare when Angelo interrupted. it's intoxicating.

She thinks she won that round. She didn't.

Not even close.

Now I get to parade her through a room full of men who'd slit throats just to have five minutes alone with her—and every single one of them will know who she belongs to.

The moment we step inside, all eyes turn to us.

The gala is everything you'd expect from the top players in the underworld. Gold chandeliers hang high above a ballroom filled with men who've built their empires on blood and betrayal and women in designer gowns draping themselves over the arms of criminals. Their jewels are worth more than most people's lives. The scent of cigars, expensive liquor, and unspoken threats lingers in the air.

This isn't a party. It's a power play.

And I'm here to remind them all who the fuck I am.

I tighten my grip on Sabrina's waist, my fingers pressing into the soft curve of her hip. She stiffens for a moment but doesn't pull away. Instead, she exhales slowly, her posture perfectly poised, chin lifted, expression unreadable.

That's my girl.

She might act like she doesn't belong, but she's already holding her own.

A few heads turn as we walk in, but one man in particular steps forward.

James Cross.

Tall and ruthless. The kind of man who doesn't bother hiding the bodies. He doesn't need to. His family runs the arms dealing empire, supplying weapons to whoever pays the most.

Right now, that's me.

"Kalel," he greets smoothly, offering a handshake. His eyes flick to Sabrina, lingering for a beat too long. "And who's this?"

I shake his hand, firm, calculated. "None of your business."

He chuckles, but there's something else behind it—curiosity. He wasn't expecting me to bring someone.

Which means I have the upper hand.

"You look like a man in a good mood tonight," Jameson muses, swirling the bourbon in his glass. "What's the occasion?"

I smirk. "Business is good."

His lips curve slightly. "It could be better."

There it is. He's waiting for an opening, for a way to push his new deal. I already know what he wants—more control, higher stakes, a bigger cut. I don't fucking share. Before I can speak, Sabrina shifts slightly against me.

It's subtle, but I feel it—the way she stiffens, the way she glances up at me, eyes sharp and calculating. She is uncomfortable. I let my thumb trace slow circles over her waist. A silent reassurance. James watches the small exchange closely.

"Why don't we discuss this somewhere private?" he suggests.

I nod once, then lean into Sabrina's ear. "Stay here. Don't talk to anyone." Her lips part slightly, but she doesn't argue.

Good.

I leave her standing by the bar. While Angelo and I follow James through the crowd, weaving between the city's richest and most dangerous men. As I turn, I glance back. Sabrina stands exactly where

83

I left her—chin lifted, fire in her eyes. And just like that, I know... I'll kill anyone who touches her.

Chapter 9

<u>Sabrina</u>

I swirl my drink in my hand, letting the ice clink against the glass as I scan the room. The city's deadliest men fill this gala, yet it remains one of the least hostile environments I've experienced since Kalel took me.

I exhale slowly, forcing myself to relax. The dress is tight; my heels are too high, but at least I have a drink in my hand and a moment of peace. Kalel is handling business, and I fully plan to enjoy the few minutes where he isn't breathing down my neck, telling me what to do, how to act, who to avoid—

"Having fun standing alone at the bar?"

I turn toward the voice, arching a brow as I take in the man beside me.

He's beautiful. Not in the hard, brutal way Kalel is, but in an artistic, almost careless kind of way. Messy dark hair, sharp eyes filled with mischief, and a smirk that suggests he was either born to piss people off or seduce them.

And to be honest, it's probably both.

He lifts his glass to his lips, assessing me. "What's a pretty thing like you doing looking so bored?"

I smirk, tilting my head. "Who says I'm bored?"

85

He leans in slightly. "I don't know maybe the way you just sighed into your drink, like it insulted your entire bloodline." He says

I let out a laugh before I could stop myself.

Shit.

He grins like he's won something, setting his drink down. "See? That's better. A face like yours should never look miserable at an event this pretentious."

I raise a brow. "And you? You look like you're enjoying yourself just fine." I say,

He places a hand over his heart dramatically. "I thrive in situations where I get to cause problems."

I chuckle, shaking my head. "Should I be worried then?" I ask. His smirk deepens. "You should be intrigued." I take a sip of my drink, eyes narrowing. "And who are you exactly?"

"Jin." He extends his hand. Like this is some kind of meet-cute and not a mafia gala. "Artist. Lover. Occasional menace." I roll my eyes but take his hand, anyway. "Sabrina." His fingers brush over my wrist before he lets go, his smirk never faltering. "Oh, I know who you are."

I hesitate. "Oh, do you?"

He tilts his head, studying me. "The woman Kalel kidnapped? The one he keeps tucked away like his most prized possession?" His smirk sharpens. "Yeah, I know you." I couldn't help but scoff. Is everyone here just as twisted as Kalel?

"That's a dramatic way to put it." I said.

His grin turns wicked. "I'm a dramatic guy."

I smirk despite myself. He's nothing like Kalel. Kalel is all sharp edges and control. Jin is playful chaos. Where Kalel watches me like I'm a possession, Jin looks at me like I'm a puzzle he wants to solve.

Dangerous in an entirely different way. He leans against the bar, completely at ease.

"Tell me, does Kalel know you're standing here flirting with me?" I raise a brow. "Who says I'm flirting?" His grin widens. "You're still talking to me, aren't you?"

I shake my head, sipping my drink, but before I can respond— Something shifts in the air. A presence that I feel before I even turn my head. Jin notices it too. His smirk twitches, like he's been expecting this. Slowly, I glance over my shoulder—and fuckkk.

Kalel is making his way across the room, murder written all over his face. His jaw clenched, his eyes locked on me. His stride was purposeful. Predatory. Why is it always me? Ugh! His hands flex at his sides like he's already imagining wrapping them around Jin's throat.

Jin watches him approach, unbothered. If anything, he looks highly entertained. He exhales, turning back to me, voice light and teasing. "Oh, look. Your owner's coming." I choke on a laugh, but Jin just grins like he was waiting for this exact reaction.

When Kalel reaches us, the heat of his fury rolling off him in waves. I swear I could hear the ice in his drink crack from the tension alone. Jin, the absolute menace that he is, tilts his head at Kalel and smirks. "Relax, big guy. I was just keeping her entertained while you were off handling your little business deal."

Kalel doesn't blink. "Leave."

Jin sighs, shaking his head. "No pleasantries? No, thank you for making your girl laugh?"

Kalel takes a step closer, and for the first time tonight, I feel real danger.

Not towards me.

Towards Jin.

Jin, however, is unfazed. Amused, even. He smirks at me one last time, completely ignoring the murderous tension radiating from Kalel. and says, "Have a good night, cutie." Then he walks away and I exhale, turning to Kalel—but before I can speak, his hand is on my waist, pulling me flush against him. His grip is tight, his fingers pressing into my skin, his voice low and dangerous.

"You think that was funny?"

I smirk, because I can't help myself. "Maybe." I say.

His eyes darken, his control slipping. "You like entertaining other men, kitten?"

I tilt my head, pretending to think. "I enjoy making you work for it. I enjoy making your life just a little harder." His smirk is slow and predatory. "You're gonna regret that." Heat coils in my stomach, my breath hitching slightly. I should back down, but don't. Instead, I lean in, letting my lips brush just barely against his jaw. "Promise?" I ask.

His grip tightens.

And just like that, the game changes.

* * *

Kalel

She's playing with fire.

Sitting there, smirking up at me like she didn't just spend the last ten minutes giggling at another man's jokes. Like she doesn't know exactly what she's doing to me. I grip my drink tighter, letting the ice bite into my fingers as I watch her. I watch the way her lips curve slightly—amused, taunting.

She's waiting for me to snap.

And I will, but not here.

Not yet.

I set my glass down and lean in, brushing my lips just over her ear. My breath is warm and deliberate against her skin. "We're leaving."

She tilts her head slightly, feigning boredom, but I see the flicker of something in her eyes. Anticipation? Good. "Already?" she muses. I smirk, my fingers grazing the bare skin of her back where her dress dips low. I feel her stiffen.

"You've had your fun, kitten." My voice is low, possessive, and deadly. "Now it's time for mine."

Her breath catches, but she schools her expression quickly. She wants to pretend she's still in control. That's cute.

She isn't.

I guide her toward the exit, my grip firm on her waist. I make sure everyone in this goddamn room sees it—sees who she belongs to. The way she moves for me; the way no other man will ever get to touch her.

Jin's smirk still lingers in the back of my mind.

I flex my fingers. I'll deal with that later. Right now? She's my problem.

On the car ride home, she barely has time to settle before I'm on her. The second the door shuts, my hand is on her bare thigh, pushing her dress up just enough to make her squirm. She gasps, twisting to glare at me. "You really can't keep your hands to yourself, huh?"

No, and why would I want to?

I smirk, tracing slow, lazy circles on her skin. "Can you tell me why I should?" I ask.

She exhales sharply. I love pissing her off. She shifts, trying to push my hand away, but I don't budge. Instead, I grip her thigh, squeezing just enough to make her breath hitch. "You forgot who you belong to tonight," I murmur, my lips just brushing the shell of her ear. "That was a mistake."

She scoffs, rolling her eyes. "I don't belong to anyone." She says. I chuckle, slow and dangerous, trailing my fingers higher. Her body betrays her, tensing, heating. I lean in, my voice a dark promise. "You will when I'm done with you." She exhales, sharp and uneven, but before she can say anything—Angelo ruins it.

"So, Sabrina." Her head jerks up, startled, as if she forgot he was still very much in the front seat. I clench my jaw, already irritated. I'm going to kill him. Angelo glances at us through the rear-view mirror, his lips twitching like he's enjoying himself.

Of course he was.

To him, I was still just Kalel. Not the head of the Marchetti family. More his brother than his boss.

"I noticed you met Jin tonight," he says casually. I go still. Sabrina blinks, tilting her head. "Yeah, what about him?"

Angelo hums. "Just wondering what you thought of him."

I shoot him a glare so sharp he should be dead. He knows what he's doing. Sabrina, completely unaware of the storm brewing in my chest. She shrugs. "He's... interesting." My fingers tighten on her thigh. She doesn't notice.

"He's funny," she continues, completely fucking oblivious. "And dramatic, but not in an annoying way." I grind my teeth. Dead, he's a dead man, because I'm going to kill him. Angelo smirks. "That's just how he is. Right, Kalel?"

My vision darkens. She turns to me, curious. "Oh? You know him?" I exhale slowly, forcing control back into my voice. "Something like that." Angelo hums, pretending to be deep in thought. "Yeah... you could say that." Sabrina narrows her eyes, looking between us. "Wait. Are you two—?"

"That's enough," I snap. Angelo smirks but doesn't push it. He knows better. Sabrina, however, is still looking at me. She tilts her head, studying me now, like she can sense the tension I'm barely containing. I don't like being studied. So I distract her the only way I know how.

I grip her chin, tilting her face toward mine, making her focus. "You're worrying about the wrong things." My voice is smooth, dangerous. Final. Her breath hitches, but I don't let her look away. "You should be worrying about what I'm going to do to you when we get back."

Her lips part slightly. I can see the war in her eyes—defiance battling anticipation. She wants to push back, but she's already losing.

I smirk, brushing my thumb over her lower lip. "And trust me, sweetheart." My voice drops. "I'm going to make you suffer."

Her thighs squeeze together on instinct.

I feel it. And fuck me, I love it.

Angelo clears his throat. "Alright, lovebirds," he says, far too entertained. "We're back." I inhale slowly, pulling back just enough to make her miss my touch. Sabrina exhales, blinking fast, like she's trying to clear her head.

I chuckle, low and deep. She thinks she's catching up to me. She has no fucking idea.

Chapter 10

Kalel

The moment we step inside the estate, I don't let go of her. Not even when the doors shut behind us. Sabrina mutters something about me being a psychotic asshole under her breath and not when Sabrina twists in my grip, glaring up at me.

"You can let go now," she says, voice sickly sweet.

I don't.

Instead, I tighten my grip around her waist, my fingers digging into the fabric of her dress, pinning her to me.

She exhales sharply; her nails pressing into my forearm. "Kalel."

I smirk. "Yes, kitten?" Her eyes blaze with defiance and attitude. My fucking weakness. "You're acting like a jealous lunatic," she bites out. I chuckle, slow and dark, dipping my head closer until my lips hover over her ear. "And you're acting like you forgot who you belong to." I say.

She scoffs. "You keep saying that like I ever agreed to it." I smile against her skin. "You did when I took you to La Morsa." She sucks in a sharp breath, her body betraying her again. I win. I feel the way her pulse jumps beneath my touch, the way she leans into me for just a second before she catches herself.

She hates this. She hates that she wants me. That only makes me want to ruin her more. I pull back slightly, just to look at her.

Sabrina.

My problem and my fucking obsession.

Standing there, fire in her eyes, challenge in her posture, acting like she wasn't seconds away from melting in that car. Acting like I didn't watch another man make her laugh. Watch another man make her fucking smile.

I flex my jaw, barely keeping my temper in check. I need to remind her why she's she's here.

I need to feel her. Hear her whimper. I need to punish her. "You didn't let Jin get in your head, did you?" I murmur, voice taunting. She narrows her eyes, lips parting, but before she can say something back, I grip her jaw. Not too rough. Just enough to make her stop.

Her breath catches, but she doesn't pull away. "Did you like it?" I ask, my voice low, lethal. "The attention?" Her lashes flutter, but her jaw tenses.

She's going to lie.

I squeeze slightly. "Careful." She glares up at me, chin tilting just to spite me. "Why? You gonna punish me again?" My smirk is slow. "Oh, kitten." My thumb swipes across her lower lip, teasing her. "I was always going to punish you."

Her pupils dilate, her chest rising in sharp breaths. She likes this. She likes when I press, when I push. When I test how far I can go before she snaps, and I intend to find out.

I release her jaw and grab her wrist instead, leading her through the estate, ignoring the way she stumbles slightly to keep up with my much longer strides.

"Kalel." she calls out.

I don't stop. She tugs against my grip. "Kalel, where the fuck are we going?" I keep walking, dragging her through the hallway, straight toward our bedroom. She digs her heels in hard. "You have a mouth to speak Kalel! Use them, god!" She yanks her arm, actually trying to fight me.

My fucking brat.

I chuckle, turning to face her. "You really think you get a say in this?" She glares up at me. "I think you need therapy." I laugh. Actually, laugh. We both do. Then I lift her off the ground. "Kalel!" she shrieks, kicking. "You can't just carry me like a goddamn caveman!"

I smirk, throwing her over my shoulder like she's weightless. "You say that like I don't do whatever I want." She screams in frustration, pounding on my back. "Put me down, psycho!"

"Gladly." I kick open the bedroom door, step inside, and toss her onto our bed. She bounces slightly, her hair tumbling into her face, her stunned glare making my chest tighten and my dick throb with satisfaction. She props herself up on her elbows, eyes burning into me. "You're insane."

I smirk, unbuttoning my shirt. "And you're in my bed."

She exhales sharply, catching the meaning immediately. I lean down, pinning her beneath me. One hand on either side of her head, my body caging hers in.

She doesn't move. She doesn't breathe.

Neither do I.

Then—she tilts her chin up, just slightly.

A fucking invitation.

I graze my lips over hers—just enough to make her ache for it.

She trembles, her nails curling into the sheets. I pull back slightly, smirking, and grip her chin. Forcing her to meet my eyes. I expect another smart-ass remark, another bratty little taunt, but she just breathes through parted lips, watching me. And that's when I see it.

The need.

The sharp edge of her desire, buried under all that attitude. She wants me to break her. She just won't say it. Fine. I'll make her scream it. I crush my mouth against hers, taking. No hesitation, no softness—just pure possession. My teeth graze her bottom lip, my tongue sliding in to taste her, and fuck, she's sweet.

Her hands clutch my shirt, gripping hard like she's trying to hold herself together. She can't, she won't. I pull back, my breath rough, trailing my lips down her throat and along her collarbone. She shivers and her fingers twitch, like she wants to push me away—but doesn't. Instead, she moans, just barely.

"We shouldn't..." she breathes, but it's weak, broken. I smirk against her skin. Liar. My hand slides under her dress, my fingers dipping between her thighs—and fuckkk, she's soaked.

I exhale sharply, my grip tightening on her hip. "Are you sure you want me to stop?" She doesn't answer. Not with words, but her hips roll just slightly, chasing my fingers, like she can't help herself. I chuckle darkly. "That's what I thought."

I slide one finger inside her, slowly teasing her relentlessly. She gasps, her body tightening around me instantly.

Fuck.

I add another curling deep. Her head tilts back, her breath catching, but when I pause. She opens her bratty little mouth again.

"What—" she pants. "Why—" I grip her jaw. "Take your dress off." Her lips part, uncertainty flickering across her face. I raise a brow, waiting. She hesitates, just for a second. Then obeys. Taking the dress off, never taking her eyes off of me.

That's my good girl.

I let my gaze drag over her, slow and deliberate, taking in every inch of exposed skin. She's intoxicating. I'm already barely in control, and seeing her like this—bare, wanting, waiting—I swear I'm about to take her.

I slide my fingers back between her thighs, rubbing slow, torturous circles against her clit. She trembles.

I smirk. Perfect. My lips trail down her stomach to her wet pussy. I pause just above where she wants me most, pressing a kiss against the soft skin.

"So," I murmur, my breath warm against her. "You like using men to make me jealous?" I ask.

She whimpers. I glance up. "Answer me, kitten."

She exhales shakily. "Yes."

Wrong answer.

I slide my fingers deeper, my tongue flicking against her clit exactly where she needs me.

She jerks, a broken moan slipping from her lips. It sends a pulse straight to my dick.

"Fuck, Kalel," she gasps. I hum against her, smirking when I feel her body shake. She's close.

So I stop.

She gasps, her head snapping up. "W—why" She grins

I grip her thighs, pinning her down. "The safe word is purple," I say smoothly. Confusion flashes across her face. "What?" I tilt my head, observing her. "The safe word is purple," I repeat.

Her lips part, her chest rising and falling in sharp, uneven breaths. She understands, but she doesn't use it.

Good.

I straighten, yanking off my shirt, undoing my belt. She watches me, her breath catching when I pull my cock free. Her eyes drop lower. She stills.

I smirk. "Something wrong?" She blinks, shaking her head slightly. "You're... huge." I chuckle, gripping her ankles, dragging her to the edge of the bed. I was big and my girth had made women question their abilities, but she's going to take all of it. Maybe next time she won't forget where she belongs.

"Yes, I am kitten and you're gonna take it. All of it." I say.

She swallows, hard. I tilt my head. "Are you on birth control?"

She licks her lips, nodding. "Yes... IUD."

Good. I smirk, spreading her thighs wider, rubbing my dick through her slick folds. She's soaking. "You ready for me, kitten?"

She exhales shakily, but there's no hesitation in her eyes now.

I lean in, my lips brushing hers, my voice dropping. "On your knees." I demand. She hesitates. Confused.

I wait.

Then—she shakes her head. "No." I chuckle darkly, gripping her hair, twisting it into my fist. She gasps, her defiance flickering. I guide her down, slow but unyielding. She resists—for half a second. Then she folds. Her lips part slightly, her breath uneven.

I smirk, brushing the tip of my dick against her mouth. "That's what I thought." She glares up at me, but before she can fire off a bratty little insult—I push inside. Her lips stretch around my throbbing cock, her eyes widening.

Fuck.

I groan, gripping the back of her head as she struggles to take me. Her fingers dig into my thighs, her lashes fluttering, and I swear, I almost lose it right there.

"That's right, look at me while you swallow my dick" I say.

Her tongue swirls over the head, sucking me deeper, her throat tightening as I hit the back.

I groan. "Fuck, kitten."

She gags slightly, but doesn't pull away. Fucking perfect. I thrust deeper, watching the way her eyes tear, the way her body fights it—but she doesn't stop.

"Who do you belong to?" I growl. She tries to answer, but she's choking on my cock. I pull out, watching the way her lips gloss over with spit, watching the drool drip from her chin. The way she gasps for air, her chest heaving.

"Who do you belong to?" I ask again, my voice calm. Commanding.

Her throat bobs as she swallows, blinking her teary, stubborn eyes up at me. "No one," she whispers.

I exhale slowly, shaking my head. "Wrong answer."

I shove back into her mouth, deeper this time, until she's choking. Until she has no choice but to take it. She gags, tears spilling down her cheeks. I groan, fucking her mouth, dragging her down until she has no escape.

I pull out just enough to let her breathe. "Try again, kitten. Who do you belong to?"

She gasps, blinking up at me, spit dripping from her swollen lips. "You," she whispers, her voice wrecked.

I smirk. "That's my girl."

Then I grab her and throw her onto the bed.

And this time, I don't stop.

I press her down against the mattress, my body caging hers in, my grip firm around her wrists as she trembles beneath me. My hard cock throbbing to be inside of her. She's still breathing hard, her body warm, her skin flushed from what I've already done to her, but it's not enough. Not nearly enough.

I need her ruined. Needing, wrecked, and fucking mine.

My fucking little slut. My chest tightens. And she's fucking perfect. I grip her hips. She's so damn soft. So ready. I push in slowly, inch by inch, giving her time to adjust. To stretch around me. My jaw clenches, my hands gripping tighter as I hold back, letting her adjust.

She gasps, her body trembling, fingers digging into the sheets. "Breathe," I murmur, my voice low and coaxing. "Relax for me, baby— let me in." She exhales, melting just slightly, and I press deeper, groaning as she takes me—all of me.

Fuck.

I thrust slowly, rhythmically. Memorizing every part of her, inside and out. "You feel that?" I murmur, dragging my lips along her shoulder. "How good you're taking me?"

"Y-Yes," she moans softly, her breath shaky, and I know she's feeling every inch of this, every inch of me. The moment I pull out and slide back in, she shudders, her walls tightening around me.

"There you go," I whisper a praise, gripping her hip, guiding her into the rhythm. "Just like that, kitten. You're doing so good for me."

She whimpers, pressing her head into the sheets. She's already falling apart, but I'm not done with her yet. I grip her hair, tilting her head back, forcing her to feel every single movement.

"You're taking it so well," I murmur against her neck, dragging my teeth over her skin. "So fucking tight." She gasps as I thrust deeper, hitting exactly where I know she needs me.

Her body tenses, then shakes. "Fuck Kalel" she moans.

She's close.

I smirk, moving one hand between her thighs, finding her throbbing clit. "Right there?" I ask, knowing the answer. She nods frantically, moaning. "Yes—right there, Don't stop—" I groan, rubbing slow, teasing circles, just enough to keep her on edge.

"You gonna come for me, kitten?" I murmur, my breath warm against her ear. She whimpers, her body trembling, desperate. "Tell me," I demand, thrusting deeper, pulling her tighter against me. "Yes," she gasps, her voice breaking. "I—I'm gonna—" she stutters.

"Come for me, baby."

And she does.

Her entire body tenses, then shatters, tightening around me so hard I have to grip her just to hold her still.

I don't stop. I work her through it, murmuring praise against her skin, groaning as she rides out every wave. "That's it, good girl. Such a fucking good girl." She collapses forward, trembling, but I'm not done. Not until I make sure she knows who she belongs to.

I hold her tighter, chasing my release, taking what's already mine.

When I finally cum inside her, I let out a low, satisfied groan, pressing my forehead against her back, catching my breath.

She whimpers, still coming down, her body limp against the sheets. I smirk, pressing a slow, lingering kiss to her shoulder. "That's my girl," I murmur, completely satisfied.

She doesn't answer—Still coming down from her orgasm.

That's just how I like her—wrecked, ruined, and too breathless to remember anyone else's name.

Chapter 11

<u>Sabrina</u>

I woke up to cold sheets.

My body is still heavy from sleep. My muscles are sore in a way that makes heat flicker through me before I fully register what's wrong.

Kalel is gone.

The space beside me—where he should be—is empty. I sit up, my heart hammering. The room is dark and silent. The only sound is the faint rustling of trees outside the massive windows.

For a second, I tell myself I'm overreacting. He wouldn't leave in the middle of the night without telling me. Maybe he's in the shower or in his office, brooding over whatever psychotic mafia shit he does at night, but deep down—I know.

He's not here. He left.

A sharp, unfamiliar feeling rises in my chest—something I haven't felt in a while. I feel my chest tighten. I know he's not, but my brain doesn't seem to know the difference between perceived abandonment and rejection from doing normal human behavior sadly.

I take a deep breath, pushing my feelings away. I fell asleep, and he disappeared. I toss the blankets back roughly, ignoring the ache between my legs as I storm out of the room.

He has to be here;

101

I check the office. Nothing. The kitchen. Empty. The gym. Still nothing. By the time I'm back in the main hall, I'm seething because it's not just that he's gone. It's that I woke up looking for him. That I wanted him and that's unacceptable. How did I let myself get to this point?

I exhale sharply, trying to force down the heat creeping up my neck. I didn't mean to fall asleep next to him like that. Didn't mean to let my body melt into his, but after what happened—after everything he did to me, the way he talked me through it, how his touch possessed me, and how he drew every single reaction from me as if I were made for him—

Fuck.

I drag a hand through my hair, my chest tight. The memories slam into me, hard and relentless. His voice, smooth and possessive—

"You take it so well, kitten. Look at you." The way he praised me; owned me. The way he ruined me for anyone else.

"Come for me, baby. That's my girl."

My stomach clenches, my thighs pressing together as heat licks at my skin, humiliation washing over me. I felt like I let him see too much. Like I was too much and now? He's the one who left. I exhale, my fists curling. "Ugh. why did you sleep with him? Why didn't you say no?" I'm spiraling.

If he thinks he can just disappear after last night—He's got another thing coming. I stomp back to the room and lay down. I don't even remember falling back asleep.

One minute, I'm pissed the hell off, storming around the house like a lunatic, cursing Kalel's name for leaving me after what we did. Next, I'm out cold, but when I wake up—he's asleep. I blink, disoriented for a second.

Kalel is lying beside me, his broad chest rising and falling in deep, steady breaths. His body beneath the sheets. I felt every feeling I've ever tried to hide all over again. I sit up slowly, staring at him. He looks... different like this.

Less sharp, less ruthless, and more peaceful. Like he's not carrying the weight of the world on his shoulders for once. I felt like maybe I should let him sleep.

I should, but I'm still mad.

So instead, I grab the nearest pillow—and smack him in the face with it. Hard. He jerks awake instantly, one hand shooting out like he's ready to kill someone, but I cross my arms and glare.

"What the hell was that for?" he said, his voice is deep and rough from sleep—and for a second, it almost makes me forget I'm mad. Almost. I felt like smacking him again.

So I do.

Kale catches the pillow mid-swing, his grip firm, his eyes sharper now, but there's something else too—amusement.

I narrow my eyes. Smug bastard. "Where did you go last night?" I demand, my voice sharp. His lips twitch like he's holding back a smirk. "Miss me, kitten?"

I glare harder. "Kalel." I said, looking unamused. He shifts, completely unbothered. Stretching his arms over his head, the sheets dipping just enough to tease the sharp lines of his stomach. He knows exactly what he's doing, but I refuse to be distracted. I cross my arms tighter. "Where. Did. You. Go." I said angrily, waiting for his answer. His smirk grows. "Are you jealous?"

I scoff, throwing the pillow at him again. He catches it effortlessly, chuckling now.

"Oh, you are," He said, his voice is pure arrogance, his eyes glinting like he's enjoying every second of this. I scowl, refusing to let him have this. "I'm not jealous." I glare at him.

"Mm." He nods, looking entirely too smug as he leans back against the headboard. "So you just hit me in my sleep... for fun?"

I purse my lips. "Maybe."

He's laughing now. Actually laughing. It should piss me off more, but it doesn't because he looks good like this. Shirtless, hair messy from sleep, his voice still deep, his smirk lazy, not a single ounce of concern in his entire being. I hate that my stomach flutters. That I want to climb into his lap and erase the fact that he left at all, but I refuse to give in. I narrow my eyes. "Where did you go?"

Kalel exhales, finally letting the amusement slip just slightly. "There was a problem I had to take care of." I frown. "What kind of problem?" He tilts his head, studying me, like he's deciding how much to tell me or if he should.

Then he sighs, dragging a hand through his hair. "Business."

I raise a brow. "Business?"

He gives me a pointed look. "Mafia business." I inhale slowly, searching his face. "Did you kill someone?" His lips twitch again. Not a denial. Great.

I exhale sharply, shaking my head. "You know what? Don't tell me."

He chuckles, reaching out suddenly and grabbing my waist, yanking me into his lap. I gasp, hands flying to his chest, but he doesn't let go. Instead, he smirks, eyes dropping to my lips. "You're cute when you're mad," he murmurs.

I narrow my eyes. "And you're an asshole." His smirk deepens. "An asshole who had you searching the entire house for him last night?" He says with a smirk.

I roll my eyes, but he grins. "You did, didn't you?"

I hate how good he is at reading me or maybe he was watching the camera.

I lift my chin, full of fake confidence. "No."

He laughs again. Then he flips me onto my back, pinning me beneath him, his mouth brushing my ear as he whispers—

"Liar." And just like that, I know exactly where this is going and I don't want it to stop. My breath catches, my pulse hammering as Kalel pins me beneath him, his body pressing into mine, his lips hovering too close.

I should fuss back at him with something sharp. Remind him I'm still mad. Still pissed that he left without a word. Show him I'm still not over the fact that I woke up searching for him like some clingy, needy—

I stop myself, hating the thought. His smirk deepens. Like he can see my thoughts unraveling. "Admit it," he murmurs, voice teasing and smug as hell. "You missed me."

I glare. "I didn't." I say smugly. He hums, completely unconvinced. "Then why'd you go looking for me?" I scowl, refusing to answer. He chuckles, his grip tightening on my wrists as he leans in, brushing his lips just below my ear slowly. "You woke up, and I wasn't there."

I bite my lip hard, fighting back tears. Tears he will never see. People have always abandoned me. I've never felt like I was ever enough. Not until Kalel. Not until he took me and accepted my anger, my sass, and my attitude. I always fall for the love bombing. Not this time.

Kalel grabs my chin, making me look him in the eye and snapping me back to reality.

"You missed me and got mad," he continues, his voice all dark amusement and dangerous control.

"Embarrassed. Probably cursing my name." He says, feeling a little too pleased with himself. I exhale sharply. The fact that he's right makes me even angrier. I twist beneath him, struggling, but it's useless. He doesn't move. Doesn't even budge. Instead, he smirks harder, pressing his weight into me like he enjoys the fight.

I glare, spitting fire. "You think you're special, don't you?"

He chuckles, dragging his nose along my jaw, his breath warm against my skin. "I know I am." My stomach flips, annoyingly, traitorously. I clench my jaw, refusing to let him win. "You really think I was out there crying over you?" I scoff, tilting my chin up. "Please. I was just looking to see if you finally got arrested."

His smirk sharpens. "Disappointed I wasn't?"

I snort "You? In cuffs? You'd probably enjoy that."

His gaze darkens, his smirk shifting into something slower, more dangerous. "Careful, kitten."

I freeze, because I know that look. I've seen it before.

The calm before the storm and suddenly, the air shifts. The teasing is still there, but beneath it is something deeper, possessive, and deadly.

"You were jealous," he murmurs, suddenly serious. "Weren't you?"

I hesitate, and that's enough for him to know the truth. Kalel chuckles low, his lips brushing against mine, just barely. "I could make you beg for me, right now," he murmurs. "Could make you forget you were ever mad." My heart pounds. I should push him away. I should, but I don't.

Instead, I part my lips, about to fire back with something smart, something to take the power back — But he beats me to it.

"Tell me, kitten," he breathes. "Would Raphael have left you alone in the middle of the night?" My blood goes cold. I stiffen instantly, my breath hitching. Kalel sees it, he feels the way my body locks up beneath him and just like that, the game changes.

His smirk vanishes. His expression darkens, fury flickering behind his eyes. He wasn't supposed to say that. I shove at his chest, hard, pushing him off me. He lets me—for now.

I sit up, glaring. "Thinking about Raphael?."

He watches me, silent, unreadable. Then, slowly—too slowly—he smirks again, but this time, it's different.

It's insidious.

Like he knows exactly what button he just pushed. If he wants to play games, I'll fucking play. I tilt my head, tapping my lip like I'm thinking really hard about something. "You know," I muse, my tone deliberately casual. "Now that I think about it, Raphael wouldn't have left me alone in the middle of the night. You're right."

Kalel's jaw flexes. I felt the way his hands clench. The way his breathing changes.

Fucking perfect.

I smirk, dragging my nails lightly down his chest—teasing, taunting. "In fact..." I let my voice drop into something sultry, something that will get under his skin. "I bet Raphael would've stayed. Maybe even—" I don't get to finish because one second, I'm smirking up at him. The next—I'm on my back, pinned against the bed, Kalel's weight pressing me down, his hand wrapped tight around my throat. Not squeezing. Not yet. Just there. Holding me still. Holding me exactly where he wants me.

I gasp, but his lips are already at my ear. "You wanna keep running that mouth, kitten?" he murmurs. "Go ahead. Let's see how far you get before you regret it." My pulse hammers, but I won't break first.

I narrow my eyes, shifting beneath him, making sure my hips graze him. I know he's already hard, I can feel it. He inhales sharply. I smirk. "He'd probably have me moaning his name." Kalel lets out a dark, breathy laugh. Then he grips my jaw, tilting my head back. "Is that right?" he murmurs. "Then why are you trembling? Are you giving in to me already?"

I am shaking, but not from fear. It's from how fucking good this feels. He sees it, feels it, and instead of backing off—he presses in closer. His thigh pushes between mine, spreading me open, pressing exactly where I'm aching for him.

I suck in a breath, my nails digging into his arms. Kalel smirks. "See, kitten?" His lips brush my jaw, taunting. "You talk about other men. But when I touch you?" He drags his fingers down my stomach, slowly, teasing. "You forget them real fast."

I let out a sharp breath, hating that he's right. That my body is already arching into his. His lips ghost down my neck, barely there, just enough to drive me insane. "You can push me all you want," he murmurs. "But we both know I'm not going anywhere."

And that? That hits me harder than it should.

Kalel grips my hips, grinding against me just right, making me gasp. He smirks as I glare up at him. Breathless and yearning.

"You're an arrogant piece of shit." I say.

He chuckles, dragging his tongue down my throat, sucking at the sensitive spot that makes my toes curl.

"Yeah," he murmurs, his voice rough, wrecked. "And you fucking love it." I know I should want him to leave me alone, but I don't. Is there something wrong with me? I grab the back of his neck and pull him down, crashing my mouth against his. He groans, deep and guttural, and just like that—he loses control.

And I let him.

His body pins me to the mattress, all muscle, dominance, and dangerous obsession. His mouth crashes against mine—hard and messy. Consuming me. I moan into it. The second he tears at my clothes, I slap his hand away. He freezes. I smirk. "You want it? Beg." His eyes go dark.

"You really want to play that game with me, Kitten?" His voice is hypnotizing. I nod and he growls and grabs my wrists, pinning them above my head with one hand while the other trails down my body. "You want to act like a little fucking brat? You want me to beg for it?" he rasps against my throat. "Fine. But you'll beg before I'm done with you. And you'll thank me for it."

His fingers slide between my thighs—rough and teasing. He strokes me through my panties, slowly and barely there. I writhe. "We'll see."

He smirks. "That's the plan."

Then he rips my panties off and drags his mouth down my body like a man on a mission. "You don't get to come until I say so," he warns and then he devours me. His tongue is sin itself, flicking, curling, pressing—his mouth warm and relentless between my thighs. I arch off the bed, moaning, panting, cursing him with every breath.

But he doesn't stop. He flattens his tongue and sucks hard at my clit, fingers plunging deep inside me as my vision goes white.

"Kalel—oh my god—" I moan.

"Not yet," he growls, pulling back just when I'm right at the edge. "You haven't begged."

"Asshole," I hiss, legs trembling and aching for more. He spanks my inner thigh—just hard enough to sting.

"I'm waiting." My pride burns, but my body is on fire. "Please," I whisper, voice wrecked. "Please let me come." As he licks circles around my clit. I feel the warmth radiating up my body.

"Louder." He spanks me. Fuck!

"Please," I moan, hips grinding against his mouth. "Please, Kalel. I need it. I need you."

That's when he breaks me. "Good fucking girl," he growls—and then drops his mouth against me again. I feel the heat burst through me, making my body tense. I come so hard I scream "Yes!". The orgasm continues, ripping through me like lightning. My entire body shakes, thighs clenching around his head, and he doesn't stop—not even when I beg him to.

He finally pulls back, licking his lips like I'm his favorite meal. "You taste so fucking good, baby," he says darkly, dragging me up the bed. "Now let's see how loud you can scream with my dick inside you." He flips me over fast, spanking my ass once—hard—and I yelp, hips jerking.

"Count."

"W-what?" He lands another sharp slap. "Count for me, Kitten."

"One," I moan.

"Good girl."

Another hit. Another moan.

"Two."

"See? You can listen." He slides into me in one brutal thrust, deep and thick and perfect, making me cry out as I fist the sheets.

"Kalel—" I moan.

"Say my name like that again," he pants against my ear, "and I'll come before I get to finish ruining you." His hand wraps around my throat again, squeezing just enough to cut off the breath in my lungs— and send another spike of heat straight to my core. I meet every thrust with one of my own, head spinning, body burning, vision going hazy.

"You gonna come for me again?" he grits, driving into me so deep I see stars.

"Yes—yes—please," I beg.

His fingers slide down between us, circling my clit, and I break. My second orgasm crashes through me like a wave, violent and all-consuming. I sob into the sheets, convulsing around him as he groans, slamming into me one last time before he spills inside me with a growl of my name.

He collapses on top of me, breath ragged, biting my shoulder and hands fisting the sheets beside me.

Then he leans in, pressing a kiss to my shoulder where his teeth left a mark.

I tremble beneath him, and I realize that I have feelings for him.

Chapter 12

Sabrina

I don't know what I was expecting when Kalel told me he wanted to introduce me to someone.

Was it a business partner? Or another scary, gun-wielding psychopath from his empire? Maybe even an overpaid lawyer who helps him launder money and cover up murders?

What I wasn't expecting was her.

Gianni.

She's stunning.

Gianni has long, wavy brown hair, warm golden skin, brown eyes that immediately assesses me with something close to curiosity. She's tall, like model tall, dangerously pretty, and carries herself with a confidence that makes it clear she knows exactly who she is.

Kalel watches us, arms crossed, his usual brooding presence hovering over us. She flashes a smirk, her gaze flicking casually between me and Kalel. "So you're the girl my brother kidnapped?"

A startled laugh escapes me before I can stop it, echoing harshly against the polished wood floors. Kalel's eyes narrow immediately, annoyance tightening his jaw. "Careful," he warns his sister quietly, voice low and full of restrained irritation.

Gianni rolls her eyes dramatically, ignoring him. She leans casually against the kitchen island, arms crossed, and fixes me with an inviting grin. "Ignore him. He's always so grumpy. It's exhausting."

Something in her attitude draws a genuine smile from me, easing the knot in my chest just slightly. "Trust me, I've noticed," I reply, leaning against the counter opposite her. "How do you put up with it?"

Kalel mutters something in Italian that I'm sure is a curse. I smirk. I like her. She looks like she annoys him just as much as I do. Gianni's sharp wit and fearless teasing remind me of myself—before Kalel, before the kidnapping, before everything.

She smirks. "It's been a long, miserable twenty-two years."

Kalel exhales through his nose, rubbing his temples like he's deeply regretting every choice that led him to this moment.

"I'm right here," Kalel interjects, clearly irritated.

"Unfortunately," I shoot back.

Gianni bursts into laughter, high-fiving me playfully. I see a shadow of genuine warmth cross Kalel's features before he quickly hides it behind his usual scowl.

But then it shifts.

She asks a question—just a simple, casual question. "So...how'd you guys meet?" Suddenly, the air changes. I felt like feel Kalel tense beside me.

I swallow, forcing a smile. "Oh, you know. The usual. We ran into each other, sparks flew, I was taken to his house with no way to leave." Gianni's smile falters. Just for a second. But I see it.

The way her brows knit together. The way her fingers tighten slightly against the table. She knows; She's not stupid.

Kalel's jaw clenches. "Gianni." His tone is warning.

She ignores him. She looks at me. Like really looks at me, and for the first time since I got here, someone sees me. Not as Kalel's possession. Not as something to be owned.

As a person.

My throat tightens. I force a smirk, shoving the emotion back down where it belongs. "Relax. I'm still breathing." I say, hoping she drops the subject.

Gianni doesn't laugh this time. She looks between me and Kalel. She's putting pieces together. Gianni's realizing exactly what kind of man her brother is.

Gianni clears her throat, stepping back. "Well." She forces a grin, but can see the tension behind it now. "I guess the rumors weren't that far away from the truth." She says, battling with disbelief.

I let out a dry laugh, but my stomachs twisting. I don't know if my isolation is the reason, but I liked her, and now I feel awful. I feel like the weight of what Kalel did to me is now somehow sitting on my chest, suffocating me, screaming at me. It's not just me who sees it now. It's his sister too.

That makes it too fucking real.

Too heavy for me.

I can feel it between us—the weight of the truth neither of us wanted to face.

Gianni knows.

She might not have said it out loud, but I saw it. The way her eyes flicked to Kalel, the way her body tensed, like she was only just realizing what her brother had truly done.

For a second, I think Kalel is going to drag me away.

Scared that Gianni is going to push. Ask more questions. Demand answers.

But then—"Ahh, my two favorite troublemakers." Angelo's voice cuts through the tension like a blade, his tone lazy and teasing. I blink, startled, as he strolls toward us, his usual grin in place.

Gianni lights up.

"Angelo!" she squeals, launching herself at him so hard he stumbles back a step. Kalel exhales, rubbing a hand down his face like he's exhausted by the entire situation. I watch, still trying to wrap my head around the fact that this is happening.

Angelo laughs and swinging Gianni around like she weighs nothing. His deep chuckle filling the room and melting the lingering unease. Kalel watches silently, exasperation and reluctant amusement flickering across his face.

As Angelo settles beside us, he winks at me. "What's the verdict? Have you two formed an alliance yet? Ready to overthrow Kalel's reign of terror?"

I roll my eyes dramatically, grinning despite myself. "We'll need more firepower for that."

Kalel growls under his breath, clearly irritated. Gianni laughs openly, linking her arm through mine. "You'd be a fantastic addition," she whispers conspiratorially.

"She already has the attitude down," Angelo teases.

I smirk confidently, enjoying the newfound camaraderie. "You'd better believe it."

Across from me, Kalel's gaze is dark and intense, his expression unreadable. He's studying me, taking in every detail, like he's memorizing this moment. It feels intrusive, overwhelming, and yet undeniably thrilling. My heart pounds in my chest, the heat of his attention unsettling and exhilarating.

I sit back, taking it in. She has no idea how lucky she is. She has no idea that Kalel is the monster in the shadows, the villain in someone's story.

In my story.

"You're staring," I snap at him, breaking the charged silence.

His lips twitch into a faint smirk, eyes never leaving mine. "Maybe I like what I see."

I scoff, ignoring the traitorous flutter in my chest. "Oh, really?"

His smile widens slightly, eyes glittering with dangerous amusement. Gianni interrupts before I can retort, nudging me playfully.

I tilt my head, grinning at Gianni. "I like you. You're way more fun than your brother." Kalel grits his teeth and smiles. Gianni smirks. "Right? He's so serious all the time."

Kalel rolls his neck like he's trying not to kill us both.

Angelo snorts in amusement. "Well. Someone has to be the boring one." Kalel's jaw flexes harder.

Angelo chuckles, raising his hands in mock surrender. "Nah, I'm just here for damage control."

Kalel rubs his temples like he's in pain. Me, on the other hand, I laugh, actually laugh. Something in my chest loosens. I needed this. I needed a moment where I wasn't thinking about why I was here. A moment where I wasn't thinking about what Kalel had done to me, what I'd let him do, or what I still fucking wanted from him. Even though I wanted to hate him. A moment where I could just breathe. I glance at Kalel. Again, expecting to see him brooding, irritated, over it and he is. But when I meet his eyes, something shifts. He's watching me.

Not just watching—studying. He's memorizing this moment like he's never seen me laugh before. As if he never would again.

I tear my gaze away first, clearing my throat. I can't think about that. I won't. So instead, I smirk at Angelo. "Alright, damage control. Where's the alcohol?" I say.

Gianni cheers. Kalel groans. And just like that, the weight is gone—at least for now.

* * *

The late afternoon sun bled across the courtyard, dripping gold over the estate. Shadows stretched long across the freshly cut lawn, the scent of fresh bread and roasted meat lingering in the thick summer air. I leaned back against the wooden picnic table, my curls in a messy ponytail on top of my head, pastry half-eaten in my hand. Across from me, Gianni lounged like she owned the world, sipping lemonade with her leg propped up, looking every bit like the mafia princess she was.

Kalel stood a few feet away with Angelo, their conversation low and constant. His eyes kept flicking toward me, like he needed to see me. Like he was memorizing the way I looked at this moment—at ease, not spitting fire in his direction. I was laughing. Actually laughing at something Gianni said. And the worst part? It felt good.

"Okay, but seriously, this whole 'prisoner' thing is working for you," Gianni teased, tipping her chin up. "You're glowing, babe."

I snorted. "Oh yeah, I'm living the dream. Hostage chic is really in this season."

Angelo huffed out a quiet chuckle, shaking his head. "You two are troublesome together."

I smirked at him. "Don't act like you don't love it, big guy."

His mouth twitched. And that's when I knew—I had him. Somewhere between him keeping Kalel from going full psycho and watching over me, Angelo had started seeing me differently. I wasn't just Kalel's problem anymore. It felt like we were family…Or something close to it.

Gianni leaned in, voice low. "He won't admit it, but Angelo's been looking out for you like a big brother. It's kind of cute."

I arched a brow at him. "That true?"

Angelo rolled his eyes like I'd just asked him for a kidney. "Don't get used to it, troublemaker."

I grinned. "Oh, I absolutely will."

Out of the corner of my eye, I caught Kalel watching. Something dark passed over his face, something heavy. It was like the sight of me fitting in—laughing, joking, slipping into his world like I belonged— did something to him.

It dug into him deep, settled in his bones, and what made it worse was that I was supposed to hate him. Maybe I still did somewhere deep

116

down inside. But this? This moment felt like a glitch in the universe. It was like something that wasn't supposed to exist. Yet did.

"It's time." Angelo murmured beside him.

Kalel exhaled, pulling himself away. His gaze lingered on me for a second longer before he nodded once. "I'll be back."

I felt him leave before I saw him leave. Am I starting to care?

Nope, not happening.

Gianni tapped her nails against the table, waiting until the men disappeared before sighing. "He's so fucked up, you know."

I scoffed. "Yeah. Understatement of the century."

She tilted her head, observing me. "You wanna know why?"

I hesitated because I shouldn't care. It was easier to keep him in the villain box, to pretend there was nothing beneath the surface. But the way Gianni looked at me was like she'd already decided I was going to hear it.

She exhaled, leaning back. "Our dad was the hardest on Kalel. Harder than you can imagine. He wasn't allowed to be a kid. Not even for a second. While I played, he trained. When I laughed, he took hits. He was born to be our father's successor, and our father made damn sure he never forgot it."

I hadn't realized I was gripping the edge of the table until my knuckles turned white. Gianni's voice dropped like the weight of what she was saying pressed down on her, too. "The only person who ever loved him like really loved him was our mom. She made him feel safe and when she got sick, I was too young to understand. Kalel knew. He watched her die slowly. He watched our father grieve her like he lost a possession, not a person. And after she was gone, he was alone in a way no one should be." My throat went tight. "That doesn't excuse what he's done."

Gianni nodded, solemn. "No, it doesn't. He's crossed too many lines." She said. Then her voice softened. "But he loves you, Sabrina.

In the only way he knows how."

Something cold wrapped around my ribs and squeezed. Love. Was that what this was? Kalel's obsession, his control—it wasn't normal. But maybe, just maybe, it was the only love he had ever been taught. I looked away, staring at the horizon. I wanted to hate him without complication. Wanted to rip this conversation out of my head and pretend it didn't change anything.

But it did.

And that terrified me more than anything.

Chapter 13

Kalel

I knew it was coming.

The second I walked away from them. I need space, air, anything to get my head straight, but that wasn't going to happen. At least, not with Gianni following me.

The meeting with Angelo had just wrapped up, leaving a sour taste in my mouth. I handled business, but my mind was elsewhere. It was on Sabrina. It's always on her. On my way back to the office, I saw Gianni speaking to Sabrina. I didn't hear the words, because I saw the expression on my sister's face—tight with frustration. Her body language is tense. I knew what the conversation was about before it even ended and didn't need to stick around and listen. I already knew how Gianni felt.

She catches up just as I step into my office, closing the door behind her with more force than necessary.

I don't turn. I just exhale sharply, running a hand through my hair. "Whatever you're about to say—don't."

She ignores me. Of course she does. "I'm not here to argue," she says. "Dad wants to see you."

I scoff. "Not interested."

"He didn't ask," she presses. "He wants you to get married," she

119

says.

That catches my attention.

I finally turn to face her, my jaw tightening. "What?" Her expression is unreadable. "You heard me. He wants you to get married."

The tension in my shoulders coils tighter. My father never made idle demands. If he wanted me married, it meant something—something that would put me exactly where he wanted me. Caged.

But that also meant I had leverage. "Fine," I say, my voice measured. "I'll go."

Gianni studies me, and I can tell she's waiting for something. Maybe an argument, maybe a fight. She gets neither. She exhales, frustrated, shifting her weight. "Kalel, look at me."

I don't, because I already know what's in her eyes.

Pity. Judgment. Disappointment.

The trifecta of people who don't understand me.

I don't want to fucking see it, but she won't let up. "This isn't love, Kalel," she says, her voice dead serious. My jaw tightens. The words claw at something buried deep and raw, but I shove it back. "I said don't."

"She's not a fucking possession." Gianni proceeds.

I grip the edge of my desk, my knuckles going white.

Wrong. She is mine. Every part of her—her mind, her body, her fucking soul was mine. Whether Sabrina accepted it or not. Whether Gianni understood it or not.

She's pushing it and I'm not in the mood. Gianni exhales, frustrated, desperate. "Kalel, look at me."

"She's not Mom," she says, voice softer now. "She's not just gonna accept whatever twisted version of love you're offering." A sharp, searing pain stabs through my chest. I turn fast, barely holding my temper. "Don't," I warn, danger humming in my blood. My voice is low and dangerous. "Don't you dare bring her into this."

Gianni lifts her chin, unflinching. "Why? Because I'm right?"

I step closer, towering over her, trying to shut this down before it goes any further. My pulse is a war drum in my ears.

"You think you know what's happening here?" I murmur, voice cold, but inside, something is clawing its way out. Something violent. Something desperate. Her gaze sharpens. "Yeah, actually. I do."

I tilt my head, my jaw tight. "You think I don't love her?"

She scoffs, crossing her arms. "You don't even know what that is, Kalel." That hurts more than it should. Something unwanted twists in my chest. I shove it down. "You don't know what you're talking about." I say, praying that she drops this.

She takes a step closer. "I know you're keeping a woman locked in this house like she's some fucking prize you won."

I smirk, slow and dangerous. "You're wrong." She blinks, surprised by my response. I lean in slightly, my voice pure control, pure truth. "She's not a prize, Gianni."

My eyes darken. The need, the hunger, the possessiveness—it coils around me, suffocating and unrelenting. "She's a possession." Her breath catches.

Good.

I want her to hear it, and I want her to understand every word that comes out of my mouth. "I don't let go of what's mine," I say, absolute.

Final.

"And Sabrina is mine." I whisper in her ear.

Gianni shakes her head like she can't believe what she's hearing. She still thinks I'm someone she can reason with. "Kalel," she breathes, voice low, pleading now. "If you care about her at all, you need to let her go."

She still doesn't get it.

Something inside me snaps. I slam my hand against the desk, the force of it rattling the objects on top. "Enough!" My voice is sharp, a growl filled with rage, obsession, and need. A desperation I refuse to name.

Gianni flinches. Just barely, but I see it.

Gianni's chest rises and falls, her hands curled into fists at her sides. But her expression shifts, something clicking behind her eyes.

This is it.

She realizes, truly realizes, that not even she can save Sabrina from me.

Smart girl.

Her lips press into a thin line, her throat bobbing as she swallows.

"I don't understand you anymore," she whispers. I shake my head, my breathing heavy, my hands still planted on the desk. "Then stop trying to." I say, She takes a slow step back, like she's finally accepting what I've known all along.

I'm beyond saving, and so is Sabrina. Without another word, she turns and leaves, shutting the door softly behind her.

I stay still for a long moment, my pulse still hammering, my body coiled tight with frustration. I finally let out the breath I was holding. My hands are shaking. Not from doubt, not from regret, but from the raw, terrifying realization that I meant every single word.

I won't let Sabrina go. Not now. Not ever.

The words she spat at me echo in my head, gnawing at the edges of my control. "I don't understand you anymore."

My pulse hammers. My grip on the glass cup tightens until my knuckles turn white. Then I throw it. It shatters against the wall, shards exploding across the floor. The sound is sharp, cutting through the thick silence of the room.

I don't care. I don't care. I don't fucking care!

I swipe the rest of the liquor bottles off the table, the expensive crystal shattering into nothing. The rage boils over, my control slipping for just a second, just long enough to let the world around me feel what I feel inside. Sabrina.

Her name alone is enough to pull my next breath tight. My hands shake, not from fear, not from exhaustion—but from the unbearable, insatiable need to keep her as mine.

Gianni doesn't get it. No one fucking does. Sabrina is the only thing in this world I can't afford to lose. The only thing that keeps me tethered. The only thing that makes sense.

I press my hands to the desk, breathing hard, my reflection staring back at me from the shattered glass on the floor.

Gianni's wrong. I'm still the same person. I always have been. I inhale slowly, pulling myself back from the edge. My rage is useless if I let it control me. I force my muscles to relax, rolling my shoulders back, straightening my spine.

There's only one solution. One way to make sure Sabrina never leaves. One way to solidify what's already mine. A slow smile tugs at my lips as the thought settles, a sharp contrast to the storm inside me. If Sabrina won't accept her place willingly, then I'll have to make sure she has no choice.

She'll hate me for it. At first, but in the end, she'll see. She was always meant to be with me.

* * *

I see everyone step into the lounge, my face composed, but the tension clings to me like smoke. The air shifts the moment I enter. Angelo's eyes flicker to me, assessing, while Gianni is deliberately looking anywhere but at me.

Sabrina, however, doesn't look away. She watches me, her hazel eyes sharp. "What's wrong?" she asks, tilting her head, studying me, but before I can answer, Gianni cuts in, voice tight. "Nothing. Just my brother being my brother." Angelo's gaze narrows slightly.

Sabrina doesn't buy it either, but they mind their business. Good. I walk straight to her. Sit down next to her, closer than necessary. My thigh presses against hers. The heat of her body sinking into mine.

She stiffens for half a second, then exhales, her lips parting like she's about to say something, but I don't give her the chance.

My hand finds her thigh, fingers tracing the soft fabric of her dress. I feel her breath hitch, her pulse stuttering beneath my touch.

She tries to play it cool, acting as if nothing is happening, as if my hand isn't creeping up her thigh, as if my touch doesn't affect her. Let's see how long she can keep this up. I can feel the way her body betrays her, the way her breathing changes. Her fingers tighten slightly on the cushion beside her.

I lean in, close enough that my lips brush the shell of her ear. "You're quiet," I murmur, my voice low, edged with something darker.

She smirks back all fake confidence and sharp edges, but says nothing. She moves closer unconsciously. It's slight, but I see it.

I smirk, my palm sliding higher, fingers pressing lightly into her skin. "Something on your mind, kitten?"

She swallows hard; her lashes lowering as she shifts in her seat. "You tell me. You're the one acting weird."

I exhale a quiet chuckle. "So, that's what we're calling it?"

My hand tightens slightly, just enough to make her squirm.

Fuck. I want her.

Right here. Right now. I don't care who's watching.

The craving is unbearable, the need to mark her, to make sure every inch of her remembers who she belongs to even when I'm not there. I can barely contain it. She's right here, and I plan to claim her in every way that matters.

She exhales shakily, and I know I have her exactly where I want her. Angelo clears his throat, but I don't look at him. I don't look at Gianni either. Right now, there's only one thing that matters.

Sabrina and the pleasure I plan to give her.

She shifts slightly, as if she's trying to put some space between us, but I don't let her. I let my fingers brush the sensitive skin just beneath the hem of her dress, watching the way her pulse flutters against her throat. Watching the way she fights against her own reaction, trying to school her expression into something neutral. She's good at pretending, but not good enough. Not with me.

I lean in, dragging my lips just barely over her jaw before murmuring, "I can feel you trembling, kitten."

Her eyes flicker to mine, something sharp and defiant flashing behind them. "You wish." She says and I chuckle lowly, my breath grazing her skin as I whisper, "Every damn night."

She inhales sharply, but before she can say anything, Gianni abruptly stands, knocking her chair back in the process. "I need a drink."

Good.

Run, little sister, because you can't save her from me.

Angelo mutters something under his breath, following Gianni out of the room, but I don't acknowledge either of them. My focus is locked on Sabrina, on the way her lips part slightly, the way she's still trying to act like my touch isn't unraveling her piece by piece.

I let my fingers trace back down, deliberately slow, feeling the tension coil between us like a live wire. "Go ahead, keep pretending," I whisper, my lips brushing against her ear. "But we both know the truth."

She exhales shakily, her body betraying her once again.

And I smile. Because I know, no matter how much she fights it—she wants me just as much as I want her.

Chapter 14

Sabrina

A few hours later, Gianni stretches her arms with a yawn, her playful energy dimmed but still present as she stands. "Alright, I should get going before I fall asleep right here."

I glance up at her from my seat, trying to ignore the warmth of Kalel's arm resting lazily across the back of the couch, fingers teasing the bare skin of my shoulder. The contact is subtle, but comforting. It should feel like nothing, but it doesn't. It's impossible to ignore.

Gianni leans down, pulling me into a tight hug. "Don't let my brother drive you too crazy, okay?" she whispers, just low enough for me to hear. There's something heavy in her tone, something deeper than her usual teasing. "Never," I whisper back.

I pull back slightly to look at her, but she's already moving on. She's kissing Angelo's cheek before turning to Kalel.

For a moment, they just stare at each other. There's something unspoken between them, something that makes my stomach tighten. But then Gianni sighs and steps forward, pressing a soft kiss to his cheek.

"Try not to be such an asshole, alright?" she murmurs.

Kalel exhales through his nose, but he doesn't respond. He only grips her arm briefly before letting her go.

Gianni flashes us all one last smile before heading for the door.

The moment she's gone, the air shifts again.

Kalel's fingers slide down my shoulder, tracing in slow circles, his heat bleeding into me. Even though every part of me screams that I shouldn't let him get to me, my body betrays me.

It always does.

I swallow hard, trying to keep my breathing steady, but Kalel's touch lingers. He knows exactly what he's doing, and the worst part? He knows it's working.

I glance at Angelo, who looks as if he's debating whether he should say something, but he doesn't. He just shakes his head and leans back, as if resigning himself to whatever the hell is about to happen next.

I exhale, but it doesn't help. Because I know exactly what that means.

My night with Kalel is just beginning.

I turned on my heel and walk to the bedroom, closing the door behind me. My skin burned with frustration, my muscles tense from holding the realization that I was losing. I was catching feelings for my captor. I needed to cool off, to scrub away the weight of the night.

Without a second thought, I yanked off my clothes, tossing them onto the floor as I stepped into the marble shower. The water blasted against my skin, hot and punishing, steam curling around me. I let out a slow breath, tilting my head back, letting the water drown out everything. Until It feels like someone is watching me.

I opened my eyes and turned my head, already knowing who it was.

Kalel stood just outside the glass, leaning against the doorframe like he had all the time in the world. Arms crossed, gaze heavy, mouth tilted in amusement like he was enjoying a private show.

"Really?" I huff. "You're gonna stand there like a creep?"

He didn't answer right away. Just stared, his eyes tracing every curve of my body. Every drop of water running down it.

Then, with agonizing slowness, he reached for his shirt, peeling it off in one fluid motion, revealing the sharp lines of muscle, the old scars that traced his ribs, his arms, his chest. My stomach clenched. He held my gaze as he worked his belt loose, unbuttoned his pants, and let them drop to the floor.

I swallowed hard.

Not because I hadn't seen him like this before, I knew what was coming.

He stepped into the shower, the heat of his body closing in, suffocating me in the best and worst ways. I pressed my back against the cool marble, a poor attempt at keeping space between us. It didn't matter. He reached me in seconds, one hand coming up, fingers trailing along my collarbone before he grabs my chin rubbing his thumb across my bottom lip.

I shiver.

"got anything to say now?" Kalel says his voice was a low rasp, thick with dark amusement.

I clench my jaw, refusing to give him the satisfaction of a reaction. Even though every part of me wants to cave. Arching slightly as his grip tightened, just enough to make my pulse spike.

"Kalel," I warn, my voice lacking any real fight.

He smirks, leaning in, his breath warm against my cheek. "You keep acting like you don't want this." He says, his other hand trailed down my waist, fingers ghosting over my stomach, making me shiver.

I sucked in a sharp breath. "I don't." I lie.

His lips brushed my jaw, then lower, trailing heat across my neck. "Then say it like you mean it."

I didn't, and he knew it.

I hated him. I hated him for making me feel this way. For making my body melt against his, even when my mind screamed at me to resist. Then he kissed me, slowly, passionately. I didn't fight it.

I let him consume me, my hands fisting in his hair, nails dragging across his shoulders. He groaned into my mouth, pressing me harder against the wall, his body flush against mine, his hands exploring my body.

Then, just as suddenly as he came, he pulled back. His touch shifting—softer now. He reached for the body wash, pouring it into his palm before smoothing it over my skin, massaging my shoulders, down my arms, and over my stomach. The heat between us didn't dim, but it shifted, turned into something deeper, something more intimate.

He washed me like I was something precious. Like I wasn't his captive. Like I was his and God help me, I let him.

I know you're probably thinking Sabrina, stand up. You'd be right. I should have fought, but I didn't. Instead, I reached for the bottle, lathering soap between my hands. My heart slamming against my chest. I know I shouldn't be doing this. I did it anyway.

I moved my hands over his chest, tracing scars I'd never asked about and smoothing muscles carved from war and violence and he let me, watching me the whole time, his gaze unreadable, intense.

It wasn't a surrender. This wasn't lust? No. This was something else. Something I wasn't ready to name, but as my hands traveled lower, as Kalel let out a low, approving growl, I knew I was too far gone to stop.

Too far gone to pretend I didn't want this.

The water scalds my skin, but it's nothing compared to the heat in my veins, the burn of his touch. My knees hit the tile before I realize I've surrendered again, before I can stop myself from giving in to him— again.

Except this time it doesn't feel like surrender.

I look up at him; the water sliding down his sculpted body. His muscles tense, his broad chest rising and falling. His eyes darken, his hand resting on the back of my head like he already knows what I'm about to do. Like he's been waiting for me to fall to my knees where he thinks I belong.

I should hate him for that. I should resent the way he's looking down at me, the way he owns me without trying.

But I don't.

I part my lips, dragging my tongue along the thick, hard length of his dick. My nails digging into his thighs as I take him deeper, hollowing my cheeks. A growl rumbles from his chest, his grip in my hair tightening. "That's it, kitten. You're such a good girl for me." He praises me, making my body ache for him.

My thighs clench, the praise breaking me like it always does. I moan around him, sucking him harder, letting him feel my need for him, my craving. He twitches in my mouth, his control slipping, and that does something to me. The way I can unravel him, the way I can make him lose control—it fuels me. Owns me.

I bob my head, my tongue teasing his tip, my lips stretched around him as I take him to the back of my throat. He curses, his fingers twisting in my curls, his hips jerking like he can't help it.

Then he yanks me up, crashing his mouth to mine, tasting himself on my tongue. He grips my thigh, lifting me against the shower wall. "You want me to fuck you, kitten?" he murmurs against my lips, voice dark, teasing. His tip presses against my entrance, teasing me. Not giving me what I need.

My hands clutching his shoulders, my legs wrapping around his waist, pulling him closer. My heart pounds against my ribs, my core aching for him, for the ruin only he can give me.

"Please," I whisper, the word tasting like defeat.

He rewards me instantly, thrusting inside me in one smooth stroke, stretching me, filling me completely. My gasp turns into a moan, my nails raking down his back as pleasure explodes through me. He groans, burying his face in my neck, his lips trailing fire along my skin. "You're so fucking perfect, Baby" he rasps. "Made just for me."

His pace is slow and deep as I melt into him. Craving every thrust as if it were my last. He slowly dragging every inch of him out before slamming back in, making me feel every devastating inch. He worships me with his hands, his mouth, his words, murmuring praise between thrusts. "Look at you, Princess. You're taking me so beautifully. My perfect little slut."

I squeeze around him. Feeling my walls contracting as he drives me higher. My head falls back against the tile, my moans echoing in the steamy space, my hands fisting in his wet hair.

"I hate you," I moan, but there's no venom in my voice, only the shattering edge of pleasure, of need.

He chuckles darkly, kissing my jaw, my neck, dragging his teeth along my pulse. "No baby, you hate how much you need me."

I do. God, I do.

His hips snap harder, his thrusts deep and claiming me. His name falling from my mouth in broken cries. The pressure builds, my body tightening around him, my breath coming in sharp gasps. His thumb finds my clit, circling it and wrecking me. Pushing me to the edge.

"Come for me," he demands, his voice rough and possessive. "Come, while I'm inside you, kitten."

And I do. My body shatters, pleasure slamming into me so violently I lose myself in it, in him. I tremble, my legs locking around him, my nails digging into his back as he chases his own release, his rhythm breaking. With a low growl, he thrusts deep, spilling inside me, his breath ragged. His arms tightening around me like he'll never let go.

We stay like that, panting, tangled, our bodies still joined. His lips kiss my forehead, his hands smoothing down my back. "You mean the world to me," he says, Like a vow, a promise, and a curse.

And as much as I want to fight it, I know the truth.

I was his the moment he put me in his room.

Maybe even before that.

His fingers trace my jaw, tilting my face up to meet his gaze. "I feel you thinking," he murmurs, brushing a kiss against my swollen lips. "Don't." He says.

But I can't help it. Can't stop the way my heart clenches, the war inside me flaring up again. I should push him away, should rip myself from his grasp before he cements himself even deeper inside me.

Yet, I melt into him, into the warmth of his hands on my skin, the way he strokes my back like I'm something precious. His touch is too gentle, too reverent, like he's terrified I'll vanish if he lets go.

Like he knows I'll run.

His breath is warm against my ear. His voice was dark with something I can't name. "Say it."

I swallow, my lips parting before I can stop myself. "Say what?"

He nips at my jaw, his fingers tilting my hips forward so I can feel every inch of him still inside me. "That you are where you belong."

The words hang between us, heavy in the steam-filled air. I shake my head, my chest rising and falling with uneven breaths. "I—"

"You are." His voice is lethal, a whisper that cuts through me. His lips find my throat, pressing kisses down the column of my neck, his body still hard, still ready for me. "I don't need you to say it, kitten. I already know, but it would be nice to hear it."

I shudder, my fingers gripping his shoulders, torn between pushing him away and pulling him closer. My resolve is crumbling, my mind foggy with the aftermath of pleasure with him.

He rolls his hips, and a sharp moan spilling from my lips. His dark chuckle brushes against my ear as he pins me tighter against the tile, his hands gripping my thighs. "Let's see how many times I can make you fall apart before you admit it."

* * *

After the shower, I step out first, wrapping myself in a towel and avoiding eye contact with Kalel like that'll somehow undo what just happened between us. The heat of his hands on my skin. The way he handled me like I was something to be taken care of rather than owned. I can't stand that I don't hate it.

He follows out a second later, not bothering with a towel around his waist like the absolute menace he is. Water drips down his chest, trailing lower. I try to whip my head away before I question my life choices again.

"You're staring, kitten," he drawls, amusement lacing his voice.

I scoff, tightening my towel. "I think we're way past that now."

"Sure." He smirks as he towels off, his movements unhurried, like he enjoys getting under my skin. And of course, he does.

I ignore him, grabbing the silk nightgown he set out for me earlier, but before I can retreat to the bathroom, he's suddenly behind me, hands bracketing my hips. His lips brush my ear, a dark whisper against my skin.

"Sleep in my shirt," he murmurs.

I stiffen. "Why would I do that?"

His grip tightens, just slightly. "Because I want you to." He says.

I hate that a thrill rushes down my spine at his words. I hate I don't immediately push him away. But most of all, I hate that I give in.

I yank one of his black shirts from the drawer and storm into the bathroom. When I return, Kalel is already lounging on the bed, scrolling through his phone like he doesn't have a single worry in the world. I scowl at him.

"Happy now?" I snap.

He doesn't even look up. "Relax, kitten. You're too tense."

My scowl deepens as I climb into bed, putting as much space between us as possible, even though I want to hold him close. But then he speaks again, his voice casual, too casual.

"I'll be gone for two days." He's says like it's nothing. It shouldn't bother me, but it does.

I pause. My body reacts before my mind does—my fingers curl in the sheets, my chest tightens. I turn to him slowly.

"Why?" I say, pushing my thoughts to the back of my head.

His eyes flick to mine, unreadable as always. "My father wants to talk to me about something. I have to go see him." He says, trying to get a reaction out of me, but he won't.

A pang of frustration hit me. I should celebrate the fact that he'll be out of my sight for forty-eight hours. But all I can think is—I have to go two days without him.

Two days without his teasing remarks, without the way he watches me like I'm something precious and dangerous all at once. Two days without his hand on my throat when I push too far.

It's maddening. I say nothing. Just fold my arms and glare at the ceiling. "Kitten," he drawls, amusement creeping back into his tone. "You're pouting."

"I am not pouting." I say, annoyed.

"You are."

I grind my teeth. "If you're gonna be gone for two days, I want a phone." I demand. He chuckles like I just handed him all the entertainment he needed for the night. "Of course you do."

I prop myself up on one elbow, narrowing my eyes at him. "That wasn't a joke. If I'm stuck in this house, I need a damn phone."

His gaze darkens. He leans in slightly, tilting his head. Kalel asks "You want to talk to me that bad?"

I roll my eyes so hard it almost hurts. "I want something to do when I'm bored." His smirk deepens, but he nods. "Fine. You can have a phone. But," he raises a brow, "you can only go out if Angelo is with you."

I exhale through my nose, already annoyed, but I don't argue. I've grown a soft spot for Angelo, and Kalel knows it.

Damn him.

"Whatever." I say as I wave a hand dismissively, settling back into the pillows, determined to ignore him.

The room falls into silence. The only sound is the occasional rustle of sheets as I adjust, trying to get comfortable. Eventually, my breathing evens out and I let myself drift until I feel the weight of an arm draped over my waist. The slow, steady rise and fall of a chest against my back. My pulse stutters.

Kalel is cuddling me, and I like it.

The warmth of his body and the way his fingers absently trace over my hip. The steady presence of his body keeping me anchored. It's comforting in a way I don't want to admit. He's feels like home.

I bite my lip, staring at the darkness of the room, trying to rationalize it. It's just exhaustion. That's all. It's not because his touch soothes something deep inside me. It's not because I feel safer wrapped in his arms than I have in years.

It's not because I'm starting to like him.

I squeeze my eyes shut, willing myself to sleep, but the battle inside me rages on. Because no matter how much I fight it—no matter how much I tell myself that I should hate him—I don't.

Chapter 15

Kalel

I wake before the sun rises, the faint glow of dawn barely seeping through the curtains. The room is quiet, the kind of silence that exists only in the earliest hours of the morning.

And then there's Sabrina.

Curled into my side, her breathing soft, steady, unaware of how beautiful she is, even when she's sleeping.

She sleeps like she doesn't have a care in the world, like she hasn't spent every waking moment fighting me. Her curls spill over the pillow, her lips slightly parted, her features relaxed in a way I rarely see when she's conscious.

I take it in, memorizing the sight before I have to leave.

She'd throw a fit if she knew I was staring. Would roll her eyes, call me a creep, maybe even throw a pillow at my head.

The thought makes me smile. God, she's got me in a way no one ever has.

She's been fighting me since day one, pushing back at every turn, and yet, here she is. In my bed. Wrapped around me like she belongs here.

I trace a knuckle down the curve of her cheek, barely grazing her skin. She stirs but doesn't wake, shifting slightly, pressing closer. My chest tightens. She'll never admit it—maybe she hasn't even realized

136

it yet—but she's letting her guard down and that's dangerous. For both of us.

Exhaling, I force myself to move, untangling from her warmth and slipping out of bed. She murmurs something incoherent but doesn't wake.

Probably for the best.

I get dressed quickly, pulling on a black button-down and rolling up the sleeves before heading downstairs. Angelo was already at the dining table, sipping coffee like he has nowhere to be. He kicks his feet up onto a chair, his gun lying casually on the table next to his eggs.

I give him a look. "You eat like that in your own house?"

"I eat like this in your house. That's all that matters," he says, with a grin.

I shake my head and sit across from him, pouring myself a cup of coffee. The steam rises between us, mixing with the scent of butter and toasted bread. Angelo eyes me over his mug, amusement flickering in his gaze. "You're up early. Don't tell me the princess kicked you out of bed."

I smirk. "No, but I wouldn't put it past her."

He laughs, shaking his head. "She's got fire. I like her."

I take a sip of coffee, my jaw tightening. "Don't get too attached."

Angelo raises a brow. "You saying that for my sake or yours?"

I don't answer.

Instead, I focus on my plate, cutting into the eggs with deliberate precision. Angelo watches me for a moment, then leans back, smirking. "So, you're really going, huh?"

"Wouldn't be leaving if I wasn't."

"Mm." He tilts his head, his expression shifting just slightly. "You sure this meeting with your father is just a meeting?" I lift my gaze to his, reading between the lines. Angelo has been with me long enough to know how my father operates. If he's calling me in, it's never just to talk. I exhale through my nose. "I'll handle it."

Angelo studies me, then shrugs. "Your funeral."

"Optimistic as always." I say.

"You know me." He grins. "Sunshine and rainbows."

I shake my head and push my plate away, done eating. Standing, I grab my jacket, sliding it on. "Keep an eye on her while I'm gone." I demand

"Already planned on it."

"Don't let her out of your sight." He gives me an exaggerated salute. "Aye, aye, Captain."

I roll my eyes, but the tension in my chest loosens just slightly.

"She asked for a phone," I add, already expecting his reaction. Angelo raises his brows. "You caved?"

I glance at the stairs before turning back to him. "She's getting restless." He smirks. "More like she's getting to you."

I don't dignify that with a response. Angelo just chuckles, shaking his head. "Man, I can't wait to see how this plays out."

I give him a warning look. "Watch yourself."

He raises his hands in surrender, still grinning. "Hey, I'm just saying. The great Kalel Marchetti, getting soft? It's history in the making." I scoff, turning toward the door. "If I come back and she's missing, so are you."

He snorts. "You wound me."

I don't linger. I step outside, the morning air sharp against my skin, and slide into the waiting car. As the driver pulls away, I lean back against the seat, exhaling slowly.

Two days.

I shouldn't be thinking about her already.

But I am. I always am.

* * *

138

The Marchetti estate is a relic of power—cold, pristine, and untouched by anything as trivial as warmth. It's a monument to legacy, built to outlast men like my father.

Staff serves dinner in the grand dining hall, where a chandelier glows above the long mahogany table. The food is perfect; the wine aged to some ridiculous number, but nothing about this place feels good.

Because he is here.

Enzo Marchetti.

My father.

He sits at the head of the table like a king waiting for his subjects to grovel. He wears a pressed suit, his hair precisely slicked back, but his cold, calculating eyes lock onto me as if I'm a puzzle he's already solved.

Gianni is across from me, swirling her wine like she'd rather be anywhere else. Smart girl. She knows how these dinners end.

Enzo takes his time, cutting into his steak, chewing, swallowing, before finally speaking.

"Kalel," he says smoothly. "I think it's time we discuss your future."

I don't react. Just lift my glass and take a slow sip. "Thought I already handled that."

He exhales like I'm a disappointment. "You've handled the family well enough. Expanded it. Strengthened it. But you've neglected something crucial." I set my glass down with a sharp clink. "Have I?"

Gianni stiffens.

Enzo dabs his mouth with a napkin, slow, methodical. "You need a wife."

There it is.

I don't blink. "And?" His lips curl slightly. "I've found one for you." Gianni sets her glass down a little too hard. I don't move. "She's from a wonderful family," he continues, ignoring the crackling tension. "Well-bred. Educated. She'll strengthen our legacy. And she'll be here tomorrow for dinner."

I stare at him. Then I lean back, my smirk lazy, lethal. "No."

Enzo raises an eyebrow. "No?"

"I'm not marrying her." A beat of silence. Then he chuckles, shaking his head like I'm a misbehaving child. "Kalel," he says, patronizing as fuck. "You're thirty-two years old. Do you plan to waste your best years chasing a fantasy?"

I say nothing.

"Marriage isn't about love," he continues. "It's about power. Stability. And you don't have a choice."

Wrong.

I lace my fingers together, tilting my head slightly. "I don't have a choice?" I ask.

Enzo leans forward, eyes gleaming. "No, you don't."

Gianni shifts, her discomfort palpable, but she stays quiet. Smart girl. I exhale through my nose. "You still think you get to decide?"

Enzo's smirk deepens. "You're my son."

I chuckle, low. "I am not your son. I' am your successor." I say, my voice dropping low. "And I have already taken your place."

His expression twitches, barely perceptible, but I see it.

"I built this empire," he says, voice cold. "You just inherited it."

"I conquered it." I say, letting the words sink in. "And you are sitting at my table, in a house that belongs to me, pretending that you still matter." The room goes still. Enzo's grip tightens on his knife, knuckles going white. His jaw clenches, but he forces out another mocking chuckle.

"And what about her?" he says, feigning curiosity. "Your little captive?"

Gianni's eyes snap to me. I go rigid. Enzo swirls his wine, watching me carefully. "What was her name again?" His lips curl. "Ah. Sabrina."

The sound of her name leaving his mouth makes my blood boil. "You will not talk about her," I say, my voice quiet but laced with warning. Enzo tilts his head, eyes glinting. "Touched a nerve, did I?"

I push my chair back slowly; the sound scraping against the marble floor. The room darkens with my presence, my rage a tangible force pressing against the air. Enzo doesn't move. But I see it—the flicker of caution in his gaze.

"I am the head of this family," I remind him, stepping toward him, slow, lethal. "Not you. Not anymore."

His smirk falters. "You still think with your dick, boy. That's your problem."

Gianni flinches. I don't. Instead, I grip the edge of the table, leaning in just enough for him to feel the full weight of my fury.

"Sabrina is mine," I say with a growl, each word sharp as a blade. "The only woman I will ever marry is her."

Enzo exhales through his nose, shaking his head in mock disappointment as he says, "A twenty-five year old captive, Kalel? Is that the best you can do?" My vision goes red. I lunge before I can think, grabbing him by the collar and slamming him against the chair. The wine glass tips over, the deep red liquid spilling across the white linen. Gianni gasps.

"Watch yourself," Enzo says as a warning, his voice low, his expression unwavering.

I tighten my grip. "You watch yourself," I snarl. "Because if you ever speak about her again, I will remind you exactly why I replaced you." A flicker of something crosses his face—not fear, but understanding. He knows me. Knows that I mean it.

I will hurt him and he knows he can't stop me.

Gianni shifts uncomfortably. "Kalel—"

"Stay out of this," I snap, not taking my eyes off him.

Enzo's jaw ticks. Then he lifts his hands in surrender, his mouth curling with reluctant amusement.

"So, this girl means something to you?" Enzo says, like he didn't already know the answer.

I release him, my breathing even but seething. "She's everything."

Enzo straightens his suit, exhaling like I'm an inconvenience. He picks up his napkin, dabs at his lip, then gestures at the spilled wine.

"Shame," he muses, voice dripping with mockery. "This was vintage."

I stare at him, my fingers twitching with the urge to do more than just warn him. He lifts his gaze, and for the first time, he looks old. Resembling a man whose reign is over. Then he sighs. "Fine," he mutters. "But if you think you can play house with a captive, be my guest. Just remember..."

He leans back in his chair. "Women like that don't survive men like us. You better hope she survives." He says, the words cut because they're true. Because she's in my world now. A world of blood and betrayal.

I don't respond. I just turn and walk out, my mind on one thing.

Sabrina.

I slam the door to my room hard enough to rattle the frame. The rage is still in my chest, coiled and tight. My hands ache from clenching my fists throughout dinner, from not snapping my father's neck when he dared say her name like it meant nothing. Like she meant nothing.

I pace once, twice. The room is colder than I remember—probably because I haven't stayed here since I took over. This house isn't home. It's a tomb and all I can think about is her.

Sabrina.

What she's doing. If she's pissed off. If she asked for more coffee or gave Angelo hell. If she's safe. She'd probably laugh if she knew how fast I pull my phone out. How fast I tap Angelo's name.

He answers on the second ring. "Did you kill him?" Angelo says jokingly.

I grunt. "No. Unfortunately." There's a pause. Then Angelo whistles low. "That bad, huh?"

"He brought up marriage. He said he had someone lined up for me." I say, running my hand over my face, sighing.

Angelo makes a sound like he's choking on something. "Oh yeah? Let me guess, she's got the personality of cardboard and the face of a well-pressed spreadsheet," he says, pretending he didn't know my father.

"I told him no." I confess.

"I know." Angelo says.

I stop pacing. "He mentioned Sabrina."

That sobers him. "What'd he say?"

"He called her a captive. Mocked the idea that I'd marry her." Silence. Then Angelo says, "Are you going to marry her?"

"I will." My voice is steel. "No one else touches her." Another pause. Then a dry laugh. "Well, I hope she likes expensive rings and expensive problems."

"She asked for a phone, like you said." He says.

"Did she get it?." I say. "Give me her number."

He doesn't even hesitate. I hear the rustle of a paper or screen. Then he rattles it off. I save it. Her name locked into my phone like a brand.

"She behave?" I ask, lowering myself onto the edge of the bed. Angelo's tone shifts—teasing, but knowing. "Define behave."

I smirk. "Angelo."

"Relax, man. She's been... surprisingly chill today. Didn't even insult me once after lunch."

That pulls a genuine chuckle out of me. "She's softening on you."

"Yeah, yeah. I'm adorable. What can I say?"

I pause, staring at the door, already feeling the pull in my chest. "I'm coming back early." I say. I know I said that she is mine, but it feels like every second that I am away from her, I am losing parts of myself.

"When?" Angelo asks.

"Tomorrow." I say my hear feeling heavy.

Angelo exhales like he expected it. "Couldn't stay away, huh?"

"I don't trust him," I say flatly.

"Your father?"

"Him. Or the world." I lean forward, resting my elbows on my knees, phone still pressed to my ear. "She's in my house, under my name. I'm not leaving her longer than I have to." Angelo hums low. "Got it. I'll keep her safe, Kalel. She's good."

I nod, even though he can't see me. "I'll call her tonight."

"She'll pretend to hate it." He said.

"I know." A small smile pulls at my lips. "But she'll answer." Because regardless of whether she's ready to admit it. She wants to hear my voice as badly as I need to hear hers. I hang up and stare down at the number glowing on my screen. Tomorrow morning can't come fast enough.

Chapter 16

<u>Sabrina</u>

I'm barely awake when he walks in, his sleeves rolled up. Watch glinting on his wrist, eyes already locked on me like he owns the morning and everything in it.

"Get dressed," Kalel says, calm but commanding. I blink, still tangled in his sheets. "Why?" I say questioning if this was another power play.

"We're going shopping." He says.

I sit up, sheets falling around my waist. "Shopping? For what?" I say, confused. He walks over, leans down, and kisses the top of my head like I'm something he wants to savor. "For tonight." He says. His voice dropping to a whisper. "We're going on a date."

A date? I never thought I'd hear him say that. Not the man who kidnapped me, stole my life out from under me, and somehow made me want to *stay.*

I arch a brow. "You don't strike me as the wine-and-dine type."

He smirks. "I'm not. But for you, I'll make an exception."

The heat in his gaze makes my heart skip a beat, but I cover it up with a shrug, pretending my hands aren't itching to reach for him. Without another word, he turns and disappears down the hall. Leaving me standing there with my stomach in knots.

A *date.*

God help me, part of me is giddy and the other part is terrified of what it means if I start wanting things I'm not allowed to have. Even after our talk last night.

I drag myself to the bathroom, flipping on the light.

The mirror catches me off guard

Eyes wide.

Mouth soft.

Hope blooming where there shouldn't be any.

ugh pathetic, I scold myself, but it's half-hearted at best.

The shower hisses to life, steam filling the air. As I strip off my clothes slowly, almost cautiously, like peeling away armor I didn't know I was still wearing. The water hits my skin, hot as I let it wash away my fears.

By the time I step out, the mirror is fogged over, my reflection a ghost of the girl I used to be. I towel off quickly, wrapping myself in soft fabric, running fingers through my damp hair, choosing a dress. Slipping on my heels, my stomach twists into knots. Why am I so nervous? It's not like this is the first time he's taken me shopping. Or the first time I've been alone with him.

Thirty minutes later, we're pulling up to yet another store that makes designer boutiques look like thrift shops. Security opens the doors like they know him. Like he's the VIP. Honestly? He probably is. I walk in beside him, pretending my heart isn't fluttering at the thought of a date. It echoed in my head all day, but I don't have long to focus on that now.

Once we're inside, the racks of clothing look more like art than fashion. Patterns. Silk. Sequins. Labels I can't pronounce.

I try on dress after dress. Gowns that wrap around my body like water. He waits outside the dressing room, lounging on a chaise like a roman god judging his muse. And then—I step out in a black slit dress that hugs my curves like sin.

And there I see it.

He's not alone.

She's tall. Pretty. One of those girls who looks like her perfume costs more than most people's rent. Her laugh rings out like she's trying to be heard, like she wants him to *look*. And Kalel? He's not paying her much attention—barely glances her way—but he hasn't shut it down either. She leans in closer, saying something flirty, but I can't hear her. Her hand brushes her hair off her shoulder, like she's giving him a full view. And something hot slices through me. Not fear. Not anger.

Jealousy.

I step out in the black dress like its armor. I know exactly how good I look. And I walk over there, hips swaying, head high. A storm in heels.

"Babe, what do you think about this one?" I say, sweetly. My eyes are only on Kalel as I come to stand between them. "Oh, who's she?" I ask

His gaze lifts to mine instantly. And it's *all heat.*

He better.

He smiles slowly, like he's been waiting for me to snap. "This is supposedly the beautiful lady my dad wants me to marry."

My stomach drops. "Oh, nice to meet you,—" I murmur, brushing invisible lint off his shoulder—the one *she* touched. "Anna, and you are" she asks. "I'm his girlfriend." I say deadpan.

Anna smirks at me "Oh so you're the famous captive."

I don't like her. I know I just met her, but she seems like a bitch. I flash her a smile, polite and disarming. "I didn't mean to interrupt you baby, I'll come back if it's important" I say as I turn to walk away, but Kalel grabs my wrist pulling me onto his lap. "It's not important," He says, wrapping his hands around me.

I swear I saw her face twitch. I know I'm not crazy.

"No, I was just telling him how happy I am that our father agreed to the marriage." She says.

"We're not getting married," Kalel says sternly, as if he was warning her. I smile uncontrollably. Then, with a casual flick of my wrist, I smooth his lapel flat and lean in, pressing a kiss to his jaw. "Looks like Kalel has spoken."

Kalel huffs a dark laugh, his hand sliding instinctively around my waist.

The girl clears her throat. "Well... I should get going."

"You should," I echo sweetly, turning to Kalel with a teasing pout. "We've got more dresses to try on. And you promised to zip the next one."

Kalel's thumb grazes my lower back. "If I help, I'll do more than zip it."

I glance over my shoulder and see the girl already walking off. Something tells me this isn't the end. I don't chase her with glares or words. I just let her leave.

I know I won, but it doesn't feel that way.

Kalel leans close, mouth brushing my ear. "You were jealous."

"I was *watchful*," I correct, spinning on my heel and heading back toward the dressing room. "And now I'm wearing the winning dress. Try not to drool, Daddy."

* * *

One I choose a dress for tonight, try on everything. Dresses. Shoes. Lingerie. I don't check a single price tag. I toss things in the assistant's arms like I'm casually redecorating a palace. Kalel watches patiently. Amused, but he doesn't tell me to stop.

And when we get to the register?

The total flashes.

$203,794.67

The woman behind the counter tries not to faint.

I look at Kalel with the pettiest smile I can summon. "Oops. Did I go overboard?"

He doesn't blink. Instead, he steps forward, slides his black card across the counter, and says, "Bag everything. Twice if she wants it."

Then—he turns to me, pulls something from his wallet, and presses it into my hand.

A card.

Black, sleek, and heavy. With my name embossed on the front.

I stare at it. "Kalel..." He steps in, so close I feel the warmth of his breath when he speaks. "There's no limit," he says quietly. "You're cute when you're jealous."

My jaw drops and without missing a beat, I say, "Then you better remember who you have at home, Daddy, or I'll bankrupt you and look good doing it."

From behind us, a voice cackles.

Angelo.

Leaning against the entrance like he's been there the whole time, watching the show unfold with popcorn and a front-row seat. He wipes a tear from his eye. "God, I love her. She's worse than you."

Kalel smirks, tucking a strand of hair behind my ear.

"No," he says, eyes never leaving mine. "She is perfect." And I feel it—right then. The weight of his words. The danger in them. And the promise, too.

The car ride home was quiet. Well, not quiet—more like the calm before a fire-breathing storm. Angelo drove like he always did—focused, unbothered, pretending like the two rabid wolves in the back seat weren't seconds away from drawing blood.

And Kalel...

Kalel was being himself.

"You know," he drawls, one arm thrown lazily over the back of my

149

seat, "the way you looked at her talking to me—I thought you were gonna rip her head off."

I didn't respond, but my jaw tightened just enough for him to notice. He always noticed. The man observed like a sniper. He fed off reactions, especially mine. I stared out the window, trying to ignore the heat crawling up my neck.

"Jealousy looks good on you, Knight."

I snap my head toward him. "I wasn't jealous." His smirk was maddening. "You were." He said. I huffed, crossing my arms. "Even if I was jealous, who did she think she was? She's happy your dads agreed to the marriage. Is she insane?" I

Kalel leaned in, his eyes glinting with that dark, slow-burning possessiveness. "I'm with you."

God, he was right. I, Sabrina Knight, had been jealous. Of some nameless bimbo fluttering her lashes at the man who kidnapped me. What the actual hell is wrong with me?

Oh right. Everything.

Before I can finish mentally diagnosing myself with a full psychotic break, I feel it—his hand sliding up my thigh.

Slow. Warm. Dangerous.

I freeze, biting the inside of my cheek when his fingers dig into the soft skin just above my knee. "You got jealous of a woman talking to me," he says, his breath brushing hot against the shell of my ear. "I wonder what you would've done if I'd agreed to the marriage."

I turn my head sharply. "I'd have celebrated."

He blinks.

I smirk. "I wouldn't say anything. I'd be free," I shrug, dragging my eyes over his face, "and trying someone else out for size." His grip tightens—hard. Not enough to hurt, but enough to send my pulse racing. His expression changes, lips still curled, but his eyes turn lethal.

"No one touches you," he says, warning me. "Anyone who even tries to touch you the way I have... will die." I inhale, and it's a mistake. He smells like smoke and spice and power.

"And what if I want them to?" I ask sweetly, tilting my head. His eyes darken. A muscle ticks in his jaw. "You won't."

"And if I do?" I ask.

"I'll make you forget their name. While you're screaming mine." He says.

Ohhh, he did not like that. The tension snaps so taut between us I'm sure even Angelo feels it. I open my mouth to volley back—

"Home," Angelo interrupts smoothly, glancing at us through the rear-view mirror. "We're home."

Thank God for Angelo. The man deserves a damn sainthood. Kalel doesn't move. His hand is still on my thigh. His body still angled toward mine like a predator staking a claim. But his voice is lazy when he says, "Don't test me, kitten. I enjoy being cruel a little too much."

I roll my eyes, but my pulse is still racing. "We'll have to test that theory."

He leans in closer, voice like steel. "Test me if you want, but don't say I didn't warn you."

And the worst part?

I didn't have a comeback. Not because he was right, but because the way he was looking at me made my thighs clench and my brain fizzle.

God help me.

The second we step through the front doors, it's like the world resets.

"I need to handle something, Kitten. Let me know when you're ready." Kalel says, his warmth disappearing faster than I'm ready for. Without a word, he jerks his chin at Angelo, the silent order between them as clear as a shout.

Business.

It's always business.

I watch them walk off, their heads low, their voices too quiet for me to catch.

Whatever world they belong to when they disappear behind closed doors... is none of my business.

Not yet. Maybe never, and to be honest, I didn't want to know.

With a tight breath, I turn and head upstairs, pretending it doesn't sting more than it should. Pretending it's fine. Because that's what I do best, isn't it?

I toss my bags onto the bed, stripping out of my clothes like I'm shedding a second skin. The bathroom is still warm from the last shower, but it doesn't stop the cold from sinking into my bones. I crank the water hotter than necessary, stepping under the spray and letting it burn the doubt out of me.

Tonight is supposed to be normal, I remind myself.

Normal-ish.

As normal as anything can be when you're living in a mansion, run by criminals.

When I step out, I'm careful—choosing the soft black dress we picked out, smoothing it down my hips, fastening delicate jewelry around my neck like armor.

My hair's still damp when I leave the room, the nervous energy under my skin impossible to sit still with.

I pad barefoot down the hall, glancing around before slipping toward Kalel's office.

The door is cracked open just enough.

I should knock.

I should wait.

But his voice catches me.

And like the masochist I am, I freeze.

"I thought nothing of it," Kalel says, his voice low, edged with something I've never heard before—something that makes my blood turn to ice.

"When he said 'I hope she survives you'... I thought he was just being an asshole. Just... spitting poison like he always did."

A pause.

A breath.

Then Angelo's voice, quieter but no less heavy.

"You really believe that?"

The silence that follows is worse than any words. Suffocating me, it's like the entire house is holding its breath. Kalel curses under his breath, the sound sharp and guttural.

"I don't know anymore." He says.

I clamp a hand over my mouth, backing away as quietly as I can, heart hammering in my ears. I don't need to hear any more. I already know what's between the lines.

His Dad didn't just hate Kalel.

He *marked* me.

And Kalel didn't see it until now?

What the hell did I do? I was kidnapped. I take a deep breath, exhaling slowly, quietly, hoping that just for one night, I could simply enjoy myself.

I slip back down the hall, my pulse thundering in my ears. Every step feels heavier, harder to control, like if I let myself stop moving for even a second, I'll collapse right there on the floor.

When I reach the bedroom, I close the door softly, pressing my forehead against the cool wood. My reflection in the mirror catches my eye. Perfect makeup. Soft curls. Pretty dress.

You look fine, normal even.

So why does it feel like you're about to be ripped apart?

I shove the thoughts deep. Far enough that maybe I can pretend they don't exist for one night. Just one. I sit on the edge of the bed, tapping my fingers against my thigh, counting my breaths until thirty minutes slide by like an eternity. The door creaks open, and Kalel steps

153

in, dressed in a black button-down and dark slacks, looking like every sin I've ever wanted to commit.

He smiles when he sees me, unaware that the ground beneath us is starting to crack.

"You ready, princess?" he asks.

I force a smile, smoothing my hands down my dress to hide the way they're trembling.

"Yeah. Let's go."

And just like that, I slip my mask back on. Just like that, I pretend everything is okay. Even as the storm brews right beneath my skin, waiting for the moment, it finally breaks.

Chapter 17

The car ride to the restaurant started off normal. Well... as normal as it can be when you're sitting beside the man who kidnapped you, made you feel like a goddamn goddess, and now looks at you like you belong to him.

Kalel sits beside me in the back seat, legs spread, fingers drumming casually on his thigh like he's bored, but I know him by now. He's not bored. He's calculating.

Angelo's in the front, silent as usual, but I see the way his eyes flick to the rear-view mirror every few seconds, like he knows Kalel is up to something. "You're quiet," Kalel murmurs, glancing over at me. "You were giggling with Angelo earlier. What changed?" I glare at him. "I'm saving my energy for the poor waiter you're going to terrorize."

Kalel grins, slow and wicked. "You're adorable. You think you can protect him."

"Right," I say, rolling my eyes.

He smirks, and the way he shifts in his seat makes my stomach tighten. Then his hand slides over my thigh again, but this time there's no warning. "Kalel," I hiss, eyes darting to the front of the car. "Angelo is right there."

"Angelo's not looking," Kalel says with a shrug. "Are you, Angelo?"

155

"My god," Angelo mutters. "I'm driving."

"You see?" Kalel's palm moves higher. "He's focused." I swallow hard as his fingers stroke the inside of my thigh, then push the fabric of my dress up higher. "I hate you," I whisper, my cheeks flushed with anger. Feel every fiber of my body calling me a liar. Kalel chuckles darkly. "You say that, but let's see what your body says."

I gasp when his fingers slide over my panties. God, I want to scream. I want to slap him; to do something so that I can win this sick game we always seem to play. But I sit there, breathing hard, thighs spreading as he presses down, slowly and deliberately.

His mouth brushes my ear. "Your so wet already? You're practically begging me."

"Fuck you," I whisper.

"Oh, you will," he says. "But not yet."

He pulls his hand away. As if he didn't just turn my entire body into a live wire. And the bastard smirks like he won.

* * *

We get to the restaurant and it's as classy as I expected. Intimate lighting, beautifully set tables, heavy silverware. A place meant for elegant meals. Kalel takes my hand and leads me in like he owns the place. Which—I wouldn't be surprised if he does.

The hostess goes to seat us, and Kalel pulls out my chair for me. "Right here's perfect," she says, placing the menus down. Kalel doesn't respond. He pulls my chair out from under the table entirely, drags it beside his seat, and sets it there like that was always the plan.

"She's too far," he says smoothly. The hostess blinks. I roll my eyes. "You know I can walk a few feet on my own, right?"

Kalel sits and tugs me into the chair next to him, so close our thighs are touching. "You're staying where I can reach you."

"Why do I feel like that has nothing to do with safety?" I mutter, and he doesn't deny it. He just smiles and picks up his menu.

We flirt through the appetizers with sharp words, challenging stares, little smirks every time I pretend I don't like his hand on my lower back. Then the main course comes, and so does the real show. While the waiter is reciting the specials, Kalel slides his hand back under the table. At first, it's casual. Resting on my thigh again. Warm. Firm.

Then—deeper.

My eyes widen, and I grab my wine glass like it's the only thing anchoring me to reality. Kalel's fingers trail up under the slit of my dress, and before I can stop him, he moves my panties to the side.

"Don't," I whisper through clenched teeth, faking a polite smile for the poor waiter who has no idea I'm about to combust. Kalel says nothing. His fingers slide between my folds, and I almost choke on my own air. "So, would you like to hear the chef's recommendations?" the waiter asks.

Kill me.

"Sure," I croak. "Go ahead." Kalel slides one finger inside me. Then another.

I grip the edge of the table so hard my knuckles turn white, nodding along like I'm paying attention while my insides clench around him. His thumb brushes my clit, lazy and slow. I shift in my seat, holding my breath, trying to play it cool while heat builds inside me like a volcano I can't contain. And Kalel? He's calm, cool, and collected. Watching me lose it with a damn smirk on his face.

"You okay, ma'am?" the waiter asks.

"She's just a little... overwhelmed," Kalel answers smoothly.

His fingers curl just right, and I snap.

My orgasm crashes into me in hot, messy waves. My thighs trembling as I try to keep a straight face, blinking hard like the light's too bright. Kalel pulls his fingers out, lifts them to his lips, and sucks them clean—right there, while staring into my soul.

I almost moan. The waiter blinks. "Would you two like a moment to order?"

Kalel leans back and says, "She's ready now." And the rest of the meal is a blur. I try to act normal. I really do, but Kalel's hand never leaves my thigh, and my brain is fried from whatever the hell just happened. As dessert comes, he leans toward me, brushing his lips against my temple.

"Marry me."

I blink. "What?" He turns, eyes burning into me.

"Marry me."

I freeze. Words stall in my throat. Part of me wants to say yes. My heart screams for it, but I remember what I heard earlier. Hearing that his father hopes I survives this. The threat still lingers in the back of my mind. How could he think I would marry him? "I don't think we should," I say softly.

"How can I marry someone when their father might want to kill me? Let alone... Marry my kidnapper."

Kalel's jaw tightens—but not in anger. In restraint. Like he's fighting every urge to tear the world apart until I say yes, but all he says is, "I didn't know you heard that? I'll deal with him. Don't worry about that. You just focus on what you want." What makes me feel crazy is that I know he will handle it. I know how crazy he is and yet part of me wants to test it. To see how much he loves me. To say yes, but I know I shouldn't and that leads me here.

And the worst part? I still don't know how to answer that.

Chapter 18

Kalel

She didn't say yes, but she didn't say no either. And yet the fact that she didn't say yes still slices through me like a dull blade. "I need time," she says, looking everywhere but at me.

Time. She needs time.

As if I haven't already given her more than I've ever given anyone alive. As if I haven't torn apart my own fucking soul just to hold hers in my hands. She's not rejecting me. At least not yet, but why does it still feel like she is?

She's not ready to surrender either and that's what I need—her surrender. The kind of surrender that has nothing to do with chains or cages, and everything to do with want. I need her to want me. To need me.

She's close.

I can feel it in the way her body leans toward mine, even when her mouth tells me to back off. When her breath hitches under my touch, I can taste it. I can hear it in the silence after I asked her to marry me. The silence that sounds like she's fighting herself, not me.

"Alright," I say, voice low and controlled. "You want time? Fine. But I won't wait forever."

She opens her mouth like she wants to argue, but I've already turned away because if I don't, I'll pin her against the God damn restaurant wall and remind her exactly what she's hesitating to say yes to.

Dinner ends in silence. Not the cold kind. The kind that hums with everything unsaid. It takes everything in me not to remind her who she belongs to.

Fucking time. That word echoes in my head. Does she not realize that I could take that 'time' away from her? That I could make her marry me without her knowing? I drag myself out of my thoughts before I spiral.

I settle the bill without blinking. She doesn't thank me, but she doesn't need to. Her body's still tense beside me as I lead us out, brushing my hand along her lower back.

Outside, the air is cooler. Sharp. It cuts through the lingering heat between us, but not enough to extinguish it. I feel her—hesitating. Torn.. But I don't say anything. I don't need to. We're both wound too tight, and one more second of her silence might break me. I won't push her anymore tonight.

Then—

Pop.

It's faint at first, but the ache unfurls under my skin like smoke, slow, insidious, already familiar.

I know that sound.

I've *lived* that sound.

It isn't firecrackers. It isn't a car backfiring. It's death—disguised as thunder.

A gun shot.

Time doesn't slow. It breaks. Shards of it catch in my throat, where regret already lives. The glint of the scope flashes like a cruel joke across the street. A shadow leans out from behind the car.

But my eyes don't go there.

They go to her.

To Sabrina.

Frozen in place, her eyes wide. Lips parted like she's seconds away from speaking a truth she'll never get to finish.

She doesn't know.

She doesn't *see it*.

But I do. And somewhere deep inside me, something rips open. I can't let this happen again. The memory comes flooding back. The fracture in my chest. A scream I never let out. A name I haven't spoken in years.

There was another girl once.

Another shot, another body that dropped because I didn't move fast enough.

I move.

No breath. No hesitation. No goddamn room for fear. It won't happen again—not this time.

It was a choice I made once—and won't let myself make again. I reach her. My body slams into hers, shoving her back, and that's when it hits me—the impact. Like fire tearing through my side. Like someone opened me from the inside out. The pain doesn't matter. Neither does the blood. The only thing that matters is that she's okay. I collapse into her, barely registering the scream she lets out, or the way she catches me before I hit the ground.

"Kalel!" Sabrina Screams.

I want to say something. Want to tell her I'm fine. That this is nothing. That I'd do it again and again if it meant she'd still be breathing, but I'm bleeding too fast.

My body's going cold.

I hear another shot—louder this time. Final.

Angelo.

I feel relieved knowing that Angelo never misses. "Shooter's down," I hear him say, but it sounds like it's coming through water. I try to sit up, but my limbs don't want to move. She's pressing into my side, her hands slippery with blood, her face twisted in panic. That's my girl.

She's crying.

And fuck... she still looks beautiful even when she's breaking.

"Are you hurt?" I manage, barely getting the words out.

"No," she sobs. "You are. You fucking idiot—why would you do that?"

I want to laugh. I think I do. "Because you're mine," I whisper. "And no one will hurt you ever again."

She's shaking. "You could die, Kalel—."

"I'd die a hundred fucking times if it meant keeping you alive," I rasp. "You don't get it, kitten. I've already died once. The second I dragged you to my house and locked you away—that was the day I chose to live."

"Stop talking," she cries, pressing harder. "You're losing too much blood."

"Say yes," I whisper. "Just once. Even if you don't mean it."

She leans down, her forehead touching mine.

"If you die on me," she says through her tears, "I swear I'll say no to you on your grave." That makes me smile. Weak and real. I don't know if I'm going to die, but at least I got my answer.

"There she is..." And then everything goes black.

The world slips away—but I don't feel nothing.

"Kalel..." She says it's faint, but it slices through the dark like moonlight through smoke. I know that voice. I *shouldn't* know that voice. But I do.

"Amy?" I say in a whisper.

I blink or think I do—but there's no light. Just her. Standing in front of me like she never left. Dressed in the same combat boots and confidence I fell in love with. Her curls are pulled back, and her green eyes glow like forest fire.

She looks the same. Untouched by time. Beautiful. Too beautiful to be dead.

"You look like shit," she murmurs with a smirk, crouching in front of me. "Didn't think you'd bleed out over another girl." Amy says.

My throat tightens. "You're not real." I say

She shrugs. "Neither are you right now."

Her fingers brush over my jaw, and I lean into the touch before I can stop myself. God, I *missed* her touch. The way she held my face like I was something she wanted to remember. Like I was someone worth *holding.*

"I didn't mean to let you die," I whisper, voice cracking. "I didn't get there fast enough."

Her smile falters.

"I was alone after you." I say, a knot forming in my throat.

"I know," she whispers.

"I loved you," I choke. Pushing back tears. She brushes a curl from her cheek. "I know that too."

"You were the only one I ever let in. You were the only one I—" I stop myself. My chest aches like the pain is clawing from the inside out.

Her hand slides to my heart. "She's not me."

"I know." I say.

"But you love her too." It's not a question. And that's what guts me. Because I do. I love Sabrina with a desperation that makes my chest feel too small. I love her in a way that terrifies me.

"Does she reminds you of me?" Amy whispers.

"No," I say hoarsely. "She reminds me that I survived losing you."

Amy tilts her head. There's no jealousy in her eyes—only under-standing. "You let her in," she says, almost in awe. "Even after me."

"I didn't want to."

"But you did." I nod.

"She's the only reason I'm still breathing."

Amy's lips twitch. "Then go back to her."

"I don't know how."

And just like that—she's gone, leaving behind nothing but her voice in my veins and the unbearable ache of being pulled back to a life I'm not sure I deserve.

Chapter 19

Kalel

The world comes back slowly. Fuzzy.

Pain first—sharp, white-hot in my side. Then cold. Then warmth. A scent hits me next—sweet, familiar.

Her.

My eyes crack open. Dim lights. Beeping machines.

A hospital. I hate hospitals.

They're too white. Too clean. It made me remember visiting my mother in the hospital before she died. Hospitals are a jinx to me, but it doesn't matter because she's here. Curled up in a shitty hospital chair beside my bed, one leg tucked under her, arms crossed, lips parted in sleep. Her curls are a little messy. Her mascara smudged under her eyes. She looks exhausted, and she's still the most beautiful thing I've ever seen.

I shift, and the motion pulls a groan out of me. My ribs scream. My bandages tighten. Her eyes snap open. "Kalel?"

I force a smirk, even though it hurts. "Hey, kitten."

She's on her feet instantly, hovering over me, hands fluttering like she doesn't know where to touch. "Thank god you're awake. You're—you're okay?"

"Define 'okay,'" I rasp, voice raw. "Feels like I got run over by a truck."

165

"You got shot, dumbass," she snaps, but her voice cracks on the last word. I grin. "Worth it." She rolls her eyes, but they're glassy. "Don't you dare say that?"

"I'd take another one right now if it meant keeping you safe." Her lip trembles. "Don't say that either."

"I mean it." I say.

"I know you do," she whispers, sitting on the edge of the bed. "That's the problem."

There's silence for a beat. Then she sighs and says, "You scared the hell out of me, Kalel."

"You stayed." I say

She swallows. "Of course I stayed."

"No. You didn't run." I say as I reach for her hand and squeeze it. "You didn't leave." Her eyes drop to our joined hands. "Someone had to keep your crazy ass alive." My smile fades, and I study her—like really look at her. She's pale under the warm undertones of her skin, like she hasn't slept, hasn't eaten properly, hasn't stopped worrying long enough to even breathe.

"Have you been here the whole time?" I ask.

She shrugs. "Left once to shower and Angelo brought me clothes." My chest tightens. "You didn't have to."

She lifts her chin, feigning calm. "I know, but I wanted to." And just like that, I want to kiss her. Want to drag her into the bed and feel her heart against mine, beat for beat, like proof she's real and mine and not going anywhere.

Before I can speak again, the door creaks open. "Look who's awake," Angelo says as he walks in, holding a black hoodie and my phone. "Took your sweet time."

"You kill the guy?" I ask.

"One shot. He didn't even get a second breath."

"Good." I nod once. Angelo nods back, then jerks his head toward

166

Sabrina. "She didn't sleep, didn't eat, and threatened every nurse who tried to make her leave. You owe her."

Sabrina flips him off without looking at him. "Snitch." She says.

I chuckle.

* * *

Later that day, we went back to the estate and the second we're inside the house, Sabrina's in full-blown dictator mode.

"Couch. Now."

"I can walk—" I say

"I said couch, Kalel. Don't make me hit you." Angelo raises a brow as he drops the overnight bag by the door. "She's terrifying."

"She's perfect," I mutter, letting her guide me to the couch. She glares at me like I'm being difficult on purpose. I am, and she knows it. "You're the worst patient I've ever seen."

"You're the hottest nurse I've ever had."

"Shut up."

She fluffs a pillow and carefully helps me sit down. Her hands are gentle. Her lips are tight. I watch her flutter around the room—grabbing blankets, pain meds, water, snacks. She's muttering under her breath. "Idiots don't listen, get themselves shot, bleed out on my dress, and now I'm playing house with a war criminal." She says feigning annoyance.

"You're cute when you're domestic," I say lazily, eyes following her every move. "Makes me want to propose again."

"You're high on painkillers."

"And yet I still feel the same way about you." She tosses a blanket over my lap—maybe a little harder than necessary. "You need sleep." I reach out and catch her wrist before she can pull away. "Stay." I say and she stills and looking at me. "Kalel—"

"Please."

Her expression softens. She exhales and sits beside me, tucking her legs under her. I lay my head against her shoulder, eyes heavy. "Kitten?"

"Hm?"

"You're taking care of me." I say.

"Don't get used to it." But her hand lifts to my hair and starts stroking—smoothly, and in that moment, I know. Like really know she's mine. She already said yes already. Whether she meant it or not.

The house is dark. Everyone's gone. Even Angelo, who finally took a hint and left me alone with her.

Sabrina's beside me, curled up on the couch. She's got one hand tucked under her cheek, her head resting against my chest like I'm not a dangerous man. Like I'm hers. The painkillers are wearing off. My ribs are screaming and my side burns like fire every time I breathe too deep, but I don't care. She's here. That's what matters.

"You still awake?" I felt the ache from my wound as I murmur.

"Unfortunately," she mumbles. "Your heartbeat's too loud." I smile, lazily. "Want me to stop it?"

"Don't tempt me." Sabrina says.

There's a beat of silence. Then she shifts slightly, nuzzling closer, her fingers brushing absently across the bandage on my abdomen.

"I should be mad at you," she says softly. "But I'm... not."

"You will be. Eventually." I joke.

"Maybe, but thank you for protecting me. "

"Thank you for staying." I stare at the ceiling. I don't know why I do it, but I start to tell her something I've kept to myself for so long. Something I'm so tired to carrying alone. "I never cried. Not once. Not even when they buried her." My voice catches. "I just stood there. Stone-faced. While they lowered the only person who ever loved me into the ground. I swallow hard, and it tastes like dirt.

168

"Part of me never left that grave." I said.

A silence settles between us.

Thick. Bare. Not uncomfortable—just heavy with the weight of things no one's ever said out loud.

Then, softer—like I'm afraid saying it too loud will bring her back. I add, "I was alone after that. For a long time."

Sabrina stays still. Her fingers trace lazy, aching circles against my chest. And maybe that's why I keep talking. Maybe that's why the next name slips from me like a sin.

"There was a girl once."

Her body tensed. Just a flicker.

But I feel it.

"Her name was Amy."

It's the first time I've said her name out loud in years.

And it cracks something wide open inside me.

"She was chaos and comfort all at once. Couldn't sit still. Didn't care who I was supposed to be. She was light... but not in a soft way. She was fire. The kind that makes you believe you can burn and still live." I said as I stare at the ceiling, blinking against a memory that still bites.

"I thought maybe—maybe—she'd be the one to warm the cold in me."

I pause. Taking a breath, feeling the heartbreak all over, reopening a wound I thought had callused over years ago.

"She died." I say.

Two syllables. One collapse.

Sabrina's hand tightens, but she doesn't speak.

And I thank God for that.

Because if she did, I might shatter.

"She died," I repeat. "And something in me went with her."

I don't tell her about the blood. Or the sound. Or how I still wake up hearing it. That I still dream about her. I don't tell her that I begged whatever god was listening to take me instead.

I just breathe. And exist. And ache.

Sabrina leans forward, presses her forehead to mine, and whispers, "You're still here."

"Barely," I rasp.

But I hold her tighter, anyway.

Because *maybe this time*, I won't have to watch the light leave. She pulls back just enough to meet my gaze. "And yet you're the only man who's ever made me feel protected."

It kills be because I don't deserve that. I don't deserve her, but I'll take it. Then her lips brush mine. Soft and devastating. It shatters something in me that I didn't know was still whole. When she pulls away, I whisper the one truth I've never said out loud.

"I will burn the entire fucking world to keep you breathing." She doesn't waver. She kisses me again. And this time, I know—she hears me. All of me.

Chapter 20

<u>Kalel</u>

The stitches itch like hell. I sat in my study, with my shirt unbuttoned, the scar just under my ribs still a deep red slash against my skin. The bullet had missed anything vital—barely. Sabrina had stayed the whole first night in the hospital. Then screamed at me for taking the hit once. Like I wouldn't take ten more if it meant she never had to feel that fear again.

The door creaked open, and Angelo stepped inside, jaw tight, eyes darker than usual. He only looked like that when he brought death with him.

"Talk," I said, before he could open his mouth. He shut the door behind him. Locking it. He walked to the desk and dropped a black leather folder in front of me.

I didn't touch it.

I waited.

He stared at me with a dead look in his eyes. "It wasn't a rival crew. It was an inside job."

It should surprise me, but I already knew. My fingers flexed. My vision tunneled. "Say it," I said, demanding he continue. Angelo's hesitation didn't comfort me.

"Go on."

"Enzo, put the hit out on Sabrina." Angelo confirms.

My blood turned ice cold. "He's been contacting some of the old guards. Men who were loyal to him before you took over. Whispering promises. Calling favors." He stood and slid a photo across the desk—surveillance stills. One of my soldiers. Someone I fed, trained, gave a life to—talking to a man I hadn't seen in years.

One of my father's enforcers. I stared at the photo. Angelo added, "They received payment in crypto."

"Enzo didn't use his name. But he didn't need to. He gave your men orders. The ones that are still too scared to let go of the past." A slow, familiar heat crept into my chest.

The kind that used to rule me. The heat that made me dangerous.

"I took a bullet," I said softly, "Because my father wanted my woman dead."

Angelo nodded. "He thought she made you soft. Knew she gave you something to lose. So he tried to take it."

My hand curled into a fist. I wasn't surprised, but I had hoped he wouldn't go that far, and he did. He tried to take the only thing in this world that made me feel human again. I stood, rolling my shoulders, the scar pulling tight. My suit jacket slid over my shoulders like armor. My voice came out calm. Colder than anything I'd used in years. "Get me the names of everyone who spoke to him."

"They're in the folder."

"I want them dragged in—alive. Family too. If they knew and said nothing, they're done."

"And your father?" Angelo asked.

I looked up slowly, eyes locking with Angelo's. "I'm going to remind him who the real fucking Marchetti is." He didn't flinch. Just gave a single nod, like he already knew a storm was coming—and I was the eye.

I didn't say another word. I didn't need to because some promises aren't spoken. They're carved into bone.

* * *

Later that night, I sat on the edge of the bed, watching Sabrina sleep. Her breath was even. Safe. Unaware. She didn't know what kind of blood I was about to spill for her. Didn't know what I was capable of—still, but Enzo did.

He raised me in fire, and now I was bringing the whole kingdom down on his fucking head. Enzo should've aimed for me. He should've made sure I died on that floor and didn't get up, because now? Now no one could save him from me. I am done playing nice.

I show up at the undisclosed warehouse. Two chairs, two traitors, and me. They were both bleeding. Tied to the iron chairs. Hands zip-tied behind their backs. Faces busted open. One of them—Marco was already missing two teeth. The other—Daniel had piss-stained jeans and a split lip that made him whistle every time he breathed. Angelo stood in the corner, arms crossed, silent and unreadable.

I paced slowly between the two men, blood-slick gloves creaking as I flexed my hands. My Glock was holstered at my side. I didn't need it yet. I wanted to talk first. "Marco," I said calmly. "I held your son when he was born. Remember that?" He said nothing. So I crouched down in front of him, face inches from his.

"You drank my whiskey. Ate at my table. Swore your loyalty to my name." His mouth twisted. "It wasn't supposed to be her." now he's lying. I laughed low.

"Who the fuck was it supposed to be, then? Angelo? Me? You don't get to pick whose life gets taken when you sell me out to the man I replaced." His eyes flinched. "Enzo never lost his grip on you," I muttered. "You were always his dog, weren't you?"

He said nothing. "Fine," I said, turning to Luca. "And you?"

"I didn't know what the job was," he croaked. "I just passed the message. It seemed like a bluff to me."

"Your mistake," I said, walking to the table and pulling out a small black case.

Inside were shears, a knife, and a blowtorch.

Marco's breathing stuttered.

I picked up the shears.

"Let's talk about loyalty," I said, grabbing Daniel by the chin. "Did your father teach you any? Or was he too busy kissing Enzo's ring too?" Daniel struggled against the restraints. "Please—Kalel—"

"Shhhh. Don't beg yet." I said as I snip the shears, cutting off one of his fingers with one sharp squeeze. His scream echoed in the concrete room. "You pass my father's order through my crew," I said, "and you think I'm going to let you breathe afterward?"

"I was scared," he sobbed. "I was scared, man—"

"You feared the wrong person," I said coldly. Then I turned back to Marco. "Hey, man, does your sister still live on 39th?" I asked quietly. His head shot up. "Don't."

"I remember her. She used to bring you coffee when you were on lookout. Sweet girl."

"She doesn't know anything."

I smiled.

"That didn't save Sabrina, did it?" He paled. I knelt in front of him again. "You betrayed me and worst of all...You almost got my wife killed."

He broke. "I'm sorry—please—please, Kalel, don't, please. I'll disappear. I'll leave the city. You'll never hear from me again—just let me live p-please." I pulled my gun from the holster. Why would I let them live when they tried to take everything from me? Huh? I tap the gun to my head, trying to stop myself from the brink of insanity.

I point the gun at him, and he froze. I looked him dead in the eye.

"You are no longer needed."

BANG.

Blood splattered the floor. His body jerked once, then slumped forward, dead weight in a steel chair. Daniel yelled "Fuck man!". I turned to him, calm as ever.

He pissed himself again. I didn't even blink. "You begging for your life?" I ask.

"Kalel—*please—* I didn't know what he wanted,"

"You still delivered the message." I pressed the muzzle to his forehead. "You chose your side."

BANG.

Silence. I stand there, chest rising and falling, blood dripping to the floor, and felt nothing. Not guilt, not rage, not even fucking regret. Just clarity. Angelo stepped forward. "You want me to clean it up?"

"No," I said, turning for the door. "Leave them here." I smiled faintly.

* * *

Next, we head to Enzo's estate. My childhood hell. I didn't knock. I kicked the doors open so hard they slammed into the marble walls and cracked the trim. Two guards moved.

They stepped aside—eyes lowered, hands shaking, because they felt it. What was walking through these halls was not a man. It was vengeance uncaged.

Enzo sat in his study. Same smug posture. Same glass of aged brandy in his hand. I would murder the world for the woman he put a bounty on. Even if that person was my Father. When he saw me, he didn't seem to care. He just tilted his head and said—

"She survived, then." The floor under my feet stopped existing.

"She," I echoed, stepping into the room, my voice quiet, masking the anger inside. "Not Sabrina. Not your son's soon to be wife. Just... she." I said.

He took a sip, calm as the devil himself. "She made you soft. You used to be efficient. Precise. You bled for her like a dog—"

Something inside me cracked the same way it did when I was a child. I moved before he finished the sentence. I lunged across the desk, dragging him over it by the throat. We crashed into the floor, and I heard something in his ribs snap. He grunted, swinging at me, and I let him.

One hit. Just one.

Then I slammed his face into the floor so hard the tile cracked.

"YOU PUT A HIT ON MY WIFE!" I roared, pounding my fist into his face. Again and again and again. Blood sprayed my knuckles. His nose shattered under my fist. "You sent men to KILL her—I was bleeding out on the ground like a fucking dog—because you couldn't control me anymore."

"She was a weakness," he hissed through broken teeth. "She turned you into a liability."

"She turned me into a man," I growled, dragging him to his feet and slamming him into the bookshelf. "You built me in your image and then you couldn't handle it when I became something better." He spit blood. Who did he think he was? Did he think he could father me now when he did nothing but hate me when I was growing up?

"You're nothing but an obsessive little boy with a gun," Enzo hisses.

My hands wrapped around his throat, and I squeezed. "I'm a man with something to lose," I said. "And you just tried to take her from me."

Suddenly, the door burst open. "Kalel!" Gianni's voice sliced through the fog. She froze at the sight—me with my hand around our father's throat, blood dripping down my arms, Enzo's face barely recognizable.

"What are you doing?!"

She ran forward, panic twisting her face. Angelo caught her just in time, dragging her back.

"NO—let me go—Kalel, STOP!" I didn't stop, not when he tried to take the only good thing in my life away from me. I slammed Enzo into the wall. Hard. The plaster cracked behind him. His eyes were bloodshot. Face broken. Lip split. I pressed the gun to his forehead.

"Why?" I whispered. His smile was hideous. "Because I knew she'd be your end." I stared at him and everything came flooding back. I remembered everything. The backhands, the punches, the manipulation. The day my mother died, and he didn't shed a single tear. The way he looked at me when I cried for her. Everything.

He looked at me like I was pathetic.

Like I was weak. I pulled the hammer back. "Kalel don't!" Gianni screamed behind me. "Please! Don't do this!"

"You don't understand," I said softly, never taking my eyes off him. "He didn't just try to kill her. He tried to rip the last piece of me that wasn't in his control out." I leaned close, so only Enzo could hear the last words. "I gave you a chance."

BANG.

The gun went off like thunder. The bullet tore through the back of his head and sprayed the wall with blood and bone. He dropped like dead weight—no glory, no ceremony. Just a hollow thud. Gianni screamed "Nooo–".

Angelo let her go, and she crumpled to the floor, sobbing over the corpse of the man who made us both. I stood there, gun still raised, my hands steady. I felt nothing. No relief. No remorse.

My priority was Sabrina's well-being; I'd destroy everything to ensure her safety. Gianni was still on the floor, sobbing, curled over the body of the man who raised her and destroyed me. Blood pooled beneath Enzo's head. His face was half gone. The shot was clean and final.

Gianni looked up slowly, her face blotched with tears and horror and something else I hadn't seen in her eyes in years—Fear. "You killed him," she whispered, voice cracked and raw. "He was our father—"

"He was a fucking threat," I said sharply.

Her lips trembled. "He was still our father."

"No," I said, voice cold, and lethal. "He stopped being my father the second our mother died and the second he tried to take Sabrina from me." She shook her head, her hands trembling where they pressed to the blood-slick floor. "You could've exiled him. Cut him off. You didn't have to—Kalel, you didn't have to—" She says panicking.

"I did," I said. "It was for the best."

Gianni stood slowly, rage blooming across her face. "Don't you dare tell me what's best. Don't stand there soaked in his blood and pretend this was mercy—"

"I'm not pretending anything," I said, taking a step toward her. "You want to be mad? Good. Be mad. Be furious. I'll give you a year." Her brows pulled tight. "A year?"

"A year to yourself," I whispered. "Rage. Run. Do whatever the fuck you need to do." Her chest heaved, anger and grief radiating from her like fire. "But when I call for you," I continued, voice like a blade, "you will come." I hissed.

Her eyes narrowed.

"Or I will send someone to get you."

Gianni's jaw dropped. Her voice shook. "I don't know who you are anymore." I stepped closer. Looking her dead in the eye. "I've always been the same person, Gianni." The silence between us turned suffocating.

"Take that as a warning if you have to."

Tears filled her eyes again, but I wasn't done. "You're still my little sister. That hasn't changed." I looked down at Enzo's body one last time. "I just did what none of you could do." Gianni covered her mouth. A sob broke out of her chest and she turned and ran—away from the blood, away from me, away from whatever line I'd finally crossed.

Angelo stood in the doorway, silent. I holster my weapon.

"Get the room cleaned," I said. "Burn everything that belongs to him." He stood, nodding once. "And Gianni?" Angelo asked.

"She'll come home when I call," I said coldly. "She knows better." Then I turned my back on what was left of my father and walk out the front door without looking back.

Chapter 21

Kalel

Once I got back to the estate, the front door creaked shut behind me. The house was still. I stood in the entryway, body stiff, every muscle taut from the violence I'd just unleashed. My hands, still covered in blood, gripped the door frame, steadying myself for a moment to take a breath. The shadows felt heavy tonight, but when I heard her soft breath from the bedroom, when I heard Sabrina—my Fiancee—sleeping peacefully, everything else faded. The rage. The blood. The body of the man who raised me only to betray me. I pushed those thoughts away because she was safe.

I'd made sure of that. No one was going to hurt her ever again. I didn't know how I knew that for sure. Maybe it was the violence that left me cold. Or maybe it was the way her presence calmed the fury that had driven me for so long. But for now, she was asleep. And so was the part of me that needed to own everything.

I moved through the dark house, toward the guest bathroom. The bloodstains on my hands were becoming real now, instead of just in my head. I turned the shower on, letting the water heat as I stripped off my clothes. the remnants of the past few hours still clinging to me, Enzo's blood staining my body.

I washed it all off.

Each stroke of soap, each scrub of skin, felt like I was cleansing myself—clearing the blood, the rage, everything that wasn't mine. I scrubbed harder, as if the anger would melt away with every inch of skin I cleaned. It was mechanical, a ritual, a way of erasing what had happened. But I knew it wouldn't. I wasn't naïve.

I stepped out of the shower and wrapped a towel around my waist, taking a long look at the bloodstained clothes on the floor. I had no need for any of this now. I packed everything into a bag, the blood-soaked shirts, pants, and jacket. No one needed to know. No one would. When I finally slipped into the bed beside Sabrina, I didn't feel relieved. I felt distant, like I was holding her close to ground myself, to remind myself of why I had done it all.

My fingers brushed her cheek, softly. She looked so peaceful in her sleep. Unaware of everything that had happened while she was lost in her dreams. "No one will get a chance to hurt you," I whispered to her, voice low and filled with that twisted tenderness only she could draw from me.

I leaned down and kissed her forehead, the warmth of her skin a contrast to the coldness that still lingered in my chest. She stirred, her face softening at the touch, but didn't wake up. I settled beside her, the smell of her skin grounding me, anchoring me back from the storm inside. I held her, pressing my lips to her hair, letting my body relax for the first time in hours.

It felt like I had just closed my eyes, but it was a few hours later, the sunlight sliced through the curtains, waking me before I was ready. Sabrina was still asleep beside me, tangled in the blankets, her body warm and soft. I watched her for a moment, the steady rise and fall of her chest, the peaceful expression on her face, and I felt the tightness in my chest loosen—just a little.

Then reality settled in and I had to get up. I had work to do. I pulled myself out of bed as quietly as I could, trying not to disturb her. The last thing I wanted was for her to know how far I'd gone, how much I'd sacrificed to keep her safe. But I couldn't stay in this bubble forever. I moved into the bathroom to brush my teeth, clean up a bit, and get dressed. By the time I stepped back into the bedroom, Sabrina had woken, stretching, a little smile on her lips as she turned toward me.

"Morning," she said sleepily.

"Morning, Kitten," I say back, my voice hoarse from a night that felt like a dream I couldn't shake. She sat up in bed, pushing her hair back and looking at me with that soft, loving gaze only she gave me. "You okay? You look... tired."

I nodded. "I'm fine. I just have to get back to work today. Things to take care of." She frowned slightly, but she didn't push. She knew when to give me space. Her hand reached out, brushing my arm gently.

"You sure? You've been through a lot lately."

"I'm fine," I assured her. "Nothing we can't handle. I'm just—" I paused, looking at her, smiling softly.

"I'm just glad you're safe."

Her eyes softened, and for a moment, I almost felt like the man I used to be—the man I thought I could be for her. But that man didn't exist anymore. The weight of everything I'd done still clung to me, but I couldn't let her see it. Not now. "I'll be back tonight," I said, reaching over and brushing her cheek with the back of my hand as she smiled up at me, trusting, unknowing, I walked away carrying the lie like a blade in my chest—because the man that came back tonight was not be the same man and would never be again.

Chapter 22

Sabrina

The morning was deceptively quiet.

The quiet that makes your skin prickle. Like the calm before a storm that already knows your name.

I walked into the kitchen barefoot, hair a mess, Kalel's hoodie swallowing my frame. I just wanted coffee. Maybe eggs. A few minutes where I wasn't being watched or touched or manipulated by Kalel. A moment that didn't feel like I had to keep on a mask.

"Morning, Kitten." My stomach dropped.

Kalel.

Great, I guess that wasn't happening.

He stood at the marble island like he owned the sun, flipping through something on his phone. Angelo leaned beside him, drinking espresso and smirking like he'd just heard the joke that I hadn't. I swallowed. This can't be good. "I didn't know this place came with an audience." I say.

Kalel glanced up, and the second his eyes landed on me, I felt it. That damn heat. The possessive weight. He put his phone down slowly, then nodded toward the fridge. "You're up early. Good. We have things to discuss."

"Like?" I ask.

He took a sip of his coffee and said it so casually I almost miss it.

"We're getting married."

Silence.

The air. My breath. The room. Everything stopped. I blinked. "I'm sorry. We're—what?"

"Start planning it," he said, voice smooth like sin. "I'll have the legal side handled. I want something tasteful. Intimate. Maybe Tuscany." I laughed. Because what the fuck? what else would you do when someone announces a wedding you didn't agree to?

"Kalel," I said, slowly, "I don't recall saying I'd marry you." He tilted his head, all mock innocence. "No?"

"No," I snapped. "You were bleeding out. I was crying. You told me to say I'd marry you even if I didn't mean it—remember that part?" He stared at me. Calm yet serious. Then set his cup down with a quiet clink and walked toward me. Each step was deliberate.

I backed until my back hit the counter. His hands rose. Not to touch me—but to trap me. Palms flat against the cabinet on either side of my head caging me in.

"and did you mean it?" he asked, voice lower now. My heart slammed against my chest so hard I heard it in my eyes. I hated that part of me fluttered. That part of me wanted him closer.

"Kalel," I breathe,

"Well?" he said again, dipping his head until his lips hovered above mine. "Did you mean it?"

I didn't answer, and that was enough. His mouth curled into a smirk. "You didn't say no." I narrowed my eyes. "That's not a yes."

"Doesn't matter," he said, voice sharp as glass. "It's not like you have much of a choice."

I pushed at his chest, but he didn't move.

"You're marrying me," he said, a slow, wicked grin spreading across his face. "Because I said so. Because you're mine. And I do what I want with my things." My stomach twisted—part fury, part something worse. Who the fuck does he think he is? I can't stand him when he acts this way.

"I am not an object, Kalel," I spat. "I'm a person. As hard as that may be for your power-hungry brain to comprehend. I am a person. And I do not want to marry you." His eyes darkened—but not with anger. With amusement. With something more terrifying. More possessive.

He leaned in, his voice like silk and smoke, his lips brushing the shell of my ear. "Then you'll be my mistress."

I froze.

"You'll live here," he whispered, breath warm against my neck. "You'll sleep in my bed. You'll take my dick, follow my orders, my devotion. You'll be mine in every way." My knees nearly buckled. His fingers tapped twice under my chin, lifting it like I was a pet. His smirk was smug and unholy.

"You will never be free from me." He pulled back, slow and confident, like he hadn't just set my entire nervous system on fire. Then he turned to leave.

"You can't make me marry you, Kalel!" I shouted after him, my voice cracking. He didn't even pause. He just looked over his shoulder, lips curling like the devil himself.

"I will, Mrs. Marchetti. Whether you like it or not."

Then he disappeared down the hall. And of course, Angelo followed right behind him—muttering, "Damn. I need popcorn for this." Am i the only sane one here? ugh. He thought he could own me? Tell me I'd marry him like it was just another line in one of his mafia contracts?

Oh.

No, no, no.

I was done playing the good little captive. The quiet storm. The girl who let him corner her and melt into his touch. He wanted to twist me into his wife?

Fine.

185

I'd twist him first. I was going to drive Kalel Marchetti absolutely insane. I waited until the evening—until the sun dipped behind the estate, casting long shadows and turning the house to gold. I slipped into the dress he bought me. Blood red. Slit to the thigh. Backless.

It clung to my body like it knew exactly what I was doing. And I let it.

I put on some lipstick, tousled my curls, and sprayed on a perfume that I knew made his pupils dilate. Then I found him exactly where I knew he'd be—his study. Back turned, sleeves rolled and jaw tight as he read something on his desk.

I knocked once. He didn't turn. "Kalel"

His head lifted slightly. "Mm?"

"I've been thinking," I purred, stepping closer. "If I'm going to be your mistress..." That got his attention.

He turned slowly, gaze dragging down my body, eyes dark and already burning.

"...then I should probably start acting like it."

He stood. Towering over me, but I didn't back down. I reached up, traced my finger down his chest, slowly. His breath hitched—but only for a second. He saw through me. Knew what I was doing.

"Is that what this is?" he asked, voice thick with warning. "Are you trying to play me?"

I smirked. "No, Kalel. I'm just asking questions."

He stepped closer. "Ask the wrong one, and I might forget how gentle I've been."

I didn't back down.

Didn't blink.

Instead, I leaned in, tiptoeing, lips brushing his jaw. "Tell me something," I whispered.

"If I'm your mistress... does that mean you get to sleep with whoever you want?" His body stilled.

Tensed.

Checkmate.

"And more importantly..." I smiled, sweet as sin. "Can I?" I ask. He stared at me. Not moving. Not breathing. So I pushed harder.

"Could I try someone else out?" I asked innocently, dragging my nail along the line of his chest. "See if someone else can make me submit? Maybe someone who doesn't have to threaten me to get what they want."

It was a shot.

A low, calculated, devastating blow.

And it landed.

His jaw clenched so tight I swore I heard the crack. The desk behind him rattled as one hand slammed down, keeping him from losing it completely.

Then his eyes lifted—and I knew I'd crossed a line I couldn't uncross. His voice was a whisper.

Deadly. "Try it."

I blinked. His hand shot up, grabbed the back of my neck—not roughly, but firmly. Commanding.

"I fucking dare you," he growled, nose brushing mine. "Let another man touch you. Let him try to make you submit."

"Kalel," I whisper.

"I'll break his fingers," he snarled, his grip tightening just enough to make my breath hitch. "One by one. I'll make him wish he never laid eyes on you—and then I'll kill him slow."

My heart thundered, but I didn't look away. I *couldn't*. I wanted to poke the bear? The bear was awake—and it was hungry.

Kalel's eyes dragged over me like a brand. "No man touches what's mine." His voice dropped lower, richer. Lethal. "No man sees you spread open, soaking wet, moaning the way you do for me."

I swallowed hard. My thighs pressed together, the ache between them unbearable.

And he saw it. Of course he saw it.

His mouth curled into a smirk. "Yeah," he rasped. "That's what I thought."

* * *

Kalel

She really thought she could challenge me.

Throw my threats back at me like it didn't own her. Teasing me. Talking about another man making her submit?

No.

No one gets that privilege, but me. She blinked at me, lips still parted from the breath she lost—and I saw it. That flicker of fear. Of lust. Of something primal that she didn't want to admit.

I grabbed her jaw, forced her to look up at me. "You wanted a reaction, baby? You just fucking earned it." I grin.

"On your knees." I demand.

Her lip twitches. Almost defiant. Almost. I wrapped my hand around her curls and shoved her to her knees.

Good fucking girl. I unbuckle my belt with my other hand slowly, watching the way her eyes track my every move. She wants to hate this—wants to—but her lips part, and that bratty little mask slips just enough to show the truth beneath it. " You remember the safe word?" I say praying she never uses it and she nods.

Good.

"Open that mouth like a good girl." She hesitated—so I slapped her cheek with my dick.

"Now." She obeyed, lips trembling as I pulled my cock free, already hard, already leaking from just looking at her. "You wanna play games, kitten? Earn the right to breathe again."

I didn't ease in. No, no, no. I shoved my cock into her mouth, groaning as the warmth of her throat wrapped around me. She gagged, hands clutching my thighs, but I didn't slow.

I fucked her mouth, forcing her to take every inch, spit pooling down her chin, her eyes watering so beautifully I could've come right fucking then and there. "This is all you're good for, isn't it?" I growled, thrusting deeper. "Your smart mouth wrapped around my dick, taking it like a little fucking whore."

She moaned around me. "Yeah. You like being used." I say as I yank her off by the hair, drool dripping down her neck. She gasped, breathless.

Then I spit in her mouth.

"Swallow."

She did.

That's my good fucking slut. I dragged her up and bent her over the desk, yanking her dress up and tearing her thong clean off. She gasped, already soaked. "Oh, you're dripping for me?" I sneered, rubbing my dick between her folds. "You need this dick, huh? You need to be wrecked?"

I slammed into her, brutally, bottoming out in one savage thrust. She screamed. Her hands clawed at the desk as I fucked her mercilessly, hips pushing into her so hard the wood creaked beneath us.

"You feel that?" I hissed. "That's what happens when you try to provoke me." I say, slapping her ass. Every slap echoed through the study. Her ass bounced perfectly. I brought my hand down—hard—again and again, each hit making her cry out, moan, and beg.

"Who's are you?" I ask.

"F-fuck, Yours" Sabrina moans.

"Louder." I command

"Y—Yours!"

I wrapped my hand around her throat and pulled her back against me, my mouth at her ear. "Come for me. Right fucking now." I say as I reach between her legs, rubbing her clit in tight, vicious circles, and she shattered, screaming my name, legs shaking, cunt clenching so tight it made me see stars.

"That's one," I growled, not even slowing. She whimpers, wrecked and shaking, and I just keep fucking her. "You're not done."

I flipped her onto her back, spread her legs wide, and kneel between them—licking up her release before diving in again. My tongue assaulted her clit while two fingers curled inside her. She sobbed, grabbing my hair, trying to escape the pressure.

I didn't let her. "Come again, baby," I said against her cunt. "Right now. I want you crying when I take your ass next." That broke her. She screamed through her second orgasm, thighs clamping around my head, tears streaming down her cheeks. I kiss my way up her trembling body and whispered in her ear,

"Now I'm going to take you like no one else ever will." I say as I slicked my fingers and worked her tight hole open, watching her face twist with pain and hunger.

"Please," she gasped. "Kalel—please—I want it. I want you."

"That's right," I growl, lining up. "You're mine. Every fucking hole."

I push in, her cries like music to my ears. She shook beneath me, overwhelmed and full, and I pause only long enough to praise her.

"You're taking it so good, baby. My brave little slut. You were made for this." Then I fuck her. No mercy. Just raw, primal thrusts that made her scream, moan, sob from overstimulation. "You love this," I snarl, spitting on her ass. "Being used. Being owned. Being wrecked by me."

"Yes—yes—Kalel, I; fuck—I'm gonna—"

"Do it."

And she coming for the third time, body convulsing around me as she cries out, completely gone. I followed with a guttural groan, slamming deep and coming hard, filling her until it leaked down her thighs. When I pull out, she collapsed, panting and broken and perfect. I grabbed her jaw, tilted her face to mine, kissing her softly—deep, filthy, possessive. "You're mine," I whispered. "You'll never belong to anyone else." And the way she looked at me?

She fucking knew it.

Chapter 23

Sabrina

The next morning I woke up sore. Not a little sore. Wrecked. My entire body ached like I'd been claimed by something primal and left marked from the inside out, because I had. The sheets were tangled around my legs, my thighs still sticky, my throat raw from all the things I let him do. Things I wanted him to do.

God, I hated that.

I blinked up at the ceiling, my mind foggy, my limbs limp. He wasn't in bed. Thank fuck. Maybe I could breathe. Think. Run. I sat up with a groan, pulling the sheets around me like a shield. I swung my legs over the edge of the bed—then froze. He was standing in the doorway.

Coffee in one hand. His phone in the other wearing nothing but black silk pajama pants that hung low on his hips, revealing the deep v of muscle I already hated myself for wanting to lick.

He smirked. "You're awake." My stomach twisted. "Don't look at me like that," I snapped, standing fast. "Last night—wasn't what you think it was." His smile didn't fade. Not even a little. "You're right," he said casually, stepping closer.

"It wasn't what you think it was."

I stepped back. so he steps closer again. I backed into the dresser and he trapped me there. Kalel set the coffee down beside me and slid his hand along the curve of my hip, fingers brushing the bruises he'd

192

left the night before. His mouth ghosted the shell of my ear.

"Last night wasn't just sex, Sabrina. It was surrender." I shoved his chest. He barely budged. "I didn't surrender shit," I growled. "You screamed my name and I spit in your mouth and came in your ass," he said, voice low, almost teasing. "You begged me to claim you. That wasn't just sex, baby. That was ownership."

I slapped him.

He caught my wrist—gently—and brought it to his mouth, kissing the inside like it was sacred. "I'm not going to fight with you this morning," he murmured. "You're sore. You're sensitive. And you're mine."

"I'm not—"

"You are," he interrupted, tilting my chin up. "You always have been. But now? Now you feel it." I tried to twist away. He didn't let me. Instead, he walked me back to the bed and sat me down like I weighed nothing. Then he knelt.

Knelt.

Between my legs. "I don't care if you're mad," he said, dragging his hands along my thighs. "I don't care if you lie to yourself." His mouth hovered over my core—already tender, already throbbing. "You'll still come on my tongue the second I touch you."

"Kalel—"

"You'll still cry my name like it's a prayer."

"I'm leaving—" I say.

"No, you're not." His fingers parted me. I gasped. Because even now—I was already wet. "You want to pull away," he whispered, kissing the inside of my thigh. "But you won't. You can't."

He licked a slow, devastating line up my pussy—and my spine bowed off the bed.

"You belong to me." he whispers.

"Kalel—don't—" He didn't listen. Of course he didn't. His mouth was already on me.

My back hit the bed as his tongue flicked over my clit with relentless precision, like he knew every nerve, every weakness, every way to unravel me. I fisted the sheets, thighs trembling as I tried to keep control—tried to fight the wave threatening to drag me under. "You're already close," he murmured, breath warm against my pussy. "You taste so fucking good."

His fingers slid inside me—deep—curling perfectly. His tongue circled, sucked, and devoured me. "Come on, baby. Give me what's mine."

"Fuck—no—Kalel—"

Smack.

He slapped the inside of my thigh. Hard my hips jumped. "You don't get to hold it," he growled. "You don't get to pretend you don't want this. Not after the way you screamed for me yesterday."

His mouth was back on me before I could breathe—tongue lashing over my clit, fingers pounding into me fast, hard, dirty. The sounds between my legs were obscene, slick, wet, and desperate.

I was falling apart right there in his bed. On his tongue. In his grip. "Let go," he ordered, voice low and commanding. "Fucking let go, Sabrina. Come for me. Now."

I screamed.

My orgasm exploded like shrapnel, tearing through every muscle, locking every joint, blanking my vision. My body convulsed, clenching hard around his fingers as he fucked me through it, milking every second like he owned my pleasure. Because he did. I gasped his name. Sobbed it.

Again.

And again.

He stayed between my legs, licking me softly, gently, until I flinched from overstimulation. Then he pulled back—slow, smug, glowing with that wicked, victorious satisfaction only he could wear so well. He kissed the inside of my thigh, his voice velvet and ruin. "That's my girl." And I couldn't say a thing. Because he was right. And I hated how much I loved it.

"Get dressed," he said, cool and collected, standing up like he didn't just ruin my morning. "Black dress. No panties." he demanded.

My mouth dropped. "Excuse me?"

He winked. "You want to play with power? Good. I'll show you what it feels like to wear it."

I should've known the black dress was a trap.

I climbed into the back of the car, arms crossed, refusing to look at him. Kalel slid in beside me, too smug, too calm.

Angelo was up front, pretending to check his phone, but I saw the smirk. "You look good," Kalel murmured, voice all gravel and heat. His hand found my thigh instantly. "You look delectable."

"Don't touch me." I say pretending to be annoyed, but of course he continues to touch me. His fingers slid up the inside of my thigh, brushing just under the hem of my dress. I bit the inside of my cheek as he grazed knuckles where panties should've been.

He leaned close to my ear. "Are you already wet?"

"Kalel—" His fingers dipped between my folds, slow and knowing. I slapped my hand over his, but he didn't stop.

"You're going to sit through this entire meeting," he whispered, "remembering exactly how I'm touching you right now."

"You're disgusting."

"And you're dripping." Kalel says.

I roll my eyes. Up front, Angelo cleared his throat. "Want me to turn the radio on?"

Kalel wasn't even phased. "She's quiet and either I'm still winning."

I nearly died.

The bakery was pristine, elegant, filled with pastel samples and

195

delicate floral designs. The wedding planner had already set up our private table. Kalel sat beside me, his hand firmly on my thigh like it lived there. The cake lady introduced herself. "Hi, I'm Callie! I'm so excited to go through these flavors with you two—oh, give me one second, I just got a call from my supplier—don't touch anything yet!"

She scurried away.

Kalel's eyes slid to mine.

I froze.

"Kalel, don't—"

"I told you not wearing panties would have consequences. No one's looking—" His fingers were already between my legs under the table. I gasped, slapping a hand over my mouth. "You told me not to wear any" I say, right before he dipped two fingers inside me, slowly, like we had all the time in the world. My back arched, knees pressing together to keep from falling apart right there on the fucking velvet chair.

"Keep your eyes on the cakes," he whispered, mouth brushing my jaw.

"whyyy," I whine, breath shaking. "Because you like it." Kalel say, rubbing his thumb found my clit. Moving in tight circles. My legs jerked.

"You want to come here?" he asked. "Right where they'll walk in? While you're tasting cakes for our wedding?" I couldn't speak because I like it. I know how sick that is, but there is something about his lack of care that's starting to attract me more than I'd like to admit.

I loved that he didn't show a sense of regard for anyone, but I also loved that I was the only one he allowed to challenge him. Even if it was only a little bit.

His fingers moved faster and I came in what felt like thirty seconds—biting down on my lip so hard I tasted blood. My thighs trembled. My breath caught and just as I finished, just as the world tilted—

Callie walked back in with her iPad. "Sorry about that! Now, where were we—vanilla bean or buttercream?" Kalel smiled like he hadn't just fingered me within an inch of my life. "We're leaning toward something rich."

I wanted to die.

Angelo, lounging in the table behind of us with a coffee, shooting me a wink. "Better pick something sweet," he said. "Sounds like you're already having dessert."

God, I hate him. I hated both of them. Yet, most of all I hated how wet I still was—for him.

* * *

I don't know why I thought I would be safe in the car because Kalel didn't let up. His hand stayed on my thigh the whole way back. Every now and then, he'd slide it up, stroke me just enough to make me squirm, then pull away.

By the time we pulled into the wedding dress store, I was shaking.

He leaned close again, voice low.

"You think I'm done with you?"

I didn't answer.

He smirked. "You're going to come in every room we plan this wedding in. In every dress fitting. Every flower appointment. Every menu tasting. Every night until you walk down that aisle— until you are legally mine."

I couldn't breathe and I couldn't wait. As I get to the car I slam the door harder than necessary. and Kalel slides in beside me from the other side like he hadn't just made me orgasm with his fingers under a tablecloth while the cake lady stepped out to take a phone call.

He adjusted his cuffs. Calm. Clean. Unbothered.

I some part of me still wanted to hate him, and I did. Or I wanted to.

"You're quiet," he murmured, his thigh brushing against mine in the backseat. "What, cake not sweet enough for you?"

I shot him a glare. "You're not funny." He grinned like I'd just called him delicious. "It's adorable when you try to be mad after coming all over my fingers."

"Kalel—"

"You clenched so hard. I thought you were gonna break."

My thighs clenched again—damn him. I scooted an inch away, but he followed. "I'm not talking to you."

"Baby, you moaned into my palm like you were praying. I think we're past the no-talking phase."

Up front, Angelo snorted and I nearly choked.

"You're enjoying this?" I snapped. Angelo didn't even try to hide it. "I'm living for it. You're the first woman who's ever given him hell—and he's never looked happier." Kalel smirked. "She's the only one I'll ever marry. It's supposed to hurt."

"I didn't agree to marry you." I say.

His voice dropped instantly. "You will."

I opened my mouth—he leaned in, his hand sliding onto my bare thigh again like it was nothing. "I'll take you in every room, every car, every corner of this city until you forget how to say no," he whispered. "You'll moan it instead. You'll beg for it."

"You're delusional." I said.

He smiled, cocky and dark. "Then why are you still wet?"

My breath hitched. And I hated that he was right. I crossed my legs, glaring out the window as the streets blurred by. He leaned back like he hadn't just mind fucked me with one sentence.

I felt his hand rise again. Higher this time. My breath caught as his fingers dragged across the crease between my thighs, lightly.

"You want me to stop?" he asked. I clenched my jaw. He leaned down, brushing his lips against my ear. "Then say it."

I didn't. My fingers dug into the leather seat as I bit back a gasp.

"See?" he whispered. "You can run your mouth, roll your eyes, but this—" his fingers pressed just enough to make me whimper, "—this always tells the truth."

The car slowed.

"Dress fitting's next," Angelo said too cheerfully, pulling into the private showroom lot. "Try not to traumatize the seamstress." Angelo Joked, but knowing Kalel—we would.

Kalel kissed my cheek with mock sweetness. "Oh, we'll behave." Kalel said as he pulled the door open and stepped out first like the devil in a tailored suit. I stayed frozen for a moment. Still flushed and confused. Still mind fucked from the ride. God help me if he follows me into the dressing room.

Spoiler: If he did, I'd let him.

Chapter 24

Sabrina

The boutique looked more like a cathedral than a store.

It sat tucked behind iron gates in a secluded part of the city—no flashy signs, no storefront windows. Just a single black awning with delicate gold embroidery: Maison Aurelia. Understated yet elegant.

Exactly like him.

A woman in all black met us at the entrance, eyes sweeping over Kalel like she already knew who he was—and who I must be. She opened the door without a word.

The scent hit me first. Roses. Peonies. Fresh-cut silk. The air inside was cool and still, like nothing here moved unless you paid enough to make it dance. The floors were glossy white marble, veined with gold. The walls were a soft, smoky gray, lined with framed sketches of gowns that probably cost more than my college education. To the left, a glass display of custom accessories—veils, tiaras, gloves, shoes so delicate they looked breakable. To the right, a lounge area with velvet chairs in deep emerald and ivory, where champagne waited in crystal flutes on a silver tray.

Everything whispered wealth, power, and submission.

We walked deeper into the space, past mannequins dressed in handcrafted bridal gowns hand-beaded corsets, illusion lace backs, skirts made of a hundred layers of tulle and silk. Each one more extravagant than the last. And at the far end of the boutique—my dressing suite.

Private. Gated off with dark velvet curtains and a gold nameplate that read Bride Reserved in calligraphy.

My stomach twisted.

Bride. I wasn't a bride. I wasn't his bride. And yet, when I stepped inside the suite, I didn't turn back.

The room was softly lit, with mirrors on three sides that reached from floor to ceiling. The center had a raised white platform—where brides were meant to stand and be admired. A small vintage chaise sat off to the side with a stack of white gift boxes and a set of ivory pumps laid out neatly.

It was beautiful and intimate.

Just like the man who'd follow me in seconds later. I should've known he'd follow me in. The second the seamstress excused herself to grab another size, I was left alone in a private dressing suite with mirrors, velvet curtains, and three different gowns I'd barely touched.

I exhaled hard, smoothing the fabric of the corset bodice down my front.

Just breathe.

The slit in the dress was high—too high. The back was open. And I'd already told them I wasn't wearing any damn underwear because Kalel wanted everything to be "authentic." God, I hate him. Which didn't explain why my body clenched the second I heard the door open behind me.

I turned and there he was.

Kalel.

Leaning against the door, watching me like he'd just caught his prey walking into a trap.

"Get out," I said, voice low.

He didn't.

He didn't say a word.

Just stepped inside, locked the door behind him with a quiet click, and turned to face me.

"You look beautiful," he said, slow and quiet, "wrapped in white." I backed up. "This is a wedding fitting. Not an invitation." I said looking at myself in the mirror as he stalked forward.

"You think I can watch you put on dresses like this," he murmured, as I turned to look at him. "and pretend that I am not seeing the most beautiful woman alive today?" His hands grabbed my hips, turning me to face the mirror. I gasped, gripping the wall for balance. Kalel stood behind me, eyes locked on mine through the reflection. His hands ran down my sides, dragging the fabric up inch by inch.

"We're getting married." he said, voice gravel and lust. "Then let's start it off right."

"Kalel—" I warned.

His hand slid between my thighs from behind, finding me wet. Already ready for him. "I haven't even touched you," he growled, voice husky. "And you're soaking."

"You don't get to just—" He bent me over the seamstress's chair in front of me, lifting the dress just enough. "If you want me to stop all you have to do is say it." Kalel says, waiting for my response. I know I should object but for some reason I am starting to lose the battle inside me. I want him. I want Kalel.

He unzipped his pants and the sound alone made my thighs tremble. When he thrust into me—slow and deep—I nearly moan his name. His hand slammed over my mouth instantly. "Quiet," he whispered, hips snapping forward again slow and deep. Teasing. "You want the seamstress to hear how much you like being taken like this?"

My nails clawed at the fabric of the chair as he fucked me pushing in slowly making me want to beg for more. He has one hand around my mouth, the other gripping my hip so tight I knew there would be bruises. Our reflection showed everything—his eyes, full of fire. My body, undone. The way he owned me. the way he's making my body want to melt on to him, God. His strokes feel so good I start to whine while I moan. tears forming in me eyes. Making me so wet its going down my thighs.

"You think any other man could have this?" he hissed into my ear. "Touch you like this? Break you open and still put you back together like I do?"

I whimpered, nearly gone. "You're mine," he growled, fucking me harder. "Say it."

"No." I whimper in pleasure.

He pulled out just enough to make me gasp and I want to beg him not to stop. Then slides into me again just enough to tease me, slowly hitting deep before pulling out again.

"Say" thrust "it." thrust and I broke my orgasm slamming into me hard. "I'm yours," I moan as his head dropped to my shoulder. He came with a groan, hand still clamped over my mouth, body shuddering against mine. And just as I started to come down— I hear a knock at the door. "Miss Knight?" the seamstress called sweetly. "Do you need help getting out of that one?"

Kalel smirked, pulling back, tucking himself away.

"I think she needs help," he called, deadpan. "But not from you." I wanted to die. I wanted to melt into the floor and disappear, but Kalel leaned down, brushing a kiss behind my ear.

"You look beautiful," he whispered. "And you're going to make a stunning fucking bride."And the room was quiet again. Kalel had finally left, his parting smirk still burning into the back of my mind like fingerprints on skin.

The moment he was gone, the silence pressed in like a weight I didn't realize I'd been holding off.

I stood alone on the raised platform, surrounded by mirrors that offered no mercy.

The seamstress returned and helped me into the final dress of the day—a gown made of liquid silk, soft and clingy in all the right places. Strapless. A subtle corset beneath the fabric that pulled in my waist. The skirt flowed around my legs like water, pooling at my feet with a small, elegant train. No beads. No lace.

Just smooth, dangerous simplicity.

The kind of gown you'd wear if you knew exactly how beautiful you were—and how powerful you'd look while being claimed. I stared at myself in the mirror. And something in me cracked. This was really happening. This wasn't a dress-up fantasy. This wasn't a bluff. I was going to marry Kalel fucking Marchetti.

Whether I agreed or not. Whether I fought or gave in. I was going to walk down an aisle and let a man I never chose slide a ring onto my finger and call me his. And no matter how many times I told myself I was playing a game, that I was going to find a way out—somewhere deep down...

I wasn't sure I wanted to.

My throat tightened. I blinked fast, refusing to cry in a damn dress fitting, but the pressure in my chest wouldn't leave. It clawed at me from the inside.

A sick and twisted longing. "You okay?" His voice shattered the silence. I spun around—Kalel had slipped back in without a sound, leaning against the doorframe.

"You shouldn't be in here," I said, too quickly. He took a slow step forward, hands in his pockets, eyes dragging down the length of me like I was art he already owned.

"I think we're past that, but I'll humor you. Did you choose this dress?" he asks.

"I didn't say yes."

"Then I think it's fine." I swallowed hard, heart racing. He hands brushing my arms. Not claiming. Not demanding. Just... there. "You look nice in this dress too," he said quietly. "More than I imagined."

"Don't." I say. He leaned in, lips ghosting the shell of my ear. "Don't what?"

"Don't be nice to me," I whispered, shaking. "It's worse then when you're domineering." He paused and for once... he listened.

He stepped back, eyes unreadable, letting the silence fall between us again. I turned back to the mirror. Forced myself to hold my reflection's gaze.

He didn't say a word. Just walked to the counter and handled it. Like he knew his kindness made me crumble.

The ride back was silent. Not the smug kind. Not loaded with innuendo or smug touches. Just... still.

Kalel sat beside me, scrolling through something on his phone, his hand resting on my thigh like it belonged there. I was still wearing the same red dress, back in my own skin, but somehow it didn't feel like mine anymore. None of this did.

I crossed my arms over my stomach as the nausea crept up slowly— soft at first, then sharper. A swirl in my gut that didn't sit right. Maybe the champagne from the cake tasting?

Maybe the adrenaline crash? My hand curled lightly over my lower abdomen. Just a light pressure. The kind you use when your body's trying to tell you something but you're not ready to listen.

Kalel noticed. "You okay?" he asked, glancing over. "Yeah. Just... tired." I leaned my head back, letting my eyes close.

* * *

The car ride home from the dress fitting had been long. Too many turns, too much perfume, too little food. The second we stepped back into the house, the pressure in my chest got worse. My stomach

205

twisted. And when I reached the stairs, I had to pause, one hand unconsciously pressing against my stomach, folding in on myself like I could physically calm the now cramping feeling rolling through me.

Angelo saw it. Of course he did, but Kalel didn't. Kalel kept walking, already barking orders at someone down the hall, completely unaware—or too wrapped up in whatever obsessive version of reality he lived in to notice I was barely standing, but Angelo? His eyes never left me. He didn't say anything. Just watched, jaw tense, brows pulling low like something clicked in his head.

I forced a breath, pushed off the railing, and climbed the stairs like nothing happened.

I didn't see him again until later that night when I was sitting in the kitchen hands wrapped around a mug of ginger tea that I didn't even want. Just trying to settle something that felt deeper than physical.

The moment he stepped into the room. It shifted. He didn't make a sound at first. Just walked to the fridge, grabbed a bottle of water, leaned against the counter like he hadn't been watching me all day.

I sipped my tea slowly. "You good?" I ask Angelo.

"I should be asking you that." He said back and I tensed. Way to make me feel better. "You looked sick earlier," he said simply. "At the stairs. Hand on your stomach. You looked like you were gonna pass out." I set the mug down. "I'm fine."

His eyes narrowed. "You sure?" I hesitated as he stepped closer. Not threatening. Not in the way Kalel dies. Just... solid and safe. "I've seen this before," he said, voice low. "Too many times to ignore it." I swallowed.

"I'm not—" I shook my head. "I don't think I'm pregnant." Angelo didn't blink. "That's not a no." He said.

I stood, instantly uncomfortable. "I don't need this right now." I murmur.

"You do." He says his tone stayed calm, but there was steel beneath

206

it. "Because if you are—if there's even a chance—you need to figure out what the fuck you're going to do."

I turned away, arms wrapped around my middle, because I couldn't look him in the eyes. "You know how he is," he said quietly. "You know Kalel." My throat tightened. "If he finds out you're pregnant," Angelo continued, "he will never let you leave. Not even in pieces." I blinked hard, jaw clenched.

"You don't think I know that?" I say.

"I think you're scared," he said. "And I think you need someone in your corner who doesn't have a fucking god complex." I slowly turned back to face him. "I'm not going to tell Kalel," He continued. "Not unless you want me to." Angelo says.

My chest heaved. "You'd keep that from him?" I asked, questioning why, but all he did was nod. "If it means protecting you? Yeah. I would." I didn't know what to say to that. So he stepped closer again, dropped his voice to a whisper just for me.

"If you need anything—anything—you come to me. Not him." I looked up at him, eyes burning. "Why are you helping me?" He didn't smile, just held my gaze with something heavy in his eyes. "Because he might be my best friend," he continues, "but you don't deserve to go through all of this alone."

And for a moment, I wanted to cry because for the first time in weeks—maybe months—I didn't feel like like I was by myself.

I felt human.

Chapter 25

<u>Sabrina</u>

Two days. That's how long I had left before I'd be married. Before my name wouldn't be mine Sabrina Knight anymore. Before I stood in front of whoever Kalel allowed to witness our union and became Mrs. Marchetti. No matter how many screaming alarms were going off inside my body. And still... none of that scared me as much as what I was about to do right now.

I found Angelo in the courtyard, leaning against the stone railing, sunglasses on, phone in hand, looking like the mafia's favorite magazine cover model. He looked up before I could say a word. "You don't look like you slept."

"I didn't."

He nodded like he already knew why. "I need your help." His brows lifted slightly. "You're not trying to run, are you? Because I can't help with that."

I shook my head. "It's not that." I glanced around. Lowered my voice. "I need to see an OB/GYN." His jaw tensed.

"I think..." My voice dropped to a whisper. "I think something's wrong with my IUD. I'm still sick. I need to know if it's still in place." Angelo stared at me for a beat too long, like he was reading every word I hadn't said.

208

Then he exhaled. "Give me twenty minutes." He said.

* * *

He lied to Kalel. Told him I needed to get fitted for a custom piece of jewelry that was running late. Said I'd throw a fit if it didn't match the wedding colors. Kalel bought it—barely and then we were in the car. Just me and Angelo. No teasing this time. No smug remarks. Just a tension that hung heavy between us like a secret waiting to detonate.

The clinic was quiet. Discreet. Hidden in a medical building that didn't scream prenatal from the street. Angelo sat beside me in the waiting room like a silent bodyguard, never looking away. When my name was called, he followed. He didn't ask if I wanted him to. He just came.

The nurse did the basics. Weight. Blood pressure. Took a quick urine sample. I didn't even register most of it. I was too busy trying to keep the bile down in my throat. The doctor came in, kind and professional. She asked a few questions, then started the scan. And there it was. The screen flickered and my heart stopped.

"You're pregnant," she said softly. "About nine weeks."

The air left my lungs.

She kept talking. Something about early care. Prenatal labs. Follow-ups. But I didn't hear it.

Because all I could hear was the memory. Of the first time. Of the last time. My hands clenched the paper sheet beneath me as the room shifted. I saw the pale blue walls of the ER. The blood. The vomiting that wouldn't stop. The look in the nurse's eyes when she told me the heartbeat was gone.

Hyperemesis gravidarum, they'd said. The said it was severe morning sickness, but it felt worse than that. It took everything. My health. My weight. My child. I had lost her at less than ten weeks. And

209

now... Now it was happening again.

My vision blurred. My throat closed. I didn't even realize I was crying until Angelo touched my shoulder. I turned my face away. "Don't. Please." He didn't push. The doctor gently explained the nausea. The vomiting. Why I'd been feeling the way I had.

HG. Again. My nightmare was back, but this time... it wasn't just me. It was Kalel's baby. His child. My chest twisted with panic—and something worse.

Guilt.

Deep down, beneath all the fear, a part of me wanted this. A part of me ached at the thought of holding something that belonged to me and no one else. "I've had a miscarriage before," I said quietly, once the doctor had stepped out. "I don't know if I can do it again." Angelo didn't speak. I wiped at my face, voice low. "Don't tell him. Please."

His brow furrowed.

"Not yet," I whispered. "I need to figure out what I'm going to do first. I need... space. I need time." He looked like he wanted to argue, but he didn't. Instead, he nodded once. "Your secret stays with me." And for the first time since the nausea started... I felt a little less alone.

The ride back to the estate was quiet. Angelo didn't say anything, and I was grateful. I couldn't take the weight of more words. Not now. Not after the news that had shifted the ground under my feet.

I pressed my forehead against the window, watching the world blur by. Me pregnant again. Nine weeks. HG. Again.

I still hadn't said the word out loud. I wasn't ready to give it form. If I didn't speak it, maybe it wouldn't grow. Maybe it would stay small. Contained. Manageable. But the truth was already living inside me. And it wasn't going anywhere.

My stomach churned again, and I took slow, shallow breaths to push it down. I couldn't afford to get sick in Kalel's car. He'd notice. And the second he started noticing, everything would unravel. He'd lock me down tighter than ever. Not just as his bride, but as the mother of his child.

God help me, the moment he found out, there'd be no space. No air. No me. I pressed a hand to my stomach without thinking.

Nine weeks.

It didn't feel real. It felt like a countdown. Ticking toward something I wasn't ready for. When we got back to the estate, I slipped inside like a ghost.

I barely made it up the stairs before I had to throw up again, breathing through the wave of nausea that punched me in the gut. Cold sweat beaded at my temple.

You're okay.

You're okay. Just pretend. Tonight was the engagement party.

Not my choice. Not my guest list. Not my world, but Kalel had arranged it like a coronation. And I was the crown. I stood in front of the vanity in the guest wing bathroom, already zipped into the pale gold dress he picked out for me. It fit like a second skin. Strapless. High-slit. Exposed in every way.

I looked perfect, but I felt like I was drowning.

My hair was curled. My lips painted a soft rose gold. My skin glowing with that bridal sheen they all loved. No one would look at me and see the storm underneath. No one would know that I was carrying a secret that was already rewriting the rules of the game. My reflection stared back at me.

Strong. Composed. Lethal in heels. A fucking lie. You can't fall apart. I tell myself.

Not yet.

I forced a deep breath, then stepped out of the bathroom. By the time I reached the staircase, the sound of music and laughter floated through the hall. Guests were arriving—Kalel's people. Men in suits. Women in diamonds. Champagne flutes already raised.

The entire estate had been transformed.

Candlelight shimmered off cream-draped tables. White roses trailed down the banisters like vines. Waiters moved like shadows with silver trays and practiced smiles. I scanned the room from the second floor landing, heart pounding in my ears.

Kalel stood near the piano, wearing a black suit and no tie, two buttons undone at the collar. He looked powerful. His eyes found me instantly. He smiled and the world spun a little harder. Because I hadn't told him. I didn't know if I could. I wasn't sure what I was more afraid of—him knowing I was pregnant... Or him knowing I was scared.

A string quartet played something timeless in the background, the champagne sparkled, and every woman in the room looked like money.

I stood near the center of it all, Kalel's hand at the small of my back like a weight. Everyone smiled at me. Everyone stared. Everyone whispered.

She's beautiful.

She's marrying Marchetti.

She has no idea what she's getting into.

They weren't wrong. My lips held a practiced smile, the kind that didn't reach my eyes. I nodded. I said thank you. I accepted compliments I didn't deserve, wore the ring like it didn't burn on my finger.

But inside?

I was unraveling.

My stomach turned violently every time the scent of food passed me. I hadn't eaten all day—hadn't been able to. The nausea came in waves now, sharp and sudden, pulling the strength right out from under me.

I kept trying to sip water between conversations, but even that made me want to throw up. Like my body wanted to purge everything I gave it. I pressed a hand to my side discreetly.

Nine weeks.

It echoed in the back of my head like a countdown. Kalel leaned in, voice low. "You good, kitten?" I nodded fast snapping back to reality. "Yeah. Just warm." His eyes narrowed slightly. He knew something was off. Of course he did, but there were people everywhere. He wouldn't call me out here. Not yet, right?

"Smile for me," he murmured, brushing his fingers lightly against my lower back. I did. I had to because no one could know. Angelo's warning was still fresh in my mind.

I lasted another thirty minutes. Thirty excruciating minutes. I shook hands with men who smelled like cigars and crime. I answered questions I didn't care about. I posed for a photo with a woman in diamonds who said I looked "exotic" like it was a compliment.

Then the room spun and my vision blurred. I blinked hard, trying to steady myself, willing my legs to stay under me. But then the lights got too bright. The air too thin and just as someone asked how we met— Everything tilted.

And then—Darkness.

When I opened my eyes, everything was a blur. The ceiling above me looked unfamiliar. Cold air hit my skin. Strong hands gripped my waist—Kalel—his voice low and sharp somewhere near my ear.

"Get me a doctor. Now!"

"Sabrina—baby, open your eyes. Look at me." He begged

I groaned. My body felt heavy and weak. He cupped his hand to my cheek. "You passed out. Do you hear me?"

"I—I'm fine," I say barely able to speak as I try to sit up. He didn't let me. "You're not fine," he growled. "You haven't been eating. You're pale. What the fuck is going on with you?" The panic in his voice wasn't just anger—it was fear. Real fear.I blinked slowly, trying to ground myself. Trying to find the strength to lie again.

But for the first time... I wasn't sure I had it in me.

* * *

Kalel

She went limp in my arms. Again. One moment, she was standing next to me in the hall, nodding like she was fine. The next—her legs gave out. Her body folded. My arms caught her just before she hit the ground. "Sabrina." My voice broke.

She didn't respond. Not even a whisper. Fuck. I didn't wait. "Angelo!" I barked. He was already moving, clearing the last stragglers out of the hallway. "Everyone out. Now."

I lifted her into my arms—her body unnaturally light, terrifyingly still—and strode toward the front door like a man possessed. Her skin was too warm. Her breath was too shallow. I didn't remember opening the door. Didn't feel the cold night air hit my face. All I could focus on was the panic in my chest and the crushing, all-consuming thought:

Don't take her from me. I can't lose her to, not like this. Not now. "Get the car," I snapped. Angelo was already pulling the keys from his jacket. "It's waiting." he said.

I laid her across the back seat, her head cradled in my lap, my hand trembling against her cheek as we sped through the city.

She stirred—barely. Her lips parted. "Stay with me," I whispered, leaning close. "Please." Angelo glanced at me from the rearview mirror. "You know what's going on?" He asked. I shook my head, jaw clenched. "She keeps saying she's fine." I say.

"She's not." He says.

"I fucking know she's not." I say and I hated how helpless I sounded. I'd built an empire from blood and fear, but I couldn't fix this. I couldn't touch this. All I could do was hold her. At the hospital the fluorescent lights made everything feel colder.

The nurses moved fast. They didn't question who I was or why we were here after hours. My name bought silence. My voice bought speed.

They took her. Hooked her up to an IV. I sat beside the bed, fingers still wrapped around hers. Her color came back slowly. Her lips looked less pale. Her breathing evened out. Relief cracked something in my chest I didn't know was breakable.

The doctor returned an hour later with a tablet in hand, eyes skimming the lab results. "I need to speak with the patient alone," he said.

"No." My voice was like steel. "You don't."

The doctor glanced at me, then at Angelo. "I mean it," I said. "I'm not leaving."

"Ms.Knight?" the doctor asked gently, avoiding my eyes now. "Are you okay with me sharing this in front of him?"

I turned to look at her, still too pale, her eyes glassy with exhaustion. Her hand was still in mine. But there was something in her face— fear. Not of me, but for me. She looked at the doctor. "It's okay," she whispered. The doctor exhaled, then looked between us. "You're pregnant."

Silence.

Cold, brutal silence.

"She's suffering from hyperemesis gravidarum," he added quickly. "It's a severe form of pregnancy-related nausea. Not uncommon—but very serious if untreated." He kept talking—about remedies, hydration, medication options—but I didn't hear him. The words you're pregnant rang in my ears like gunfire. I looked at her.

The woman I'd torn the world apart to keep. The woman who had fought me with fire and still crawled into my arms when her body gave out.

The woman who was carrying my child.

I couldn't breathe.

The doctor left. I stood slowly. She sat up, weakly, IV still taped to her arm. "I thought you had an IUD," I said quietly. Her lips parted. "I did."

"Then how—"

"I didn't get it checked," she whispered. "Not when I was supposed to. It must've... fallen out." My stomach dropped.

"You knew."

Her eyes widened. "Kalel—" I took a step back.

"No," I said, voice shaking now. "You knew you were sick. You felt it. And you didn't tell me."

"I didn't know how to tell you I was—"

"You Knew." I say interrupting her. She didn't deny it. And that's when something snapped. "You lied to me," I whispered. "You lied, you kept this from me, and you stood beside me in front of hundreds of people like everything was fine while you were suffering and carrying my child."

She opened her mouth. I wasn't listening. "I would've moved the wedding. I would've protected you. Changed everything, but you decided for me." My voice got louder. Harsher.

"I trusted you to fight me, to sass me, to make me lose my fucking mind—but I never thought you'd hide something like this."

I stepped forward. Angelo moved between us in a flash, hand on my chest. "Kalel," he said quietly. "You need to breathe." he warned.

"She lied, Angelo." I said trying to control the fury i am feeling inside.

"I know."

"I would've given her everything. Everything." My hands shook and my chest hurt. It felt like betrayal. But worse. It felt like fear. Because if I hadn't found out tonight... If she hadn't fainted... what else might she have kept from me?

I looked at her. She was crying now and that undid me more than anything else. I wanted to hold her. I wanted to scream. I wanted to crawl inside her skin and protect her from everything, including me, but all I could do was stare. And hurt.

Chapter 26

<u>Sabrina</u>

The car ride home was silent. Not the comfortable kind. The kind that presses on your chest like a brick. That makes every breath feel like a mistake. I sat on the far end of the backseat, staring out the window like the blurred lights of the city could answer the questions pounding in my head.

Kalel hadn't looked at me once since we left the hospital. Not a glance, not even a word. He sat with his hands clasped in his lap, jaw locked so tight I could see the muscle twitch every time he swallowed another emotion. I'd never seen him like this. Not even when he was angry. This wasn't anger. This was... distance.

And it felt so much worse.

Angelo drove in silence, eyes forward, jaw tense. He could feel it too. The frost in the air. The ache beneath it. I curled my fingers around the edge of my seat to keep them from shaking.

I wanted to speak. To reach for him. To fix it. But I didn't know how. I had broken something. And I didn't know if it could be put back together. The second we walked through the front door, Kalel started upstairs.

I followed.

"Kalel—please," I called after him. "Can we talk?" He stopped on the landing but didn't turn around. "You mean now?" He said his voice, low in a way that didn't make my skin tingle—it made my heart drop.

"Yes, Now." He turned slowly. His face was calm, but I could see it in his eyes.

The pain.

The betrayal. He was bleeding, and I was the blade that cut him. "You should've told me the second you suspected," he said. "Not lied. Not fainted in my arms. Not waited until a doctor told me while you sat there acting like it was no big deal."

"I was scared," I said softly. "So was I," he snapped. "When you collapsed in front of me. When I carried you out of that party thinking I was about to lose you."

"I didn't know for sure—" I said.

"But you knew something," he growled. "And you kept it from me." I took a shaky breath. "I didn't want to give you a reason to cage me even more than you already do." His face hardened.

"You think this is about control?" he asked. "I wanted to take care of you, Sabrina." He laughed once—humorless and broken. "But maybe I'm the fool for thinking you'd ever let me."

"That's not fair." I said.

"No?" He stepped closer. "You're the one carrying my child, and you let me walk around thinking everything was fine while your body was shutting down in silence."

I swallowed, tears burning behind my eyes. "I didn't do it to hurt you." I said.

"Didn't you?" he said coldly. "Because it feels like you wanted to keep this from me. Like you didn't want me to know until it was too late." I flinched. And then he said it. The words that cut deeper than anything else. "Maybe this was your way of reminding me I'll never really have all of you."

Silence.

Dead, suffocating silence. I opened my mouth, but he didn't wait. Kalel turned and walked down the hall, disappearing into one of the guest rooms. The door slamming shut.

And I stood there—alone. Cracked wide open.

* * *

After a while I laid in bed, staring at the ceiling, wrapped in the sheets he usually pulled me into, but tonight?

It was cold and empty.

I turned over, hoping he might appear, but he didn't. Hours passed and the silence became unbearable. At some point, I got up. Walked down the hall bare feet and in a silk robe, praying I was wrong. That maybe he'd come back. Maybe he was just cooling off. I opened the guest room door slowly.

The light was off, but I saw him on the bed. Broad shoulders. Still fully dressed. Lying on top of the covers. Facing the wall.

I didn't go in. I couldn't. I closed the door just as quietly. Returned to our bed and broke. The sob hit before I could stop it, curling me into the sheets, into the ache, into the emptiness he left behind.

Because I had hurt him, and for the first time since Kalel Marchetti dragged me into his world... I didn't know if he would ever reach for me again.

The next day I stood outside his office door for a long time. Long enough to rehearse what I wanted to say a dozen different ways.

None of it sounded right. None of it softened the truth, but I couldn't keep doing this. Not for me and not for the child growing inside me. I took a breath and knocked once. I didn't wait for a response. I pushed the door open.

Kalel was behind his desk, phone in one hand, pen in the other, a sharp shadow in his perfectly tailored shirt. He didn't look up.

"I'm busy." He said.

"This won't take long," I said. His jaw tensed. He set the phone down slowly, eyes lifting—cold and unreadable. I closed the door behind me. Then I said it. "I don't want to marry you." The air between us stilled. His face didn't change, but his eyes did. They darkened like storm clouds.

He leaned back slowly in his chair, like he was holding something back. Something dangerous. "You don't want to marry me," he repeated flatly.

"No." I said

He nodded once. Like he was processing it. Then stood. Calmly. Too calmly. He walked around the desk toward me. "You don't want to marry the man who's fed you, protected you, and kept you safe when your world fell apart?" he said, voice low and controlled covering the storm inside, but I held my ground.

"No, I want to protect myself now. And my child."

His jaw twitched. "You mean OUR child." I flinched at the emphasis. "You think walking in here and telling me this makes you brave?" he said, eyes narrowing. "You think this makes you a fucking hero, Sabrina?" He asked.

"I think it makes me honest." I respond and he laughed. "Honest?" he echoed. "You lied about being sick. You lied to my face. You let me plan a wedding while your body was falling apart and said nothing."

"I was scared!" I shouted. "Of me!" he snapped.

"And that's the problem." I said.

Silence rang in the room. Tight and choking. "I'm not going to raise a child in this," I said softly. "With a man who treats me like property one second and like glass the next. I can't do this anymore." His face changed then. Harder. Colder. Something unrecognizable

. "Then don't," he said quietly.

"You don't want to marry me? Fine. Don't. Raise your bastard kid on your own. You can leave too."

I froze. Air punched out of my lungs and he saw it. He saw the pain hit and didn't stop it. He didn't take it back. I took a shaky step back, tears blurring my vision, but my body didn't wait for permission to break. My stomach lurched. I barely made it to the corner of the room before I dropped to my knees and threw up in the trash can.

The weight of everything I'd carried all week—fear, betrayal, heartbreak—rushed out of me in waves, my body heaving until there was nothing left but acid and silence.

I wiped my mouth with the back of my hand, still kneeling on the floor, trembling. Kalel didn't move. Didn't speak. Didn't come near me, and that was the moment I knew: This wasn't love anymore.

This was war.

* * *

The silence between us was thick—bruising. He stood like stone while I sat on cold tile, body hollowed out and raw, as if the act of purging had stripped me down to something skeletal. Something survival-bound.

I'd thrown up four times by noon. Nothing stayed down. Not toast. Not crackers. Not even water. My stomach churned constantly, my body shaky from the weight of holding everything in—my tears, my fear, and the thing growing inside me.

Kalel hadn't spoken to me for the rest of the day. Not a word since he broke me this morning. I was curled on my side, trying to breathe through another wave of nausea when he walked in sharp in a black dress shirt and a silver watch.

"You have fifteen minutes to get dressed," he said.

I didn't move. "What for?" I croaked, voice raw from being sick.

"There's an event. We're making an appearance." He said.

"I'm not feeling well."

He didn't flinch. "That wasn't a request." And then he left. Just like that. Fifteen minutes. Like my body wasn't falling apart. Like he hadn't broken me into pieces and left me in our bed alone. Like we didn't matter anymore. Like he didn't call our child a fucking bastard.

But I got up.

I put on the dress laid out for me—black silk, thin straps, fitted. It swallowed me whole. I hadn't even realized how much weight I'd lost until that moment. I couldn't keep my hands steady, putting on makeup.

When I walked out into the hall, Angelo was waiting by the door, checking his watch. His eyes met mine and froze for a second. He saw it. The fatigue. The paleness. The way I held my stomach like I was trying to keep myself from caving in, but he didn't say anything.

Not with Kalel standing behind him, sunglasses on, jaw locked like stone. The ride was silent. Not tense. Just hollow. Like nothing lived between us anymore. The venue was some private rooftop lounge in the city, all clean lines, white furniture, and money in the air. Everyone was smiling. Toasting. Talking in low, expensive voices.

Kalel stepped out of the car without waiting for me. I followed and the second we entered the crowd, he disappeared.

Off to shake hands with people who mattered. People who weren't me. He went off to play king in a world I didn't belong to. I stood still for a moment, my stomach turning. The sun was too bright. The air, too thick. I felt like I might collapse again if I didn't sit down.

I spotted a white bench tucked near the edge of the rooftop. I headed for it, heels clicking against the stone, every step heavier than the last.

I sat down and breathed.

Trying not to throw up again. Then I heard his voice. Smooth. Familiar. "Should I be offended? You look like you're dying at a party

223

I'm attending?" I looked up.

Jin.

He was leaning against the glass railing, dressed in all black, not a wrinkle out of place. His dark hair curled slightly around his temple, and that crooked smile hadn't changed.

He slid onto the bench beside me without asking. "I'm fine," I muttered.

"You don't look fine." He replied

"I haven't had a good month."

"I heard." Of course he did.

I looked at him sharply. He shrugged. "People talk. Especially about Kalel Marchetti's stolen bride." I swallowed hard. "You shouldn't be talking about me or to me." I say slightly annoyed.

"Why? Because your overbearing captor might shoot me?" He asks.

"Something like that." I say feeling every ounce of strength leaving my body. He tilted his head, eyes trailing down my form—not in a gross way. more of a curious and concerned look.

"You're pale."

"I'm pregnant." He blinked "Shit." Jin said shocked.

"Yeah."

He was quiet for a second. Then he said, "You don't look happy about it." I didn't answer, because I wasn't. I didn't know how to be happy anymore. Then I realized something.

I looked up—and across the rooftop, Kalel and Angelo were walking toward a small building on the far end of the lounge. A private meeting space. Two suited men followed behind them.

A meeting. I watched the door close behind them. A window opened in my chest.

A chance.

"I have to go," I whispered suddenly, standing. Jin blinked. "What?"

"I have to leave. Now. While he's in that meeting." I said.

"Why?"

"Because if I don't do it now, I'll never get away."

His eyes searched mine. Then—something dangerous sparked in him. "Alright," he said, rising with me. "Where do you want to go?"

"I don't care. I just need to not be here."

He didn't hesitate. He grabbed my hand, tucked me into his side, and whispered, "Follow me."

We slipped through the crowd like smoke. No one looked twice. Jin smiled at the right people. Nodded at a security guard. Then ten minutes later, I was in the passenger seat of his matte black car.

Free.

For the first time in months. I didn't know where I was going. Or what would happen next, but I finally breathed and it felt like living. The city blurred past us in streaks of steel and sunlight. Jin drove fast.

Not reckless—but smooth. Like someone used to running, used to staying just ahead of something that could eat him alive.

It fit him.

The silence stretched, but not uncomfortably. He didn't rush me. Didn't ask questions. Just let the music hum quietly from the speakers while I stared out the window, trying to piece myself back together.

Eventually, he said, "How long have you been trying to leave?" I didn't answer right away. Then, softly, "Since the beginning." Jin's hands tightened slightly on the wheel. "That long?" I nodded. "He really is such a fucking dick?"

"Yes, yes he is." I say with a smirk.

He let that settle. No judgment. Just acceptance. "And the baby?" he asked gently. I hesitated. "Nine weeks. Maybe ten."

He exhaled slowly, eyes still on the road. "I've been sick every day for days." His jaw flexed. "And he still dragged you out?"

"Kalel doesn't like being questioned." I say.

"No, I don't imagine he does."

I closed my eyes, head resting against the seat. "He used to make me feel like I was powerful. Like I could fight him and win. Like he wanted me to." I say, as I sigh looking out the window.

"And now?" He asked.

"Now he's just... trying to win."

The car fell quiet again, but the silence between us wasn't hollow. It felt like something alive. Like something waiting. Then Jin said, "I know somewhere safe." I turned to look at him. "Why are you helping me?" He glanced over briefly, his eyes too perceptive. "Because you asked." he says with a smile.

"That's it?" I questioned.

A small smile tugged at his lips. "You're not the only one who knows what it feels like to be close to him." I didn't ask what he meant. I just let the quiet sit between us. Let the road stretch out like a lifeline. For the first time in months, I wasn't being watched. I wasn't being followed. I wasn't being owned.

I was sitting beside a man who didn't want to control me. And that alone made me want to cry, but I didn't. Not yet at least, I wasn't safe. Not really. Not until I was somewhere he couldn't find me.

Thirty minutes later Jin's car pulled into a private, gated drive at the edge of the city—modern, sleek, and surrounded by tall hedges and trees. A fortress disguised as a home.

"Yours?" I asked.

He nodded. "My city base. It's not registered to me. So, he won't find you here." I stepped out, legs still shaky, stomach queasy.

Jin came around and opened the door for me—not like I was helpless. Like I mattered. "Come on," he said softly. "Let me get you inside. You can rest. Eat. Throw something at me if I look at you wrong." He joked.

I cracked a smile. The first one in days. He led me in, flicking on soft lights. The inside was clean, minimalist, black-and-steel with warm floors and big windows. A place built to hide and breathe at the same time.

He gestured toward the long couch. "Sit. I'll grab you some water." I sank into the cushions with a sigh, my body finally giving out from the adrenaline. When he came back, I took the glass, hands still trembling. "You okay?" he asked. I nodded, but my voice betrayed me. "No."And then I whispered it again "No. I'm not."

Jin didn't touch me. Didn't offer empty words. He just sat across from me, his voice quiet but certain. "It's okay to not be okay." And for the first time in forever, I believed it.

Chapter 27

Kalel

The meeting ended without incident. Numbers. Territory. A few veiled threats. I wasn't listening to any of it. My mind hadn't left her since I walked away from her this morning. Since I said something I could never take back. "Raise your bastard kid on your own and you can leave". The words echoed in my skull like gunshots.

When the final handshake was made and the doors opened, I scanned the rooftop. Looking for her. Looking for my girl so that I could apologize for what I said, but when I went to the spot where I'd last seen her was empty.

No black silk. No soft curls. No fire behind her eyes. Just empty space. I started walking, slower at first. Then faster.

"Sabrina."

Nothing. I moved through the clusters of people, searching faces, scanning corners. Nothing. A chill licked down my spine. She wasn't here.

She wasn't fucking here. She hadn't just wandered off.

She was gone. I turned sharply toward the security near the edge of the rooftop. "Did you see my fiancée leave?" I demanded. They froze. "Sir—"

"When?" I said sternly.

"Maybe thirty... thirty-five minutes ago," one said. "She was with a man." Everything went still. My voice dropped. "What man?"

"Uh—dark hair. About six feet two inches. Black suit. Smiling. Looked... Korean?"

Jin. Fucking Jin. My chest went cold.

Then hot and I snapped.

She was gone. Fucking Gone and she left with Jin. No note. No message. No trace. And not just gone from the rooftop. Gone from me. Gone from the world I built to keep her wrapped in silk and steel. Gone from the house where she slept in my bed and carried my child.

She had left me. She fucking left me, but the worst part was that she didn't leave alone. I'm going to kill him. Not even his father can save him from what I am going to do when I get my hands on him.

I let out a sinister chuckle. Fucking Jin.

That smug, cocky bastard with his pretty face and quiet charm. She smiled at him. I saw it. I saw her smile at him like she hadn't spent the last few months curled in my arms moaning my name. As if I hadn't broken myself into pieces trying to keep her alive. She smiled at him and now she was gone.

Angelo stood to the side of me on the rooftop, tense but still breathing like this wasn't the end of the world. I wasn't breathing at all. I was burning. "Get me every camera in a three-block radius," I said, voice low.

"Kalel—"

"Every plate. Every face. I want to know what car he drove, which direction he went, and where he's hiding her."

"We'll find her—" he said.

"She didn't just disappear, Angelo," I snapped. "She was taken."

His brows lifted.

"She made a choice," he said carefully.

I took a step forward, fingers twitching.

"He's had his eye on her from the beginning. Always too close and

229

way too polite. Just waiting for his chance."

I smiled then. Dark and ugly.

"He thinks he can keep her. That he can touch what's mine and live." I said still smiling.

"Kalel."

"She's pregnant, Angelo. With my fucking child, and he helped her run."

I wasn't just going to find them. I was going to make him pay. I was going to rip the smile off his face and make her watch. Then I am going to pull her back into my arms and remind her who she belonged to. She can cry. She can scream. She can say she hated me a thousand times, but she is still mine.

And I was going to prove it.

Even if I had to chain her to my fucking bed to make her stay.

Angelo was silent for a long time before he finally asked, "What happens when you bring her back?" I turned slowly. "Then I remind her that no matter where she runs, no matter who helps her—there's no world where she's free from me." I smiled again. Sharp.

Final.

"Because if I can't have her..." My voice dropped to a whisper. "...no one can."

I take a deep breath as we head to the car slamming the door shut with a force that felt like a verdict.

The silence inside the SUV pressed in thick and heavy, like smoke from a fire that hadn't finished burning. Angelo slid into the driver's seat. The engine roared to life, and we pulled off, leaving behind nothing but the echo of her absence. My hand rested on my knee, twitching. I couldn't stop it.

I felt it again.

That itch.

The one that crept up my spine, whispering violence in the space where calm should be. I'd only ever felt it one other time—when I lost Amy. But this? This was different. This was worse. Because Sabrina *chose* to leave. She made a decision.

And she made it with him.

I stared straight ahead, eyes unblinking, watching the blur of Bellavora streak past the tinted windows. I didn't see buildings. I didn't see people.

I saw her.

In that red dress.

The one I bought her.

On her knees for me. Moaning my name like a fucking prayer and now she was gone. Taken or worse—she left *willingly*.

Angelo didn't speak at first. He knew better, but I could feel his glance flick to the mirror every few seconds. Like he was trying to assess just how close I was to snapping, but he didn't need to look. I was already broken.

"Kalel," he finally said, his voice calm—measured. "You don't know that Jin—"

"She left with him," I said. My voice was hollow. Void of emotion. The kind of empty that only came after you gave too much of yourself and still got abandoned.

"She didn't leave a message. No goodbye. No hesitation. Just gone. It took thirty-five minutes. That's how long it took for her to disappear from my life like I was nothing."

"You treat her as if she's nothing to you." Angelo says. I turned my head slowly toward the rearview mirror, locking eyes with him.

"She's everything." I say pushing away whatever feelings I still left. That shut him up.

I let the silence crawl back in, wrapping around us like a noose.

I whispered, more to myself than to him. "I bled for her. Killed for her. Made enemies disappear in the middle of the night without leaving a trace. All so she could sleep safe."

My fingers curled into fists.

"And she *ran*."

Angelo adjusted his grip on the wheel. "You don't —"

"She was pregnant," I snapped. "With *my* fucking child. And she ran."

That word tasted like poison now.

Ran.

She left me standing on the edge of a rooftop like a fucking idiot with a ring in my pocket and a grave in my heart.

"She smiled at him," I said. "Like I didn't matter. Like all of this— everything we've been through—meant nothing."

The leather of the seat creaked as I leaned forward, elbows on my knees, rage curling in my gut like a second spine. "He thinks he can keep her? That he can hold what's *mine* and live?"

A dark laugh escaped me—quiet and guttural. "He has no idea what I become when someone steals from me."

"She's not—" Angelo started, but I cut him off.

"She is," I growled. "She's mine. I branded that woman with my fucking soul. And she can lie to herself all she wants, but she'll never escape me."

"She's not a possession, Kalel."

"No," I said softly. "She's worse."

Angelo hesitated. "Worse how?"

I leaned back, staring at the ceiling like it might have the answers I couldn't find in myself.

"She's an addiction," I whispered. "The kind that burns you alive and makes you *thank* it."

Every thought I had led back to her. Every breath I took since the second she walked into my world had been hers. I didn't know how to function without her orbiting me like a damn star I couldn't reach.

"You going to kill Jin?" Angelo asked again, quieter this time.

"No," I said, a cruel smirk tugging at the corner of my mouth. "I'm going to destroy him."

He said nothing. Because there was nothing left to say.

The rest of the ride was quiet. The kind of quiet that happens before someone sets a match to a city. I sat in the shadows, the heat of my fury pulsing under my skin like wildfire—silent, patient, inevitable.

Sabrina thought she could leave.

Jin thought he could take her.

And me?

I'd make them both regret believing I'd ever let them go.

Chapter 28

Kalel

It's been three months. Three fucking months since she vanished and every hour without her felt like a noose tightening around my neck—slow and suffocating. I hadn't slept. Not really. I'd moved into my office, maps, CCTV feeds, and vehicle logs spread across every surface. My phone buzzed non-stop. My men reported hourly. My tech teams worked around the clock.

Nothing. Not a trace. Like she'd fallen off the face of the earth. Like she was hiding.

From me.

Like she was happy to be gone. The thought alone made my teeth grind. I stood at the window, staring out over the estate, jaw clenched, a half-drained glass of whiskey forgotten in my hand.

Behind me, the door opened and Angelo stepped in, but I didn't turn. "You found her?" I asked quietly. He hesitated a little too long.

"No." He said.

He's a fucking liar.

My eyes narrowed at the glass. "You sure about that?" I asked, as Angelo moved farther into the room. "She's hiding well. No digital trail. No card use. It's like she knew how we'd track her."

"She didn't do this alone." I said.

"No. Jin helped."

That name again. I set the glass down slowly on the windowsill. Angelo cleared his throat. "Kalel..."

"Don't," I warned. He fell silent, but I heard it. The thing he wasn't saying. The thing eating at him. I turned slowly. "You saw her didn't you?"

He said nothing, but that was all I needed. "You saw her," I repeated, stepping forward, voice low. "Where?"

"I didn't speak to her. Was she with him?" He stated, but he didn't answer.

My chest twisted. Not from surprise. From the confirmation. "And?" I asked tightly. "How did she look?" Angelo shifted. "Healthy." He said trying not to look at me.

I stopped. Blinking once. "What?"

"She looked... better." He was trying to downplay it. Soften the word, but I saw through it. "She looked happy." I asked.

Angelo didn't respond. That was the truth, She looked happy. Without me. My jaw locked. My fists curled. "I gave her everything," I said quietly. "I tore down my own rules for her. I let her in. And she—she ran."

"You said she was scared—"I said to Angelo

"But, she's mine," I snapped, stepping closer. "I don't care if she's scared. I don't care if she hates me. She doesn't get to smile for another man while I'm tearing this city apart looking for her."

Angelo didn't flinch, but I saw it in his eyes. The shift. The calculation. The concern. "I want her back," I said. "I don't care how you do it. I don't care what it costs. But if you don't bring her to me in the next few days..."

I leaned in. Voice like a death sentence. "...then I'll bring her back here myself." I said as I turned and walked past him and the silence that followed? It felt like the calm before a war.

I didn't bother taking a moment to regain my composure. I needed the walk. I wanted the staff to see me—wanted the fear in their eyes. Let them whisper. Let them know that their king was spiraling.

I reached the garage and slid into the front seat of the matte-black SUV before Angelo could catch up. The door barely shut before I slammed it in gear. I didn't tell him where I was going.

He knew.

I needed to see her. Even if it was from a distance. Even if I had to watch her smile for another man while my hands were empty and shaking from not touching her.

It had been three months, and I still couldn't sleep without her scent in my sheets. I couldn't walk past the guest room she stayed in without pausing, waiting, hoping to hear her voice again.

And now she was out there. Breathing, laughing, *living*. As if she hadn't buried me alive the second she walked out. I pulled onto the main road, tires screeching like a goddamn declaration of war. It was reckless I know, but I was past being cool now.

She was mine. And I was done pretending I could live without her.

I parked at the top of the hill overlooking the long stretch of gravel. It was quiet, and that's what I needed to calm the thoughts in my head. If I came for her would she look at me with hate? With fear? Would she run again? I almost hoped she stayed because that would mean I didn't have to chase her and I didn't have to hurt Jin.

Chapter 29

Sabrina

For the first time in days, food didn't make me want to cry.

I was halfway through a bowl of fruit—real fruit, not the kind drenched in syrup and lies—curled up in one of Jin's oversized hoodies on his penthouse balcony, and my stomach wasn't trying to kill me.

Small wins.

"Do I get credit for this?" Jin asked, leaning against the railing in designer sweats and no shirt, like his abs were part of the architectural aesthetic.

I rolled my eyes. "For buying fruit?"

"For saving your life," he said dramatically. "I mean, let's be honest. If you had to suffer under Kalel's cold, brooding silence one more day, you probably would've just walked into traffic." I laughed—an actual laugh—and set the bowl down. "You're not wrong." I say. He turned toward me, that cute grin of his lighting up again.

"Good. Now get dressed." I blinked. "What?"

"I'm taking you to the beach."

"I'm—what?"

"You need salt water and serotonin. I've decided." Jin says.

"I'm still recovering."

"Exactly. And you can do that while standing in the ocean looking hot and dramatic. I'll even bring an umbrella and feed you grapes like a Greek goddess."

I blinked again. "...You're insane."

He winked. "Only a little." I hadn't realized how heavy everything felt until I was in the water. The second the waves touched my skin, something in me loosened. Jin had dragged me to a secluded cove thirty minutes from the city—white sand, no people, endless sky. It was the kind of place you only find if you have money, secrets, or both.

I let the salt water lap at my legs, my arms outstretched as I walked deeper in. The nausea? Gone. The tightness in my chest? Lighter. And when I turned and saw Jin throwing a towel dramatically over one shoulder like he was about to walk a runway? I smiled. "What?" he called, arms out like he was inviting applause.

"You're so—much." I said.

"And yet, you're still here."

I laughed again. He came toward me, barefoot in the surf, water hitting his calves, curls dancing in the wind. "You're smiling," he said, eyes crinkling.

"Don't get used to it."

"Oh, I already am," he teased. "If I get you to laugh three more times, I'm proposing." He says with a smile.

"Hard pass."

He clutched his chest. "You wound me."

"You love it."

He grinned. "I really do." We stood in the shallows, waves tugging at our ankles, sun warming our skin. And for the first time in so long—I didn't feel trapped. Just... still. Like I existed again. "Can I ask you something?" I said softly. He tilted his head. "You can ask me anything."

"How do you know Kalel?" The smile faltered. Just a fraction.

"We grew up together," he said after a moment. "Used to be best friends." I blinked. "Wait—you and Kalel?" I asked unable to believe

238

what I just heard.

"Shocking, I know. I had color in my soul, and he had... trauma."

"Still does." I say looking down

"Tragedy never goes out of style," Jin said dryly. "But you're nothing like him." I say, he looked at me, eyes narrowing slightly and something shifted. A flicker. A warning. "Don't be so sure," he said, voice lower. "I haven't decided if that's a good thing yet."

I stared at him. He smiled again—lighter, but something behind it lingered. Something hungry and suddenly I realized:

He wasn't just helping me. He was watching me. Wanting me. Maybe more than he should. I didn't realize how far I'd waded into the water until the breeze tugged my wet hair off my shoulders and I was almost waist-deep.

The nausea had faded to a low hum. Manageable. My skin didn't feel like it was burning from the inside anymore. And for once? I wasn't thinking about Kalel. I wasn't thinking about the wedding being canceled. Or the way his voice had cracked when he realized I'd lied. how his eyes had gone cold right before he said something that would haunt me forever.

"Raise your bastard kid on your own."

Instead, I was here. In the ocean. With Jin. Watching him try to skip rocks into the waves and dramatically curse every time they plunked straight into the water with zero grace. "This beach is cursed," he declared, hands on his hips.

"Or you just suck at skipping stones."

"I resent that," he said, brushing sand from his fingers as he stepped closer. "I'll have you know, in middle school, I had the best rock skip out of my entire gang."

"You had a gang in middle school?" He smirked. "Of course. We stole vending machine snacks and made mix tapes. Very elite."

I snorted, covering my mouth. He grinned wider. "There it is again."

he says.

"What?"

"The laugh. You've been doing it more." I looked down at the water. It swirled around my thighs, cool and grounding. "Feels strange," I admitted. "Being happy." He didn't say anything right away. Then, softly, "You deserve it." I glanced at him. He wasn't smiling now. Not in that smug, cocky way he usually did. His eyes were on me. Really on me.

Like he was cataloging the way the sun hit my skin. The way my chest rose with each breath. The way I existed. "I'm starting to think Kalel's a bigger idiot than I thought," he added. I raised a brow. "You think you're not?" I ask.

"I know I'm an idiot," he said with a grin. "But at least I'm the charming kind." I turned to walk back toward the shore, letting the water fall away from my legs. Jin followed, close behind.

When we reached the sand, I dropped down onto the blanket we'd brought. My body already felt lighter. My muscles less tense. It was the first time in weeks I didn't feel like I had to flinch every time someone said my name.

Jin laid back beside me, arms folded under his head. "You ever think about just... staying gone?" he asked casually.

"All the time."

"Then maybe you should." He said and I turned to look at him. He didn't look smug now. He looked serious. Like the idea of me staying gone—of staying with him—was becoming more than a favor. More than curiosity. "You keep looking at me like that," I said slowly, "and you're going to catch feelings."

"Cutie," he murmured, gaze flicking to my lips, "I already did." My breath caught. He didn't move closer. Didn't press. But the air between us changed. Shifted. Something dangerous and warm and tempting stirred in my chest and for a second? I let myself wonder what it would feel like to choose someone gentle.

Someone who made me laugh. Someone who didn't make love feel like war.

By the time we got back to Jin's place, the sun was starting to dip behind the skyline—casting golden light across the tall glass windows of the penthouse. It should've felt like a cage. All the glass. The height. The walls I didn't own. But somehow, it didn't. It felt like breathing.

* * *

Jin tossed his keys into a bowl by the door, peeled off his sweatshirt, and headed straight for the kitchen like he'd lived here a thousand lifetimes. I hovered near the couch, still wrapped in the towel I'd used to dry off, salt water drying at my hairline. "You want tea or juice or... wine that you'll probably judge me for?" he called. "I'm pregnant, remember?" He peeked around the kitchen wall. "So... tea?"

I smiled. "Tea."

He disappeared again, and I let myself sink onto the fluffy couch, the kind that practically swallowed you whole. My body felt light, like the ocean had washed away some of the weight I'd been carrying for months, but that didn't mean I was safe. It didn't mean Kalel had stopped looking. He's out there and he'll come for you.

I glanced toward the front door. No sounds. No shadows. Just Jin. Making tea like I wasn't the mafia's runaway bride. Like I wasn't a ticking bomb. "Here," he said a minute later, handing me a steaming mug with lemon. "Organic. Hand-picked. Probably overpriced. You're welcome."

"Wow," I said, smirking. "You're just... so husband material."

"I know," he said dramatically, settling onto the couch beside me. "And yet, tragically single. It's a crime, really." I laughed—again. He turned toward me, arm along the back of the couch, body relaxed in that effortless way that made you forget just how sharp he really was. "I like seeing you like this," he said.

"Like what?"

"Not flinching. Not looking over your shoulder. Just... you." He says. The words hit deeper than they should've, because I hadn't felt like myself in weeks. Maybe months. And yet here, with Jin, barefoot and still damp from the beach... I wasn't surviving. I was living.

"You should rest," he added, softer now. "You look better, but you're still pale."

"I'm fine." I rebuttal

"You always say that." he says as he smirks

"And you always call me out."

"Because someone has to." He says with a chuckle. I looked at him. Really looked at him. Messy wavy hair. Gold chain. Lazy grin that hid too many secrets. He was beautiful. Trouble, and maybe—just maybe—dangerous in a way I didn't mind. "Thank you," I whispered. "For today." Jin's smile faded, replaced by something quieter. Something more... real. "You don't have to thank me," he said. "Just let me keep you safe."

I didn't respond. Not because I didn't want to.But because some part of me was starting to believe he meant it and another part was terrified of what that might cost him.

After our talk Jin kisses my forehead and walks away.

* * *

Thirty minutes later, I smelled food before I heard the sizzling. My stomach didn't twist this time. Not violently, at least. I padded out into the open kitchen, still wearing one of Jin's hoodies—this one black and oversized, swallowing me down to my thighs. My hair was damp from a long shower. I looked less like someone on the run and more like someone recovering.

Progress. Jin stood at the stove, barefoot, focused, a dish towel over his shoulder like someone's too-sexy husband. Which was annoying. And a little bit unfair. "You're cooking again?" I asked, voice still soft from the nap I took earlier. He turned with a grin. "Don't sound so surprised. I'm a man of many talents. Did you know I once got a Michelin chef to say I had 'potential'?"

"Was this before or after you bribed him?" He winked. "No comment." I glanced at the pot, then at the plate he was prepping with grilled chicken, roasted sweet potatoes, and plain jasmine rice. "Looks good," I said. "Smells better," he replied. "But I know you're still nervous to eat." I leaned against the counter, crossing my arms. "I just don't want to throw it all up again. I already ate earlier. Pushing it feels... risky." I say.

He turned toward me fully, holding something in his hand.

A pink Benadryl tablet. "Take this first," he said. "It should help." I frowned. "Where did you get that?"

"Pharmacy two blocks from here."

I stared.

He added, "I looked it up. Found a couple of OB's online talking about how it can help with morning sickness when Zofran's too heavy. Said it's safe in early pregnancy if used short-term. I triple-checked." My mouth parted. "You... researched it?"

He raised a brow. "You thought I was just here for vibes?"

I blinked fast, something in my chest tightening, because Kalel hadn't done that. Not when I was fainting. Not when I was sick every morning. Not even after he found out I was pregnant, but Jin... Jin went and looked up how to help me. "You okay?" he asked, his voice gentler now.

I nodded, lips pressing together. "Yeah. Just... surprised." He didn't push. Just handed me the tablet and a glass of water. I took both. And for the first time in days, I wanted to eat. We ate on the couch, our plates balanced on the coffee table, legs tangled under a shared blanket while a movie played in the background—some ridiculous early 2000s romcom that Jin insisted had "life-changing cinematic value."

He watched it like it was Shakespeare. I tried to keep up, but my body was finally relaxing. Warm food. Real comfort. Safe company. It was too much. I didn't even notice when I drifted off. Didn't feel myself leaning into him, my head against his chest, his arm sliding around me like it belonged there.

* * *

Jin

She fell asleep on me. One hand curled against her stomach, her lashes fluttering like she was still dreaming. And God help me—I was already addicted. To the way she softened against me. To the way she trusted me just enough to sleep. To the way I felt like I'd kill anyone who tried to take this away from her.

Even him.

I shifted gently, cradling her against my chest. Then, as quietly as possible, I stood and carried her to the bedroom, placing her down on the cool sheets like she was made of glass. She didn't stir. Didn't pull away. I pulled the blanket over her slowly, brushing a curl off her cheek. "I've got you," I whispered, so low I almost didn't hear it myself. And for once? It felt like maybe I really did.

My phone buzzed. I glanced at the screen, expecting it to be one of my men.

Angelo: He wants to meet. Midnight. Pier 17. Come alone.

I stared at the message, expression flat typical Kalel. Always demanding and expecting things to go his way. I sigh, then reply.

Tell him I'll be there.

Then I locked the phone, slid it back into my pocket, and let my gaze fall back to her. Still sleeping.

Still safe.

Chapter 30

Kalel

The moment I see Jin I want to rip his head of. He stood in front of me like he wasn't afraid to die. That was his first mistake."You've had her for 3 months." I say, my voice was calm. Jin leaned back against the wall of the rooftop terrace like we were discussing the weather and not the fact that he had taken what belonged to me. "She came to me," he said evenly.

"She doesn't belong to you."

"She doesn't belong to anyone." he corrected me like she wasn't my fiancee. My hands curled into fists. I hadn't touched him yet, but I wanted to. God, I wanted to knock that smug fucking smirk off his face and grind it into the concrete.

"Let's not play games," Jin said, arms crossing casually over his chest. "You're not here for negotiation. You're here because your ego can't handle the fact that she ran and didn't look back."

I took a slow step forward. "She's pregnant. With my child. and you helped her run."

"I helped her breathe." He said and I snapped.

My fist collided with his jaw before I even registered the swing. He staggered—but didn't fall. He grinned, blood at the corner of his mouth.

"There he is," Jin said, wiping it away.

246

"Kalel Fucking Marchetti. I was wondering when the real one would show up."

I lunged again—this time he ducked and landed a sharp hit to my ribs. The pain radiated, but I don't care. We crashed into each other like fire meeting gasoline. The fight wasn't clean—it was personal. This wasn't about who hit harder. It was about who hurt more. I shoved him against the wall, forearm at his throat.

"You think you've won?" I hissed. "You think a few dinners, nights with tea, and quiet smiles makes her yours?" I ask.

He spat blood to the side.

"She'd rather be sick and free with me than caged and heartbroken with you."

That did it. I slammed him against the wall—hard, but before I could follow through, a voice roared behind us.

"Enough!" Angelo said as he yanked me back by the shoulders, slamming me against the railing.

"Get off him," he barked.

"Now."

Jin coughed, pushing off the wall. Angelo turned to him next. "I should let you two kill each other," he snapped. "But neither of you deserve her if this is how you're going to act."

"She chose to leave," Jin said, panting.

"And I'm choosing to take her back," I growled.

"Like hell you are." He argues.

"She's mine." I demand trying to repress my anger.

"Not anymore."

That landed harder than any punch could. I went still only my chest heaving. Was he right? Did i push her to run? And to Jin of all people? I lick my lip feeling the blood in my mouth. My knuckles are raw. Jin looked certain. Certain that she was gone. and that? That was worse.

Angelo stepped between us, breathing heavy. "This meeting's over."

No one moved. Not at first, but I turned and walked away. Because next time? I wasn't bringing words. The second the car door shut, I lost it. "She'd rather be sick and free with me," I hissed, replaying Jin's voice in my skull like a curse.

"She'd rather be—fuck!" I slammed my fist against the dashboard. Again and again. "Kalel—"

"Don't."

Angelo gripped the steering wheel tighter but didn't say anything. I could feel the judgment radiating off him, but I didn't care. Jin's blood was still on my knuckles, but it wasn't enough. I'd left the pier without her. I let him get in my head. Because I saw something in his eyes I hadn't seen since before I took her—Hope. And that's what broke me most. That she might be giving him what she refused to give me.

When we got to the estate i walked straight to my office to get a drink then went to the living room.

By the time Angelo came in, the bottle was half empty. My shirt was unbuttoned. The living room lights were off, and I was slouched in the armchair, staring at nothing. Whiskey burned down my throat, but it didn't do what I needed it to. It didn't shut her face out of my head. It didn't erase the way she looked when she slept in my bed. Didn't silence the echo of her voice when she said, I don't want to marry you.

You broke her. I poured another glass.

"You're spiraling." Angelo's voice cut through the dark like a blade. He was leaning against the doorway, arms crossed, still dressed like he hadn't stopped working, because he hadn't. Because someone had to hold the empire together while I fell the fuck apart.

"I don't remember asking for your opinion," I muttered.

"No," he said. "You don't ask for much of anything anymore. You just demand." I looked up slowly.

"What did you just say?"

"I said," he snapped, stepping inside, "you've become everything

248

your father was, and worse. At least he had the decency to admit when he was being a bastard. You? You act like she owes you her love."

My breath caught.

I stood slowly, glass still in hand. "You work for me." I growled.

"No—I stood by you," he fired back. "I was your brother when no one else would be. But don't get it twisted, Kalel—just because I've fought beside you doesn't mean I'll follow you off a cliff."

"Watch your mouth."

"Or what?" His voice cracked. "You'll hit me? Hurt me? Kill me? Go ahead. Add me to the list of people you've destroyed."

I said nothing. He stepped closer, eyes blazing. "You're not the only one who lost her," he said. "I did too." That stopped me cold. "What?"

"I lost her," he repeated. "She was becoming family. I watched her soften you. I watched her try to love you, even when you made it impossible. Then I watched you rip her heart apart. You fucked it all up. Why? because you couldn't handle her being human? Being scared." The words sliced deep.

"She lied to me," I said quietly. "She kept the pregnancy from me—"

"Because you scare her!" Angelo shouted. "You think you own people, Kalel. You think love is something you can trap, or threaten, or chain. But it's not. And now she's gone. Because of you. No one else, but you." He said.

I was silence.

My throat was tight. My hands shook, but I couldn't let it show. Because if I did... if I let that crack open... I might never close it again. Angelo's voice softened—just enough to twist the knife.

"I loved her like a sister," he said. "And you pushed her out of this house like she was a problem to solve. Like she wasn't the only good thing you've ever had."

He turned away and just before he left the room, he added one final blow:

249

"You're not a king, Kalel. You're a scared boy with a crown made of ashes." And then he was gone.

Leaving me alone with the bottle, the silence, and the truth. That I fucked up. And now she is gone with Jin. The door slammed behind him. Suddenly, the silence didn't feel like control anymore. It felt like punishment. I stood in the center of the living room, glass shards at my feet, Angelo's words still bleeding through the air.

You scare her. You want control.

You're worse than your father.

I lost her too.

I couldn't breathe. My chest felt too tight. My throat felt raw. My hands ached from clenching too hard. I turned and stumbled down the hall. Past the library. Past the office. To the one room I hadn't walked into since she left.

Ours.

The bedroom door creaked open like it was mourning her too. Everything was still the same. Her hairbrush on the vanity. One of her necklaces draped across the nightstand. Her scent sweet, floral,and soft still clung to the sheets, and that was what broke me. I dropped to my knees. One hand clutched the edge of the bed. The other tangled in the blankets where she used to sleep. Where I used to hold her. Where she used to tremble in my arms and curse me, kiss me, need me.

Gone.

She was gone.

And I had no one to blame but myself. I buried my face into the sheets, chest heaving, the pain ripping through me in waves so deep I didn't recognize the sound coming out of me. It wasn't rage. It wasn't control. It was grief.

It was love, rotting from the inside out.

And for the first time in years, I didn't want to be Kalel Marchetti. I wanted to be someone she could've loved, but it was too late and I was still the villain.

Even when I'd give my life to be the one she ran to instead of from.

* * *

<u>Sabrina</u>

The sun had just started to dip below the skyline, casting everything in soft gold when I heard the door open.

"Jin?"

I walked out of the guest room barefoot, Jin's hoodie sleeves swallowed over my hands still warm from the shower, my hair wet at the ends. Jin stepped into the penthouse like he wasn't bleeding, but I saw it the bruises,the split lip, the slight wince in his left shoulder.

"Oh my God." I rushed to him. "What happened?"

He waved it off with a dramatic smirk. "Pier sparring match. I lost to concrete."

"Jin—"

He exhaled slowly. "Kalel found out you're with me." I froze. "He didn't come here," he added, voice quieter now. "Had Angelo set up a meeting first, but you know Kalel—he doesn't meet. He warns."

"And?" I ask part of me already knowing the answer.

"And I poked the bear." I touched his arm, gently. "He hit you?"

"Not before I hit him first." He tried to make it a joke, but there was a shadow in his eyes. Something unsettling. "He's not going to stop," I whispered.

"No. He's not." Jin agrees.

"Then I need to leave."

His eyes snapped to mine.

"I'm not putting you in danger, Jin. Not after this." I say. He studied me for a long moment, then agreed. "Okay," he said. "Then we leave tonight." Jin made a few calls and within an hour we were getting on a flight to the new safe house.

* * *

The new safe house was quieter. More remote. Tucked into a grove of pine trees near the mountains, with air that actually smelled like something real.

No traffic. No eyes.

Jin had gone overboard, of course—floor-to-ceiling windows, black-and-cream decor, a fireplace he absolutely did not know how to use without nearly burning the house down the first night.

It was... safe, but not safe from my thoughts. Not safe from the ache that hadn't left my chest since I walked away from Kalel and never looked back. It had been three months. Fourteen days of silence. Fourteen days without a phone call or a threat or a trace. Somehow, that scared me more.

I sat on the edge of the couch, staring out the window at nothing, one hand absentmindedly brushing over the slight curve of my stomach.

"You're brooding again," Jin's voice called from behind me. "I thought we agreed I'd be the dramatic one in this situationship." I turned my head. He was standing in the doorway of the art studio he'd set up in one of the spare rooms, sleeves rolled up, a paint smear already on his jaw.

"You're always the dramatic one," I muttered.

"And yet you're stealing my brand," he said with mock offense, sauntering over and plopping beside me. "You've been sulking for days. What's going on in that beautifully chaotic head of yours?"

I looked down. Then sighed. "You know what it is."

252

He tilted his head. "Kalel?"

"And what he did to you. Because of me." I say. Jin's smile faltered. Just a fraction, but then he leaned back, legs spread lazily, voice softer than I expected.

"I'm fine."

"You're still healing." I rebuttal.

"I've had worse. Once I dislocated my shoulder trying to recreate a Magic Mike move."

I snorted despite myself. "That's not the point." I say. Jin reaches out, nudging my arm. "Then what is?" He asks. I didn't answer. He watched me for a second. Then stood up. "Come on." He muses. I blinked. "Where?"

"To paint." he said like I should have known

"I don't—"

"Nope." He says, as he hold up a finger to shush me. "No excuses. No pouting. I have soda, wine, brushes, canvases, and enough passive-aggressive energy to create a masterpiece of emotional repression. Let's go." He says, as I stared at him. He arched a brow. "You've got all these feelings locked up in that pretty little head of yours, and it's not good for you. Or the baby."

My chest tightened. "I'm not an artist."

"Okay. I just pretend to be one. I paint the most when I'm heartbroken or overwhelmed or in need of an aesthetic Instagram post." He held out a hand. I looked at it for a while, then took it.

* * *

Twenty minutes later we were both covered in paint. Neither of us had touched the canvas seriously. "You're not supposed to throw paint, you maniac!" He yells. I laughed as he dodged behind the easel.

"Says who?" I laughed. "Jackson Pollock could never!" he shouted

"You just got paint on your eyebrow!"

"Adds to my charm!"

Eventually, the chaos slowed. We painted side-by-side. Jin painted something abstract and loud. Something beautiful. Me on the other hand, I something softer and smaller. Like I was afraid to take up space.

Jin noticed.

Of course he did.

"Let it go," he said gently, voice low now. "You don't have to hold it all together here." I stared at my brush. Then at the color on the canvas. My hand moved slower, more sure. I didn't realize I was crying until a tear splattered across the blue. I sniffed. Jin didn't say anything. He just kept painting.

And that—that—was why I was starting to feel safe with him. Not because he rescued me. Not because he fought for me, but because he didn't try to fix me.

He just let me be.

We painted for a while in comfortable silence, occasionally flicking color at each other like unsupervised children. Jin stood a few feet away, head tilted, staring at his finished canvas like it belonged in a museum.

"I think I just invented a new movement," he said solemnly. "Jinism. Bold. Raw. Unapologetically chaotic." I looked at his painting. Which was, in fact, just bold strokes of purple, black, and gold thrown together like his brain exploded.

I smirked. "Looks like a fever dream."

"And yet I can feel the jealousy radiating off you." He says.

I turned back to my own painting—softer lines, a stormy sky meeting calm ocean. Still unfinished.

"You know," he added dramatically, "some might say you're intimidated by my artistic genius."

"Some might also say you need to be humbled."

"Oh?" He looked up just as I dipped my brush in orange and flicked it at him. The paint landed square on his cheek. He blinked. Touched his face slowly.

"You've made a powerful enemy today."

"I'm shaking." I said through a smile. He lunged. I squealed and tried to run, but my socked feet slipped on the hardwood, and before I knew it—

Jin caught me and tickled me to the floor. I was breathless. Laughing. At some point Jin hovered over me, one hand pinning my wrist above my head, his other bracing against the floor beside me. His curls hung in his face, streaked with paint,

and his hoodie had slid up just enough to show a line of toned skin beneath. My breath caught. His did too. The laughter faded into something... quiet. Our eyes met. Neither of us moved. Then his gaze flicked to my lips and mine to his. The kiss wasn't soft. It wasn't planned.

It just happened—a crashing, breathless, paint-streaked kiss that felt like relief and tension and confusion all colliding at once. His hand tangled in my hair. Mine fisted in his hoodie. When he finally pulled back, he was breathless. So was I. He stared down at me for a beat, then whispered, "Shit." My heart pounded.

"Sorry," he added. "I was gonna say something chill, like, 'That was unexpected,' or, 'You taste like orange paint,' but instead... I think I'm catching feelings for you." My chest tightened. He smiled, softer now.

"Which is honestly terrifying, because you're hot, pregnant, emotionally complex, and you might shank me in my sleep. And yet... here we are." I didn't know what to say, because I liked him too.

I liked the way he made me laugh when I didn't think I could. I liked that he gave me space to fall apart. I liked that he didn't try to tame me.

But...I also remembered Kalel's voice. His hands. His rage. I knew he

255

wasn't done. Not yet. Still, lying there under Jin's weight, chest rising and falling beneath him, I let myself whisper the one truth I did know.

"I'm scared." I said. He didn't flinch instead he said. "I'll be strong for both of us. You just be here."

Chapter 31

Kalel

They were gone again. She was gone again. I wasn't angry. Anger was too soft. Too human. What I felt now? Was clarity. A silence in my chest that rang louder than any scream. Sabrina had made a choice. So had Jin. Now it was my turn.

I stepped into the back alley of a known safe house on the edge of the city—one of Jin's old drop spots. The man tied to the chair in front of me was bleeding from the mouth, his left eye nearly swollen shut.

I crouched beside him slowly, like we were having a quiet conversation. "You saw them leave," I said calmly. He shook his head. "I didn't, I swear—"

Bang.

The bullet ripped through his kneecap. He howled, tipping forward in the chair. "I'm not here to be lied to." I said. Angelo stood behind me, arms crossed, silent. Watching.

Judging.

But he didn't stop me, he knew better. I grabbed the man's face and forced him to look at me. "Where did they go?" I ask.

"I—I don't know—he said something about the coast, maybe—"

"Where?" I interrupt

"North—north of the city. A beach house—he's used it before. That's all I know, I swear—"

"Thank you." I say as I pulled the trigger. One shot between the eyes clean. I stood slowly, wiped the blood from my cheek, and turned to Angelo. "Burn the building." Angelo didn't move for a second. Then he nodded. He didn't speak, but he looked at me like he didn't recognize me anymore.

Good.

He wasn't supposed to. I wasn't Kalel anymore. I was the consequence.

* * *

Later that night we stopped a man outside a bar who'd once moved money for Jin. He denied knowing anything. I watched his eyes. His pulse. The way his voice trembled just slightly. He was lying. I pulled the knife from my coat.

"Wait—please—don't—"

The blade was under his chin before he could finish. "You're shaking," I said softly. "You shouldn't be scared. You should be terrified." And when he didn't talk? I slit his throat.

Angelo stepped back, breathing hard. "You're not giving them a chance," he muttered.

"They had one," I said, wiping the blade clean. "They chose wrong."

They think she's safe. They think hiding her behind false smiles and soft hands makes her untouchable, but I see her. In every shadow. In every nightmare. I see her sleeping in his arms. Smiling in his passenger seat. Laying in his bed like she isn't mine. Like I didn't build a world around her.

For her.

I didn't take her to ruin her. I took her because no one else deserved her, but if she wants to see what freedom looks like? I'll show her. I'll paint the streets red with every man who tries to protect her and when

I finally find her? She won't run again.

She won't have a chance to because I'll remind her who I am. And she'll never forget again. I stared at the paused frame on the screen in front of me. Jin's car. Pulling off a side road two towns north of the city. A blurry flash of dark hair in the passenger seat.

Sabrina.

"You sure it's them?" I asked. The hacker nodded, swallowing. "Yeah. I traced the burner phone to a tower near that range." I nodded once. Then pulled out my gun and shot him in the head. Angelo stepped back. "Fuck, Kalel"

"I told you," I said coldly, turning to face him. "Anyone who helps her disappears."

"Then why am I still breathing?" I ask.

"Because you still have use."

His jaw clenched, but he didn't argue. I stepped around the blood pooling beneath the hacker and opened the folder on the table. Property records. Supply drops. Cash withdrawals made by proxies tied to Jin's shell company.

He thought he could hide her in the trees? Make her smile? Make her laugh? Make her forget *me*?

No, no, no.

I didn't break her just to let someone else piece her back together.

She's mine, and if I have to take her again?

If I have to chain her to the fucking bed? So be it. Because this time? I'm not bringing her home. I'm keeping her.

* * *

Once we got to the next person who helped him take my wife, my fiancee away, the old man was already scared. He shook as he lit a cigarette with trembling fingers, like the flame might save him.

"I already told you—I didn't know who the girl was. I just sold him the cabin." He pleaded.

"Jin." He nodded quickly. "Yeah. Yeah. Jin." I looked around the shed. It's small and isolated. It reeking of dust and regret. The perfect place to make someone disappear. "You said the cabin was in Ridge Valley," I murmured.

He nodded again, smoke curling up past his sunken eyes. "That's right. North road. Past mile marker sixteen. Secluded. Real quiet." He says.

I stared at him then smiled. "Thank you."

His expression faltered. "Wait, so I'm good to go?"

I took the cigarette from his hand, lifted it to my lips, took a drag, and blew the smoke into his face. Then shot him in the chest. He slumped to the ground before he could even scream. I dropped the cigarette on his chest. "Should've asked for more."

Later that night The map was in front of me. Ridge Valley. Mile marker sixteen. The cabin. I tapped the page twice with my finger, then looked at Angelo.

"Go." He raised a brow. "You want me to bring her back?"

"No," I said. "I want you to watch."

"Kalel—"

"Find them. Follow them. Watch them." I demand.

"And when I see them?" Angelo questioned.

"You know what to do."

I stood by the fire, watching the logs crackle as Angelo stepped into the room. He didn't speak at first. He didn't have to. I could feel it in the silence. "Well?" I said quietly. "They're there." He paused. "And?" I ask, waiting for him to continue.

"They kissed." He says and my world tilted. The blood in my ears turned to thunder. "They kissed?" I repeated.

260

Angelo nodded once. "She didn't stop him."

The fire snapped. So did I. I grabbed the nearest bottle from the shelf and hurled it across the room. Glass shattered against the wall, liquid spilling like a wound. "He touched her?"

"Yes." Angelo said.

"She let him?" I ask, not trusting what I heard because that couldn't be right.

"Yes." He said.

Something inside me split, not cracked. Split kike a dam collapsing. The last shred of mercy I had for the world burned in that single word. "She's mine," I whispered. "She's mine."

"Kalel—"

"I want his heart on a fucking plate." I demand. She kissed him and something inside me died. I didn't scream again. Didn't throw anything. I didn't rage like I did when Angelo first told me.

No. I went quiet. I sat on the edge of my bed in the room that still smelled like her, still had her brush on the vanity, her perfume on the sheets, and I stared at the wall until the light outside disappeared and darkness swallowed the room.

She kissed him.

After everything. After I tore my soul open to protect her. After I bled for her. After I begged her to stay. She kissed him. And she smiled. She smiled like she hadn't watched me break for her. Like she hadn't buried her heart in mine and set it on fire before walking away. I clenched then unclenched my hand. Breathe. But I couldn't feel it, any of it. Not the grief. Not the betrayal. Not even the rage. Just... Silence.

That terrifying silence in my chest. The kind I hadn't felt since I was a boy. Since my mother died. Since I stopped letting myself cry. I stood up and walked into the bathroom. The mirror caught my reflection. I didn't recognize the man staring back.

Eyes hollow. Jaw clenched. A monster in a silk shirt and somehow?

That made it easier, because if she was going to kiss him like I never existed—

Then I'd erase the man she used to know

* * *

A few hours later Angelo stood at the counter, arms crossed, watching me pour another glass of whiskey. "You're really doing this?" he asked quietly. I didn't answer. "You're shutting down." Still nothing. "Kalel."

"I'm done," I said finally. His face shifted. "Done with what?"

"Feeling." I drank. Let it burn. "If she wants to see what I'm capable of without the pieces she softened, then she'll see." He stepped forward. "Don't do this."

"She broke me."

"You're doing this to yourself."

"No," I said, voice low. "She did this the second she let someone else touch what was mine." He stared at me and I knew what he saw. Not the man he grew up beside. Not the friend. Not even the leader, but a weapon.

A ghost; and I didn't care. Because the man who loved her? He died the second she kissed Jin. Now? All that's left is what she made of me.

It was 3:47 a.m. And I hadn't slept a second. I lay in the middle of the bed—our bed—my eyes burning as I stared at the ceiling, the shadows, the nothingness pressing in around me. My body was still, but my mind? Ripping itself apart.

She kissed him.

I could still see it—vivid, branded behind my eyelids. Her fingers curled around his sleeve. The way she tilted her head slightly. The soft look in her eyes before her lips met his. What's worse—how she didn't pull away.

She didn't stop it. She wanted it. She let him.

I turned my head slowly toward her side of the bed. The sheets were still slightly creased, like her ghost had been lying there just minutes ago. I used to hold her here. Used to run my hands down her back until she fell asleep.

Used to feel her breath on my chest, her body curling into mine like I was her home. Now I was just a place she ran from. And he—he—was where she rested her heart. I clenched my jaw. Tried to close my eyes. They snapped open again. The kiss. The smile after.

Her smile.

The one she gave to me in pieces. The one she gave him whole. I sat up slowly. Swung my legs over the edge of the bed. My bare feet hit the cold floor.

I didn't move.

Didn't breathe. Just sat in the silence. And let the grief turn to fire. Let the fire turn to ice. Let the ice seep into my blood, because if I didn't? I'd feel everything and feeling would break me worse than she ever could.

* * *

An Hour Later, I stood in the hallway. Lights dim. Everyone's asleep except me. I walked into the security room, motioned the tech out with a single look, and pulled up the last images Angelo sent. There they were. Sabrina and Jin. Eating dinner on the porch. Her curled up in his hoodie. Laughing. And then—The kiss again. I stared at the screen. At her soft smile. The way she looked at him like she was finally safe.

Like she finally had peace and it made me hate her for a second. Hate her for making me love her so completely. Hate her for choosing someone else to be gentle with. I leaned forward slowly, resting my knuckles on the console. Then whispered, "Sleep while you can, kitten."

"Because when I come for you..." My eyes stayed locked on hers. "...you won't wake up in his arms ever again."

Chapter 32

Sabrina

It had been a perfect day. The kind that felt like it didn't belong to me. We'd gone into the tiny nearby town—Jin insisted on getting ice cream even though it was freezing, and I gave in because he made puppy eyes and said "I'm deprived, Sabrina. Do you want that on your conscience?"

We strolled past little bookshops and antique stores. He made me laugh so hard I nearly dropped my cone. And for a while, just a little while—I forgot the world outside existed. I forgot Kalel existed.

We pulled up to the cabin just before sunset, the trees glowing amber and gold in the fading light. Jin unlocked the front door first, waving me in like a royal guest. "After you, my tragic queen." He said.

I rolled my eyes with a smile and stepped inside— And stopped. There, on the couch, arms resting on his thighs, eyes dark and unmoving Sat Kalel. The room went still. My heart plummeted. He stared at me. Then his voice cut through the silence like a blade.

"Time to come home, Sabrina." He said.

I froze.

Jin stepped up beside me. "No," I said quietly. "I'm not going anywhere with you." Kalel's jaw clenched, a flicker of something terrifying in his eyes. His gaze shifted to Jin. And that's when I felt it. The shift. The storm. Kalel stood. "You kissed her?" Kalel asked. Jin

265

tilted his head, arms crossed. "Pretty sure she kissed me back." He responded, and that was it. The next few second was a blur of fists and fury. Kalel lunged. Jin met him halfway. This wasn't a warning. This was war. Bodies slammed into walls. Glass shattered. A lamp hit the floor.

Jin got a hit to Kalel's ribs. Kalel grabbed him by the collar and drove a punch into his stomach. I screamed."Stop it!" Neither of them listened. Kalel went for another hit—rage in every movement— And that's when I stepped between them.

"Kalel, no!" I yelled

He froze. His fist stopped inches from my face, breathing hard. Chest heaving. His eyes locked on mine. Not rage now. Not fury. Just hurt. Real. Raw. Gutting. "You're protecting him?" he said, voice barely above a whisper. I swallowed.

"Kalel..."

His jaw twitched. His eyes burned. "You're protecting him?" he repeated, louder this time. "You're mine. My Fiancee. The mother of my child." He took a step forward. I didn't give in.

"You were supposed to love me, Sabrina."

"You tried to own me," I whispered. His face cracked. He looked at me like I'd just put a knife in his chest. Maybe I had, but no matter what I said next, I knew—This was the moment that would change everything.

The room spun. I didn't even get a word out. One second I was trying to breathe. Next, my legs went numb. My vision blurred, pressure building behind my eyes, like the air was too thick, like my body wasn't mine anymore.

"Sabrina?" Jin's voice.

Far away and muffled. My chest squeezed. My knees buckled and then I was falling. But I didn't hit the floor. Someones arms caught me. I blinked once. His face swam in front of mine.

Kalel?

He was shouting. I think; But I couldn't hear the words anymore. Only the pounding in my ears. Only the panic clawing at the edge of my fading mind. His hands cupped my face. His lips moved.

"Stay with me, kitten. Stay awake—please." Kalel pleaded. I tried, but the dark pulled harder. And this time, I didn't have the strength to fight it.

* * *

Kalel

She collapsed in my arms, one second she was fire. Next, she was cold. Her skin was clammy. Her breathing was shallow. Her lips pale. I didn't think. I just carried her. To the car. To the hospital. Through the fucking storm in my chest that made it feel like I couldn't breathe until she did.

The doctor's voice blurred in the background. Words like dehydrated and stress-induced episode and we stabilized her, but none of it mattered until I saw her eyes open. Until I saw color return to her face. Until I knew she was going to live.

I sat in the chair beside her hospital bed, staring at her hand resting in mine. She looked so small. So fucking breakable and for the first time in my life, I didn't want to own her. I just wanted her to be okay. The door opened behind me. I didn't look up.

"I brought coffee," Jin said softly.

"Not thirsty."

He stayed quiet for a second, then sank into the chair across from me. We sat like that. Not talking. Just watching her. Finally, he asked, "Do you really love her?" Jin asked.

"Yes." The word was a growl. A prayer. A curse.

Jin exhaled "I think I do too." That made me look at him.

267

He didn't care though. "She already chose me," he said quietly. "You know that." I looked away, jaw tightening.

"I didn't want to fall for her," he said, voice steady despite the anguish in his eyes. "I didn't plan to. But it happened."

I clenched my fists so tightly it hurt. "If you're here to rub it in—"

"I'm not," Jin says cutting me off gently. "I'm saying that if I step away... you need to give her something real. Not obsession and not fear."

"I will," I said fiercely. "I'll change. I'll give her anything. Everything."

"You always say that." He rebuttals.

"I mean it," I growled, meeting his eyes. He studied me carefully for a long moment, then slowly nodded.

"She can't handle this war between us. Not like this."

"I know." I say, looking at Sabrina.

He stood slowly, hesitating as if his own legs didn't want to carry him forward. "I'm walking away," he said finally. "Not for you, but for her." He turned toward the bed. I watched him kneel beside her and gently take her hand, cradling it as if it were precious porcelain.

"Hey," he whispered softly, stroking her skin with his thumb. "There she is. The strongest girl I've ever met." He says. Her eyelids fluttered, barely opening. Her breath shuddered. He smiled down at her, but his eyes were glassy with unshed emotion. Slowly, he leaned forward, kissing her forehead like it was the last chance he'd ever have.

"I love you, Sabrina," he murmured, voice rough with quiet pain. He closed his eyes, resting his forehead gently against hers, breathing her in one final time.

"Always remember that." Her lips trembled, eyes flickering open fully this time, searching his face in quiet panic.

"Jin...?" Her voice cracked, weak and fragile. "W-what do you mean?" She asked.

His breath hitched, shoulders visibly tightening, but he managed a faint, gentle smile. "I just...have to make an important call," he whispered, voice barely holding steady. "I'll be back."

She tried to hold his hand tighter, eyes pleading, confusion swimming beneath the surface.

"Don't go," she whispered, voice breaking softly. A single tear slipped silently down her cheek.

My heart twisted violently. Jin leaned forward, pressing a tender, lingering kiss to her knuckles. His lips brushed her skin reverently, as if savoring a final goodbye.

"I'll always love you, cutie," he whispered, voice shaking now. "Even when you don't see me."

He stood, turning away swiftly as if he couldn't bear another second without breaking. He paused at the door, fist clenched tightly, struggling visibly to keep himself from turning back around.

A long, shaky breath left him. Then he walked away without looking back. Leaving me sitting there.

Heart breaking.

And for once? I didn't stop him, because he gave her something I never could. Peace.

The room was painfully quiet after Jin left, the weight of his absence heavier than any silence. Sabrina stared at the door, tears pooling in her eyes, slipping down her cheeks in quiet surrender. Slowly, I leaned forward, gently brushing away the tears with my thumb. Her gaze shifted to me, heartbreak shimmering in her eyes.

"He really left," she whispered hoarsely. "For you," I said, voice raw. "Because he loves you that much." She took a shuddering breath, closing her eyes briefly. When she opened them again, the intensity of her sadness nearly broke me. "What happens now?" she asked softly.

"I'm taking you home," I said quietly.

Her eyes narrowed slightly, irritation flashing across her face, replacing the sorrow.

"It's not like I have a choice anymore," she muttered bitterly. The words cut deeper than any blade ever could, breaking something inside me. I swallowed hard, my throat tight. "Sabrina—" I started, but she turned her face away, refusing to look at me, her silence speaking louder than words ever could.

* * *

Sabrina

The flight was silent. Kalel didn't speak, and I didn't dare look at him. I stared out the window, clouds drifting beneath us, wondering if this emptiness was what disappearing felt like. When we landed, the silence lingered, thickening like fog.

A car waited, sleek and ominous. I sat in the backseat beside him, curled against the door, my body angled away, building an invisible wall between us. He didn't try to touch me. Didn't try to speak. Maybe he felt it too—that something inside me had dimmed, leaving behind nothing but ashes.

When the car pulled into the driveway, my chest tightened painfully. The gates opened slowly, revealing the mansion bathed in golden lights and deep shadows. It didn't look like home. It looked like a cage.

The car stopped, and Kalel stepped out first. I hesitated, suddenly exhausted, then sighed heavily and followed him. Every step up the stairs felt heavier than the last, as if chains were wrapping around me.

He opened the door. I walked inside without glancing at him. The air smelled familiar. Clean. Rich. Expensive.

And suffocating.I didn't wait for him. I started moving toward the guest room. I couldn't—wouldn't—sleep in his bed tonight.

"Sabrina." His voice stopped me. I turned slowly.

Kalel stood in the foyer, shadows carved sharply across his features, his eyes watching me with a quiet intensity. "I know this isn't how you wanted it," he said carefully. "But I meant what I said. I want to make you happy." I stared at him, weary and numb. "And you think dragging me back here after I collapsed is the way to do that?" His jaw clenched briefly. "I brought you home to protect you." I said.

"No," I replied softly. "You brought me back to control me."

He took a step forward, desperation threading through his careful composure. "I'm trying. I'm trying to do this right." He said.

"Then let me go."

Silence filled the space between us, thick and final. His eyes darkened, and tension radiated from every muscle in his body. But he didn't move, didn't speak. He just stood there, watching me as if I was slipping through his fingers because I was. Without another word, I turned and walked away. I didn't look back.

Chapter 33

Sabrina

I didn't trust the quiet in me when I stormed down the hall, fists clenched, heart hammering violently in my chest. I couldn't cry, I wouldn't. Not again. The guest room door slammed behind me, shaking the walls. My back hit the wood, breaths ragged, vision blurring. I hate this house. Hate these walls, this suffocating silence— how everything here seemed to swallow me whole, stealing pieces I'd never get back.

I stepped toward the bed, but before I could move another inch—The door opened. I spun around, anger scorching my throat. "I—" But the words died instantly, because Kalel was already sinking to his knees. Right there, at my feet.

I froze, my heart skipping painfully. He didn't push. He lingered looking up at me through eyes so red and raw that I felt them carving into my chest. Eyes that for once didn't mask the torment I always sensed but never saw.

"Sabrina," he whispered, voice fracturing like he hadn't spoken in a lifetime. Then his head dropped.

His broad shoulders shook uncontrollably, fingers gripping his dark hair in desperation. He looked so unsteady, so utterly broken, I thought he might shatter right there on the floor. "I can't—" His voice splintered, falling apart. "I can't fucking do this anymore."

"Kalel" My voice shook, a plea and a warning all in one. He lifted his eyes again, and what I saw stripped the air from my lungs.

"I can't keep pretending," he rasped, anguish staining every word. "Pretending like I'm okay with you walking out that door, acting like I'm not dying every time you look at me like you wish I was someone else." He said as he pressed his hands against the floor as if trying to steady himself against an invisible storm.

"You can scream at me, Sabrina. You can fucking hate me, hit me, tear me apart—but please," his voice cracked again, and my stomach twisted painfully, "please don't leave me again. I— I won't survive it. I swear, I won't." his voice cracked.

My legs trembled. Breath halted painfully in my chest. He stared at me, eyes glistening, vulnerable, and breaking with every heartbeat. "I love you," he whispered, voice shredded raw. "I love you so fucking much, Sabrina. It's eating me alive. It's killing me every single day." Tears welled, thick and shimmering in his eyes—but they didn't fall, because Kalel never cried. Kalel bled, Kalel shattered, but tears? Never.

His chest rose and fell raggedly as he struggled for air. "I haven't slept in weeks," he admitted, voice strained, painfully hollow. "How could I sleep knowing someone else gets to see your smiles, hear your laughter— feel your warmth? Knowing you were breathing easier without me?" He said as he reached toward me, hand trembling violently, stopping inches away. Like he wasn't allowed. Like he had lost that right forever.

"You're the only thing—the only fucking good thing—I've ever wanted for myself. The only one who's ever seen past the darkness. And when you left..." His voice faded, the silence choking him, the truth bleeding him dry. Everything inside me fractured. I cracked wide open and I hated myself for how much it hurt to watch him suffer.

His voice dropped, haunted and thick with grief. "Everything went dark again, Sabrina. Darker than before. I didn't know how deep it could go until you showed me—until I lost you." A single tear finally broke free, sliding down his face like a silent confession.

"I'm sorry," he choked out, his head bowing in surrender. "I'm sorry for hurting you, for breaking everything good in you. For loving you too selfishly and too violently to keep you safe." Silence echoed between us like an endless ache.

I wanted to scream at him. To hit him. To run far away, but I didn't. I couldn't move because, God help me, some sick, twisted part of me still loved him. Still wanted to wipe that tear away and pull him into my arms. And that realization was the cruelest wound of all. Slowly and painfully, I forced my shaking legs to move, sinking down in front of him until we were eye level.

"Kalel" I breathed softly, heart aching, voice breaking. My fingertips brushed his jaw, felt the harsh tremors beneath his skin. "If you want me—if you really want me back—you have to earn me. You have to prove it." I said

His eyes met mine, filled with desperate hope, determination sparking to life through the pain. "I will," he vowed hoarsely, fiercely. "Whatever it takes, Sabrina. Whatever it takes." After everything, the tears wouldn't stop. Not loud, desperate sobs. Just quiet, relentless grief that burned behind my eyes and settled like lead in my chest.

I laid in the bed and I curled into the sheets, holding my stomach protectively, face buried in the pillow scented faintly with lavender. It wasn't Kalel's pillow, wasn't his bed—that was deliberate. Yet the ache I felt wasn't for him.

It was for Jin.

For the teasing smile that always softened his features. For the way his eyes held mine, making me feel seen, truly seen, in a world intent on breaking me. For the silent goodbye he gave, without ever speaking the words.

"I love you, Sabrina. Always remember that." I did. I always would.

It was agony, because Jin was gone, and he wasn't coming back. Grief didn't scream—it sank. Slow and deep, suffocating from within.

By sunrise, I was spent. Body heavy, limbs numb. With a shaky sigh, I pushed myself up and stumbled toward the door, needing water, air—anything to feel alive again. But when I opened it, I froze.

Kalel was slumped against the wall, head tilted back, lips slightly parted, breathing evenly in sleep. My heart twisted painfully at the sight. He looked broken, exhausted—as if he hadn't known peace in months.

Carefully, quietly, I knelt beside him, noticing a faint bruise on his hand, likely from the fight with Jin. When I touched his shoulder, his eyes flew open, wild and alert, before softening immediately at the sight of me. "Sabrina," he rasped, voice rough with sleep. "Are you okay?" He asked.

I withdrew my hand quickly. "Shouldn't I be asking you that?"

He blinked, trying to separate dreams from reality. "Didn't mean to fall asleep here," he muttered, embarrassed. "I just... couldn't leave you."

"You need real sleep," I whispered.

He shook his head, honesty raw in his voice. "I can't sleep without you, Sabrina. I haven't slept properly since you left—not even once." The confession hit me harder than I wanted it to. "I don't think that's a good idea," I murmured.

nodded stiffly, acceptance heavy in his eyes. " I get it—"

"I'll stay," I interrupted softly. "Just until you fall asleep." Relief filled his eyes, painful in its intensity. Without touching, without speaking, we lay together, separated by an invisible barrier of pain and unresolved words. Soon, Kalel's breathing deepened, sleep finally claiming him. I watched him, heart heavy. He looked peaceful in sleep, yet it only reminded me how complicated things had become. Quietly, I slipped away.

* * *

In the bathroom, hot water cascaded over my skin, scalding grief and confusion from my bones. Jin's absence remained a brutal ache, but Kalel's quiet vulnerability unsettled me more. I wasn't supposed to feel safe near him. Yet I did—and I despised myself for it. After the shower, I studied my reflection in the fogged mirror. Still hollow, still hurting, but somehow stronger than yesterday. I dressed in simple, fitted clothes and opened the bedroom door again to find Kalel awake, sitting on the bed's edge, shirtless and disheveled.

Without a word, I let my gaze linger deliberately over his form, slowly watching heat spark in his eyes. I smirked softly and walked away. Heading toward the kitchen when I collided with Angelo.

"Dang, Sabrina," he breathed, steadying me gently. "Warn a guy next time." I laughed weakly. "I need food before I commit homicide." He chuckled, eyes gentle. "You look better."

"Define better." I said squinting my eyes

"Less ghost, more badass menace."I smiled faintly, peeling the banana he handed me. A quiet moment passed before Angelo spoke again, sincerity evident.

"I missed you, Knight."

My chest tightened, and I nodded softly. "Missed you too." Silence stretched heavily between us. Then, carefully, Angelo asked, "Are you okay?" I hesitated. "I don't know. I feel bad for hating him, but he hurt me so much." Angelo's nod was understanding. "You're allowed to feel both." He said.

I swallowed hard. "He took everything from me. My choices, my freedom, my life. But then I see him, and he looks just as broken as I feel, and I hate myself for caring."

"Knight," Angelo said gently, eyes compassionate, "you loved him. Maybe part of you always will. That doesn't make you weak." Tears slipped free, hot and relentless. "I just want peace," I whispered. "For myself. For my baby." Angelo hugged me tight, his voice firm. "Then let us help you find it. Whatever it takes." A quiet, familiar voice from behind made me stiffen.

Slowly, I turned. Kalel. He stood in the doorway, barefoot, shadows lingering beneath his eyes, his powerful frame tense and still—as if one wrong move might shatter something fragile. But it was the raw, unguarded longing etched across his face that nearly stole my breath.

"I didn't mean to interrupt," he said quietly, voice barely audible, like a whisper begging permission to exist.

Angelo glanced between us, sensing the weight of unspoken things. He gently squeezed my shoulder. "I'll give you two some space."

He stepped out leaving us alone. Again.

"I don't know how to trust you anymore," I whispered, voice trembling. "You broke me." Regret flashed in his eyes, raw and unfiltered. "I know. And I'll spend every day making it right, if you'll let me. Even if it takes a lifetime."

His sincerity made my heart ache in a way that was almost unbearable. "Let him try, Kitten," Angelo murmured softly. "You deserve peace."

I look away, swallowing the lump in my throat. "It's not that easy." Kalel took a cautious step forward, voice gentle yet firm. "Nothing worth having ever is. But you're worth everything. And I'll prove it to you—no matter how long it takes."

Kalel moves toward me, cautiously as if I might bolt if he moved too quickly. "I just wanted to say... I'm sorry. Again."

I didn't respond. Didn't move. His gaze locked with mine, pleading. "Not just for what I said—but for how it made you feel. You never deserved any of it." I looked away, blinking back tears.

"You made me feel like I didn't belong to myself anymore," I whispered. He flinched visibly, as if my words were blades slicing into him. "I know," he said roughly. "And I'll regret that for the rest of

277

my life."

My arms crossed tightly around myself, battling between screaming and breaking down into sobs. He took another careful step forward, eyes swimming with regret. "There's something else..." he exhaled shakily. "I need you to know—I'm happy about the baby." I blinked, caught off guard. His gaze lowered reverently to my stomach, as though it was his lifeline, the only thing anchoring him.

"I spent my whole life terrified of becoming like my father," he confessed, voice breaking slightly. "Cold, cruel, and empty." He pushed a hand roughly through his hair, eyes shadowed by his own fears. "When I found out you were pregnant... for the first time, I didn't feel like a monster. I felt like maybe, I could be more."

My chest tightened painfully.

His eyes searched mine desperately, open wounds begging for healing. "I know I haven't earned a second chance. But I'll spend every moment trying anyway." He said.

I swallowed hard, trembling slightly.

"I don't know if I can forgive you." I said as I sigh looking at the floor.

"I'm not asking you to. Not yet."

"What are you asking, then?" My voice shook, vulnerable and exhausted. His expression softened into something heartbreaking. "Just don't give up on me." And somehow, that simple plea unraveled me more than anything else ever could. I stared at him, fighting the burn behind my eyes, my voice cracking as I spoke. "Don't."

Kalel froze, confusion and pain washing across his face. My heart thundered in my chest. "Don't stand there telling me you're happy—not after what you said."

"What—?" he began, bewildered. "You called our baby a bastard." Shock bled through his expression. "Sabrina, I—"

"You said it like it meant nothing," I snapped. "Like it wasn't real.

Like it wasn't precious." He opened his mouth, but no words came. "I lost a baby before," I choked out, my voice barely above a whisper. The admission hung in the air between us, heavy and painful.

"I was 10 weeks along. Then one day, when I woke up unable to breathe, throwing up blood." I trembled, feeling the ghost of that agony grip me all over again. "HG. I didn't even know what it was until it robbed me of everything."

Kalel stepped instinctively closer. I moved back. He stopped immediately, his eyes shadowed with grief. "I saw the heartbeat," I whispered, throat tight, tears slipping freely down my face. "And then it was gone." Kalel's jaw tightened, anguish darkening his eyes.

"I never told anyone. Not even the bastard who knocked me up and walked away when things got difficult." My voice cracked. "I didn't think I'd ever get another chance. And when I did—I was terrified. I still am."

I met his gaze, raw and unfiltered. "When I heard you say that word—that cruel, careless fucking word—it broke something in me." I said. Pain shattered his composure completely. Kalel closed the space between us slowly, approaching as if I might shatter into pieces.

"I didn't mean it that way," he said desperately, voice ragged. "Sabrina, I swear. I was hurting, angry, and ignorant. If I had known—"

"You think that makes it hurt less?" I interrupt.

"No," he breathed, agony etched in every line of his face. "No, it doesn't. But I'm sorry." His voice cracked, raw with regret. "I'm so fucking sorry." I saw the tears pooling in his eyes. Yet I couldn't let it go—not yet.

"I can't lose this baby," I whispered, heartbroken. "Not again." Kalel reached for me again, slower, gentler. And this time, I didn't move away. His palm touched my stomach—warm, tender, reverent—and I watched as his eyes closed briefly, as if trying to memorize the feeling.

"You won't lose this one," he whispered fervently, looking back up at me, eyes blazing with fierce determination. "I promise, Sabrina—I'll do everything in my power to protect you both."

In his eyes, I saw a vulnerability I'd never imagined possible from him—the boy hidden beneath the hardened man, desperate for redemption, for a chance to love something right and for a moment, a brief, fragile heartbeat—I almost believed him. His touch lingered, imprinting warmth onto my skin even after he slowly drew back, but the weight of his apology, of his grief, was suffocating, overwhelming. "I... I need to go," I whispered, suddenly unable to bear any more.

Kalel's eyes flared with urgency. "Sabrina—"

"Don't." My voice was soft, yet firm. I stepped back, retreating from the ache of his gaze. Not because I wanted to hurt him—but because the pain, the hope, the raw vulnerability, were too much to handle.

Turning away, I head to the room without another word. With every step, my heart fractured just a little bit more.

I closed the door softly behind me, the quiet click echoing in the silence that enveloped the space. Leaning against the cool wood, I shut my eyes tightly, breathing in slow, deliberate breaths, trying to steady the trembling in my chest. The warmth of his gaze lingered, a phantom touch that traced invisible paths along my skin. It wasn't fair—none of this was fair.

* * *

After a moment, I pushed away from the door and stepped further into the room. Familiar surroundings, once comforting, now felt foreign and accusatory. My gaze caught on small gestures, subtle tokens scattered around, each one a silent message I wasn't ready to decipher.

At first, I thought it was guilt.

The flowers in the hallway. The fresh clothes folded neatly at the edge of my bed. My tea, always hot and waiting when I woke, sweetened exactly how I liked it even though I'd never told him.

Guilt. That's all it was. Or so I kept telling myself.

But then it continued.

The first time I caught him, he was kneeling in the garden, dirt coating his hands, sweat soaking through his shirt. I didn't even know Kalel knew how to plant things. I stood frozen, watching him carefully settle lavender into the soil as if it were glass.

He didn't acknowledge my presence, and I didn't speak. Maybe he knew I was there, maybe not. The next morning, the scent of lavender greeted me as I stepped outside.

Another night, insomnia drove me into the kitchen. There he was—barefoot, his back turned to me, silently baking the shortbread cookies I loved.

From scratch.

He handed me a warm cookie, brushed a soft kiss atop my head, and walked away. I sat at the counter for fifteen minutes, pulse erratic, pretending my heart hadn't just shattered and rearranged itself. Every time my gaze lingered on something longer than five seconds, it appeared in my room. A book. A fuzzy robe. The lip gloss I lost weeks ago—replaced without comment.

I never asked and He never explained.

Then came the dog.

A casual remark about wanting one—nothing serious. Two days later, a floppy-eared rescue mutt with a crooked tail appeared in the sun room alongside a note:

"He bites everyone but me. Figured you'd relate." I say jokingly. I named him Chaos and Kalel calls him our son.

He started reading. I found his bookmarks scattered through every romance novel I'd left behind—highlighted passages, notes in the margins, written questions like love letters he never dared to send.

"Is this how she wants to be loved?" "Would she ever let me touch her like this?" I read his handwriting and had to physically lie down to breathe. Partially because it was funny but mostly because it was sweet.

Every night, he stayed outside my door. Not to guard me. Not to listen.

Just to be close.

One night at 2 a.m., I found him half-asleep on the floor, head resting against the wall, hands uncertain in his lap. I asked him why without looking up, he quietly confessed, "Because I miss hearing your voice, even when you're cursing me." I closed the door and cried until dawn. Kalel doesn't say "I'm sorry" with words. He apologizes through actions. Through patience. Through restraint.

Through holding his love like a knife, cautiously waiting until I'm ready to be touched again.

Maybe I shouldn't forgive him. Maybe hatred should still hold my heart.

But I saw him in our babies unfinished nursery, gently cradling a baby book, mouthing the words to himself—slowly, trying to learn something he never thought he'd need to know.

And I knew he wasn't fighting for forgiveness. He didn't push. He was fighting to become better.

For me. For us.

And as my heart quietly drifted back home, I realized I didn't know how to keep hating him anymore.

Chapter 34

Kalel

She hadn't looked me in the eyes in three months, not really. Not like she used to.

Not like when I remembered. She ate more now—barely—but each bite was quiet. She moved around the house like a shadow, a ghost haunting a place she once loved and I despised myself for it. I hated the version of me that dimmed her brightness, but hating myself wouldn't fix her.

So I started small.

That night, I sat alone in my office, illuminated only by the blue glow of my laptop screen, typing words I never imagined I'd search.

"Hyperemesis gravidarum – making her feel safe."

"Supporting pregnant partners through trauma."

"Regaining trust after emotional wounds."

I read until the letters blurred, and exhaustion blurred my edges. I learned which scents unsettled her stomach, which foods might soothe, which vitamins could stay down. Five different pregnancy-safe teas arrived the next day, each carefully selected for nausea, sleep, and comfort.

The following morning, I purged every scented candle from the house and replaced them with unscented ivory pillars. I instructed the kitchen staff to avoid garlic altogether. My cologne, the one she'd once said she loved, disappeared into the bottom drawer.

It wasn't enough, but it was a start.

Days later, I watched her quietly pause by an open window overlooking the garden. It was brief—a hesitant glance, almost accidental, but I saw it.

Her fingertips gently pressed against the glass as she took in the lilies and roses the gardener had planted earlier that week. And for the briefest heartbeat, a whisper of a smile curved her lips. It pierced something deep inside me. I knew then exactly what I had to do.

* * *

Three days had passed before I stood at her bedroom door, palms damp, pulse hammering through my veins. Every instinct screamed I was risking too much, too soon. But Sabrina was worth every risk. With a gentle knock, I kept my voice careful, unassuming.

"Sabrina?"

No answer.

"I... I have something to show you." I said. Silence lingered like a breath held, but then the door cracked open, just enough to let her cautious gaze meet mine. Those hazel eyes were wary and distant—yet there was something else, something hopeful.

"Do you trust me?" I asked softly.

She didn't answer with words, but she allowed me to gently cover her eyes with one hand. The scent of her shampoo stirred memories I ached to relive, yet I remained careful, deliberately guiding her barefoot down the hallway.

Her slender fingers curled into my forearm, hesitantly but grounding. I treasured the weight of her hand, a quiet reminder that she hadn't entirely given up.

My heart was a wild drum by the time we reached the courtyard. I stopped in front of the carefully planned surprise and whispered, voice rough with nerves, "Okay. Open your eyes."

As soon as she did, Sabrina's breath caught, eyes widening at the spectacle before her.

I had transformed an entire section of the estate into her own private garden. Rows upon rows of lilies, roses, and fragrant lavender stretched elegantly across the grounds. Stone pathways twisted gently between blooms, guiding her steps through colors of delicate blush, pure white, deep violet, and muted gold. Lavender shrubs lined the borders, their gentle fragrance perfuming the air, offering comfort and tranquility.

Alive.

Warm and beautiful. Just like her.

Her lips parted in awe, her eyes brightening with unshed tears. "Kalel.... how did you...?"

"I saw you," I admitted quietly, chest tightening with vulnerability. "When the gardener planted those flowers near the window. You stopped and smiled."

Her gaze swung to mine, startled by the realization.

"I never forgot," I said, throat tight with sincerity. "My mind forgets many things. Horrible things. Painful things, but never you. Not the way your laugh lights up the room. Not the way your presence fills empty spaces. And never the way you looked at those flowers—as if they were the first beautiful thing you'd allowed yourself to see in far too long."

A tear slipped down her cheek, glittering in the sunlight. My fingers twitched with the urge to wipe it away, but I stayed still, unwilling to push her further than she was ready to go.

"Thank you," she whispered finally, a genuine, breathtaking smile illuminating her face. And for the first time in forever, I dared to hope that maybe, just maybe, we hadn't completely broken after all.

She held my gaze a moment longer, the fragile intimacy between us lingering like a delicate thread, easily snapped but desperately precious. Eventually, she looked away, her lashes casting faint shadows across her cheeks. With a gentle nod, she turned, moving slowly down the hallway, the quiet echo of her footsteps resonating softly, each step drawing her away yet somehow closer to me.

I stayed there, rooted in place, heart pounding unevenly as I watched her retreat. My breath hitched with the sudden realization of just how deeply she'd embedded herself into my very being. A quiet hope stirred within me, cautious but undeniable, threading its way into the spaces between my fears and regrets.

When Sabrina stepped quietly into our room, my heart stopped. She stood there, hesitant, uncertainty shadowing her eyes, hand lingering on the doorknob like she might turn around at any moment, but she didn't. She closed the door softly behind her and crossed the room without a word.

I didn't dare breathe too deeply, didn't risk breaking whatever fragile peace had brought her back to me tonight. Instead, I watched her silently, my pulse thrumming with cautious hope.

Without meeting my gaze, she slipped beneath the covers, curling into the sheets with a quiet sigh. My heart thundered in my chest, relief and joy flooding through me like sunlight piercing a storm.

Carefully, I joined her, keeping space between us until she shifted slightly closer. I hesitated only briefly before gently wrapping an arm around her waist. When she relaxed against me, something within me settled for the first time in months.

I laid awake long after she drifted off, memorizing every curve of her face, every subtle flutter of her lashes, the soft parting of her lips as she breathed. Moonlight bathed her features, highlighting her beauty and vulnerability.

"I'll do anything for you, Sabrina," I whispered softly, barely audible. "I'll do whatever it takes to earn your love again. I'll become the man you deserve—the man our child deserves. I swear."

Sleep eventually claimed me, peaceful for the first time in too long, with Sabrina safely in my arms.

Morning came gently. I woke first, sunlight filtering warmly through the curtains. Sabrina lays beside me, still peaceful in sleep, her hair cascading across the pillow. Tenderly, I brushed a strand away from her face.

"Sabrina," I murmured softly, pressing a careful kiss to her forehead. "Wake up, Kitten. We have an appointment today."

She stirred slightly, eyelids fluttering open. Her hazel eyes, soft and sleepy, met mine, and my chest tightened.

"What time is it?" she asked, voice husky from sleep.

"Time to get ready," I replied gently, smiling down at her. "We're going to find out if our baby is a boy or a girl today."

Her eyes widened slightly, excitement chasing away the last traces of sleep. A beautiful, cautious smile graced her lips. "I almost forgot."

"I didn't," I promised softly, brushing my thumb lightly along her cheek. "I've been counting down the days." She held my gaze, warmth flickering in her eyes. "Me too." We lingered just a moment longer, savoring the closeness, before she pushed herself up and stretched with a small, contented sigh.

"Let's go meet our baby," she said softly.

My heart swelled impossibly, and as I followed her from the bed, I silently vowed to cherish this second chance she'd given me—and never let it slip away again.

The moments after were quiet, filled with tender anticipation as we dressed and prepared to leave. Sabrina moved with gentle deliberation, occasionally glancing at me, a soft smile playing at her lips. Every shared look felt like a silent promise, fragile yet resilient, binding us closer together with each passing second.

As we stepped outside, sunlight filtered gently through the clouds, casting a warm glow over everything around us. Angelo was already waiting by the car, offering a reassuring smile as he opened the door for Sabrina. She slid into the seat gracefully, settling comfortably as I joined her.

The car ride to the OB felt surreal. Sabrina sat beside me, eyes bright with anticipation. Angelo drove quietly, his presence comforting as always. The tension from recent months seemed to fade with each mile we traveled, replaced by tentative joy and hope.

"So, what do you think we're having?" I asked Sabrina, unable to contain my curiosity. She smiled, glancing down at her stomach thoughtfully. "I don't know. Sometimes I feel like it's a boy, but other times, I swear it's a girl."

"I think it's a boy," I admitted softly, warmth filling my chest at the thought. She nodded slowly, her eyes distant with contemplation. "I like Greyson or Romeo for a boy. If it's a girl, maybe Isabella or Valentina?" I smiled warmly, the names resonating deeply. "I love those names. They're perfect." Sabrina turned to look at me, eyes searching. "What about you?" She asked.

"I've been thinking about names too. But honestly, as long as our baby is healthy and you're happy, the name doesn't matter as much to me," I confessed sincerely. She smiled softly, her gaze tender. "You're going to be a good father, Kalel." Emotion tightened my throat, gratitude and hope swelling painfully. "I promise I'll be everything you both need." In the rear-view mirror, I caught Angelo smiling knowingly, a quiet approval in his eyes. I smirked back, heart full and hopeful. Today felt like the beginning of something new—something precious I would protect fiercely, no matter the cost.

* * *

<u>Sabrina</u>

I wanted a girl.

I had a whole plan: tiny bows, soft pinks, sparkly chaos, and a little version of me who didn't take shit from anyone—including her mafia daddy. Kalel wanted a boy, of course he did. He didn't say it directly, but the way his lips twitched every time the word son came up? Yeah. That man was dying to pass down the Marchetti crown to someone who would probably come out of the womb with a scowl and a superiority complex.

But when the ultrasound tech smiled and said "Congratulations, it's a boy," Kalel froze.

I braced myself for the smug grin, the I told you so—

And then I saw it. He was smiling. Not cocky. Not smug. Soft. Like his whole damn world just shifted under his feet and he liked where it landed. He didn't push. He squeezed my hand, kissed it, and whispered, "He's gonna have your eyes."

I rolled mine. "Let's hope he doesn't get your control issues."

Kalel laughed like I'd complimented him. He kept holding my hand, even as the nurse left us alone in the room. We didn't speak much after that. We didn't need to. There was something in the silence that felt... full. His thumb brushed over my knuckles, and for the first time in a long time, I didn't feel like I had to fight the stillness. I let it settle over me, warm and strange, like slipping into something I didn't realize I missed.

When we left the clinic, Kalel didn't say where we were going. He just opened the car door and gave me that look—the one that dared me to trust him without forcing me to. And for some reason, I did.

After that, he took me to a baby store. A real one. With clean white walls and shelves stacked with ridiculously overpriced onesies. I didn't want to admit it, but I was kinda... into it.

Kalel watched me the whole time—like I was the fragile one, not the

289

fetus. I touched a little gray set that said mama's boy, then a pair of soft navy baby socks I couldn't stop staring at. I didn't buy anything, though. I just looked. He didn't push me. Didn't say a word.

What I didn't know? That sneaky bastard whispered something to Angelo when I wasn't looking. That night, I passed out early. Blame hormones. Or maybe peace. It's weird, feeling safe in the same place I once wanted to burn down.

When I woke up, he wasn't in bed. I found him hours later—eyes red, shirt covered in paint, tools on the floor, and a fucking nursery built like something out of a magazine. Blue and gray. Gold accents. A crib made of wood, love, and stubborn obsession. I didn't say anything because I didn't want to ruin it.

* * *

The next morning, he covered my eyes with those big hands of his and whispered, "Don't peek, kitten." I tried to be chill. Cool. Untouched. "Unless you're surprising me with brunch and an epidural, this better be good." I said.

He chuckled against my ear. "Trust me." When he pulled his hands away, I opened my eyes— And it hit me. Stars dangled from the ceiling. The chair in the corner was one I'd sat in at the store—just once—and left behind.

He bought it. He bought everything. My throat tightened. Vision blurred. The tears came fast, ugly, and loud. I cried like someone had ripped me open and stuffed me full of joy. Kalel turned to me so fast I barely blinked before I was in his arms, held like I might shatter from happiness.

"You okay?" he asked, brushing a tear off my cheek. I sniffled. "No, I'm crying in front of a mafia king. This is humiliating." He smirked

and kissed my forehead. "You're allowed to cry. It's okay you love me."
He joked.

"Don't get cocky."

"Too late." I leaned against him, hands on my belly, his chin resting
on top of my head. And for once in my wild, chaotic life... I didn't feel
like running. It felt like home.

Chapter 35

Kalel

I found her in the garden again. The garden I built for her, one bloom at a time. Every flower, every fragrance chosen meticulously—with Sabrina in mind. It was my silent plea, my desperate apology whispered through petals and leaves because spoken words felt inadequate.

She was sitting on the bench beneath the blooming jasmine vines, her bare feet gently grazing the soft grass beneath her, relaxed. The weight she'd carried for months, the weight I'd forced upon her shoulders, seemed lighter somehow. She looked peaceful. Like the entire world had finally decided to grant her a reprieve.

My heart clenched with longing. Maybe... just maybe... she was beginning to forgive me, but God she is beautiful.

It wasn't the fleeting beauty that simply awakened desire. It was deeper, profound—the kind of beauty that brought a man to his knees, made him whisper prayers of gratitude just for the privilege of seeing her like this. My chest tightened with the painful sweetness of hope and regret entwined, nearly choking me. "Hey," she said softly, breaking the quiet with her voice, cautious but gentle. It wasn't sharp with bitterness or cold with resentment.

"Hey," I murmured back, my voice tight, strained as I moved closer, taking a seat next to her, careful to leave enough space in case she needed it.

She didn't move away. Didn't stop me, she didn't even stiffen.

Instead, she... looked at me. Her gaze held a softness I hadn't seen in months, her eyes quietly seeking something within mine. It felt like she was seeing me clearly again, not the monster I'd become, but the man I'd desperately fought to reclaim.

Her hand moved, resting gently over the small, precious bump of her belly. My eyes followed instinctively, utterly captivated. That tiny, growing life had completely shattered me in the most humbling, profound way. It had made me believe in redemption, in hope, in something better than the darkness I'd lived in.

"I've been thinking about names," she said, breaking the silence gently, her gaze fixed on the flowers in front of us.

My heart stuttered, anticipation coiling tightly within my chest. "Yeah?"

She smiled softly, her fingers caressing the subtle curve beneath her palm. "What do you think about Greyson?"

Greyson.

The name was a sudden, powerful wave that crashed over me, filling me with an ache of pure, unfiltered hope. Greyson sounded like peace, like the quiet moment of calm right before dawn breaks, chasing away shadows and nightmares alike.

"Grey," I whispered, tasting the syllable reverently. "Like the sky, just before the storm breaks, beautiful and strong."

She looked at me then, truly looked at me, her expression shifting subtly. The careful armor she'd worn so diligently around me began to soften, revealing glimpses of the woman I'd loved fiercely, recklessly, and far too selfishly. "Exactly."

My hand moved before I could think, slowly reaching out, trembling with uncertainty as I gently laid my palm over hers, pressing it lightly to her belly. I braced for rejection, expecting her to pull away, to reject my touch as I deserved.

But she didn't.

She let me touch her, let me connect with the tiny miracle we'd created, and my heart splintered in the most beautiful way. She was letting me in again, giving me a chance I knew I didn't fully deserve but would spend a lifetime earning.

"Greyson Marchetti," I murmured quietly, my voice thick with emotion, reverence in every syllable. "He'll know he was born from something wild, something fierce, something real."

"He'll know he was born from love," Sabrina whispered softly, lifting her gaze, meeting mine. The vulnerability, the honesty in her eyes completely unraveled me. Then she said the words I'd been desperate to hear, the words I'd convinced myself she'd never really say.

"I love you, Kalel." She said.

Everything inside me halted abruptly, frozen by the sheer force of her declaration. My heart thundered painfully in my chest, a fierce, aching rhythm. Those four words eclipsed every scream, every gunshot, every broken bone I'd experienced. Nothing had ever impacted me as profoundly as Sabrina's quiet confession.

Emotion surged uncontrollably inside me, threatening to break free in tears. Instead, purely driven by instinct and overwhelming joy, I reached out, scooped her gently into my arms, and spun her slowly around. Her surprised laughter echoed softly around us, and I felt her grip tighten, felt her lean into me with a trust I had long thought lost.

Setting her carefully back onto her feet, I cupped her face gently in my hands, kissing her deeply, desperately, like a drowning man finding air. I kissed her like she was the beginning and end of everything good I'd ever known.

"I love you too," I murmured fiercely against her lips, my voice hoarse with emotion. "So much, Sabrina. You wrecked me, you healed me, you made me whole."

I knelt slowly, reverently, pressing my lips softly to her belly, feeling humbled beyond words.

"I promise you both, I'll love you the way I should've from the very start. I'll protect you, cherish you, give you every piece of myself."

She inhaled softly above me, her fingers sliding tenderly through my hair, and I felt her finally lean into my touch fully.

"Forever," I vowed softly, fiercely. "You have my word."

Her quiet sigh was all the answer I needed. For the first time, she didn't move away from my promise. Instead, she held me tighter.

I stood again, drawing her close, her head resting comfortably against my chest, the steady beat of my heart soothing and constant beneath her ear. We stayed that way, holding onto each other, letting the silence speak the truths our words could only approximate.

I had come so close to losing her, had nearly destroyed the one person who truly mattered. Yet here she was, giving me a second chance I knew I didn't deserve. It was a gift I didn't trust the quiet in me when I swore to treasure for the rest of my life.

"I'm sorry, Sabrina," I whispered fiercely, pressing another gentle kiss to her temple. "For every mistake, for every hurt. I'll never stop making it up to you."

She tilted her face upward, her eyes soft and trusting. "Just don't stop loving me."

My throat tightened, raw with sincerity and devotion. "Never."

She smiled then, fully, beautifully, and I felt my heart heal completely in that one moment. "Then we'll figure out the rest together."

"Yes," I breathed softly relieved and hopeful. I will forever be endlessly grateful. "Together."

Standing in the garden I'd created as a haven for her, wrapped in each other's arms, our unborn child nestled safely between us, I finally allowed myself to believe wholeheartedly in redemption. In forgiveness. In forever.

This was our beginning. This was our peace and I'd spend every moment of forever ensuring Sabrina never regretted trusting me again. I hesitated, then stepped back just enough to see her face fully. My heart was hammering so loudly I was sure she could hear it. "Sabrina," I said softly, taking both her hands in mine, "will you marry me?"

She froze, eyes wide.

"I know I asked before," I rushed, voice breaking. "And I didn't deserve a yes. I didn't deserve you then. But now... after everything—after the way you've let me earn even a piece of your heart back—I want to ask you again. Not because I need to keep you, but because I want to spend the rest of my life loving you the right way. As your husband. As the father of our son. As your home." I said.

Her lips parted, tears forming in her eyes—and then, she smiled. A full, radiant, breathtaking smile. "Yes," she whispered, voice thick with emotion. "Yes, Kalel. I'll marry you."

My heart cracked wide open. I pulled her into me again, holding her tighter than I ever had, as if the answer alone could sew every broken part of my soul back together. And maybe it did. Because this time, when she said yes—she meant forever.

* * *

Sabrina

The ring sparkled on my finger, but it was his eyes I couldn't stop staring at. Kalel was still on one knee, like he didn't believe it. Like if he stood, I might change my mind. His hand was still trembling in mine. This man—this dark and twisted man who once took everything from me—had just given me the one thing I never thought I'd want from him.

A future.

"I said yes," I whispered, blinking back tears that were absolutely not falling. "You can breathe now." He let out a laugh that sounded

296

more like a shaky exhale, his forehead pressing against the back of my hand. "I just... needed to hear it again."

"Yes," I said, louder this time, threading my fingers through his hair. "I'm going to marry you."

He stood slowly, cautiously, like I might vanish if he moved too fast, but I didn't. I stayed. And when he kissed me, it wasn't fire this time. It wasn't possessive or punishing or desperate. It was soft.

Loving.

He rested his forehead against mine. "You saved me," he murmured, voice low and cracked. "I tried to own you, and you... you ended up owning me." I touched his cheek, the one without the scar, my thumb brushing across the man I'd hated, fought, and finally fallen for. "You were never mine to fix," I said, tears finally falling. "But you let me love you anyway." He said.

His hands fell to my stomach, warm and protective, and his voice dropped to a whisper meant only for the three of us. "You and this baby... you're everything to me."

I smiled through the tears, cupping his jaw. "Then protect everything, Kalel."

His eyes darkened with something primal. "Always."

* * *

That night, we didn't speak much more. We didn't need to. Kalel guided me back to our room with his hand resting protectively at the small of my back. We undressed slowly, movements gentle and deliberate, like we were memorizing the feel of each other all over again. Once we were in bed, he wrapped himself around me like a shield, his hand never straying far from my belly. The weight of everything that had happened settled between us like a shared exhale. For the first time in a long while, I fell asleep feeling safe.

—

The sun crept over the horizon, casting soft golden light through the curtains. A new day.

One that didn't begin with tension or silence, but with breath. Steady, shared breath. Skin against skin. The quiet aftermath of surviving something brutal together and still choosing to stay.

When he kissed me again, there was no war left between us. Just the ruins of what we'd survived—smoldering, beautiful, and finally at peace. His mouth was soft where the world had made him hard. He kissed up my thighs like he was memorizing me all over again, but this time not out of greed—out of reverence. Out of love.

"Kalel" I gasped, threading my fingers through his hair. He looked up from between my legs, lips swollen, eyes blazing. "Let me worship you, Kitten."

Then he buried his face in me.

My head fell back with a strangled moan, hips rolling against the slow, devastating stroke of his tongue. He licked and sucked like he had all the time in the world—and I think, for the first time, he did. There was no threat of losing me. I was his.

His tongue circled my clit, then flattened against it in a slow, torturous glide. "You taste like everything I've ever wanted," he groaned against me.

I whimpered, tugging his hair. "Mmm" I moan

He didn't stop. He held me open and devoured me until my legs were trembling, until my thighs clenched around his head and I cried out his name like a prayer. He licked me through it, gently, until the aftershocks subsided, then rose to his feet—face glistening, satisfied.

"You always fall apart so sweet," he murmured, kissing me before I could catch my breath. I tasted myself on his tongue and moaned again, needing him closer. I tugged at his pants, and he helped me out of my clothes, slow and deliberate, like he was unwrapping something fragile. Something his.

When he finally pushed into me, it wasn't hard or brutal—it was slow and deep. I gasped, arching into him, and he kissed my throat, my jaw, my cheek.

"I've had you before," he whispered, voice hoarse, "but never like this."

"Like what?" I panted, wrapping my legs around his waist. "Loved." Thrust "Wanted." Thrust "Chosen." My heart cracked wide open. His thrusts deepened, rhythm steady but powerful. He cradled the back of my head, his other hand stroking the curve of my stomach. His child. Our child.

He moved like he was making a promise. "I'll never hurt you again," he said through gritted teeth, sweat dripping from his brow. "I'll protect you. Love you. Forever."

"You already do," I breathed, tears slipping free as my second climax built. "Kalel—I'm gonna—"

"Let go," he growled, grinding deeper. "Come on my cock, baby. Show me who owns this pussy now."

I shattered. My body clenched around him, pulsing with pleasure and something deeper—something sacred. And when he followed with a groan, burying himself to the hilt and spilling inside me, it felt like a vow. He didn't move for a long time, just held me against his chest, his forehead pressed to mine.

"Mrs. Marchetti," he whispered.

I smiled through the afterglow. "You better get used to hearing that." His smile was all teeth and worship. "Oh, I will. Every night, on your knees, moaning it while I—"

"Kalel"

"Yes, Kitten?" I bit his lip. "Shut up and do it again." He did.

Kalel's mouth was between my thighs, and I was already unraveling. He licked me like I was made of sugar and sin—slow and hungry. His tongue teased my clit until my back arched off the mattress, and he groaned like he couldn't get enough of me.

"That's it," he murmured, tongue stroking deeper. "Look how sweet this pussy gets for me. So wet—fuck, Kitten, you were made for my mouth." My fingers threaded in his hair, tugging. "Kalel"

He growled against me, pulling my hips closer. "Begging already? You know what that does to me."

"Say it again."

"Please." His tongue flattened, licked a long, slow stripe from my entrance to my clit, and I nearly sobbed. He slid two fingers inside me, curling them just right while his mouth locked on to my clit and sucked.

"That's it, baby. Let me hear those sounds. You're so good for me. My perfect wife."

I came fast and hard, thighs trembling, a breathless cry falling from my lips. He didn't stop—kept licking me through it, fingers working me open like he wanted to memorize the way I fell apart. "You taste like heaven, but you're mine," he growled, voice thick and low as he crawled up my body. "Mine to fuck. Mine to love. Mine to protect. Mine to break."

"Then take me," I gasped. "I want you inside me." His mouth crashed to mine, and I tasted myself on his lips—raw and hot and shameless. He lined up and slid into me in one thick, slow stroke that had me moaning his name like a prayer. "You feel that?" he rasped, moving deep, deliberate. "This cock belongs to you. I'd give you anything, Sabrina. Fuck, you feel so good wrapped around me."

I whimpered, nails digging into his back. "Kalel—oh my god—"

He cupped the back of my neck, holding me still as he fucked me slow and deep. "That's it. Take all of me. You're doing so good, baby. So tight. So fucking perfect." I clenched around him, overwhelmed by his size, his voice, the way he spoke to me like I was sacred.

CHAPTER 35

"Your body was made to take me," he whispered, lips brushing my ear. "Every inch of you is mine. You hear me? My sweet, beautiful girl. My wife."

"Yes," I moaned, nails dragging down his spine. "Yours. Always."

"That's my girl," he growled. "Come for me again. I want to feel you break around me." He reached down and rubbed tight circles on my clit with his thumb, and it was over—my body locked around his, walls fluttering, orgasm crashing through me so hard I saw white.

"Fuck, you're perfect," he groaned, fucking me through it, losing rhythm as his control snapped. I gasped, legs wrapping tighter around him. "Come for me. Make me yours." That was all it took. Kalel groaned like a man finally home, burying himself to the hilt as he spilled inside me, warmth flooding my core. His mouth crushed mine as he whispered, over and over—

"You're the best thing that ever happened to me."

Kalel's body hovered over mine, eyes locked on me like I was the only thing that had ever made sense. His hands cradled my face, thumbs stroking my cheekbones as if I were delicate. And maybe I was, just a little. "I want to see you," he whispered. "All of you. No walls. No fear. Just you and me." My heart thudded against my ribs. "You already have all of me." His mouth curved into something sinful and soft. "Then let me love you the way you deserve."

He kissed me—slow, deep, claiming. Then he moved lower, kissing the swell of my stomach, whispering, "Thank you for giving me this. For staying. For choosing me." Tears stung my eyes. Even after it was over, his voice never stopped. "You're everything. You hear me? Everything I never knew I needed."

Chapter 36

Sabrina

I woke up to lips on my shoulder and a hand on my ass.

"Kalel" I muttered into the pillow, "if that's your way of saying good morning, I'm gonna need a minute."

He chuckled against my skin, warm and smug. "You've had all night, Kitten. You slept like the dead."

"That's because someone decided to 'praise me into oblivion." I mimicked his voice, low and gravelly. ""You're so perfect, Sabrina. Let me make you come until you forget your name.'" I turned over and smirked at him. "Congrats. You did."

Kalel looked utterly unrepentant, eyes glinting with mischief. "You're welcome." I rolled onto my back, the sheet falling to reveal one bare breast—and his gaze dropped immediately.

"Eyes up here, fiancé," I teased. His hand slid up my thigh. "Can't help it. You're glowing. Might be the pregnancy... might be the five orgasms."

"Three and a half," I said sweetly. "That last one was more of a whimper."

He growled low in his throat and leaned in, brushing his lips over mine. "Then I guess I owe you a proper forth."

"Kalel—" But he was already moving, dragging the sheet off me and nuzzling my stomach. "Good morning, little one," he murmured,

302

kissing the spot just below my navel. "Your mama's being a brat." I swatted him with a pillow. "Don't you start turning our kid against me before they even have ears."

He grinned like a devil. "Too late. He already knows Daddy runs this house." I snorted. "Daddy runs nothing. Mommy's just letting him think he does so he doesn't cry." Kalel pounced, pinning me under him with a wicked smirk. "Say that again."

"Mommy's in charg—" He kissed me mid-sentence, tongue sliding deep and slow, shutting me up in the most unfair way possible. When he pulled back, I was breathless and scowling.

"Cheater." I said.

"Winner," he corrected, eyes darkening as his fingers traced my hip. "And you're the prize I'm never letting go of." I sighed, faking exasperation as I dragged my nails down his chest. "You're so clingy now."

"You said yes," he murmured, kissing my nose. "You're mine now. Clinginess comes with the ring."

"And the baby," I added.

"And the sex. Especially the sex." He said excitedly making me laugh, and it hit me how rare that sound used to be around him. Now it came so easy. So did love. After thirty minutes of cuddling Kalel tells me that he has some business he has to take care of and gets ready to leave.

An hour later the front door clicked shut and I didn't freeze for the first time in a while. Kalel kissed me on the lips, then knelt to kiss my belly, whispering something to our son.

"Take care of Mama for me. I'll be back soon." And then he left. No guards shadowing the hallway. No locked rooms. No lingering sense of danger creeping up the walls. Just quiet.

Warm, golden, safe quiet. I stood in the middle of the living room for a few seconds, waiting for the old panic to surface—waiting for the weight to crush my chest the way it used to whenever I was alone. But it didn't come. I pressed a hand to my belly. The baby shifted—small, fluttering movements—and for the first time in this house, I felt... still. Not caged. Not watched. Just still.

Free.

I wandered into the kitchen barefoot, hair still messy from sleep, wearing one of Kalel's shirts over a pair of shorts I couldn't button anymore. The marble counters used to feel cold. Now they held the Tea I made myself, the bananas I kept craving, and the ugly little magnet Gianni had stuck to the fridge that said Hot Girl, Tired Soul.

I smiled.

I walked through the sunroom, where Kalel had installed a swing chair just for me. I sat in it now, the weight of pregnancy making the sway slow and soothing. The light poured in through the windows, touching everything—my skin, my thoughts, the baby growing in me.

The same house where I once plotted escapes and whispered threats under my breath... now held my favorite blanket. A half-read book. Pictures Gianni snuck onto the mantle of me and Kalel laughing, him with whipped cream on his nose, me fake-scowling at the mess.

I hadn't realized it until now, but—

The house didn't feel like a cage anymore. It felt like a beginning. When the door opened again, I was curled on the swing with my feet propped up and a sleepy smile on my lips. Kalel walked in fast, like he was expecting something to be wrong. His eyes landed on me, then scanned the room like he was looking for shadows.

"I'm fine," I said before he could ask. "Promise." He crossed to me slowly, crouched down in front of the swing, and rested his head against my belly. "Missed you."

"You were gone for six hours." I said.

He looked up at me, gaze soft. "Longest six hours of my life." I ran my fingers through his hair. "You don't have to worry so much."

"I always will," he said quietly. "But if I ever forget... just remind me how peaceful you look when you finally feel loved." My heart stuttered because he wasn't talking about today. He was talking about the woman I used to be. The one he hurt. The one he almost lost. And now—he saw her healing. I leaned down and kissed his lips, slow and certain. "I'm home," I whispered.

Later that night I convinced Kalel to have a movie night with me. Well if you can count asking him with puppy eyes and him saying yes without hesitation convincing. Kalel's fingers were tracing idle circles on my stomach again. We were curled up on the couch, wrapped in one of his expensive cashmere blankets, watching some over-the-top action movie he kept pausing to make fun of.

"This man just jumped off a helicopter with no parachute, landed in water, and walked it off. I call bullshit," he muttered, pressing a kiss to my temple. I laughed as I snuggle deeper into his chest. "Says the man who once took a bullet and stitched it up himself with whiskey and dental floss."

He didn't push. He tilted his head like he was considering it. "Touché." Greyson kicked suddenly—hard enough to make me flinch. "Ow," I muttered, hand flying to my belly. "Okay, that one was new." Kalel shifted immediately, alert. "You okay?"

"Yeah. He's just... being feisty."

Kalel smirked. "Told you. Marchetti blood." But a few seconds later, another cramp hit—and this one didn't feel like a regular kick. I sat up straighter, trying to breathe through it. Kalel—danger's smile faded. "Sabrina?"

My hand gripped the couch cushion. "I don't know. That one felt... different." Then something warm and wet rushed between my legs.

I froze, but Kalel didn't. He was already off the couch, eyes wild. "Was that—?"

"My water just broke," I whispered, heart hammering. He blinked. "You're not due for another three weeks."

"No shit," I snapped, breath hitching as the next contraction rolled through me like a freight train. "Tell Greyson that." Kalel moved fast—grabbing the hospital bag, tossing on a hoodie, helping me stand even as I leaned over in pain.

"Okay, okay. We're going. I've got you. You hear me?" His hand didn't leave my back. "You're doing amazing. We're gonna meet our son."

* * *

Kalel

I've been in shootouts. Watched men die. Took bullets and didn't feel a think, but nothing—nothing—prepared me for the sound of Sabrina screaming in pain as I held her hand in that hospital room. She was drenched in sweat, curled forward, her entire body trembling through another contraction. Her nails dug into my arm hard enough to break skin, but I didn't let go.

Not even for a second.

"You're doing so good, baby," I whispered, brushing hair back from her face. "Just breathe. I've got you."

"I can't—" she panted, voice cracking. "Yes, you can," I said, barely holding my voice steady. "You're the strongest person I know. You brought me to my knees and built me back up. You can do this." She looked at me, eyes glassy with tears, pain etched into every line of her face. But there was fire in her, too. That same unbreakable fight that made me fall in love with her in the first place.

The doctor's voice was a blur. I heard "pushing," "rotation," and "early delivery," but all I cared about was her. "You need to push, Sabrina," the nurse said gently. "He's coming fast."

She cried out again, and I wanted to do something just to make it stop. But I held her tighter. "I'm right here," I whispered. "Every step. You won't do this alone."

She pushed. Screamed. Cried. I broke into a thousand pieces watching the woman I love fight to bring our son into the world.

Then— A cry, high-pitched. Real.

His.

Greyson.

I didn't realize I was crying until Sabrina looked at me and smiled— exhausted, tear-streaked, absolutely wrecked—and said, "We did it." I laughed, choked, nodded like a fool. "You did it, baby. You gave me everything."

They placed him on her chest, small and red and perfect. His fists curled tight like he was already ready to fight the world.

My boy. Our boy.

I couldn't move. Could barely breathe. Sabrina cradled him close, her voice a soft hum against his cheek, and I watched them like I was seeing life for the first time. The nurse turned to me. "Do you want to hold him, Dad?" I'd never heard anyone call me that. Never thought anyone would. I nodded, blinking fast, and reached out with shaking hands.

He was so small.

He fit in my arms like he was made for it. Like he'd always belonged there. "Hey, little one," I whispered, voice rough. "It's me. Your dad." Greyson blinked, and I swear—swear—he looked right at me. "I'm gonna protect you with everything I am," I told him. "You and your mama. Always."

Sabrina was watching me, eyes filled with something deeper than love. And for the first time in my life, I felt whole. I'd held guns. Knives. Broken men, but nothing in this world had ever felt heavier than the seven-pound miracle they placed in my arms.

Greyson. My son.

My chest ached the second his tiny fingers curled around mine like they'd been waiting for me. Sabrina was sleeping, exhausted from labor. Her hair clung to her forehead, cheeks flushed, lips parted. She looked like hell. She looked like a goddess.

And she had given me him.

Greyson stirred, letting out a soft grunt, and I stilled like the world might end if I moved wrong. "You okay, little man?" I whispered, brushing a finger down his cheek. "Tough night, huh?" He didn't answer. Just breathed. Lived. I swallowed the lump in my throat. "I didn't think I'd make it this far. I didn't think I deserved to."

He blinked, like he was listening. Like he knew.

"You're gonna grow up strong," I told him, voice thick. "Smart. Dangerous, maybe. Just like your mom." A tiny smirk tugged at my mouth. "And if anyone ever touches you or her the wrong way—"

"Kalel," Sabrina murmured sleepily behind me. I turned and she was watching, smiling like she'd never seen me before. "Don't threaten murder during your first father-son moment." I walked to the bed, careful, and sat beside her. "He's perfect," I said, placing him back into her arms.

"He's ours," she whispered and in that moment, I realized something terrifying.

I would die for them. I would kill for them, but more than anything—I would live for them.

Epilogue

<u>Sabrina</u>

Six Years Later

There was glitter on the floor. Again.

Somewhere between Roman trying to make "slime soup" and Valentina deciding the glitter was fairy dust that needed to be in her hair, the kitchen had turned into a war zone. A beautiful, loud, chaotic war zone that somehow felt like peace.

I stepped over a tiny plastic sword—Greyson's, obviously—and picked up a stuffed unicorn wearing sunglasses. Also Valentina's.

From the living room, I heard the boys arguing over who got to be the dragon in whatever fantasy battle they were staging. Probably with Kalel's help. He encouraged the chaos way more than I did.

"I said I was the dragon!" Roman shouted.

"You were the dragon yesterday," Greyson fired back. "You can be the knight this time."

"Knights are boring!"

"Knights save people—"

"Dragons burn stuff—"

I smiled and turned back to the kitchen counter, fingers tapping the side of my coffee cup, heart fluttering in a way I hadn't felt in years.

Not since Greyson.

Not like this.

The pregnancy test was tucked behind the blender. I hadn't meant to take it. It was just... instinct. The feeling was familiar. The cravings. The soreness. The emotional breakdown I had yesterday because I stepped on a Cheerio barefoot.

I wiped my hands on a towel and glanced at the clock. Five minutes. I could do five minutes.

Except I couldn't, because right then, Valentina came toddling in with her curls in a wild halo, wearing her tutu and Greyson's oversized hoodie, dragging a baby doll by its foot.

"Mommy, Daddy say you're the queen of the castle," she declared.

I grinned. "Did he now?"

She nodded seriously. "So I said I'm the tiny queen."

"Well, obviously."

Kalel appeared in the doorway behind her, barefoot, in joggers and a black tee that stretched across his chest in all the best ways. His hair was a little messy from playing with the kids, and his eyes—those storm-colored eyes I once feared—lit up the second they landed on me.

"My wife," he said, voice deep and amused. "Looking suspicious in the kitchen."

I raised a brow. "Suspicious?"

He walked over, wrapped his arms around my waist from behind, and nuzzled his face into my neck. "You're hovering near the coffee and look like you're keeping secrets."

"Maybe I am." I said playfully. He hummed. "Is it the kind of secret I can unwrap off your body later tonight?" Valentina made a blegh face and skipped away, clearly uninterested in adult conversations. I turned in Kalel's arms and smiled. "Actually, it's the kind of secret that pees on a stick."

He stilled.

His entire body froze, his jaw twitching as he processed what I'd said. Then— "Kitten," he breathed, cupping my face. "Are you serious?" I reached behind the blender, grabbed the test, and held it up.

Two lines.

Positive. His eyes shimmered. "We're having another baby?" I nodded, heart full. "Yeah. Looks like the Marchetti empire's expanding again."

And then—God—he dropped to his knees in front of me, just like he had with Greyson, with Roman, with Valentina. His hands slid under my shirt and over my barely-there bump, like he needed to feel it to believe it.

That night...The kids were asleep—somehow, miraculously. Kalel had threatened to ban dragons from bedtime if they didn't stop the fire-breathing battle by nine, and that had finally worked.

Greyson was curled into his Spider-man sheets, one hand still wrapped around his plush lion like it was a weapon. Roman had passed out mid-sentence with toy cars scattered across his blanket. Valentina? She'd refused to go down without Kalel singing that stupid lullaby twice—and only fell asleep after tucking her stuffed bunny under her pillow.

Now, the house was silent.

"Four kids," he murmured. "I know," I said, laughing softly. "Who are we?" He kissed my neck. "We're everything I didn't think I'd ever want." I leaned back into him. "We're the life we fought for." He turned me around, eyes still reverent and possessive after all these years. "You still take my breath away, Sabrina." He said.

"You're still ridiculous," I whispered, grinning. "And mine."

"Forever," he promised, pulling me closer. "And when this baby is born..."

"Don't say it." I murmur.

"I'm getting a vasectomy." I burst out laughing. "You say that every time."

"I mean it this time," he said, dead serious. I leaned up and kissed him, slow and deep. Kalel was looking at me like he hadn't touched me in years. He closed the bedroom door slowly, locking it with a click that echoed through my body. Then he turned to me—shoulders broad, eyes dark with purpose— collapses beside me on the bed, pulling me into his chest.

"You're glowing," he whispered, brushing hair from my face. "Six years, three kids and you're still the most beautiful woman I've ever seen." I smiled as he continued

"You're perfect," he breathed. "Every inch of you. Every moan. Every tear. Everything." Brushing the hair from my face, eyes soft and full of awe. "You were mine to break," he whispered. "But more than that... mine to keep." I smiled, kissed his jaw, and whispered, "Forever." And in that bed, in that house, in the arms of the man I once swore I'd never love— I found everything I never knew I needed.

Kings of Ruin Series

Want to know what happened to Jin?
Mine to Break—coming February 2026

About the Author

I'm Zara Blackwell—a mother, a storyteller, and someone who's always believed that fiction is the safest place to face our real-life monsters.

I started writing dark romance because I needed somewhere to put the pain, the questions, and the parts of myself that didn't have a voice growing up. Every twisted man I write holds a piece of someone I once knew. Some broke me. Some taught me. All of them bleed into the page as a way of healing—and maybe even helping someone else feel seen.

My female characters? They're emotionally repressed and sassy as hell—different versions of myself I've met at different stages of my life. Women who laugh through the trauma, hide behind sarcasm, and fight like they've got nothing left to lose. And I love them for it.

I don't write to be nice. I write to make you *feel*—to make you scream, cry, laugh, hate me, or clutch the book like it's the only thing keeping you breathing.

When I'm not writing, I'm lost in music, daydreaming, or plotting my next obsession.

Come get ruined with me.

www.ingramcontent.com/pod-product-compliance
Lightning Source LLC
Chambersburg PA
CBHW010532100726

47903CB00011B/2978